CELTIC
Advance Praise for CROSSING

"A vast tapestry of inter-woven stories that link the past with the present, the saint with the sinner, the living with the dead, *Celtic Crossing* invites the reader on a quest to find the true Cross. To read this novel is to embark on a pilgrimage that takes us to an unexpected and holy place."
—SUZANNE M. WOLFE, award-winning novelist,
author of *A Murder by Any Name*, *The Confessions of X*, and *Unveiling*

"*Celtic Crossing* is simultaneously a tale of a disabling family tragedy and an urgent quest for a life-altering, missing relic dating back to the very foundation of Christianity. In tracing the mysterious path of the cherished relic from the Crucifixion to medieval Ireland and the Vatican, Mattano weaves a story of faith under challenge, new-found love, faith redeemed, and ultimately the resiliency and healing power of the human soul."
—RAYMOND J. HUTCHINSON, MS, MD,
Professor of Pediatrics, University of Michigan

"Weaves together the Christian messages of hope and healing with a cast of endearing, believable characters drawn together on quest to help a sick child at a time of crisis. As the story unfolds, those involved are forced to confront their individual struggles, their belief in the reality of God, and their relationship with God."
—REV. THOMAS F. X. HOAR, SSE, PhD,
President and CEO, St. Edmund's Retreat, Enders Island, Mystic CT

"Len Mattano's brilliantly researched story transports the reader between ancient and modern places and times. Despite betrayal, loss and fear, his characters fight to preserve their faith, even when overwhelmed by the helplessness and desperation that comes when a child is diagnosed with cancer. While humanity struggles to understand why a loving God allows such things, Mattano's messengers offer God's miraculous gifts of faith, hope, love, belonging and the wisdom that the path home lies through him."
—KATHLEEN RUDDY,
CEO, St. Baldrick's Foundation | Conquer Childhood Cancers

To Tricia

CELTIC CROSSING

A NOVEL

Beannachtaí

LEN MATTANO

L Mattan

PARACLETE
FICTION

PARACLETE PRESS
BREWSTER, MASSACHUSETTS

2019 First Printing
Celtic Crossing: A Novel
Copyright © 2019 by Len Mattano

Interior art: John Jude Palencar
(Frontispiece *Skellig Michael*, Dedication *Aideen's Pendant*)

ISBN 978-1-64060-305-9

Paraclete Fiction is an imprint of Paraclete Press, Inc., the Paraclete Fiction
name and logo (wing) are trademarks of Paraclete Press, Inc.

Library of Congress Cataloging-in-Publication Data
Names: Mattano, Len, 1958- author.
Title: Celtic crossing : a novel / Len Mattano.
Description: Brewster, Massachusetts : Paraclete Press, 2019.
Identifiers: LCCN 2019014684 | ISBN 9781640603059 (pbk.)
Subjects: | GSAFD: Christian fiction.
Classification: LCC PS3613.A84348 C45 2019 | DDC 813/.6—dc23
LC record available at https://lccn.loc.gov/2019014684

10 9 8 7 6 5 4 3 2 1

Published by Paraclete Press
Brewster, Massachusetts
www.paracletepress.com
Printed in the United States of America

CONTENTS

PART III

———

DIGITAL CONTENT AVAILABLE ONLINE AT www.CelticCrossingBook.com:
- CONTEMPORARY CHARACTERS
- GALLERY OF FEATURED ART
- FURTHER DISCUSSION GUIDE QUESTIONS

LINEAGE OF THE CURING CROSS

Abbán Gallagher
Oonagh [Shea] Gallagher, 1693-1751

Sé Gallagher, 1720-1779
Miren [Ryan] Gallagher

Marcán Reid
Aine [Gallagher] Reid, 1752-1821

Padraig Reid, 1773-1832
Treasa [Quinn] Reid

Fionan Reid, 1798-1831
Maire [Byrne] Reid

Malachi Reilly
Fiona [Reid] Reilly, 1816-1876

Seamus O'Donnell
Maire [Reilly] O'Donnell, 1850-1949

Padraig Brennan
Siobhan [O'Donnell] Brennan, 1871-1913

Aidan Brennan, 1898-1940
Ida [Sweeney] Brennan

Sean Callaghan
Aideen Fiona [Brennan] Callaghan, b1940

- - -
Caitlin Maire Callaghan, 1968-2003

Michael Sean Callaghan, b2000

IRELAND

⛰ 477-512 AD GALLARUS

⛰ 512-1191 AD SKELLIG MICHAEL

⛰ 1191-1578 AD BALLINSKELLIGS

⛰ 1578-1866 AD IVERAGH & DINGLE

ATLANTIC
OCEAN

Armagh ★

Drogheda ★

Dublin ✧ Dublin Bay

Galway Bay

Kildare ★

∧ ∧
∧ ∧ ∧
WICKLOW
MOUNTAINS
∧ ∧ ∧★
∧ ∧

Glendalough

Shannon Estuary

Ard na Caithne

Cashel ★

Gallarus/Reask ——— ★ DINGLE

Dingle Bay   ★ Killorglin

Cahersiveen   ✦ IVERAGH   Ballinskelligs

Skellig Michael ▲ ▲
Little Skellig

BEARA

CELTIC
SEA

Ballinskelligs
Bay   Bantry Bay

GAUL

⚠ 44-314 AD LA SAINTE-BAUME

⚠ 314-477 AD ISSOIRE

NORTH
SEA

★ Tournai

Ocsimor

AREMORICA
or BRETAGNE

★ Paris

★ Autun

★ Auvergne
★ Issoire

ATLANTIC
OCEAN

La Sainte-Baume

Arles
★

MEDITERRANEAN SEA

TO

All my angeli dei—
in heaven and on earth

PROLOGUE

Tuesday, 19 March 1191, Skellig Michael, Éire

Brother Murrough prayed silently as the westering sun descended into the sea and nightfall arrived. Few waves broke against the granite crags seven hundred feet below, washed gray by the late winter moon. At this height the winds were forceful and constant, gusting freely through the deep horizontal window. Chilled, he lifted the weathered alder plank, thrust it into a shallow groove on the sill, and secured it firmly with jamb wedges. It was at best a partial shutter against the cold.

In three cautious strides the monk was across the dark chamber, a barren stone hut set precariously on a narrow cliff in the shadow of the island's peak. The sole furnishings were a low, shoulder-width wooden platform draped with a scrap of blanket, and a small stand sufficient for a tallow taper, a rosary, and the monk's parchment-leafed breviary.

Light seeped from a candle cup that hung pendulous on a soot-black hook at the door. With his left hand he groped for the unlit taper and brought its wick to the flame. Holding the cup tipped, a flare erupted as melted mutton fat puddled aside. He placed the taper on the stand, pushed fast the door, and swiveled the latch into the drop handle.

It was time to begin Vespers.

The thirty-two-year-old Augustinian was alone on Sceilig Mhór: jagged, desolate, far from shore. Alert against the return of Viking raiders, he kept constant watch, his only sleep stolen as fragmented naps during sunlit hours. He knelt weary at bedside—hands illumined by a dim arc of wispy candlelight—and opened the breviary to the First Vigil. Softly, softly he began to chant the litanies designated for the Feast of Saint Joseph.

In nomine Patris, et Filii, et Spiritus Sancti . . .

Peace ached to enter his anxious heart. At last he surrendered—tranquil, silent, carried aloft in spirit by the lilt of Latin to mystical reverie, then unintended slumber.

Rest was brief. He awoke instantly to the crushing sounds of a score of men marauding about the nearby abandoned monastery, their anger rising in foreign tongue as they discovered little to plunder and raged into the wilds.

He extinguished the taper, hand quaking in fear of discovery. The candle cup had guttered out and the room became pitch. Clasping the rosary, he pressed the crucifix to his lips and began to pray fervently for the safety of the venerated relic under his guard.

PART I

CHAPTER ONE

WHITE BLOOD

Friday, 25 June 2010, Rome Fiumicino International Airport

"Padre! Padre!"

The Vatican limousine driver left the engine running, door wide open, as he padded off after the priest. His short legs and heaving belly guaranteed he would never catch up—not with Kevin's head start and determined intent to make his flight. "Padre Schaeffer!" Neither would his yells reach the priest over the barrage of horns and spewing curses: Italians have no tolerance for transport strikes despite—and paradoxically assuring—their frequency. He finally relinquished and returned to the black sedan.

Without breaking stride, Kevin swung the duffle strap over his left shoulder and wove deftly between the mass of idled vehicles spread across Via Leonardo da Vinci, flexing kinks from his sore hand as he went. Picketers brandishing *sciopero* signs had slowed traffic back in the Eternal City, but the chauffer made decent time speeding along A91 until reaching the airport exit where they came to a halt, just within sight of an imposing sixty-foot statue of the famed artist and inventor. After twenty minutes he knew he'd do better hoofing than fuming. If he were destined to miss his noon flight back to Dublin, at the least he hoped to vie for a later departure home this same day.

As he rounded a curve near an Alitalia hangar, his iPhone vibrated in the breast pocket of his cassock. Hearing the chauffeur's voice, he knew immediately why the call: his briefcase had been left on the rear seat.

He cursed, knowing he could hardly abandon a week's worth of notes—even though twice already he'd threatened burning them, for the paltry value they meant to his doomed research. A week wasted at the Vatican library and rooting about the Secret Archives, not to mention the expense. Suddenly deflated, he sighed and headed once again toward the limo, shrugging that it really didn't matter when he left Rome.

Saturday, 26 June 2010, Dublin

"Damn unions," Kevin muttered as he fell exhausted into the back seat of a Diamond cab at the Dublin International Airport.

It was now after midnight. He'd missed his original flight, and the next one, routed through Heathrow, was not only over-booked but delayed: a tide of events that transformed what should have been a tolerable two-hour trip into virtual medieval torture. To cap it off, he'd just waited dead last in a line of vexed passengers who'd rushed the underserviced taxi stand. The only positive tonight would be the quiet of deserted residential streets in this otherwise frenetic Irish capital.

"Oldham House off Dartry Road, Rathmines, thanks."

Like the Roman traffic he'd just left behind, Kevin's sabbatical at Trinity College was at a standstill. A dusty two months digging in the stacks of the Old Library and the past week's search of yet-older codices at the Vatican had led nowhere. In his fatigue he despaired he'd need to abandon his treatise, provocatively titled *Apostolic Apostasy*—and the planned mainstream book he'd counted on as his ticket out of teaching. Approaching fifty, he coveted the chance for change, for a much-needed reassignment. This year away from Boston, away from academics and far from the ever-present reminders of his mother's merciless death a year earlier, tantalized as a segue to new life. Stillborn, it now seemed.

Yet he was never one to cower. He sat up and reconsidered. Perhaps his hypothesis was wrong that the disciples had lost faith in Jesus after the crucifixion. If instead their faith truly had been "rendered impenetrable through the miraculous power of the Holy Spirit," perhaps so too could his. A ray of hope emerged.

As they sped across the Samuel Beckett Bridge, its steel cables and spar rising harp-like from the center span, he decided on a premium bottle of Jameson to thank his lifelong friend Marco for hosting his stay in Italy. The Old Distillery over the River Liffey would be the place to shop, and he could certainly use the long walk through town after a night's sleep—if only to sort out next steps in his work.

Soon the taxi pulled to a stop. With a light sprinkle falling, he tipped the driver and walked briskly to the house entrance several buildings down the empty pedestrian road. Boisterous laughter from a few inebriated undergrads sparring in the TV room spilled into the foyer. He collected his mail then left the party behind, climbing the stairs to his flat.

Stagnant air awaited him. He opened windows an inch or two over the bed and by the dining table, which he'd left heaped with papers. Immediately a damp cool draft scented lightly from the gardens at Palmerston Park began to freshen the small space. As a Boston College professor, he was lucky to have snagged housing usually reserved for students of the school's Centre for Irish Programmes. Absent this academic perk, he could never have afforded research abroad or had access to key original documents.

After grabbing a chilled bottle of Evian and stripping off the long buttoned cassock—not his usual garb—he leaned

back against the counter and flipped through flyers, coupon
sheets, and the glossy campus weekly. Among the detritus was
a business-sized interoffice mailer, addressed in youthful cursive
simply to *Fr. Kevin—Oldham #12*. He recognized at once the
writing as Stephanie's, his BC summer intern. It was her first
time abroad, a fact that shone in pure enthusiasm like the gleam
of her smile

Setting aside the rest of the mail, he unwound the string tie
and lifted the flap. Tucked inside were a newspaper clipping and
a plain white envelope with a yellow sticky note:

> Father –
> a woman stopped by this morning
> asking for you. She was disappointed you
> weren't here and insisted that I get this to
> you today. She needs help with a personal
> matter but didn't say what. Hope you had a
> good flight. Here's the Irish Times
> write-up on you. Nice! See you Monday.
>
> – Steph

In silent protest to what seemed at that moment an insolent
demand, he intentionally glanced at the article first. It spanned
three columns and extended down a full half page. The
introduction centered on the worldwide popularity of his debut
book, *Acts Two: The Post-Biblical Lives of Jesus' Companions*,
and prominently featured the cover of the European edition.
Interview-style questions and answers about his current project
followed. He was pleased with the extent of coverage but cringed
as he read through the optimistic replies he'd given the editor.
Much had changed in the few weeks since.

With a sigh, he cast the clipping onto his work pile and rather dejectedly ripped open the sealed envelope, cutting his finger in the process. The single sheet of stationery within bore the centre's logo—clearly the visitor hadn't come prepared to leave a note. And in rather striking contrast to Stephanie's loose contemporary hand, the woman's writing appeared tense, or more precisely, constricted: the chatty sentences were crammed into the top of the page. It was signed Aideen Callaghan.

> Fr. Schaeffer,
> Your kind assistant said you're expected home from a trip this afternoon. I'm so sorry to bother you at week's end, especially to ask for help. I read yesterday's Times article about your research and must talk with you. Is there any way we can meet tomorrow? Please ring me at Our Lady's Children's Hospital, Crumlin. Ask for Michael Callaghan's room. I'm there most of the time.
> God's blessings to you.

Kevin reread the brief note and berated himself for his premature knee-jerk irritation at the woman. Still, he puzzled at the oddity of a stranger, who had apparently just learned of his research, suddenly—even urgently—requesting his help.

What in the article had triggered her interest?

Who for God's sake was Michael Callaghan?

Perhaps most perplexing at this late hour: What possible relevance could there be in a bit of biblical history dating back two thousand years?

He was cautiously intrigued but far too tired to think more about it until the morning.

His visit to the distillery gift shop might need to wait.

Saturday, 26 June 2010, Rathmines

It was a quarter after nine before Kevin awoke. Having slept through the night, he should have felt more rested. After a quick bite of toasted soda bread with currant jam, he showered, pulled on a pair of black joggers and a light gray tee, and headed north in his sneakers to the Insomnia Coffee Company two kilometers up Lower Rathmines Road.

This was his first run in months, and how quickly his pace slacked was disheartening. He adjusted his earbuds, chose a calmer playlist, and walked. Soon, though, he found that his stamina for concentrating was equally poor.

Into this void of ordered thought—as stealthily as in sleep— slithered the hydra of grief through unguarded gates. A flush of face, a catch of breath worked its venom: gut-punched with unwaned intensity by his mother's loss was its effect.

He paused. And on he walked.

By the time he arrived, the sidewalks were dense with families, couples, and raucous teens drawn out by the sun and warmth following the overnight rain. The queue extended out the café door, but unlike weekday mornings, the mood was pleasantly relaxed. Once inside, he joined the separate line reserved for those only ordering coffee straight up.

There was an empty stool at a row of tall tables pushed together to form a counter facing the window. He dug his iPhone out from his back pocket along with the folded envelope and sat down.

With renewed sharpness bolstered by a half cup of Sumatran blend, he reconsidered the letter. As before, its vagueness left him apprehensive—what he could now name as an uneasy, yet likely irrational, sense of vulnerability. While the appeal seemed sincere, the recent media attention did make him an easy target for fanatics. *I read yesterday's* Times *article about your research and must talk with you.* Still, priestly compassion dictated he not dismiss the woman's request without learning more, particularly if a child were involved. The least he could offer was a listening ear.

The call took a minute to connect. He was greeted by the children's hospital operator who confirmed that, yes, there was an inpatient named Michael Callaghan, and yes, of course she would be very pleased indeed to patch him through.

She answered on the first ring.

"Hello, this is Aideen." Her voice was calm, and she spoke quietly.

"Hi, Aideen. This is Kevin Schaeffer—"

"Father, thank you. Thank you so much for calling. Can you hold just a second?" There was a muffled pause. "So sorry. I needed to step away from Michael's bed."

"That's all right." He swirled the coffee slowly, fragrant vapors rising. "You're at the hospital. Is your child ill?"

"He is, Father, quite. Actually, Michael is my ten-year-old grandson whom I'm raising. He's been fighting leukemia for two years and doing really very well. Unfortunately, we've just learned that the cancer's come back."

"I'm saddened to hear that," Kevin said, genuinely moved.

"Father, can we possibly meet this afternoon? There is some family information I want to share that I hope will interest you. With it, I think you may be able to help Michael."

"This afternoon . . ." In the pause of hesitation he heard her inhale quickly.

"Or Monday. Whenever."

"Aideen, I'm not sure—I don't understand how it is I could help." His finger tapped the rim of the paper cup in soft, irregular bursts.

"I'm sorry. I must sound desperate." She cleared her throat, then spoke in measured words. "I know it's an imposition, but this can only be explained in person."

He thought for a moment. With his research stalled, there was no compelling reason to work the weekend. Moreover, he longed to believe this woman. Setting apprehension aside, he yielded to curiosity.

"I'll be free at one o'clock. Where would you like to meet?"

Saturday, 26 June 2010, Dublin

Kevin was three-quarters of an hour late finding the rosarium at Iveagh Gardens, having guessed wrong that it was near the children's hospital and off he'd gone by bus, only to return downtown close to where he'd started.

Adorned by an ivy-laced stone entry tucked away off Clonmel Street, the iron gates to the Victorian park stood open. Once past a narrow walled corridor and a canopied path deep in shade, sunlight drew him rightward: an expanse of green stretched forth, edged crisply by broad bands of crushed-stone paths. The harshness of rectangular lawn was artfully dominated at either end by identical angels, winged bodies weathered gray, each figure bearing aloft a censer of overflowing water that collected in large pools about the feet. Beyond a stand of mature trees, half-hidden in the distance, was the rosarium.

His immediate impression of Aideen as she approached was of youthful grace overlaid with fatigue. Her auburn hair was parted to one side and hung in waves just brushing her shoulders. She wore a knee-length muted floral skirt and a soft white cotton blouse under a thin yellow sweater with the sleeves pulled up to mid-forearm. Her gait was easy, almost carefree: no doubt reflecting less an absence of anxiety than her welcoming him in friendship.

He felt as though he had known her always: at once embraced yet overcome by a mournful image of his mother, equally vibrant until insidiously masked by dementia.

"Father . . ." She extended her hands and grasped his tightly, leaning forward slightly, her head tilted down but with a somber smile, her tear-filled eyes looking directly into his.

"Aideen, I'm glad you were able to reach me—sorry about being so late."

She looked down and acknowledged his kindness with a gentle nod, then let go of his hands and indicated with her eyes the path to the bench where she had been sitting. "Father, I want you to know how grateful I am, even if there is nothing to be done."

They sat on the beige honeycomb throw Aideen had draped over the wooden seat, surrounded by quantities of roses blooming on shrubs, clambering vines, and hedges.

No more than a moment passed before she began. From a hand-sewn quilted satin case she withdrew an oversized volume bound in deep red, finely grained burnished leather, and placed it carefully on her lap. It was embossed in gold with two large Greek characters: A•Ω.

"I inherited this Bible from my great-grandmother, Maire O'Donnell—I called her Maw Maw—who was born in 1850. She was given it by her grandfather, Fionan Reid, born in 1798. It dates back several generations before that, to the late sixteen hundreds." She opened the cover as she spoke, voice subdued. "Our family history is recorded inside."

The front endpaper was vellum, of a red matching the cover. On the title page were imprinted the words *An Bíobla Naomhtha*. Kevin guessed this tome represented a rare early Gaelic printing of the Bible—exceedingly rare in such pristine condition.

She leafed through several pages until she came to one with two parallel columns of ruled horizontal lines. Centered above were the words *Beannaigh an Leanbh*: "Bless This Child," she translated. On each line was a name written in ink, followed by the years of birth and death. The baptismal list continued onto the successive pages.

Aideen let him gaze at the entries in silence. He was instantly captivated, inspecting them up close and tracing his finger lightly across some—each a face, each a soul. When he came to the end he saw the names *Aideen Fiona Brennan 1940* and *Michael Sean Callaghan 2000*, and between them, *Caitlin Maire Callaghan 1968–2003*. He sighed, sat back, and shook his head slowly. "Amazing." He had seen many age-old books, but none with this degree of personal human connection.

"Many lives lived, Father," she said, brushing away a tear. "Maw Maw also gave me this." She removed her necklace and held its shimmering silver pendant gently between thumb and forefinger. Kevin saw that it was perfectly triangular in shape and easily measured two inches from tip to base. Inscribed deeply on the front were tarnish-black lines in the shape of a cross within a circle.

Only when she placed it in his hand could he appreciate its heft.

It was of significant size for a precious metal object and certainly carried value beyond sentiment alone. The edges were worn smooth but the corners remained sharp, lending it a vintage, timeless appearance. He examined it as closely as he had the Bible entries, running his thumb along the lines, then returned it to her palm.

His eyes were again drawn to the Bible. There in the margin next to some of the names appeared letter-height versions of the identical symbol, which had escaped his attention at first. Baffled by the apparent coincidence, he looked to her for an explanation.

"Father, Michael is not the first member of my family to suffer from cancer. His mother died with a brain tumor when she was thirty-five. My daughter, Caitlin—" The pain in her voice was unmistakable as she touched the name. "I've been

Michael's guardian since we lost her seven years ago. He was only three at the time."

Kevin sat attentive as she gained composure.

"My mother was six months pregnant with me when my own father, Aidan, died of a brain tumor."

After a long moment her head lifted, eyes dry, and she spoke without emotion. "When Michael's doctor first told me he had leukemia, I refused to accept it. How could it possibly be true? Father, I was also eight when I was struck with leukemia. My nightmare—mine—inflicted on my grandson."

Instinctively, Kevin reached out and placed a hand over hers, quickly offering a silent prayer that she find peace.

"Maw Maw gave this to me when I became sick," she said, clutching the pendant to her chest. "Can you believe she was ninety-eight at the time and healthier than me? She cried, but I had no concept of cancer—or death, for that matter. I felt her love, that's for sure."

Aideen now looked out at the horizon, her vision inward.

"Then she apologized, repeating over and over that *the cross was lost*. From her dress pocket she brought out a drawstring pouch. I remember thinking it was for coins—that she might be giving me a gift—but it was just jewelry. A child's thought." Again her gaze drifted. "She pressed it into my hand and told me to wear it always, to protect me from harm. She said she'd received it as a symbol of the wood of Christ's cross: blood-stained wood that by mere touch had cured many of our ancestors from cancer—and had cured her from *white blood* as a young girl. But then the cross disappeared from our land. Vanished from history, it seems."

Kevin listened intently, trying to assemble the many pieces of her story into a whole. Most extraordinary was the professed healing power of what sounded to be wood of the true cross and its presence in Ireland. But there was more—that which involved Michael: her great-grandmother had called her illness *white blood.* In Greek: *leukos haima.* In Latin: *leukemia.* For Aideen's family, cancer was a connection between generations—the wood of the cross, a salvation.

She continued, startling him as she pulled him from his thoughts.

"Yet I was so young I didn't know enough to ask what she meant. What did she have to apologize for? I just didn't ask. It was years later, long after she'd passed on in her sleep and I'd been cured by a new medicine—a miracle itself, really—that I turned to her Bible."

"What did you find?"

"Father, I wasn't looking for religion. I was looking for answers to a riddle—the real meaning of the pendant." She closed the book and slipped it back in its case, then looked up. "I hope I've not offended you."

Kevin raised his eyebrows, shaking his head as though her comment were senseless.

"At any rate, I looked hard, but found no answers. Instead I discovered just what you noticed moments ago: woven through my family tree is a string of ancestors whose names are embellished with the symbol of this pendant: a triangle about a Celtic cross." His gaze turned again to the necklace in her palm. "I saw that many in years past died very old, like Maw Maw. Not so with my grandmother Siobhan. Or my father, or my daughter."

She paused, then spoke deliberately.

"The written symbol only marks those who were cured by the cross. Do you see, Father? Certainly you must—you're a biblical scholar."

His eyes betrayed confusion at what she was requesting, but also a deep yearning to understand.

"The curing cross has been lost. I need you to find it in time to save Michael."

CHAPTER TWO

SEVEN DEMONS

11 Kislev, AD 29, Cana of Galilee

Preparations for the wedding of Samaan's son had created a festive atmosphere throughout the village of Kana for weeks. Except during Sabbath, family and relatives had bartered gifts, baked matrimonial desserts, and assembled tables for the feast. The bride's family made ready a home for the new couple as dowry. Now candles and torches were lit. It would be a memorable evening.

According to custom, Samaan and his wife had invited a large number of friends to celebrate this most holy ceremony. Many guests walked a day or more to attend. Samaan seemed especially pleased when his son's villager friend Nathanael arrived with the group from Nazareth. Nathanael had spent much of the winter in Bethany as a disciple of John, a prophet and baptizer, but had recently become a follower of Jesus, a Nazorean. Samaan was curious to learn more about the man Jesus, who everyone knew was simply a carpenter by trade.

After the promise of vows, traditional songs burst forth and wine was poured for all. Samaan's wife retreated to the galley tent, where she directed the setting out of the meal. Should she fail her husband's expectations, she would bring shame to him as host. At her side was her devoted cousin Mary from Magdala, a nearby village on the Sea of Galilee, who was staying at their home to help with the innumerable tasks.

It was an hour past sundown when a steward entered the tent seeking Samaan's wife, who had stepped away. Mary approached him and asked his concern: The supply of wine was almost spent, yet the day's celebration would not conclude until past midnight. What would the host have done? She promised to get word to Samaan.

A hand gently touched her arm. Turning, a flow of peace bathed her as she looked into the eyes of Jesus's mother. *My son will help.*

Tuesday, 29 June 2010, Trinity College

Kevin entered the Old Library through the faculty entrance on the west side and climbed the stairs to the third floor reading room. The Manuscripts and Archives Research Library had just opened for the morning and already half the tables were occupied. He was relieved to see that his favorite spot was still available, near a north-facing window that framed a view of the Campanile. He settled into the same straight-backed wooden chair as the day before, carefully took Aideen's Bible from his briefcase, and resumed work from where he'd left off.

The archives had been his primary research source during the past two months. The Keeper of Manuscripts had taken a particular interest in his topic, directing him to first-millennium texts that might validate the premise, and they had previously arranged to meet at eleven that morning. A substantial number of relevant volumes had been added to the collection since 1592, when the institution was founded by Queen Elizabeth. Its Protestant affiliation and charter purpose to impose Anglican domination in the strongly Catholic Ireland of the sixteenth century did not interest Kevin in the least.

Now, however, Kevin's research had taken a different tack. On a fresh legal pad, Kevin transcribed the names and dates from the baptismal list, indicating with an asterisk those who had been marked in the original as cured. He also noted the kinds of cancer that had afflicted some of the relatives, according to an oral history provided by Aideen. The direct lineage from Oonagh Shea Gallagher, born 1693, to Michael Sean Callaghan represented twelve generations. These names were underlined in the Bible, linking their relationship. The entire list totaled fifty-three, which included siblings of the primary descendants. In all, sixteen names were marked by the symbol of the cross, the last being Maire Reilly O'Donnell, Aideen's great-grandmother.

His natural approach was academic—methodical and decidedly remote from mystical.

Kevin leaned back in his chair and closed his eyes to concentrate. Clearly this family was plagued by cancer. Tracing the string of cancers through twelve generations had created a pattern that, to his mind, was best explained by inheritance, not random ill fortune. To decipher the mystery further he would need expert help.

Sitting up, he decided to page through the Bible looking for notations in the margins and for any papers inserted over the years that could yield more information. Halfway through Genesis he heard the bells of the Campanile chiming eleven o'clock. He gathered his items, walked to the keeper's office, and knocked gently on the partly open door.

"Come in."

"Hi. Is this still a good time to chat?"

"Kevin, it's good to see you. Please, sit down. Welcome back, my friend. I've been anxious to hear about your visit to the Vatican. Any progress?"

"Progress . . . I suppose, in a way. I confirmed that my theory is likely a bust. Which is good news for Christianity. Less good news for my sabbatical."

"Ah. You have my full sympathy. I was hoping for a triumph. Be that as it may, is there perhaps another angle you can pursue? Anything I can do to help at this point?"

"Thanks. I appreciate that. I need to give the whole thing some thought. In the meantime, I've gotten involved in a side project. I'd like your thoughts on this Bible, if you would be so kind?"

"Of course." He rose, pointing to the oak table opposite his desk, and cleared space on the surface for Kevin to place the Bible.

A mere glance at the cover was sufficient to capture his attention.

"Kevin, what on earth have you brought me? There's nothing like an old book to capture my intrigue on an otherwise dull Tuesday." He lifted his head slightly and looked down to bring the cover into focus through his bifocals.

"Ah, calfskin. Expertly tanned. Dye, even and rich. Minimally worn. Spine solid. Gilt lettering. Fine craftsmanship. Very old. Let's have a look inside." He opened the cover and ran his gloved fingertips professionally over the front endpapers, then examined the back endpapers. "Lambskin."

At the title page he stopped cold: Gaelic. "Kevin, I suspect you anticipated my reaction. You're quite familiar with rare volumes."

"I'm pleased you're as excited as I am."

"I would date this between 1695 and 1715, and local, not German. We'll take a look at the leaves for condition. Assuming there's no damage or untoward aging, I'd say you're looking at early retirement in style."

Kevin grinned. "For the owner, possibly. I doubt she'd let go of it at any price."

"A donation, then, as a priceless addition to our collection?"

"I'll mention it to her." While he spoke he turned to the baptismal list. "What do you make of this?"

The keeper again took in the details on the page. "These appear authentic. The inks are of varying age, particulate concentration, and color. The handwriting differs for all but a few sequential entries. Birthdates were written in the same hand as the names, and the dates of death entered later. Lettering styles are consistent with the birth eras. Kevin, what do the triangular symbols represent? I've not seen these elsewhere. Are they astronomical in nature?"

"I believe they're religious." He left it at that.

"So, an incomplete answer for the moment. Please do share more, when the time is right."

He nodded as he stood and extended his hand. "As always, I am indebted."

Tuesday, 29 June 2010, Crumlin

Kevin left campus through the Nassau Street gate and crossed over to the neighborhood Insomnia for a spicy ham-and-goat-cheese panini. Not yet a convert to tea and glad for the thriving java culture among urbanites, he ordered an iced coffee to go, then stepped back out into the strong midday sun for the short walk up to the bus stop off Grafton.

Compared to the there-and-back route he'd taken to meet with Aideen on Saturday, Kevin now found the way to Crumlin remarkably straightforward. He exited near the children's hospital. It was almost 1:50, safely past the restricted lunchtime visitor hours.

A nurse was just leaving Michael's room as Kevin arrived. With the door open he could see Aideen sitting in an upholstered bedside chair. The privacy curtain was drawn, and he could make out the silhouette of Michael's feet through the bed linen.

"May I come in?"

Aideen looked up with a smile and greeted him at the doorway.

"Father, let me introduce you to my grandson." They walked toward the window and around the curtain. Michael was half-sitting, his head resting on the inclined mattress. He was a handsome child, with light brown hair and hazel eyes. His face was pale, there were scattered bruises on his lower arms, and he appeared tired: otherwise Kevin could easily visualize him playing with classmates in the schoolyard or riding a mountain bike along hilly roadside paths.

"Michael, this is Father Schaeffer."

After a protracted moment of nonresponse and a prompt from Aideen, Michael finally set down his electric blue Nintendo DS, the kinetic music stopping as he paused the game. The room was suddenly quiet.

Kevin leaned against the bedrail. "You can call me Father Kevin. Do you go by Mike?"

His eyes blinked upward, then away. "My friends call me Mickey."

"Mickey, then." The boy hinted a smile. "Mickey, what are you playing?"

"Just an adventure game. I have a lot of action games too." He picked up the console tentatively.

"Sounds fun." There was no reply. "I hope we get to talk again sometime."

"Sure." Michael pressed play and music ended the brief exchange.

Aideen affectionately pinched Michael's blanketed toes and shook his foot. "I'll be back in a bit, okay? Ring for the nurse if you need help," she said, tucking the call button into a fold of blanket near his hand.

Once in the hall, Aideen shook her head forlornly as an apology for Michael's behavior.

Kevin laughed. "It's great to see he's acting like a healthy youngster."

"Yes—perhaps again, one day."

About them a passel of afternoon visitors streamed by. It seemed most knew their way: those who joined the staff in pacing brusquely past the uninitiated and darting in front of the slow. Kevin stood aside as Aideen maneuvered to the nurses' station to report she was leaving the ward. They then took the elevator to the ground floor and found their way to the tranquility of the chapel.

The sun high, abundant light fell through its windows: bright swaths rising from sills far above the eye's reach and stretching upward to the coffered ceiling. She led, Kevin behind in slow procession, past row after row of empty chairs. Ahead, the altar: looking down, a diminutive crucifix floating lost against an expanse of marble.

At the side aisle, votive candles stood lit in red array next to a statue of the Christ child. She leaned back and rested on the wall, hands tented over her face, eyes searching, slowly, behind closed lids.

Softly, Kevin ventured a question. "Aideen, tell me more about Michael's mother."

"My tempestuous Caitie," she said with energy, dropping her hands. "She was a strong one. She made me a strong parent." Again they walked, each step a moment to itself. "My husband died in a car crash on the back roads coming home from work one night. Caitie turned five a month later. The few memories she had of him were intense and I think happy, but growing up without him led her to be a risk-taker. Ironically."

The extent of her loss—no less the boy's—left him numb.

When they reached the far aisle she sat. He turned a chair and faced her, noting the contours of her cheeks, the delicate lines about her brow. "And now you're raising a second child alone." For Kevin it was a thought beyond imagining; for a priest, doubly so. Her shoulders shrugged resignation. "What about his father?"

She sighed. "I suppose it's for the better that Caitie told me nothing about him. Maybe she didn't know much herself. If she had any relationships before the cancer, she kept them secret. After surgery her personality changed subtly, from risk-taking to what I considered simply reckless."

"In what way?"

"Well, most of the tumor could be removed, but not all. She refused radiation despite my pleading: she didn't believe it would help and wanted nothing to do with side effects. Instead she sold her apartment, moved her things back home, and took off to Istanbul. She came back pregnant. He's been a blessing to me. I just hope—" A tear traced a path to her chin. "I hope I've been enough for him. That I've loved him enough."

Aideen's energy was spent. A minute later their solitude was broken when a chaplain ushered in an elderly woman and what looked to be her middle-aged daughter, both crying.

"Let's get back to your grandson," Kevin suggested. They stopped at the café briefly, strolled the garden, then returned to Michael's ward—Aideen now smiling in the telling of happier memories.

"Father, I've written down my cell-phone number and home address in County Kerry for you—it's anyone's guess when we'll be going back. I don't know how to thank you for trying to help."

"I'll do what I can." He tucked the notecard in his shirt pocket. "Aideen, do you think it would be possible for me to talk with Michael's doctor? About your family's history?"

"Of course. She knows some of the details, but not all. Our focus has always been on Michael. I'll ask the ward clerk to call her office, and you can fix a time. Her name is Lenore Thomson. You'll like her Scottish accent."

Wednesday, 30 June 2010, Smithfield

"Thanks for coming here to the clinic, Father Schaeffer. Sorry I couldn't meet with you at the hospital yesterday." The pediatric oncologist removed her readers as Kevin sat down, giving him a quick once-over while shoving the door closed—an easy reach from her desk.

"On the contrary, this worked out perfectly. I'd been meaning to stop by Jameson's up the road—for a gift, I should explain."

"Aye, right. And who would expect to find a physician's practice located in the Market?" Both smiled. "But, it's convenient for many of our patients, and the lease was priced right after the economic downturn." Her chair squeaked softly as she swiveled toward the table cramped into a dark corner of her office, Kevin tight against the wall. She switched on the green-shade lamp and folded her hands. "So, you're here to ask after Michael Callaghan."

"That's right. I do have Aideen's permission to speak with you."

"Yes, that's my understanding."

Kevin's eyes narrowed in a friendly crinkle before breaking her gaze. Easing back, he noted the austerity of her looks: graying hair cropped short, nondescript marble-rimmed glasses, lips gently lined with mauve-stained creases—stark features all, yet embodied by such warmth that outward beauty seemed relegated to afterthought.

He straightened, retrieved a folder from his briefcase, and set before her the list he'd prepared. "Doctor, you may not be aware of the full extent of cancers in Michael's family history. This seems extraordinarily unusual to me."

A frown gradually emerged as she examined the paper. After a moment, Dr. Thomson raised her eyebrows and took a deep breath.

"Father, where did you come by this information? How reliable would you consider it?"

"It's as reliable as the family's Bible and Aideen's memory." He mistook her silence for skepticism. "I should add that a friend of mine, an expert at the Old Library, does not doubt the authenticity of the entries made in the baptismal record."

"Nor would I—although I imagine a broader family tree would demonstrate even more cases among cousins and distant relatives." Their eyes met. "Father Schaeffer, I don't need a blood test to tell me this is a type of inherited cancer syndrome."

Suspicion confirmed, he simply nodded.

"Thank goodness it's rare, but for these unfortunate families it is devastating. Affected relatives are at an extremely high risk of developing cancer—sometimes even more than one kind—often at a very young age. And as you can see with the Callaghans, inheritance from either the mother or father is sufficient. It is a dreadful autosomal dominant disease."

Kevin pondered what had been said, overwhelmed with the vast degree of suffering, of grief, of unfounded guilt inflicted across the years. "So Michael had no chance."

"Actually, he had a fifty-fifty chance of inheriting or not inheriting the condition—this predisposition for cancer—from his mother. Not until his leukemia occurred would one know for sure. Without genetic testing, that is."

"And this could go back generations."

She sighed. "As far back as descendants continued bearing children."

Wednesday, 30 June 2010, Rathmines

It was well past sunset. At his dining table, Kevin twisted side to side and stretched, hoping to relieve the soreness in his lower back. He had been working his way through Aideen's Bible, continuing his search for notations and finding none. He would finish Luke, wash the neglected three-day stack of dishes, then rest for the night.

When he reached chapter 8, he immediately saw a heavy red line drawn beneath the words of the second verse: *chomh maith le mná áirithe a bhí leigheasta ó dhrochspioraid agus ó éagruais: Máire ar a nglaotar an Mhaigdiléanach, a raibh seacht ndeamhain imithe aisti.* In his own Bible he read the verse in English: "and also some women who had been healed of evil spirits and infirmities: Mary called Magdalene, from whom seven demons had gone out."

Luke, the physician from Antioch, had spoken over a distance of two millennia to reveal an enigmatic clue in the mystery of the cross.

CHAPTER THREE

CROWN OF ROSES

Tuesday, 7 December 476, Kildare

She sat on the cover of the old stone well, a quarter mile distant from the small domed oratory. Next to her, sheep had gathered at the trough to slake their early morning thirst before meandering haphazardly to the grazing fields. Erratic bleats, some playfully childlike and others ornery as old men, rose and fell in waves, sending clouds of winter wrens aswirl from the massive barren oak only to disappear moments later into convenient branches of leafless trees farther from the din.

The sun was now twenty degrees above the horizon, streaming light and warmth into the clear sky and onto her back. Highlights of the knee-high stone foundations of the new monastery were just becoming visible from their silhouettes. Brigid was pleased. As abbess, her life of holiness and caring for the poor had inspired a score of girls to adopt the habit in a life of service and prayer. The building under construction was a dire need. Soon she would begin work on its twin for the multitude of young men who yearned for solitary monkhood.

In her heart, the twenty-five-year-old was passionately devoted to asceticism. Together, she and Father Padraig of Armagh had begun a monastic movement that was destined to spread throughout Éire and the vast reaches of Western Christianity. The Holy See was patiently observing this experiment from afar, eager to nurture any saintly endeavor that might solidify its central authority during the inevitable disintegration of the Roman Empire.

She would christen this place *Cill Dara*, Church of the Oak.

On the fringe of her thoughts she became aware of a faint rumbling of the ground and air that quickly resolved into hoofbeats. Turning around, she could make out the shadows of four riders as they approached along the dirt path from the east. Soon their pace slowed to a trot, then a walk. The first figure dismounted and circled around her, bringing his familiar face into the sun.

"Brother Tomas, welcome. It is good to see you again. Have you ridden the night through? How is Father Padraig?"

"Sister, all is well. Be at peace. Padraig dispatched us with a message of importance. Our journey was made with haste."

"Then please, come with me to the residence and rest. We will break fast with the sisters and you can share the message in quiet."

Inside, the scent of boiled mutton and potato pancakes met them at the entry. The hut was no more than twenty by thirty paces, divided into a partitioned room with sleeping quarters to the left, and a larder to the rear. The central fireplace was open to all rooms, providing warmth and ready access from behind for cooking. They removed their cloaks and sat on benches drawn up to both sides of the plain wooden plank table.

"Sisters, we thank you for your graciousness on this blessed morning," Tomas said. He offered grace, and two meager platters were placed before them. Hushed activity in the larder could be heard, hinting that additional food was being prepared for the unexpected visitors. They ate in silence.

Following the meal, Tomas brushed away crumbs with his shirtsleeve. From his dusty brown leather satchel he brought out a sheet of sun-bleached parchment folded lengthwise thrice on itself and wound closed with a green woolen tie. Brigid accepted the letter and read its contents to herself.

Greetings, Brigid, dear sister in Christ!

Since we celebrated Mass together at Easter, I have received word of the magnificent work you have accomplished in Druim Criaidh. The fruit of your labors will shine the light of truth on many. May your blessings continue without bound. Our numbers here have likewise multiplied. Many are those who desire to walk in the path of the Lord.

Sister, this evening a messenger from our Holy Father Simplicius arrived. He brought tidings that Emperor Romulus Augustulus has been deposed in Ravenna by Odoacer, a Germanic warrior of wide disrepute. This took place days before the fall equinox.

Alas, the Empire is finally no more.

In the wake of this event, Papa fears for the stability of his holy realm. Prayers and incense have been lifted heavenward without ceasing in his private chapel, and he is taking caution to protect all sacred documents and possessions in Europe against pillage.

To our joy, we will be entrusted with the care of an especial relic. Its identity and present location were unstated, and I can conjecture not. His Holiness has ordered that we prepare a secure place for its keeping. Without question, any knowledge of it must be kept hidden from all excepting those who guard its safety until it be called to Rome.

Our period of preparation is until midsummer. In the morrow I will send my trusted servant Tomas to you with this letter and oral instructions. I will send as well my obeisance to His Holiness, with a recommended harbor for arrival of the carrier ship. Of certainty, it will not be Drogheda as it is the primary port in use and poses great risk for any who must travel covertly.

You may be anticipating that I place this task in your hands, as I am no longer fit for strenuous undertakings and am committed to tending my flock at the cathedral here.

Please send written word back with Tomas to acknowledge your understanding. Make plans and send messengers on the even months with news. Easter next will be one of great discussion with you here in Ard Mhacha.

May the grace of God abide in your heart and bless your every act.

Your brother in Christ, Padraig

His signature was embossed with the imprint of his seal, three rounded triangles joined at the apex.

Brigid refolded the letter, tied it fast, and stood. Tomas arose. Without speaking she led him to the adjacent empty room. In quiet tones, Tomas delivered the rest of Padraig's message: The relic would be brought into the remote western harbor Ard na Caithne, where the summer seas were calm. She should depart for her first journey there within a fortnight, accompanied by Tomas and his companions, to select a worthy site for settlement in late spring. Brigid would leave the sisters in the care of Brother Conlaeth.

She searched her heart and rejoiced at God's abundant love shining light on her path.

It would take ten days by horse to reach the peninsulas of Ciarraighe. For Brigid, the new year would dawn on the mountainous Atlantic coast.

Friday, 2 July 2010, Crumlin

Across the conference table from Aideen and the social worker sat Dr. Thomson and Petra, the specialty nurse assigned to Michael's care. Petra had immigrated to Dublin from Belarus fourteen years earlier but retained her singsong cadence of speech. Aideen found it mildly amusing to hear the two in conversation.

"Let's get started, then," said Dr. Thomson, glancing at her watch. "Mrs. Callaghan, I trust you've taken my suggestion and have been staying nights at the guest house?"

"I'd intended to." She paused, looking down. "No, not yet."

"Well, we need to move that along. It's nigh difficult to be an encouragement to your grandson without quality rest. Emily, please help Mrs. Callaghan settle into her room this afternoon." The social worker nodded and gently placed an arm around Aideen's shoulder.

"So, we started Michael's treatment three weeks ago as of Monday next. On the positive side, he's holding his own without any worrisome complications. Honestly, I expected him to be on antibiotics by this time." After a moment she continued, leaning forward, giving weight to her words. "Still, I'm disappointed that his leukemia doesn't seem to be showing much of a response." Her steady gaze was on Aideen, whose head remained bowed, tears now falling onto clenched hands.

"We'll give it another week. Let's try to keep him out of trouble. Maybe we can get him home for a while after that." The devastation these words had brought on Aideen was clear to all. A reassuring tone and subtle reference to failure could not mask the fact that Michael would likely die from his cancer.

"Last time we talked some about marrow transplantation. Finding a donor is proving to be quite a challenge—there aren't too many Irish Turks on the registry, unfortunately. Our first order of business, though, is beating the leukemia into remission."

Petra gently pushed a box of tissues toward Aideen. "Doctor, I'll stay and answer any questions Mrs. Callaghan might have." Dr. Thomson quietly gathered her papers, reached over and gently patted Aideen's hands, then rose and left her colleagues to comfort the weeping woman.

Wednesday, 7 July 2010, Trinity College

Kevin was excited in a way that only an unexpected turn of events can elicit. Thinking over his career, he considered the three years spent researching and writing *Acts Two* the most personally fulfilling—far and away more than lecturing. Remarkably, he had brought new context to the apostles and the closest friends of Jesus by examining their lives after AD 63, the final year reported by Luke in Acts, which had ended in a cliffhanger: Paul imprisoned in Rome awaiting trial for treason as a champion of the kingdom of Christ.

The book had become a sleeper bestseller. With permission of the provost, college president, and archdiocese of Boston, Kevin had complied with the publisher's incessant requests for speaking engagements, media interviews, and author signings. He accepted praise with humility, and contributed all profits to his order, in keeping with his Jesuit vow of poverty.

Now, in the midst of a tangibly different—and floundering—project, he had happened onto the profound misfortunes of a family an ocean away. Incredibly, the life of a ten-year-old boy depended on his delving once again into the world of the fledgling Christian church. He wondered if this were a sign, a beacon meant to guide him past deep personal loss: to be eased of recurring dreams of his dying mother that a year later still invaded his sleep. With no siblings and his father gone forty years, Kevin's sabbatical was an academic venture, a respite—and perhaps an escape to new life.

Since discovering the underlined passage in Aideen's Bible a week earlier, Kevin had immersed himself in determining its relevance. He hadn't thought to bring a copy of *Acts Two* with him from Boston, so on Thursday he'd checked the Old Library electronic card catalog and was disappointed to discover it wasn't listed. Neither did the library bookstore carry the popular title. He did find two copies at Easons on O'Connell Street and bought both, reminding them kindly to restock. He spent the bulk of the afternoon at the centre with Stephanie, explaining her new assignment compiling data and familiarizing her with the book and its numerous references—without mentioning any connection to Aideen. The other copy of *Acts Two* he kept for himself.

His first effort was to reconstruct a plausible historical outline of Mary Magdalene's whereabouts following her last appearance in the New Testament, when she revealed to a skeptical Eleven that "I have seen the Lord." Research led him to believe that she had, in fact, traveled with Lazarus and sister Martha from Judea to Gaul, fleeing Jewish persecution after the tumultuous beheading of John's brother, James. Less compelling to him was the traditional account of their being set adrift in a rudderless boat and miraculously landing on the coast of France.

Kevin's new focus, though, was not her circumstances of travel, but what Mary of Magdala had brought with her from Judea.

It was in June 2007 that Kevin had stood entranced before her bony relics at La Sainte-Baume, Provence. Here was the saint's skull with its gaping, eyeless sockets, a skull once adorned by the luxuriously long, perfumed hair of New Testament fame. He then visited Charlemagne's great cathedral at Aachen, joining throngs of pilgrims to see the Virgin Mary relics, which had not been on public display for seven years. The existence of these artifacts spoke to Mary's very human maternal love for her son. Here were his swaddling clothes, the loincloth he wore on the cross, her own cloak from when she last held him close, and even the beheading cloth of John the Baptist, his cousin who had announced Jesus as the promised Savior.

To Kevin, knowing that the Virgin Mary had never ventured beyond the Holy Land meant that someone else had carried these cherished items to France, items so precious that she would have entrusted them only to John the Beloved or to Mary Magdalene. And it was well accepted that John died in Ephesus in the year 100.

Yet in all these historical details there was no link to the cross.

This morning at the archives he had stumbled on a series of leads while searching through translations of early monastic documents for clues. Starting with Patrick, Ireland's patron saint of the fifth century, seemed logical to Kevin. An Old Irish passage in the Book of Armagh described Patrick's friendship with fellow patron saint Brigid as having been so great that they had "but one heart and one mind." Interest piqued, he then dug into what was known about Brigid and learned she had founded a scriptorium at her Kildare abbey, which became renowned for producing rich illustrations that were "the work of angelic, and not human skill," according to a twelfth-century writer.

Asking whether the Old Library had access to any of these works of art, the keeper took Kevin to an interior windowless office and proudly sat him before the panoramic screen of a recently acquired iMac. With a few quick clicks he pulled up an entire library of high-resolution scanned images. Handing over the mouse, he dimmed the overhead lights, closed the door, and left the priest in privacy.

In the darkness of the room, Kevin was stunned by the vivid clarity and vibrant colors rendered on the monitor before him. It was as though these hand-penned drawings had been created in the recent past, not twelve or more centuries ago. He spent three-quarters of an hour examining every aspect of the first several images, then picked up the pace by forcing his attention toward content, not technique. If this foray proved to be a fascinating blind end, he did not want it to consume an entire day.

At half past ten he came upon an illustration that would define the course of his quest.

The file was systematically titled kildare_loose46_5c _marymag_2006armagh.tiff.

The image was that of a full-page multicolor fifth-century illustration originating from Kildare and kept at Armagh. The scan extended beyond the edges of the paper, showing clearly that this was an individual sheet separated at some point from its book. In the left margin was a penciled notation: #3572.

Filling the right half of the picture was a seated woman crowned with a ring of white roses. Draped on her lap was the lifeless body of a man bearing crimson wounds on the chest, hands, and feet. Her expression was of graceful acceptance: a holy pietà. Kneeling before her was a woman with waves of hair to the waist. In silhouette, only a portion of her face was visible, with head bowed and the trace of a tear on her cheek. On her cloth belt written in thin pale ochre script was the Hebrew word *Migdal*.

Mary Magdalene's arms were outstretched, palms upward. Encircling her left hand was a wreath of thorns. In her right were two fragments of splintered wood, one on the other, forming the shape of a cross.

By tomorrow afternoon he would be in Armagh. There he knew would be the greatest collection of surviving artifacts from Saint Patrick himself. What might be among them he could not guess.

CHAPTER FOUR

ARD MHACHA † ARMAGH

To: Marco Giordano <m.giordano@arcsacra.va>
From: Kevin Schaeffer <kevinschaeffer999@yahoo.com>
Date: July 7, 2010 21:18:34 IST
Subject: Jameson

Buongiorno, Marco!

Hopefully you've received the superlative bottle of Jameson I sent and have had a chance to imbibe a dram or two. The helpful lad at the distillery gift shop assured me that the Black Barrel Reserve would be a perfect introduction for your Chianti palate into the creamy caramel world of Irish whiskey. Enjoy. It is a meager offering of thanks for your many kindnesses during my stay last month.

Of late I've found myself mentally leafing through my autobiography. Midlife crisis, you say? Self-assessment at least, prompted I'm sure by our recent conversations and of course the shadow of my mother's death that hasn't quite lifted after almost a year. It's remarkable the divergent paths you and I have taken since our thesis years working with Cardinal Ratzinger on the *Catechism*. He certainly recognized your brilliance and has made full use of your talents ever since. I remain impressed with all that you have accomplished in his office. Whether I believe your stories about him wearing Levis under his papal robes and hanging his halo on a hook at night, well . . .

Marco, you know I was ambivalent from the start about my current sabbatical, even with my yearning for change. I felt none of the happy exuberance associated with sourcing and writing *Acts Two*. Now that I'm confronted with having to modify or even abandon the theme of *Apostolic Apostasy*, I feel strangely at peace. It is as though setting it aside has opened time and mental space for another purpose, one of deeper meaning and consequence. Maybe a spiritual nudge—I don't know quite yet. Keep me in your prayers.

Tomorrow I leave for Armagh, where I will attempt to channel Saint Patrick. My next email may be filled with amazing tales of conquest and discovery! And perhaps a favor or two to ask of you.

Ciao, amico mio . . . Kevin

Thursday, 8 July 2010, Ballinskelligs

Aideen sat in her car, engine off and lights on, relieved to have reached home safely. The pale yellow cottage always took on a reddish hue at the close of long summer evenings.

She had hoped to leave Dublin by eleven to avoid rush-hour traffic around Limerick but didn't merge onto M50 until two. Dr. Thomson's repeated apologies for rounding late had almost angered her when an explanation would have sufficed: Michael's test results came back at noon and showed no sign of infection despite Monday's fever. The doctor had insisted she could reasonably be away from him for a week while he remained in hospital for observation. With teeth clenched, Aideen had been determined not to display ire when Petra added, "You need to get home while you can."

The driver's door of the faded red 1998 Ford Fiesta coupe creaked as she pushed it open with her right foot. Caitie had bought it secondhand after Michael was born and put on almost sixty-four thousand kilometers, along with multiple dents, commuting to her waitressing job in Killarney four nights a week until her first seizure. Over the next year Aideen added another twenty-thousand kilometers on the frequent trips to Saint Luke's Hospital in south Dublin. Later, according to her daughter's wishes, Aideen spread her ashes in the graceful Wicklow hills they had so often looked upon together from the hospital campus.

Reaching toward the dash, she flipped off the headlamps and withdrew the ignition key. Clustered on the rear floor were a half-dozen plastic bags of fresh food bought at Centra across from the memorial church in Cahersiveen. She took what she could with one hand and walked the twenty feet to the side stoop.

The door was unlocked. Barely inside, she stumbled over a black trash bag and slammed her left shoulder into the end-cabinet of the kitchen counter, scattering oranges across the hardwood floor. Not having energy to pick them up just then, she set down the bags and returned to the car for her small suitcase and the remaining groceries.

Aideen had last been home five weeks earlier. Having convinced herself that Michael's symptoms could not be due to a relapse of his leukemia, she had set out that day for his Dublin appointment with just an overnight case. When it was clear they would not be back anytime soon, she relied on neighborhood friends Peg and Danny to send clothes, clear perishables, and trim the lawn. Aideen preferred to tend the many flowerbeds herself.

The cottage was built in 1934 with craftsmanship meant to endure. Aidan and Ida Callaghan were the first owners, passionate newlyweds planning to fill the second bedroom with two or three children before inheriting the Sweeney family farm from Ida's parents. Six years later and weary from multiple miscarriages, the couple silently rejoiced when it appeared at last that this pregnancy was healthy. Ironically, Aideen was born to a mother grieving the sudden death of her husband from a brain tumor that went undetected until it triggered a massive stroke. Ida had insisted on an autopsy, hoping that it wasn't cancer—that the baby she carried might be spared the Callaghan family curse.

Aideen moved through the darkened house instinctively, turning on the bedroom light only briefly to change into her nightclothes. She then poured herself a modest glass of Baileys, dropped in three ice cubes, sat in her favorite upholstered living room chair, and somberly watched the horizon turn to indigo over Scariff Island and the Atlantic beyond.

Friday, 9 July 2010, Armagh

As requested, the reception desk rang Kevin with a 7:30 courtesy call. By then he'd already been awake for an hour, had showered, and was on his second cup of coffee while watching BBC One. Apparently the bulls running in Pamplona were friskier than usual due to a quite prolonged Continental heat wave. Hungry, he slipped on his shoes and readied to leave.

The key fob—brass and sufficiently bulky to qualify as a weapon—was on the bedside table next to his wallet. What he could not immediately find was the card he'd been given at Saint Patrick's Cathedral when he'd arrived yesterday for his supposed appointment with the curator: Gearalt, which the secretary had pronounced with a soft *g* as in *garrulous*, who was never sick, had called in sick, and it would be best to ring him in the morning to save a trip if he were still sick, wouldn't that be sensible, and here's his number. Figuring he must have left it in the car, he turned off the TV and took the claustrophobically small elevator to the lobby in search of breakfast, hoping this day would be more productive than the last.

The Charlemont Arms was a centuries-old family hotel in the center of town. Not knowing the area, he'd chosen it strictly by location and found it quaintly pleasant. It would be an easy walk back to the cathedral on the hill. While waiting for his room to be readied after check-in, his gaze had lingered on the hotel crest that hung proudly over an archway. It pictured two red dragons on hind legs, their hooves planted on a banner proclaiming in Latin: DEO DUCE FERRO COMITANTE, which he took to mean "With God as my leader and my sword as my companion."

This morning a sign pointing guests toward the dining room entrance was posted on an easel near the elevator. He gave the waiter his room number and was seated at a table for two. Moments later the customary pot of tea arrived and the extra place setting was cleared. He opened the menu and began narrowing his choices.

"Father Schaeffer?" Startled by the nearness of the gravelly voice and familiar use of his name, Kevin looked abruptly over his shoulder to see who had called. He did not recognize the older gentleman, who approached smiling, hand outstretched.

"Yes, good morning. I don't believe we've met?" He stood and accepted the vigorous handshake.

"No, no, 'course not, that's right. I'm hoping you don't mind I sought for you here. Truth be told, I get my daily exercise parking the car down the hill away from the church a bit, and this is on my path. I'm Gerry Frasier, the curator—Lynn in the office said you'd been by yesterday."

A quick smile formed on Kevin's lips as his head lifted slightly upward in understanding. "Yes. Thank you for stopping in. Gerry, is it? Please, won't you join me for breakfast?" He pulled out the second chair and encouraged him to sit.

"I don't mind a spot of tea. Much obliged." The waiter promptly brought a second cup, utensils, and a cloth serviette. Kevin ordered oatmeal, melon slices, and juice.

"You're feeling better, I take it."

"How's that?"

Kevin's smile turned a shade puckish. "Lynn said you were ill."

"The tooth, you mean? Drilled and filled—and a mite poorer for the pain."

"I'm glad to hear it's nothing serious," he said, pouring for them both. "Gerry, how long have you been curator?"

He chuckled under his breath, double chin swagging. "Now that's quite a question. Here in Norn Iron, well, let's say we don't mobilize like you Americans."

Kevin's quizzical look threw the storyteller off cadence. "Sorry, Norn—"

Gerry's equally quizzical response transformed to a broad grin. "Now, that I'll have to keep for the pub," he said with a tap to his head. "*Northern Ireland* it'd be in your language."

The absurdity of his Queen's English pronunciation made them both laugh.

"As I was saying, I've been working at the cathedral since I was a wee lad at my da's knees, as Mum would tell. Truth is, Mum parked me there after school to keep me out of the Troubles. Smart too, she was. Da had been curator since '58, so I just grew into it. He passed twenty-three years ago, come August. Sorry to say, I'm the end of the Frasier line, Father, as best I know." He winked.

"Well, you can certainly be proud of the fine stewardship you and your father have provided in caring for the church's manuscripts. I've seen some of the scanned images. They are incredible. Were you involved in cataloging them?"

"That's the first thing Da had me do. Cheap labor, I was, back then. Boring job."

Gerry emptied his cup, poured more, and artfully dribbled a good teaspoon of honey: then more after tasting. Kevin quietly observed while wondering whether this dedicated servant of

Irish monastic history was of Protestant roots—and graciously tolerant of the intrusive demand of a Roman Catholic priest on his time—or if he too were Catholic and had somehow weathered the storm of politics literally under radar, working as he did for the Church of Ireland. In either case, wise indeed his mother and reverent her son.

Gerry continued. "Truth be told, they didn't know what they had, the vicars. Sure, they knew up here," he said, pointing to his right temple, "but to them nothing could compare to the book itself. And that's long been off in Dublin."

"The Book of Armagh, you mean?"

"Well, sure—ninth century, it is. But by God almighty, we have some old ones!"

"Back to Saint Patrick, I'm aware."

"As they've been dated, sure. Or near to. The thing is, Father, everyone loves the manuscripts. To me, it's the other items that matter, in here." He pointed to his chest.

Kevin felt his pulse quicken. "Other items, Gerry?"

"Yes, 'course. Saint Padraig founded his order on the very spot that our old cathedral sets. None of the structures are from back then, mind you. It was Ard Mhacha to the pagans, but Padraig, he came along in the four hundreds and claimed the spot for Christ. And by God it's been his ever since. Christians, Catholics like yourself, all come knowing that here was the true beginning of Irish faith."

Kevin leaned back in his chair as the waiter set down multiple plates, each with oversized portions, all crowded on his side of the table. Gerry did not object when Kevin moved the toast and jams before him.

"So what kinds of items date back to Patrick's time?" Kevin probed.

"Well, personal things—correspondence, mostly," he said between bites. "The better-preserved ones are lambskin. It holds up better, not as fragile after 1500 years. Lord knows we've never been short on lambs round here."

"I imagine not. And the manuscripts—you also helped catalog those?"

"Correction—I cataloged every one. Took me most of my twenties. Da sent me off to Paris for preservation courses at the Louvre too. Amazing place, that. I learned a lot. The leap for ward was in the '80s, when we really modernized with humidity and light control, air quality, all the rest."

Kevin was impressed. "When were the documents scanned?"

"Well, Father, that we just completed last year. Truth be told, we started a dozen years back, but scanners weren't what they are today, resolution-wise. So we started over in '04. Took us five years. Plenty of Trinity students have helped. Gloves or no, they love working with the books."

The waiter returned with a fresh pot of tea and yet more toast.

"The letters—where are you at with them?" he asked, eager to hear details.

"We finished the illustrations first, then the text. Letters will follow soon enough, for use by scholars like yourself. Those we won't be postin' to the web."

"They'll be a treasure for research, certainly." The curator nodded tacit agreement—a trivial gesture in itself but done with the persuasive earnestness of an ally: Kevin sensed no guile, no inclination in him to be anything less than helpful and trust-worthy. "Gerry, there's one illustration in particular I'd like to learn more about. The digital scan I saw indicated that it was a loose page, originally from Kildare. It was numbered 3572."

"Ah, and a gem it is, Father. The finest—I know it well. Our Lady and our Lord. It's truly inspired. I heartily believe it was God's hand working through Saint Brigid. History-wise, there's no record I can find of its coming to Armagh. But it must have been early."

"How's that?" he said, leaning close.

"Mostly deriving from the fact that there was a stained-glass window patterned after it for the first church here. I'm guessing the book was sent to Padraig directly, along with one of her letters. Sad to say, now we have neither the window nor the book. You picked a good one to ask after, for sure."

"With one of her letters," Kevin softly repeated to himself. "Gerry, I would very much like to see the original illustration, and take a look through Patrick's correspondence."

"Father, I am at your service."

+++++++++

Gerry was waiting outside when Kevin returned from his room with notebook in hand. He quickly dropped his cigarette to the pavement, ground it out, and reached forward to open the door for the priest.

They walked along Upper English Street for less than a block, then darted through workday traffic to trek up the quieter Abbey Street. Rounding the corner, the roadway became a single lane bordered oppressively on each side by an unbroken succession of stuccoed two-story buildings. The sky above was cloudless, which cheered the mood substantially. They kept single-file on the narrow cobbled walk, made nearly impassable where cars parked over the curb. Gerry led, his breaths growing heavier as the way climbed and curved leftward.

It wasn't until Castle Street that the road broadened and trees appeared, although the incline remained steep right past the cathedral gate and up to the entry door. Kevin turned around momentarily to glimpse the hilltop view of the town center before following Gerry into the surprisingly bright sanctuary.

"Nice and neat, they say. Too much plaster for my liking. It's a medieval cathedral, truth be told. This renovation dates to the 1830s. Money talked, even then," he said, referring to the wealthy benefactor and his chosen architect. In the nave Gerry pointed disapprovingly to a display showcasing a copy of the Book of Armagh. "People ask about it," he shrugged.

Minutes later and with heads crouched, they descended a length of dimly lit stone stairs to the crypt. The arched ceiling in the main corridor was equally low. Between support pillars on either side branched shallow alcoves, and as they passed Kevin could see plaques marking individual resting places.

"Now, isn't this what you might expect of an old church? The crypt itself is from 1268, but we don't know when it was first excavated. The choir is directly above us."

On reaching the emergency-exit door at the end, they turned right into a darkened hallway. Overhead fluorescents came on automatically, revealing ceramic tile floors and plasterboard walls. The transition from ancient to modern was jarring. Fifteen feet along on the left was a steel door painted white. Gerry unlocked the deadbolt, pushed the door inward, and pressed several dimmer switches located at the bottom of a large service panel. A gentle light flooded the room as he closed and locked the door behind them.

"Mission control, I like to say, Father. Now, to those letters."

CHAPTER FIVE

GALL IORRAS † GALLARUS

⬭

Friday, 31 December 476, Ard na Caithne

Dawn broke somewhat earlier on this eve of the new year than at the previous week's solstice, but on awakening the traveler could only see dark snow clouds overhead. The horses were nosing away inches of light flakes that had fallen overnight, their occasional snorts creating miniature flurries that quickly settled again at their forehooves.

Alill mac Nad Froich had risen first, venturing out from the goatskin shelter to stoke the smoldering birch embers back to full flame. He then packed each of six metal flagons with fresh snow and set them beside the fire. As he reached into the provisions bag for a packet of smoked mutton, Tomas walked past briskly toward a private stand of trees eighty yards off. He returned moments later, fingers cold from having cleansed them in the snow.

"Good morn to you, Tomas. Gladly our slumbers were undisturbed in the night. Warm yourself as I prepare breakfast, such as it is. Perhaps its scent will rouse our companions."

"I thank you, Alill." He knelt and rubbed his hands together in the heat. "Once again, let me extend our great gratitude for your willingness to depart Caiseal and guide us safely across the breadth of your kingdom. We are indebted."

"You do me more homage than is merited. We Eóganachta are proud of our barony, but it is hardly a kingdom. And I am hardly the king, as my brother Óengus makes known to all. The Castle of the Rock is under his reign."

"He has led wisely: Munster has found peace since he and others accepted baptism at Father Padraig's hand after your father's death. The Spirit of God has not left your side."

"This is true. Our people have prospered. We are thus obliged to assist you now in your need, as the Church has aided us in ours."

"Sir, it is the endurance of your people's faith that gives you strength."

Tomas stood and examined the horizon. To the south were forested mountains broken by barren granite peaks. Stretching to the east was an open plain that gave rise to gentle hills undulating in the distance, the path they had followed here yesterday. Just off to the northwest was a boot-shaped harbor, rimmed at its sole by a sandy beach. Fir trees extended to the water's edge on both sides of the rounded cove, which narrowed to create a northward outlet to the sea. This was *Ard na Caithne*—known to sailors as *Gall Iorras*, Peninsula of the Foreigners, a place of safe anchorage on the desolate Ciarraighe coast.

Hearing hushed voices, Tomas turned toward the shelter. Brigid emerged, draping a woolen blanket tightly around her shoulders against the cold.

"The sky would seem to argue with our plans, Brother Tomas."

"Possibly. Yet it is a dry snow of early winter. Our efforts today should be unimpeded. We have adequate supplies if our return journey is prolonged."

"Even so, while the others are rising I should like to assess the harbor when we may." With a nod to Alill, she drew a cord about her waist, tying it fast as she walked toward the horses. Tomas followed.

Their path to the water was flat and clear of brush. Once at the beach, Padraig's wisdom in choosing this as the future arrival port for the relic-bearing ship was readily apparent. Whitecapped waves foamed incessantly on the ocean's surface, then calmly yielded their energy to the stillness of the inner harbor's depths.

"Sister, in giving thought to our preparations for summer, I have been deeply inspired by the stone oratory you use for worship. Please share with me how you undertook its construction."

"Tomas, a chapel was our foremost desire as the priory was established. We were twelve in number, with no less zeal for Christ than his apostles. Our labors were earnest but our physical strength limited. The planting field about us was strewn with gourd-sized rocks, which were gathered into border fences as they were not usable for building. There was also a hill, an upheaval of earth, weathered on one side exposing fragments of slate."

"'Upon this rock I will build my church.'"

"'And the gates of hell shall not prevail against it.'" They dismounted and walked along the strand, horses in rein behind. "Through grace we were provided with stones that we could lift, carry, and stack. It is a small chapel, no taller than it is wide, but it is strong and dry. We laid the cornerstone in midsummer that first year, and the tapered walls met above in time to shut out the autumn rains."

Beneath their feet the sand gave way to hardened snow-covered ground that jutted roughly into the cove for several hundred feet. They crossed the mouth of a broad freshwater stream and continued along the cove.

At the apex of the jetty there was an abrupt drop-off toward the water. Looking down they noticed layers of eroded brown limestone piled one atop the next, many deposited haphazardly from millennia of tidal force: a cache awaiting this moment of discovery for greater purpose.

"Tomas, you spoke rightly of inspiration," Brigid said, her eyes meeting his assured glance regarding the provision of stone well suited for building at the precise moment of need. "What do you envision for our work ahead?"

"Let us return here in May after your Easter stay at Ard Mhacha. We will bring with us ten brothers. Together we should readily complete our oratory by summer's end." He pointed toward Alill's fire, embers rising high with the billowing smoke. "I suggest it be built upon the elevation used for this day's encampment. It will need to be of sufficient dimensions to house the protectors of the relic while a permanent monastery is readied, likely a year or longer in duration."

"We are so agreed. But do hold this in confidence. The others would not now benefit from knowledge of the plan. And I sense from our guide that his Christian allegiance is forced, unlike that of King Óengus."

"Yes, sister, I have felt the same."

They rode back in silence, following the stream south toward a frozen marsh, then uphill to a site Tomas indicated might be appropriate for the eventual monastic settlement. Snow began to drift down, iridescent flecks celebrating in sunshine as the clouds moved east.

Friday, 9 July 2010, Armagh

"Father, pardon me for disturbing your thought. Might you be interested in a bit of lunch?"

It took a moment for Kevin to orient himself to the present. Looking at his watch he realized he'd been focused on the Brigid letters for over three hours.

"Gerry, of course. Thank you for your extraordinary patience. I've been completely engrossed in these remarkable documents." He swung the gooseneck LED magnifying lamp toward the wall and flipped the toggle switch off. "Okay if I leave these out?"

"'Course, Father. No one has the key except me and the office."

Kevin stood, stretched, and pushed the metal swivel stool under the desk. He followed Gerry through a maze of bookshelves, lateral drawer files, and horizontal portfolio cabinets. At the opposite end of the room was a long flight of stairs that led to an exit opening into the church's robing room. Once outside, they crossed Castle Street and descended a series of steps down onto Market Square.

"If you don't mind takeaway, I was thinking we might stop at Hester's Place round the corner to pick up sandwiches, then maybe eat here since the weather's so mild. Working downstairs I've come to appreciate the outdoors more than most, I suppose."

"That'll be fine, Gerry." He stopped, reached for his wallet, and withdrew a twenty-euro note. "In fact, please order two of your choice along with drinks and I'll wait for you here, okay?"

Gerry shook his head and patted Kevin's offering with both hands. "I'll be ten minutes at most. You rest in the sun, then." He turned and strolled downhill toward Upper English Street.

To Kevin's right a towering stone cross dominated the public square. It had drawn his attention immediately from atop the stairs and he was anxious to study it more closely. Rising from a low pedestal, the plain base tapered skyward to support a large circle upon which was superimposed a perfectly symmetric cross. There was no historical marker, but to Kevin it did not appear ancient. He sat and leaned comfortably against it.

A short while later Gerry arrived carrying two paper sacks and a handful of napkins.

"I bring you a choice of corned beef or ham, each with butter and goat cheese."

"Wonderful, Gerry. I'll try the ham, thanks." He unwrapped the sandwich, spread the wax paper on his lap, and set the small container of warm chips next to the Coke bottle on the step.

"What can you tell me about this cross?"

"Not much, Father. It's said to show what Saint Padraig's high cross might've looked like in better days. There's little to go by—you saw the sad remnant of the original back in the cathedral—a real millennial, that, meaning a thousand years at least. But this one's surely true to Padraig's spirit, him having carved the first Celtic cross in 450 or so." He broke off some bread crust and tossed the pieces to a threesome of gulls who had been threatening to swoop down if not fed.

"The circle and the cross: the eternal saving grace of Jesus's crucifixion. Patrick was fond of this particular symbol?"

"Obsessed, more like. That and clover."

"The Holy Trinity."

"As is said." Gerry nodded.

They finished their lunch in silence. Kevin's thoughts were riveted on Saint Patrick's chosen symbol, the Mary Magdalene illustration, and Aideen's pendant. *The curing cross has been lost. I need you to find it in time to save Michael.*

"Shall we return to the dungeon?" Kevin teased.

With a loud laugh, Gerry rose and threw the rest of his chips to the impatient gulls.

+ + + + + + + +

Once again seated at the utilitarian workbench, Kevin turned on the study lamp and sorted through the fragile fifth-century letters. Each page was sheathed individually in a sturdy archival polyester sleeve, sealed on two edges. There were nine in all, a few preserved quite well and others barely legible, faded and with small fragments missing. Three of these were attributed to Brigid. With Gerry's help before lunch he had deciphered portions of the text of two, in which the young nun described the founding of her abbey in Druim Criaidh, later named Kildare. Now he set about reading what he could make out from the third.

The greeting itself heralded a change in tone compared with the earlier letters. Brigid wrote with respectful formality but now expressed warm familiarity and mutual reliance.

In the second paragraph she reported on a recent winter journey to the western coast, accompanied by several of Patrick's monks and in whom she entrusted delivery of the letter. The group was led by the brother of a king whose name Kevin did not recognize.

"Gerry, do you know anything about King Enzus, if I've read this correctly? It's here," Kevin said, pointing with the tip of an unsharpened pencil.

"A Gaelic scholar you're not, I'd say. This says Óengus, one of the Celtic baron kings. We'll have to look him up if you'll be needing more detail."

"I'll add it to the list, thanks." Kevin had already concluded that he would depend on his friend at the Old Library for a literal translation and historical reference, as he was well beyond his rudimentary knowledge of the archaic language used in the documents. He continued his way down the page.

"*Ciarraighe*. Kerry, correct? And Gall Iorras?"

"That exact spelling I haven't seen elsewhere. 'Course *Gallarus* is what they call the ruins of an ancient stone church out on Dingle in County Kerry. Must be what she's talking about. It wouldn't surprise me if it was that old."

"And *taisí*?"

"Ah, now that's one I won't be needing to look up, Father, seeing as it's my life's work. In Gaelic *taisí* means *relic*."

Friday, 9 July 2010, Rathmines

She came to him in the night: a breath, a breeze, gentle on his cheek as a kiss.

He peered into formless haze—eyes temporal closed—and saw
Garden verdant, suffused with rose-sweet bouquet: Iveagh reborn;
Fountains twin: serpent crushed beneath winged spirit's heel;
Bench soft with drift-down petals: canes pruned, smoldering,
*   thorns burnt low.*
He lay curled, cradled—temple pulse rapid—hand gentle on his cheek;
Lifeblood coursed natal: hers, his, then at once away.
Too soon distant: unseeing, unseen—obscured beyond scales of
*   senility.*
Now away, away: eyes bright not with single color but all,
*   gaze gentle on his cheek.*

Without awakening he turned and slept dreamless, secure in the arms of a newborn angel.

CHAPTER SIX

BAILE AN SCEILIG † BALLINSKELLIGS

13 Shebet, AD *30, Capernaum of Galilee*

The morning air had not yet taken on the heat of day. Still, the woman lay in bed shaking with fever. Mary set the damp blanket on the floor next to her wooden stool and covered Simon's mother-in-law with another that had been set out to dry several hours earlier. Since Mary's arrival from Magdala yesterday noon, she had not left the house even for morning synagogue, where Jesus would be teaching. Now her concern was no longer on preparations for Simon, Andrew, and the Master. Instead, she feared that her friend might not survive the worsening delirium and stupor.

As Mary pulled back the darkly striped bed drape, the woman's daughter awoke from a fitful, brief rest. *Watch over your mother. I must speak with Simon. He will want to know.*

Few people wandered the stone pavements on Sabbath, and the paths were utterly barren during the reading of Scripture. She hurried through the market, her scarf floating heavily across the surfaces of empty tables still strewn with debris carelessly left behind from vendors who'd eked out every last sale before Friday's sunset. Ahead the street narrowed as it zigzagged amidst apartments, corner gardens, and communal stables.

She could hear murmuring as she approached the synagogue courtyard. A crowd had gathered about the entrance, whispering excitedly about the teacher from Nazareth who had arrived that morning, bringing with him a trail of followers who believed him to be a prophet.

Mary entered the sanctuary. A multitude of men and women stood uncomfortably close together, pressed shoulder to shoulder. They were silent, listening intently to the second reading from the sacred scrolls. She edged her way to the right rear corner, then moved forward along the side wall until she was nearly within arm's reach of the village rabbi in his chair.

Standing among the people who had encircled him in rapt attention, Jesus held a scroll open to Isaiah but recited the holy Scripture from heart. His voice was soft yet carried across the room. As he spoke, he looked deeply into the eyes of the hearers, lingering from one to the next. Mary felt herself falling into his words, and peace came upon her.

From the back there were sudden cries and hollers. A disheveled man barking curses lurched left, then right, forcing his way toward the front. He spat upon those he passed, raising his head upward from a hunched posture.

Jesus closed the scroll and gave it to the rabbi. He walked to the possessed man, placed his hands on the man's head, and closed his eyes.

Ah! What have you to do with us, Jesus of Nazareth? Have you come to destroy us? I know who you are, the Holy One of God.

Be silent, and come out of him!

The man became still. His grimace loosened, and his countenance became serene. After a moment he stood to his full height, faced Jesus, wept, and embraced him.

Come, let us walk in the sun.

Jesus led the man out of the synagogue. Only as he entered the courtyard did those left inside begin to talk in wonder about what they had witnessed.

Mary followed quickly after Simon, who was making his way through the congregation to keep pace with the Master. Andrew joined them at the door.

Simon, you are needed at home. Your mother-in-law is gravely ill. Please, ask for his help.

The brothers immediately pushed into the crowd to find Jesus. Mary stood and looked out over the mass of people. Her gaze was drawn toward a cypress tree at the foot of the stairs. He was there, beckoning her gently with an open arm. *Show me the way to Simon's house.*

Saturday, 10 July 2010, Ballinskelligs

The daylilies clustered in masses along the stone fence separating her side yard from Peg's were just beginning their summer show. The first wave of yellow blooms had awakened with the sunrise, and the rest of the stalks sagged with the weight of multiple green buds.

Aideen sat on the dewy grass, gloved hand searching under the lily foliage for the base of a particularly tall weed. Finding it, she tossed it into the bushel basket and stepped back to assess her progress. Already the gardens were taking on a tended appearance. Next she would clear the peonies of their spent flowers. Unexpectedly her eyes welled at having missed the vibrant pastel blossoms and with the realization that Maw Maw's Waterford crystal vase had gone empty the entire month of June.

Shears in hand, she crossed the rear lawn to her rose garden. The trellis was pink with miniature blooms, and the height of the tea roses was masked by the floribundas thriving beneath. She gathered a bouquet of three dozen or more laden stems, clipped away the thorns, and walked up the steps to Peg's kitchen door.

"Sweet Addy, you're home! And look at those roses!" Peg held the door wide and gave Aideen an affectionate hug with her left arm. "I have missed you! How is Michael?"

"He's okay, for the moment. I really shouldn't have left him—they insisted."

"Don't you worry yourself to an early grave, Addy. He's a strong boy. You can trust on that, saints be blest." She took an iridescent blue ceramic ewer from the corner cabinet, filled it with water, and arranged the roses as she talked.

"I'll wet the tea as soon as Danny gets back from Browne's. Can you imagine, brewing our way through two boxes since last week, just the two of us! He's to bring back a loaf of whole-grain bread, if they have it, and I'll toast up a feast! Look at you, Addy, just a waif." She centered the vase on the table. "Juice, Addy? Orange or apple?"

"No, Peg, thanks. Do sit. I'll wait on the tea."

"And the toast, then, too." Peg leaned forward and grasped Aideen's hands in her own. "Addy. Dear Addy. I worry about you. Do plan to eat dinner with us. Every night, while you're home. Won't you, now?"

"You are kind. Tonight, at least."

"That's a start, then. Now, tell me about your young man." Aideen sighed.

"Peg, I thought the first time was rough. It's so much worse once you've let down your guard." Her gaze drifted to the window, and she followed the flight of a chaffinch swooping down to the suet feeder. "I won't survive burying Michael. Not after Caitie." She felt Peg's hold on her hands tighten firmly.

"We'll come through this together, we will. Danny and I, count on us as family."

"You know I feel the same. Thank you."

"There's no thanking to be done. Ah! That'll be Daniel."

They both looked reflexively toward the front hall, having heard a car door closing on the drive. Danny strode into the room carrying two sacks, one in each arm.

"Set those down and greet Addy, luv. I'll dig out the tea." Aideen stood and accepted a warm embrace.

"Good to see you, Addy. Peg practically squealed when we saw your car out front after getting back from my sister's place in Clifden last night. Did she wake you? I'm jesting, of course. Welcome home."

"It's good to be home, Dan. I'm so grateful for all you both have done for us. We left rather abruptly." She smiled as he shrugged acknowledgment. "I'll try to give you proper warning next time, which I expect will be week's end." As Peg poured boiling water into the pot, the deep aroma of Assam blended with the sweetness of the bouquet. A moment of serenity wafted past Aideen, and with it a hint of new hope.

"Addy, why don't you and Danny set the dining table and I'll finish with the toast. Take these too—they've been sitting in the drawer waiting for a special occasion, and here we are!" She handed Aideen a new pack of vibrant paisley paper napkins and ushered the two out of the kitchen. Danny pointed Aideen toward the sideboard for tableware while he opened the stereo cabinet door. Soon the subdued opening refrains of Smetana's Moldau undulated in the background.

"How perfect for a sunny morning, Dan. It's one of my favorites." She placed the ivory Belleek dessert plates aside the napkins and returned to the sideboard for cups and saucers. Peg entered carrying the full teapot in its cozy, which she set down on a wooden trivet along with a small jug of milk, then disappeared back into the kitchen.

"Peg is such a dear. You're lucky to have found her, Dan." He caught her glance momentarily, then focused an absent look on the empty plate before him.

"She's my life, Addy. I never expected to be blest twice. Eanid is here, though, in my heart, never far. There's room for both." They listened as the flutes introduced a placid interlude, followed by a soft echo from the strings. "I drove over to see Father Finnian last week." He looked up to watch her response. "We don't see him much, now that he's being cared for at St. Joseph's in Killorglin. He asked after you." She sat silent, only her infrequent slow blinks breaking her stare. "Addy, he's eighty-eight."

"I'm sorry to hear he's failing," she said softly as she began to fold the napkins in half diagonally. "When did he leave the rectory?"

"Well, it must be nearly three weeks now. Another minor stroke. He can't manage getting into the wheelchair anymore, not with his weak legs. It was time."

"Yes. Maybe so." Just then the kitchen door pushed wide and Peg appeared with a platter of toast and a caddy of three jams.

"Danny, luv, why don't you grab some spoons for us and we can get started." Reaching back, he pulled open the sideboard drawer for the silver. "Addy, a blessing?"

"Of course." With heads bowed, they held hands. "'May the Lord bless this food and fill our hearts with the warmth of friendship. Amen.'"

"And you've surely brought your blessing on this house, Addy. Thank you for sharing breakfast with us." Peg handed out spoons to each and offered the jams to Aideen.

"Peg, I was telling Addy about our drive to Killorglin."

"Father Finnian! Sharp as a wit, can you believe, and filled with compassion. A saint in our midst." She crossed herself, then continued. "Danny, whatever would have happened to you without Father's prayers when Eanid was ill? I faint to think." She smiled somberly at her husband.

"Or without you to lift me from my loss." He touched her cheek with the back of his finger. "Now, it's a bright summer morn. Let's speak of happier times."

"I'm fine talking about him, really," Aideen said, more loudly than intended. "Dan, you are right, of course. He's only getting older. And Peg, I believe Father is committed to his flock." She paused, then drew a quick breath. "Caitlin was not an easy child, and to be sure I was hardly an easy parent to console. I have no one to forgive but myself." The confession sounded hollow even to her. "I'd like to see him. Monday. I'll visit him Monday."

"There, now. Good for you." Peg stood, refreshed their tea, and opened the window. As cool air breezed in, the room instantly filled with odors of the salty Irish coast.

+++++++++

Aideen zipped her jacket and donned its hood. The shadows cast by the red sun were long, and the winds blew off the water at will.

No one wandered the abbey ruins this evening as she reminisced over childhood games of hide-and-seek. There were hundreds of spots to silently crouch behind, never knowing if discovery was a breath away and with it being turned to stone by a pursuer's touch, or if one would escape and be declared the victorious Monk Hidden Amonkst Us.

Walking along the outer perimeter of the rectangular stone church and its field of grave markers, she brushed her hand lightly across the centuries-old roofless walls. Fragments of legends filled her thoughts, bits of stories still embellished by youthful fantasies first dreamt when the memories were laid.

When she reached the exterior corner of the ruin, her destination stood solemnly ahead. Essentially a mausoleum, these stacked stone tombs held the ancient bony remains of Augustinian monks. The upper layer was set back a few feet, creating from the lower tombs a knee-high ledge that begged one to sit and contemplate.

Aideen approached the burial site slowly, reverently, and swept away dirt from her chosen place on the ledge. Sitting with eyes closed, she envisioned Maw Maw beside her. Around her neck, then as now, hung the silver pendant given her by the elderly woman. Maw Maw told the tale of the cross as it had been handed down over the generations, of monks living on these grounds, charged to protect the hidden relic and its healing power. Aideen strained to remember forgotten details. At the end of the telling, Maw Maw cried tears of gratitude at having been cured, and tears of sadness from the untimely loss of descendants who had not, and would not, be cured by the cross that could no longer be found.

That September, Aideen had held her Maw Maw's arthritic hand as a youthful Father Finnian administered Last Rites. Despite the child's unquestioned belief in the holy oils as magical and life-sustaining, Maw Maw died. Decades later, his anointing did nothing to halt the fatal illness of her cherished Caitlin.

Now, at seventy, she struggled to understand Father's earthly limitations and his call to charity. Although holy oils had twice failed to cure, she prayed instead that he might hold a key memory of Maw Maw's history, a light on the distant past, that could help Michael. Soon she would ask.

CHAPTER SEVEN

SCEILIG MHÓR † SKELLIG MICHAEL

Friday, 15 June 512, Reask

The wolves were restless. In the full moon, their silhouettes moved erratically on the crest of the mountain. Conlaeth usually had little fear of the innumerable packs that methodically stalked the immense uninhabited wilderness of Éire. Tonight their behavior was unsettled and less predictable. Already anxious from travel and the urgency of his assignment, he fought to settle but sleep eluded him.

He sat, leaning back on the upwardly curved wall of the stone hut. As abbot he was privileged to have a small clóchan for himself during his occasional stays at this isolated monastic outpost. Others were shared by two or three monks, and the double huts by twice that. The woolen bed sacks and token storage chests were laid closely astride each other. Occupants crouched as they entered, then crawled to their beds. In winter the confined space gladly preserved warmth; in summer the stone retained cool.

Conlaeth's muscles ached. He was no longer accustomed to riding horseback days on end, and his body adjusted poorly compared to years past. Now in his seventh decade, he had finally chosen a successor for his role as bishop and abbot of Cill Dara. With Brigid's approval, on this journey he would begin to groom Fionán for the burdens associated with leadership. If the younger, somewhat rash monk proved worthy through accomplishing a task of great challenge and importance, in three years time Conlaeth would reveal his plan and gradually ensconce Fionán in the many responsibilities of the job. Once retired, he could at last make his long-planned pilgrimage to the Holy See in Rome.

Outside the air hung heavy. Dew collected on the fence that encircled the half-dozen huts of Riasc. It reached only thigh height, the limit of human strength for lifting the dense rocks into place, but deterred many animals from approaching. With one foot on the wall, he looked to the east. There, illuminated in the strong moonlight of a cloudless mid-June night, stood Gall Iorras, the freestone oratory built thirty-five summers prior by Brigid and Brother Tomas. Of the ten monks who had helped cut and carry the stone slabs from the shoreline of nearby Ard na Caithne for its construction and later the monastery, three remained, ever-steadfast in their commitment to protect the relic originally entrusted to them. Novice monks were assigned to Riasc in rotations of five years, after which they returned to Cill Dara filled with humility and purged of desire for earthly things.

This night Fionán and novice Broccán guarded the oratory and relic. Seeing no wolves on the plain, Conlaeth set out with a quick pace. The mile-long path was broad and worn, compacted earth solid beneath his stride. As he approached, candlelight flickered through the open door, which at five feet rose to only a third of the full height of the impressive peaked structure. In the silence, his footfall against the path was readily heard.

"Father, is there cause for alarm? What purpose draws you out in the night?" A young man with dark short-cropped hair emerged through the opening, head slightly bowed to miss the lintel. In the pale light his familial resemblance to Padraig was unmistakable.

"Broccán, I am only an old monk whose sleep fails with the brevity of his dreams. I seek the company of Fionán, if he would join me for a walk."

"To be sure, to be sure I shall," Fionán said as he came forward. His hushed voice, well suited to the hour, bore a nasal quality acquired from recent years in Wales. He put a hand on the younger monk's shoulder. "We'll not wander far. Beckon us in need."

Broccán nodded, then returned inside as the two set off.

"Brother Conlaeth, it is good you are here. Please, share any news that you may have felt restrained from speaking earlier in the presence of others." They slowly followed the path, eyes down but ears alert against prowling animals. "I have missed our conversations."

"As have I, Fionán." He waited until they were more distant from the oratory before continuing. "How fares Weylyn? Do not let your respect for the old man taint your words. He has served long and well, yet none of us is beyond the menace of age."

Fionán sighed deep and long. "Sire, I will speak openly, then, yet with sorrow: his mind falters. Since my coming I have of need carried his duties. The novices suspect his weakness and it drags on their hearts. Surely there are trials enough without fearing for the safety of the cross."

Stopping, Conlaeth turned and looked intently into Fionán's eyes. "You are perceptive in many ways—his letters of late raised no small concern." He paused, brow tightly furled. "When did you last verify that the amphora lies sealed and undisturbed?"

"Easter morn, eight weeks past."

"We will let it rest for now." He resumed their walk. "Fionán, perhaps you have intuited that my visit is not wholly administrative. As you yourself saw in Wales, Arian heretics are afoot, empowered by the death of Clovis. His kingdom in Gaul is fractured, and the holy alliance with Pope Symmachus has ended. Vandals threaten our lands." Again he stopped. Again their eyes met. His words were measured and firm. "The relic cannot remain here."

Fionán stood, arms crossed, eyes cast downward as he sought to comprehend the implications of these events. "This is grave news indeed. What must be done? They will not dare remove it to Rome?"

"Decidedly no—Odoacer may be dead, but Roman antagonism to the Church is not." He pointed them back toward the oratory but took no step. "Fionán, Brigid and I trust in your talents. We believe God's hand guided you back to us at this precise time from your sojourn abroad. My son," he paused, somber, "are you willing to sacrifice greatly for your faith, even if unto death?"

"Such is my life, Father. His will be done."

Hearing the monk's ardor, Conlaeth wrapped his hands about those of his ecclesial heir. "So it shall. And in your task you will not be alone: Broccán has his uncle's tenacity—while I lament that you did not know Padraig, it is truly a blessing that you know his nephew. As I trust in you, know that you must trust in his faith and undaunted strength."

Fionán bowed agreement.

The moon shone on the land. Conlaeth gestured far to the west, far beyond Riasc, out beyond the hills to the unseen coast. "Together you will make habitable a rocky eminence rising abruptly out of the sea. It will be a defensible monastery, a hidden sanctuary, for the cross of our Lord."

Monday, 12 July 2010, Dublin

Stephanie arrived at the centre early to prepare for her 9:30 meeting with Kevin. She yawned one on the next, having worked past dark all the previous week then exploring the exuberant nightlife of the Temple Bar district with an energy sustained only by youth. Her ever-larger circle of friends contrasted with her rather solitary lifestyle in Boston. Whether a new Steph was emerging in the social freedom of living abroad or if she simply drew the intrigue of others as the single American in her clique: this had yet to play out.

Now at her desk, she sorted her notes into three neat stacks. Research on Saint Patrick had been easy, so much having been written about him and with the abundance of primary sources at Trinity. While many details of his life and legend were new to her, what she had assembled was a basic catalog of known information. There was even more available on Mary Magdalene, and much of that clouded in controversy—just the endless debate whether Mary of Magdala and Mary the sister of Lazarus were one and the same filled page after page.

The smallest stack on her desk was a summary of everything she could find about Brigid of Kildare. Kevin had mentioned the saint's name literally in passing as he explained Stephanie's new assignment before leaving for Armagh. *You should probably see what you can dig up on Brigid too.* This footnote comment at the end of an hour-long lecture on Mary and Patrick seemed a tease—a prod that riveted her focus on the least known of the three.

Spending the summer in Ireland had been a last-minute change to her academic plan. Even during spring break she'd reassured her parents that she would be home preparing to retake the MCATs in September: without better scores there was little chance of her getting into medical school. Her Scriptural Dialogue class with world-famous Professor Schaeffer and the offer to intern had upended it all.

The quiet of the empty centre was abruptly extinguished by the sudden whistling of a teakettle down the hall. It was not yet 7:30 and staff usually didn't start arriving for another hour, especially on Mondays. Stephanie sat silent, listening attentively to the clinks of spoon in cup, a muffled clearing of throat, and the tap of approaching steps that softened as they crossed from tile to carpet.

"Stephanie, I didn't expect you'd be here quite yet. Good morning."

"Father, you surprised me too. How was your trip? When did you get back?" She stood and feigned a casual pose, leaning awkwardly with her thigh against the hard edge of the desk.

"Late Friday. I learned a great deal. Actually, I spent the weekend at the library getting ready for another jaunt, this one westward." Stephanie's face flushed red with anticipated embarrassment at having nothing to contribute to Kevin's own research. "How about I grab my notebook and meet you in the conference room in five?"

With barely a moment to get ready, she hurriedly drew open the uppermost file cabinet drawer, selected three brightly colored folders—one for each stack—sharpened her pencil, and rushed upstairs. She turned on the light and waited.

"So, tell me about Brigid." Mug in hand, Kevin walked the length of the narrow room, raised the mini blinds with enough clearance to open the casement window, and sat in the round spindled armchair at table's end. A light breeze wafted the spicy scent of his chai tea about, and an unexpected image of Good Friday Mass, air heavy with purifying incense, broke upon him: perhaps the reason he was drawn to it but not black tea generally.

"Okay, sure." She opened the lime green folder and scanned her notes. "Her life is pretty interesting. I couldn't verify some of the details. For instance, it's unclear if she was born in 451 or 453. She's depicted a lot in stained glass—here are three I found posted on Wikipedia." He cleared his throat as she handed him the color prints, leaving her to wonder if it was the strong tea or a comment about her source of documentation.

"These were the paintings of their day," he said in a professorial tone. "Window art vividly told the stories of saints and biblical events to peasants in a way the Latin liturgy never could." He examined the prints thoughtfully as she continued her report.

"Did you know her mother was baptized by Saint Patrick? Her father was a pagan." She passed another printout to Kevin. "This is a Brigid's cross. According to legend, she made the first out of reed as her father lay dying. He asked to be baptized, but she hoped it would also save his life. The cross has been her symbol ever since."

"A curing cross . . ." Kevin murmured. Two reeds of equal length were woven together at the center, vaguely reminiscent of a four-armed pinwheel.

"I'm sorry?"

"Stephanie, great work. This is terrific. Wikipedia, eh? Terrific." Taking the printouts, he stood and made his way toward the door. "I want to hear the rest of your findings. If you could write a brief summary, that would be perfect. Promise, no grade involved." He smiled, indicating with a wave for her to lead the way downstairs.

"And Stephanie, if you wouldn't mind terribly? The woman who stopped by here when I was in Rome—her grandson is in the hospital. I think she may have gone home for a few days, and I bet he'd enjoy some company. Let me tell you about Michael."

Monday, 12 July 2010, Killorglin

Traffic was light on the Ring of Kerry for a Monday morning, considering it was high tourist season. The skies were spectacularly clear, and Dingle Bay glinted brightly with the rising summer sun.

Aideen had passed just one bus on N70, and that as it pulled off to a scenic overlook a few kilometers west of Glenbeigh. By 9:15 she reached Killorglin and turned left onto Bridge Street. Rather than trying to parallel park in a spot too small even for her Fiesta, she drove a block toward the bridge and into a lot facing the River Laune.

For several minutes she sat, feeling the rough idle of the compact's four-cylinder engine as her hand rested on the shifter. The river was broad and shallow here and the water smooth. Beneath the old iron train bridge downstream where the course narrowed, white-foam turbulence about the stone piers was visible even at this distance.

This was a visit born of necessity. Aideen sought details of events long buried in another's memory. Father Finnian was an old man, fragile and ill. Difficult as it might be, she was determined to set aside her lingering resentment, to recapture the recently kindled spark of forgiveness she felt toward him. And regardless of whether she failed that, she would not fail Michael.

Walking the short block back toward Jack's Bakery, she crossed the street opposite Laune Health & Beauty as the string of cars heading east came to a brief standstill behind a double-parked delivery truck. Surprised to see the salon open on a Monday, she pushed the door open and entered.

"M' gosh, Aideen, don't be sayin' it's time for your trim and tint already?"

"No, Karin, just driving through. Are these new hours? I expected you'd be out."

"Summertime, y' know. There was a call for it. People coming back from holiday and wanting to spruce up when they can. We can't afford ladies traipsin' over to Killarney for convenience."

"I imagine not." She turned toward the glass display case against the window. The array of jars and bottles were silhouetted by light streaming in. "While I'm here, do you happen to carry my shampoo in travel size?"

"Sure, and wouldn't you know it's on sale today? Consider it a bon voyage gift. Second shelf on the right. Where will you be off to?"

"How kind of you. Thanks. Dublin, actually. Michael's there."

"Summer camp, then? My boy adored Clongowes. One session's all we could afford—it's not easy on the pocket book, don't you know? Is he bookish or sports-minded?"

"Quite bookish, I'd say." Aideen returned to the counter and with a gentle wave gestured the maroon container between them, ending the topic. "Are you sure I can't pay?"

"Bring a new customer with you next time. How's that? Enjoy visiting your boy."

"I'll certainly try, Karin. Thanks again."

Jack's was a few doors down on the corner. She entered the festively painted red building from the side street, where several metal café tables were placed under the awnings. A young couple sat at one, in casual conversation over coffee. The others were empty.

Inside, three boisterous women greeted customers, hands gloved and aprons dusted with flour.

"And for you?" Aideen looked up abruptly from the display case, not expecting the immediate service. She glanced behind her and saw no one else waiting.

"Yes, thanks. I'll have a latte, please, low fat, with double espresso. I'm sorry, I haven't quite decided the rest. Do you have pound cake today?" As she asked, the irony of her order made her catch her breath in a short, soft laugh.

"How does Baileys with a caramel glaze sound?"

"Ah, like a heavenly way to start the week."

"Will this be takeaway or for here?"

"I thought I'd sit outside."

"Go ahead, then, and I'll bring it directly." Aideen pulled two napkins from the dispenser and went out. She chose a table one away from the couple and sat facing the traffic coursing along the Ring.

The last time she had seen Father Finnian was at Caitlin's memorial service. There was no Mass, at Aideen's insistence. It did not seem right to raise prayers to God in the depths of grief. Oddly, the fact of her daughter's death following weeks of painful decline seemed to arrive with a suddenness that caught her unprepared. The planned cremation stole from her all but a few moments to say goodbye. In this void of mourning she recognized the solace found in a traditional Irish wake.

A scrape of chairs against granite returned her thoughts to the present. She listened as the couple's voices receded up the street. A minute later her order, utensils, and a half-dozen sugar packets were set before her with rushed efficiency and barely a nod.

The tall glass mug felt uncomfortably warm as she raised it to her lips, then placed it back down without a sip. Instead of hunger a slight queasiness swept her. Estimating the total and adding a generous tip, she left a cluster of coins next to the plate and walked quickly back to her car.

Saint Joseph's was only a kilometer north of the village center, but the river road was narrow and the going slow. Ahead of her a rusted white linen delivery truck inched forward as it passed through the car-width train bridge underpass, its missing rearview mirrors absent witnesses to the hazards of such Irish motoring. She and the driver had the same destination. Following behind until the truck turned into the rear entrance, she continued on and parked in front.

The nursing home was immaculate, an odor of disinfectant light on the air. Overhead the ten-o'clock prayer was being recited. From the lobby Aideen caught glimpses of sisters working in silence as they scuttered between residents' rooms.

An elderly nun cloaked in a deep green summer-weight cotton shawl greeted her from the visitors' desk. Hands clasped tight, she cleared her throat and approached the woman.

"I'm afraid I didn't call ahead. I was hoping to visit Father Finnian, if that's possible? I was told he's here."

"My dear, visitors are welcome at any time. How do you know Father?"

"He was parish priest at my family's church in Ballinskelligs."

"How happy he will be to see you, then, to be sure. His spirits will be lifted for days. So few come this way, the modern day being what it is. Bless you." She handed Aideen a pen and positioned the guest registry for her to sign.

"I haven't seen Father for several years—I don't want my visit to upset him. Is he quite frail?"

"His strength is from the Lord." Extending her hand, she rested it on Aideen's. "Be at peace, child." Aideen stood quietly for a moment, then nodded slightly. "Come with me to the sitting room and I'll have Sister Consolata bring Father along shortly."

She sat in the room alone, waiting. The simple space seemed overfilled with two small upholstered chairs, an end table between them, and a floor lamp, but the window was broad and let in abundant light. On the wall opposite was a framed print of the crucified Christ.

Aideen recognized it immediately. A lithograph of the same oil by Velázquez hung in the hallway outside her bedroom with its faded inscription, "To Maire from Seamus, at the birth of daughter Siobhan—1871." There, it was a fixture, an object known yet not appreciated. Here, in solitude and without distraction, she was entranced by the rich detail. Against a near-black background, the pallor of Jesus's lifeless body, the red of his wounds, and the umber grain of the pine cross leaped out. Each barb on the crown of thorns tapered vividly to a terrifying point. Above, in full clarity on the plaque were printed the Latin words

IESVS NAZARENVS REX IVDÆORVM with their Hebrew and Greek translations. As she gazed at this representation of the transcendent Christ, her hand clung instinctively to the pendant beneath her blouse.

"Hello, Aideen." With a start, she looked and saw at the doorway an aged, weakened man crouched forward in a too-large wheelchair. His left hand rested flaccid in his lap. Moved, she went to him, brushed back strands of hair, and kissed his forehead.

"Father."

The nun bowed and left. Aideen wheeled the priest farther into the room and pulled her chair close to his.

"Father, forgive me. I've not held you kindly in my heart. I'm sorry." She looked down.

"Addy, the Lord makes his ways known to those who love. He is at work in your heart. The forgiveness you seek is his, not mine."

She sat in silent confusion, at the moment unable to wend her way through a tangle of conflicted emotions. Not knowing how to respond, she walked to the window and stared out. Gradually her thoughts turned to the reason she had come. Reaching under her hair, she unclasped the necklace, removed the pendant from its chain, and showed it to the priest.

"What do you remember my great-grandmother telling you about this?"

With widened eyes, the priest took it from her with his good hand and held it up in the light.

"It is the crag, Aideen. The crag." He placed it in her up-turned palm and traced the edges of the triangle with his finger. "I've not seen this since your great-grandmother brought it to me for a blessing. You were ill. Maire prayed it would keep you safe."

"She told me to wear it always, and I have."

"Her prayers were answered. Here you are."

"Yes, here I am, Father. Alive, having lost a daughter and about to lose a grandson."

He closed her hand around the pendant and pointed to the portrait of Christ.

"*Misericordia*. Mercy. Through his merciful heart, salvation."

"*Misericordia*." Again she was dumbstruck. "Mercy for Michael."

"Through his grace, faith."

Her hand was clenched so tightly that the fingers blanched white and the corners of the medallion dug into the skin. She relaxed her grip and looked once again at the figure in her palm.

"You said this is the crag. What does that mean?"

"The crag—Skellig Michael. Did she not tell you about the cross?"

At mention of the cross, Aideen erupted into tears, then sobs. To that point the priest had spoken in the abstract, her emotions held barely in check. They now overflowed: the pain of her impending loss real, the cross her last hope.

Father Finnian leaned forward, picked up a box of Kleenex from the table, and set it on Aideen's lap.

"I'm sorry, Father. Thank you. I'm sorry." Wiping her eyes, she let herself calm. Slowly she meted out half sentences with a tremulous, then full-throated, indictment.

"Maw Maw told me she was the last in our family to be cured by the cross. That's all I can recall of her stories. Father, I must know more. My grandson is dying of cancer. What happened to the cross? What do you know?"

Pushing himself back in the wheelchair with his right hand, the priest sighed deeply and shook his head.

"Addy, I'll tell you what I can, but I don't know where the cross went."

"Please, whatever you know," she implored.

"What I know is the oral history of our Augustinian order, passed down through the centuries." The words came slowly, yet without faltering. "A cask bearing pieces of the true cross was sent to Ireland during the time of Saint Patrick. The great saint himself received it and placed his seal lest it be opened. The monastery at Skellig Michael—the crag, as I told you—was built for its protection, a rocky fortress in the violent sea. From afar the island appeared as a remote pyramid rising out of the water." He touched the pendant. "None of that stopped attack by the Vikings when they braved the oceans."

"So you think it was stolen?"

Shaking his head, he continued. "No, Addy—remember, this was eight hundred years ago. The attacks meant the island was no longer secure. It was then that the Ballinskelligs Abbey was built near to shore and the cask taken there, where it could be guarded by a host of monks. Soon all knew its power to heal, yet the monks were still charged with its safety: thus the ill were brought under veil of darkness in what became a sacred ritual of rumor." The strength of his voice faded, and he stopped to catch breath.

Her thoughts turned to Maw Maw's Bible, to the baptismal list, to those marked by the symbol of the relic. The revelation that others beyond her family or the peninsula of her childhood might have touched the cross and been healed was a solace that only intensified her sorrow at its loss.

Father Finnian moaned softly as he shifted in his chair, then hastened to finish the tale. "Sadly, though, the stronghold was turned to rubble with the Protestant Reformation, and the order disappeared into the hills. They lived in small stone huts and were forced to move the cask from place to place across Iveragh and Dingle, keeping it hidden but for healings." His eyes sank. "In the aftermath of the great famine its location was known to none."

Her gaze followed his downward. "Maw Maw was cured when she was sixteen. That would've been in 1866 or '67. So this all fits," she said, momentarily resigned. Then with renewed vigor: "Father, Maw Maw said she actually touched the cross."

Again he paused. "I have to believe your great-grandmother was delirious and near death when she was taken to the cask. It might have been the saint's seal she touched, that I can't say, but surely it was the true cross inside that healed. That's what she would have remembered—being healed by the cross."

"Perhaps so. Still, she told a convincing story, at least to me." Her tone turned sardonic. "And exactly how does one misplace an ancient cask?"

In the face of skepticism, his shrug was weak, asymmetric. "Imagine it lying hidden, with only a handful of old monks watching over it. Imagine a few years going by, a decade, then two, without it being moved, those monks who knew gradually dying off and carrying their secret to the grave."

Aideen was fascinated by the details of a history she had never heard, of great events that literally occurred in her village and surrounding hills. She knew these ruins, the stone huts that dotted the landscape, the tombs of monks who may have died protecting the cross.

Yet she was no closer to saving Michael's life.

CHAPTER EIGHT

CABLE O'LEARY'S

7 Adar, AD 30, Magdala of Galilee

Z ebedee stood at the water's edge on the northernmost shore of the Sea of Galilee. Behind him a crowd of six hundred exclaimed farewells as Simon and Andrew pushed their boat free from the sand, then set sail for Magdala. The thriving village was on the western coast and a mere four miles distant, but this was a heavy wooden vessel built for fishing, not speed. With the day's light wind and thirteen men aboard, Simon did not expect to arrive until dusk.

Today had been a revelation for Zebedee. For months he had watched with great skepticism as his sons James and young John, in whom he entrusted his fishing business, abandoned their work and follow a would-be prophet. It was beyond reckoning. From Capernaum to Nazareth and farther to the border cities of Tyre and Sidon, there was foment. The populace thirsted for freedom from Roman domination, and many were willing to accept nearly any zealot who professed to be the promised Messiah.

Now all had changed. That morning he witnessed Jesus preach a message of love and peace to thousands who gathered on the surrounding desolate hills, then was amazed as the multitude was fed their fill with a few fish and loaves of bread. He felt the teacher's words deep within and came to believe as truth that which his sons and wife had accepted long before.

John sat at the stern, watching the image of his father on shore slowly disappear. As the youngest of the Twelve, and with several in their thirties, he felt scared and alone.

Turning, he looked toward the bow and into the eyes of the Master.

Be not afraid. I am with you.

He rose, worked his way to Jesus, and gently leaned against his chest.

The sea was calm and the fishermen dragged their nets for a dinner's catch as they neared Magdala. Oil lamps were already burning in many of the homes and the evening streets were quiet. Greeting them were twenty or more disciples who had followed the boat's progress from shore.

In their midst was Salome, Zebedee's wife. She waited for James to anchor the boat and reach land. Arrangements had been made for the Master and apostles to eat at Mary's home at the edge of town. There would be room for all to rest the night. Salome called for John to walk ahead with her and help prepare the cooking fire. They set out immediately.

The dark of night was complete with still a half mile to go when Martha came rushing forward to meet them, crying. *When will my Lord arrive? Mary has fallen asleep, and I cannot rouse her. John, go in haste and bring him directly. Tell him one whom he loves is ill.*

The youth left them and went running back toward the village. Salome returned with Martha to Mary's bedside.

A short while later Jesus and the Twelve came up to the house and were received at the door by a follower known to Jesus.

Rabbi, Mary has been possessed by demons these past days. She burns with the fire of Gehenna and moans with voices of the lost. The pallor of death is upon her, and the marks of Satan bruise her flesh. Blood froths pink from her mouth, and below she is unclean. Her belly swells with sin.

The disciple stood aside as Jesus entered and was shown to Mary's room, where Martha waited. Leaning over the sick woman, he touched his cheek to hers, laid his hand on her abdomen, and breathed over her.

Mary, be well.

The woman stirred, then opened her eyes.

Rabbouni. You have anointed me.

It is you who will one day anoint me. Your faith has saved you. Rest now in peace.

Monday, 12 July 2010, Dublin

Kevin walked at a quick pace up Rathmines Road, grabbed an everything bagel and double latte from Insomnia, then slowed to eat as he continued the last block to Alan Hanna's. If he didn't dawdle at the bookstore, he'd be able to visit Michael and still leave for Ballinskelligs by midafternoon.

Entering the store, he knew at once he'd be back. The densely packed shelves spanned floor to ceiling. Browsers lounged at leisure, books held with a tenderness that suggested strong disdain for electronic media. An adjacent coffeehouse stood just beyond a peaked arch: he was in his element.

The noise level grew as he approached the children's section—not with the sound of video games but of parents reading to toddlers and older siblings shouting excitement over which books they'd chosen. He leaned down to pat the well-groomed flank of the resident dog before scanning the youth adventure titles for something that would engage Michael's interest.

Most were new printings, yet it was the used that made him pause and investigate.

The lowest shelf had him kneeling and bent, head askew. Third in was the once-white spine of a slightly marred hardback, its library label still adhered. *Book 1 in The Chronicles of Narnia* appeared at the bottom of the front cover, and when opened the book emitted the anticipated sturdy, studious smell. With the thin volume bought and bagged, he headed out the door for the bus stop.

++++++++

Michael's nurse was taking two-o'clock vitals when Kevin arrived. Shortly the thermometer beeped, the blood pressure cuff self-deflated, and she jotted down the flashing numbers on her palm for later entry into the computer record.

"All set. Vanilla for your shake, you said?"

He nodded without a smile. Strands of hair dropped ash-like onto his nose from a fast-thinning scalp, his cheeks now plumped and pink from medication. Kevin's emotions jarred momentarily at the transformation of appearance from earlier— but just one glance into his eyes and the image of the boy he remembered was restored.

She turned and saw Kevin by the door. "It looks like you have a visitor." And to Kevin: "He's been a grouch since his grandma left, fours days steady. Isn't that right, Mickey?" she teased. "Yes, and there's the 'go away' look. Let's see if your friend can cheer you." Off she went with a gentle laugh.

Kevin came fully into the room and leaned back against the window seat, watching as Michael dragged a towel across his face then shook loose hairs to the floor.

"So your grandmother is away for a while? Home, is that right? I've not been there, to Ballinskelligs, but I'll be going after lunch." Michael glared. Immediately Kevin wished he'd not attempted casual conversation.

After a minute he picked up the book from the seat cushion— the crisp crinkling of the paper bag breaking the silence—and worried in the offering that the generic rectangular shape might be mistaken for a more high-tech gift. "I brought you something. You said you like adventures—maybe you haven't read this?"

At once Michael's mood lifted. He held the bag aloft by its corners and the book flopped onto his lap. He rushed to pick it up and stared at the cover. "What's it about?"

Kevin sighed relief and moved closer to the bed. "Well, it's about a lion who's actually much more than a lion, and a witch who may be pretty but is evil in her heart." He paused. "I should say that they're not from this world: the only way from here to there is through a magic wardrobe—we have closets in America, but I think you have wardrobes, right?"

Michael nodded vigorously, eyebrows bouncing acknowledgment and yet more hairs drifting down. "Sure we do. Mine's big too. I sometimes hide there—don't tell Maw Maw."

"Never," Kevin promised. He reached and pointed to the children pictured on the front. "These are the travelers: two brothers and two sisters."

Michael grew sullen. "I don't have brothers or sisters."

"See now, that's the magic of books. Read this and you'll have four," he said cautiously.

"I guess."

Kevin looked directly at him. "It's true, Mickey. It will be very much like having siblings of your own. And you'll be transported with them to another world."

The door shushed open and the nurse breezed in with Michael's shake, then as quickly breezed out.

Ignoring the shake and without looking up from the book, Michael quietly said, "Thank you."

"You're welcome, Mickey." Kevin brushed a hand softly across the boy's head. "I'm glad you like it."

They chatted a bit more about the story, then about Michael's friends back home. Time passed. At quarter to three Kevin reluctantly rose to leave, stopping at the door. "Mickey, there's a student from Boston who's working with me this summer. Her name is Stephanie. Would it be okay if she came to visit?"

Michael's face shone. "Yes, please."

Monday, 12 July 2010, Ballinskelligs

It was far along the N70 turnoff toward Ballinskelligs, past hairpin turns and dense thickets of trees, before the narrow two-lane road emerged from its forested tunnel. Kevin found himself suddenly driving within feet of the water's edge. He eased up on the accelerator and momentarily took in the tranquil view. Across the estuary the Beara peninsula peaks stood in the silhouette of early evening. Beyond lay open ocean. He was elated at having made reservations at an inn on the bay, regardless of the extra expense.

An hour later he pulled into the inn's parking lot and was surprised to find most of the spots taken by patrons of the adjacent pub, Cable O'Leary's. It was late and he was hungry. Entering the pub, he was quickly ushered to a table near the bar.

"A pint to start?"

"Most definitely. Dark, please." The barmaid tapped the edge of a folded laminated menu perched upright between bottles of brown mustard, malt vinegar, and tartar sauce.

"Plenty in here to choose from. The dailies are on the board. Can't go wrong with the fish 'n' chips. If you're in a hurry, you'll be wanting to order before the band arrives and the place really gets crowded. Murphy's good for the stout?"

"That'll be fine." Even before he finished she was off.

Kevin looked about. A row of booths lined one wall. In the opposite corner a drum set, microphones, and a scuffed amplifier awaited their performers. Square tables crammed the space between, each with more diners than there was room for place settings. It was a lively group, with a degree of familiarity that suggested most were locals. He settled in his chair and observed. The dark décor, blazing turf fire, and rowdy chatter spoke of Ireland as much as lambs bleating on the hillside.

"Bud, it looks like we'll be joining ya. Ronnie, and over there's my mates." With a slight nod, Ronnie set his beer on Kevin's table and yelled out toward the bar. "Sam!" and then in a louder voice, "Sam! My God, man! Sam!" and then to Kevin, "Hold onto these seats for us, will ya? Sam!" Kevin was suddenly in a cheery mood, made all the better by the arrival of his Murphy's and a basket of brown bread.

"Sorry this took awhile—Darren's backed up with orders. The bread's freshly fried and the best in Ireland. You won't find salted Guinness goat curd dip anywhere else, to be sure. Now, have you decided on dinner?"

"The shepherd's pie sounds good, thanks. And perhaps another basket of bread for my new friends?" Ronnie had returned, with two tousled-looking men in tow.

"Did you hear that already?—we're his new friends! Kelly, see how wrong you've pegged us?" Ronnie's exaggerated pout for the barmaid's benefit was met with backslaps by Sam and Kyle standing just behind. "We're a harmless sort, though I do admit we like a bit of craic. But who can blame us?"

"Sir, if this trio gets unpleasant in any way, wave me over and I'll set 'em straight—that or give 'em the door." Kelly gave a pursed-lips smile and shook her head. "Them's the bane of my life since Sister Mary Margaret's class, bless her soul. Another round for you boys?"

"Yes, Miss Kelly," Sam replied sheepishly as they sat. Then winking, "Do keep our friend's glass full."

Standing, Kevin reached over and shook hands. "I'm Kevin. Ronnie, and Sam, correct? And—?"

"Kyle. Glad to meet ya. You're American, right? On holiday?" Kevin's flat accent was telling.

"Yes and no. Yes, American. From Boston, actually. No, not on holiday. I'm in Dublin for the year doing research." He'd decided to dress casually for this trip, preferring to maintain a lower profile than his clerical collar would allow. Tonight he would remain simply Kevin.

"Research? Like on mice and such?" Sam was fascinated.

"Less exciting than that, I'm afraid. Just rooting around old stones and huts."

"Well, you've come to the right place, to be sure! We've plenty of those around here," said Ronnie. "One right in my backyard, even. And the standing stones just up the way." With his index finger he pointed back over his right shoulder, then searched through the breadsticks for a suitably large piece, coated it thickly with cheese, took a bite, and continued. "So, Dublin. We were over to Naan this weekend. Just got back, matter of fact. Hellish weather for the festival. Were you there?"

"Pardon?"

"The festival—music." Ronnie's head bobbed with an imagined beat, arms swinging in time. "Best lineup yet. But man, the mud. And getting back was agony—the traffic. Did you come over on M7 today, then? Could'a walked faster."

"So that was the problem. There was a tie-up on the Dublin loop at the interchange—I assumed it was an accident. Anyhow, I opted for the scenic southern route along the coast."

"Good man. Longer on average but I guarantee you saved time today."

Their talk was interrupted as Kelly approached with the drinks. "One Guinness, one Bud Light, and one double Jamie neat." Sam grimaced with suspicion at his amber-colored pint, holding it up to the candle for closer inspection.

"Kelly, don't you be fooling with me—"

"A Bud in honor of our guest." She smiled. "Nah, don't fret. 'Course it's Finnegans. I'll be back for your orders in a blink. Sir,—"

"Kevin."

"Kevin, okay if I bring everything out together?"

"Perfect. Thanks." She tucked the serving tray under her arm and left.

A sudden cheer broke out at the tables by the door as two of the musicians walked in. Sam turned to check, then stood and pushed in his chair. "Joey's here." He grabbed his beer and headed over. Kevin looked on.

"His older bro," Ronnie explained. "He leads on guitar. Bryan's harmony, that's him with the fiddle, and Tim plays drums—I don't see him yet. Celtic trad, mainly."

"They do have a following, that's for sure. Been together for, what, maybe ten years? Since high school, anyway." Kyle drained his glass. "Saw 'em fill the opera house in Cork."

"Prime it was. Kevin, you picked a good night at Cables." The spotlight came on. Ronnie laughed and rapped the table with his knuckles. "I spoke too soon. Sam looks to be filling in on drums."

There was a break in conversation as the band tuned up and Kelly set out the second round. Kevin raised his glass.

"A toast to Sam. Cheers." They clinked and drank. Ronnie and Kyle reached for the bread.

"Have either of you been to the ruins in Dingle? Gallarus, perhaps? I'm driving up there tomorrow." Though casually asked, he was keen on learning what he could of their local knowledge.

Ronnie grunted. "Are you kidding? Those school nuns, that was their idea of a regular excursion. Same thing every winter, off we'd be to muck around the fields, sometimes knee-deep in the snow."

"Every year?"

"In February. Like we'd discover something new. But nothing there ever changed. That's the thing about ruins."

"How do you mean?"

"Well, think about it, now. Those pile of rocks sat there for eons, undisturbed in the wilds. What did they expect would happen one year to the next?"

"That's not why we went, Ronnie," Kyle said with a soft sternness. "The nuns were honoring their founding mother, the woman who built that chapel. The first of February is Saint Brigid's day."

The microphone squealed abruptly. Joey quickly apologized and the band launched into its first set.

+++++++++

Kevin leaned back on the hood of his rental car and looked out at the bay. It was midnight. The sky was thick with clouds, and the only light reflecting off the water was from a lamp mounted high on the rear wall of the inn. He rested, his ears slowly adjusting to the quiet after a high-volume evening.

A chance meeting in a pub, on the night of his arrival, with someone knowledgeable about Brigid seemed improbable. That a ready connection was drawn for him between Brigid and Gallarus seemed incredible: yet so it was.

Kyle appeared reserved compared to his easygoing friends but sincere in his wanting to help Kevin, even offering to take him on a tour of the ruins in the morning. While the band played, Kevin had thought of myriad questions to discuss on the trip. Tomorrow would be a good day.

His upstairs room was chilled and damp, a wisp of breeze coming in through the open windows. They had expected him earlier—and earlier he would have appreciated the fresh air. Instead, he hunted for a blanket.

There were three missed calls and two messages on his iPhone. Ignoring the number he didn't recognize, he tapped on the first message, left at 7:03 that evening. "Hi, this is Stephanie.

I went over to visit Michael today, but they wouldn't let me see him without permission. I wrote down my name and cell-phone number and also your name, in case they call his grandmother to check. Okay, well, let me know if you talk with her and I can try again. So, thanks and . . . talk with you soon."

The second message came in at 8:40. "Father Schaeffer, this is Aideen. The hospital called just now. Michael is fine, he's fine— I've been talking with him at least twice a day and bothering those poor nurses far too often. They won't want to see me back. Anyhow, they asked if I knew a girl named Stephanie Lambert and of course I didn't, but then they said she works for you. Is she the pretty one I met at your office? Please tell her I would be happy for her to visit Michael. It was so kind of her to stop by there this afternoon. Thank you. . . . And I'm doing okay too. It's hard being away from the hospital. But I'm getting some sleep, at least. . . . Have you been able to find out anything about, well, let me know. Thanks. Thanks again. . . . Oh, you have my number, so call if you need to, or can. Thanks."

Kevin squeezed the bridge of his nose, chin on chest and eyes closed, scolding himself as he imperceptibly shook his head with the realization that he hadn't been in touch with Aideen for nearly two weeks. Worse, he'd only visited Michael once—just today— during that entire time. His ability to focus energy on a single project to the exclusion and often sheer neglect of others had long been a source of personal disappointment. He resolved to call her later in the day, perhaps with a bit more to report depending on what he would learn about Gallarus. If she were still here at her home, as he expected, he would suggest dinner out.

Turning his phone sideways to enlarge the virtual keyboard, he texted Stephanie an update. With her in Dublin and him in Ballinskelligs, grandmother and grandson might each be welcoming visitors tomorrow.

CHAPTER NINE

AN RIASC † REASK

Tuesday, 18 August 576, Kildare

"Áed, the bellows. Pump!" Startled, the young man's attention abruptly returned to the task he'd been given. He grasped the paddle with both hands and using all his weight brought it forcefully toward the ground. A blast of air rushed into the kiln and the fire flamed white-hot.

"Good, good. Now, again!"

At ninety-two, it was with difficulty that Bréanainn recalled the tortured anxiety of being sixteen. Áed's urgent concerns did not dissipate upon being named king of Leinster.

"Lad, set aside your worries—they will await tomorrow. Mind your work. Three more pumps and it should be ready."

The old monk held the iron tray high, into the hottest part of the kiln, tipping it slowly in each direction. From experience he knew that the mixture of sand and oaken potash was now molten liquid glass. Wanting this slab to be colorless yet clear of entrapped air, he would need it to remain in the oven beyond frothing but before tinting began.

"Come and let us see how we did." Áed emerged from around the rear of the oven. It was a double-walled structure of flat rock stacked six feet high, taller by a foot than the young king. Bréanainn inched back several steps to withdraw the tray from the heat, then shuffled clockwise a quarter turn and bent at the knees, keeping the slab level as he set it on the stone bench to cool. He gently slid the wooden-handled iron spatula out from under the tray and leaned it against the oven.

"This will do, lad, this will do." They inspected the glass from a yard's distance, the radiant heat keeping them from standing closer. "Did you mind how that was done, Áed? The next will be yours, and I shall work the bellows. Now, to the mosaic."

Abundant midday light filled the chapel annex, which served as the sacristy for the adjacent small sanctuary. Bréanainn had wisely chosen this as his workspace. In the center he had erected a waist-high table. The sideboard along the wall had been cleared of patens, sacramental cruets, and purificators and instead was covered with jewel-toned pieces of translucent glass.

At random Áed selected an irregularly shaped, coin-sized red fragment and held it up to the window. Sunrays streamed through the crystal, casting a vivid red image on the boy's linen shirt. "It will be a wonderment to see the mosaic in the same light," he mused.

"Remember, lad. Seven parts sand, two parts wood ash, one part quicklime." Áed nodded, earnestly memorizing the formula. "And the quicklime—tell me how you would make it."

"From shells, Father. Oyster shells, white and clean as can be. I would grind them into a powder and fire it in the kiln."

"Yes. Let the powder settle first, and do not disturb it as it bakes. Use it at once after it cools—it will not stay active for long." Bréanainn smiled upon the child, seeing in him a leader of faith quite unlike his pagan predecessors, including his now-dead father, Colmáin.

"One day before autumn I shall take you to meet Cóemgen at Gleann Dá Loch. There the monks live as hermits, yet their barren monastery is cradled in the beauty of God's mountains. It is not more than a half-day hike up to the lake with pure white sand." He reached over to a large wooden bowl, lifted a pinch of sand, and gently sprinkled it down. "Let the color of the glass be of your choosing, not that of the sand."

Bréanainn paused to let the lesson be learned, then opened a sideboard drawer and removed a leather-bound volume. He placed it on the center table, untied the bindings, and leafed through the parchment sheets, stopping at one of the last illustrations.

"This is our window, lad." Áed immediately drew close to the book, gazing at the details of the image. After a few moments Bréanainn returned from the sideboard with an array of colored glass. "Donn, for Mary Magdalene's hair." He laid out vertical rows of russet-colored glass tiles on the table. "Tawn, for Our Lady's skin. Pallid ash gray, for the Lord." An outline of the virgin holding her dead son took form. "Red, for his wounds." Ruby-colored pieces were added to Jesus's side, hands, and feet. Shards of crimson dripped down his forehead.

"And the clear glass we made today?"

"Ah, for the white roses on Our Lady's head." Bréanainn ran his finger along the wreath in the illustration. "It was a talent of immense grace your cousin Brigid had, Áed. There are no greater pictures than hers. They appear to have the breath of life, even in what would seem to be a lifeless body." He touched Jesus's wounds, and for some time they stood, silent in thought.

"So, let us resume our work after midday prayer."

The noon hour had long passed and the chapel was empty. When their eyes had adjusted to the dim light, they approached the tabernacle and knelt on the stone floor. Bréanainn intoned the Our Father followed by a prayer of veneration to Mary. Even as he recited them a second time, Áed did not join in.

"Lad, why do you not pray? Is your heart burdened with sin?"

Áed closed his eyes, and tears dripped from his bowed head.

"Speak, child. What is wrong?"

"Father, I have not been taught in the faith. My mother is a believer and I have desired it for myself, but it was not allowed."

"Have you not received baptism, then?"

"No, Father."

Bréanainn placed his hand on the young man's shoulder, then rose and walked to a small shelf next to the altar. On it stood a vial of perfumed sacramental oil, the chrism blessed on Holy Thursday. Holding the vial in his left hand, he removed the lid and went back to the kneeling boy.

The old monk dipped his thumb in the oil and traced a cross on the king's forehead.

"Áed Dub mac Colmáin, today I claim you for Christ."

Tuesday, 13 July 2010, Ballinskelligs

Kevin was asleep when the hotel phone rang at 7:15. He was not accustomed to the shrill vintage triplet of quick rings and momentarily fumbled for the alarm clock. The old handset felt unreasonably heavy as he dragged it to his ear.

"Mr. Schaeffer, Kyle Dorrian is at the desk for you. Shall I have him wait?" The clerk rightly discerned that the guest had been awakened by the call.

"Oh, God." He muffled the receiver and cleared his throat. "Yes, I'm sorry. I'll be down in fifteen minutes. Offer him some coffee, or maybe breakfast? Thanks." He lay unmoving, arm over his eyes to shutter the light. After a few deep breaths he hung up the phone and rushed to shower and dress.

"Kyle, good morning." Kevin found the young man just outside the main door. "Poor excuse—I overslept." He rubbed his unshaven face apologetically.

"I was tempted myself. No worry at all. I can wait if you haven't eaten."

"Thanks. Maybe just for a moment, then—I'll see what they have to go. Can I get you a coffee? Tea?"

Kyle shook his head decisively and patted his stomach. "I'm good. That's my gray Jetta over there—she's not much to look at but she runs, as they say. I'll drive up."

A few minutes later Kevin was back, a cheddar scone balanced atop his new travel mug that bore the inn's logo. He opened the rear door and tossed his backpack on the floor, then climbed into the left front passenger seat. "All set."

Kyle put the car in gear and turned right onto the main road. "This time of morning we should be there before ten. Straight up 566 to N70, then west out of Castlemaine toward Dingle."

"I appreciate you driving, Kyle. I'll play the gawking tourist." He bit into a corner of the scone. "So, have you always lived here?"

"Yes and no." Kevin smiled at the reference to last night's conversation. "My da's farm is off the Ring west of town. If you see any stray sheep with red splotches on their rumps, send 'em home." He laughed. "Nah, they all have registration tags these days." He tugged at his earlobe to illustrate. "The colors do help us find ours at a distance, though, even on hills a mile off." He accelerated and shifted into fifth as the narrow two-lane road became rural.

"The guys last night, I went all through school with them. They'd be gone off to Dublin in a flash if they could. Their ladies wouldn't take kindly to that."

"And you?"

"And me—no. I'll stay put, thanks."

Kevin sat quietly, taking an occasional sip from the mug. As they drove, light and shadow were at constant play on the mountainous terrain to the east.

"See, I learned by leaving that I wanted to come back." Squinting, Kyle turned his visor to block the sun, then opened his window partway. Cool air breezed into the car. "My room looks out over the sea, with Puffin Island to the right. Straight off are the Skelligs. What's not to love?" A defensive tone in his voice made the question sound more than rhetorical.

"It's good to know where you belong," Kevin offered. Kyle nodded in agreement.

"Are you liking Dublin?"

"I am, Kyle. It's a bit like Boston—plenty of Irish." They laughed. "I enjoy the traditional academic atmosphere at Trinity College. Dublin is a vibrant, literary city. Do you know it?"

"Not well. I studied for a while at Saint Patrick's College in Maynooth. There was a shuttle into town for shopping. Mostly I took in the library and museums."

"I'm fond of the Old Library, myself." He paused briefly. "Saint Patrick's—that's quite a campus." Kevin had been surprised at mention of the school. His first trip to Ireland was as guest lecturer there, following the international release of *Acts Two*. Saint Patrick's was not only a private Roman Catholic university: it was the National Seminary of Ireland. There was much to learn about Kyle.

"You've been there, then?"

"A couple of years ago. I'd just published a book and they invited me to speak."

"You wrote a book?"

"On my research at the time. It was about the apostles of Jesus in later years. 'The rest of the story' kind of tale."

Kyle gasped. "Was that you? You're a priest?" Incredulous, he looked at Kevin in a series of quick glances while trying to focus on the road. "We read your book in freshman theology class. Seriously, that was you?"

"I'm glad it made an impression—good or bad, do you think?"

"And us talking the way we did last night." Face blushed, fingers pressed hard against his temple, he looked anguished at having inadvertently embarrassed himself.

With some regret at not having revealed his vocation earlier, Kevin moved on to ease Kyle's obvious discomfort. "Tell me about your studies." It was several minutes before Kyle responded.

"I got a scholarship. I'd been talking with our pastor for a while about seminary, and he wrote a letter. So I went." They drove in silence past the turnoff to Valentia Island. Roadside placards advertising businesses in Cahersiveen began to appear.

"I worked with my da the next summer and seriously started wondering if I'd made the right decision. They let me switch programs. I found out pretty quick I didn't really like philosophy. After that I kinda ran out of steam. So I didn't go back last semester."

Kevin's immediate impulse as a professor was to counsel Kyle through his indecision. But Kyle was an acquaintance, not a student, he reminded himself.

"And what will 'the rest of the story' be for you?"

"Well . . ." The answer hung suspended, Kyle motionless in thought. "Well, that part's not yet written," he replied softly.

They entered Cahersiveen at eight o'clock. It seemed every villager with a car was on West Main, impatiently waiting to dart single-file around outsized trucks making their morning deliveries to the numerous shops fronting the street. Half an hour later they had maneuvered along the dozen blocks and mercifully reached open road.

Just past the outskirts of town, the River Fertha widened broadly to meet them on the left. Kyle pulled off at a small waterside park.

"A favorite spot for gawking," he explained, once again offering Kevin a warm smile.

They strolled along a paved path at the river's edge, Kevin focusing his iPhone camera on the mountain opposite that swooped dramatically into the valley, its reflection clear on the still waters.

"You'll want a photo of this too." Kevin turned to see Kyle heading toward a life-sized monument of a crescent-shaped boat resting on eight metallic rods. In the boat were four cloaked monks. A center mast and its bare yard rose skyward, echoing the cross on Calvary.

"Impressive."

"Saint Brendan the Navigator. It's said that he sailed his curragh from Kerry all along the coast of Ireland, then over to England and even Brittany, spreading the faith."

"To France? When was that?"

"Must have been in the five hundreds. Saint Finnian was his teacher, and I know he built the old monastery on Greater Skellig about then."

"Kyle, I'm glad to have you as a guide. You're a font of knowledge."

"I just live here, is all. And I pay attention." Kevin walked to the road to capture a photo of the curragh backdropped by the river and mountain, then returned.

"This was a good stop. Thanks."

"It's nothing." He pointed to a granite marker at the base of the monument. "It says here that Bréanainn lived from 484 to 577. That's Brendan's old Irish name. So, onward?"

+ + + + + + + + +

"Watch your head, now," Kyle said as he ducked under the low lintel of the ancient Gallarus oratory. The rectangular stone structure was no more than fifteen feet in length, but soared to an equal height along its peak. Kevin entered the dark chamber cautiously, at first making out few details. A muted puddle of morning light was cast onto the ground through the single east-facing window, much of its intensity lost traversing the opening's depth. The air inside was cool and smelled of night.

"It's brighter in February, with the sun low on the horizon." Kyle moved along the inner perimeter, examining the stacked freestone with quiet reverence. "Even empty, abandoned eons ago, this place is still a chapel. Can you feel it?" Reaching forward, he touched a waist-high stone, then the one above, and the next. "Saint Brigid and a few monks."

Kevin stood bent at the window, looking out toward the nearby hills. "Why here? Why did they choose a site so far from their abbey in Kildare?" In the distance sheep grazed on summer grass, occasional bleats echoing across the meadow.

Hearing footfall on the crushed stone path outside, Kevin looked about and saw that Kyle had left him alone in his pondering. He reflexively crossed himself before he walked out into the sunshine.

The structure was surrounded by a small walled-in yard. A mile to the northwest he could see Smerwick Harbour at Ard na Caithne, dotted by moored boats.

"The monks who built Gallarus are buried here." Kyle was studying a narrow three-foot-high pillar standing on the edge of a large plot of smooth rocks along the oratory's north side. "This ogham stone—can you see the markings?" Kevin approached, then squatted to look closer.

Inscribed into the upper third of the pillar was an encircled equal-arm cross.

"Patrick's cross . . ." Kevin's voice carried the hush of awed discovery.

"Sister Mary Margaret told us this was his first. She said he placed it here himself after Saint Brigid finished the chapel."

Kevin ran his finger in the circle's shallow groove, then the intersecting segments of the cross itself.

"Wow. Kyle, this is really something." He stood momentarily, stretching his legs, then sat semi-reclined on the ground to examine the faint lower inscriptions more closely. "What do these mean?"

"Names of the dead, maybe?" He shrugged. "Stick-figure writing shows up on all sorts of megaliths, but they aren't all that readable. To me, anyhow."

Staring at the cross, Kevin reviewed what he had learned in Armagh, salient facts uncovered from his own research, and the lore passed on through generations of nuns as had been told to Kyle: *Brigid's illustration depicted wooden remnants of Christ's cross in Mary Magdalene's upturned palm, fragments that she may have eventually brought with her to France. Brigid's letter claimed that an outpost at Gall Iorras had been built specifically to receive a holy relic from the European continent. Sister Mary Margaret and Gerry both regarded the pillar before him to be the original Celtic cross of Patrick, an image of which was echoed in Aideen's pendant.*

It was a compelling yet incomplete scenario that for Kevin raised a series of significant unanswered questions: *Had the relic of the cross actually been brought to this site and acknowledged by this marker? Was this the destination of Aideen's ancestors who sought to be healed?* And most importantly: *Where had the cross gone from here, and where was it now?*

He sat in silent trepidation: uncertain if he were on the threshold of truth—or abyss.

"The monastery at Reask isn't far, if you want to see it," Kyle urged after some time, then wandered in the direction of the car. Kevin nodded, took a few photos of the stone, and followed.

The roads zigzagged along the flat lowlands, nearly double the distance of the walking path that had originally connected the two sites. Ever-present were views of the harbor across the open plain.

They stood in the center of the ruins. Around them was an outer stone wall ringing a knee-high inner wall that meandered the perimeter. Like pearls on a string, along the lower wall were singlet and doublet circles enclosing grass.

"They lived here, Fionán and the other monks. This is what's left of their huts," Kyle indicated as he strode over a wall into one of the smaller circles. "Just a stroll to the chapel." He pointed off toward Gallarus.

"Fionán—Saint Finnian?"

"'Course. On leaving here he built the Skellig Michael monastery. We can go out there tomorrow, unless the seas are rough."

"If you have the time, yes, I would enjoy that very much."

"It's nothing. I haven't been out yet this summer, and it's not like I'm working." Taking a step up, he walked along the remains of the hut's wall, arms outstretched as though he were once again a boy of twelve. "The boat leaves most days at eleven, from the town pier. It can be a dangerous crossing. Not at all like the waters of the harbor," he explained, eyes looking northward. "Except during a storm, it's always calm. That's why Saint Brendan anchored here. He could venture close along the coast, then set a direct course to the mainland."

"France, you said."

He nodded. "Others before him did the same. Monks trekked to Brittany to pick up novices waiting to study in Irish monasteries and returned here. This was called the peninsula of the foreigners—Gall Iorras."

"Gallarus? Or did you say *Gall Iorras*?" Kevin exaggerated the pronunciation, excitedly recalling Brigid's letter and wanting to verify if he had heard the name correctly.

"*Gall*—that means foreigner. And *Iorras*—peninsula."

"It was that active a port?"

"Well, I guess if you were a monk. The trade routes all went east."

"So a landing here could go unnoticed."

Kyle rounded the fingers of both hands and drew them up to his eyes like binoculars.

"Ah, now there you're wrong. Nothing would have snuck past Brigid's watchmen."

CHAPTER TEN

CONVERGENCE

[∞]

11 Nisan, AD 30, Jerusalem

It had been a taxing day.

The City of David teemed with pilgrims preparing to celebrate Passover. At dawn the reverence of Sabbath observances abruptly faded, overshadowed by the chaotic fervor of a quarter million Jews rushing to register, make a compulsory annual contribution to the treasury, and most importantly, purchase a year-old unblemished male lamb or goat. Sacrifices for the Feast of Unleavened Bread were exorbitant in cost and immense in profit.

As members of the ruling Sanhedrin, Nicodemus and Gamaliel had spent the morning quietly patrolling the courtyard of Herod's temple, aiding those who did not know their way and settling the many disputes that inevitably sparked into flame at the haggling tables. Their lavish ceremonial prayer shawls, heavy with holy tassels, distinguished them from the commoners. Voices lowered immediately whenever their presence was noted.

By the time the sun reached its zenith, the still air was fetid with the odor of animals and dung. The rabbis sought respite under the colonnades near the thirteen fluted golden treasury boxes. It was also a vantage from which they could watch the goings-on of the entire court.

Nicodemus eyed the Eastern Gate directly opposite. Each minute five hundred or more men entered through the twin rectangular passageways. Some veered off left or right to do business, but most now walked in an acceptably ordered fashion straight across the long open plaza, then under the imposing Nicanor Gate and on into the temple itself to await the start of afternoon prayer.

At the same moment both he and Gamaliel leaned forward to intensify their gaze at a man they recognized as Jesus of Nazareth. Word of his unorthodox ministry had reached the council, and many considered him a persuasively dangerous false prophet. Five weeks earlier Nicodemus himself had been sent to Galilee to investigate, reporting back to an enraged Caiaphas that the man was no threat. He did not reveal his growing personal belief that Jesus was in truth an enigmatic holy man of God.

Jesus moved with slow majesty, projecting an aura of pious authority. His disciples followed silently. Thirty feet beyond the gate he stopped, bowing his head in anguish over the shameful greed on display so near the Holy of Holies.

Suddenly he was in the midst of the merchants, upsetting tables. Coins and papers fell scattering onto the stone floor. Animals were loosed. The din grew as merchants reacted, hastily pushing men aside and dropping to their knees in a dire scavenge for lost money.

Gamaliel started, but Nicodemus stretched out a halting arm before him. They stood unmoving as Jesus approached.

The Nazorean stood in front of Nicodemus, taller than the older man by a hand yet with his sandaled feet a step below at courtyard level. His reddened eyes held tears, his voice a whisper.

Take these things away. You shall not make my Father's house a house of trade, a den of thieves.

The words were few but searing to Nicodemus. The words were those of the great prophet Jeremiah, who with them had warned Jerusalem to repent else be destroyed. With what authority did Jesus speak? Was there truth to the apparent allusion that Zion would fall as it had to Babylon six hundred years ago, Solomon's temple razed and the Jews in exile?

He determined to know.

+ + + + + + + +

One hour past sunset the rabbis met in the Upper City as arranged, two darkened streets from Caiaphas's villa. Joseph, a council member from Arimathea and a fellow Pharisee, joined them. Gamaliel feared retribution if found out. Reluctantly, Nicodemus agreed to cancel the visit if suspicions were aroused.

All appeared quiet as they passed the villa in silence. It was the practice of the high priest to retire early, allowing the guards to dine in the residence. With no one following, they turned at the next corner and proceeded to the house where Jesus was staying.

Lamplight shone through the windows of the upper chamber. From the gate shadows could be seen on the ceiling, their movement suggesting active conversation at table.

The maid Rhoda had been told to expect guests. Without speaking she led them through the garden and into the entry hall, then bowed and left. Moments later a dark-haired youth greeted them with a degree of formality that accorded their status.

Great rulers, in my mother's name I, Mark, offer our peace and greetings. You have come to see the Master?

At that word, Gamaliel visibly straightened with a perceived indignity. Unperturbed, Nicodemus smiled and stepped forward.

I would be most honored to speak with the Teacher. My friends will remain here.

Mark nodded, brought forth two chairs, and ushered Nicodemus upstairs.

The chamber was large, spanning the full length and breadth of the house. Dominating the room was a single, low wooden table, around which reclined eight men to a side and two on each end. Lampstands radiated soft light from the room's corners, and tallows glowed yellow amidst the plates and cups.

Master, your guest has arrived, Mark announced, then took his place against the wall.

Jesus rose and turned toward Nicodemus.

My Lord, Nicodemus uttered in unexpected and complete humility. He bowed deeply, overwhelmed by a cleansing baptism of spiritual rebirth.

Tuesday, 13 July 2010, Crumlin

"Let's go!"

Michael smiled so broadly it echoed through the halls as Stephanie weaved his chair hurriedly past obstacles human and inert. A break in the clouds was all the prompt they needed to escape outside. For a time, however brief, they would leave behind hospital woes for fresh air at the park off Dromard.

During morning rounds "silent Michael" had finally spoken, asking Dr. Thomson if he might be allowed to go walking with a friend. The order was written, transfusions given, and every bit of the midday meal finished. Stephanie arrived wet with rain and they waited for their chance—which came just as they were dealing the first hand of German whist.

She parked him in the center of the grassy field, handed him the orange Frisbee she'd brought as a surprise, and ran off a good distance. "Okay, Mickey—like I showed you," she bellowed.

The disk took flight, wobbled, and landed close enough to her feet for Michael to brand her a lousy catch. On the next toss she slipped, feet flying, and sat hard. "Bum catch! Bum catch!" he chanted between torrents of giggles.

When the drizzle drove them in, he insisted they stop at the Jelly Bean Café, and on their way back to the room he sucked sips of iced orangeade slurry through a wide straw stuck into a hole Stephanie had made in the dense white respirator mask.

No talk of leukemia. No lamenting loneliness or absence of friends.

"I had fun today," he whispered as she hugged him goodbye.

Tuesday, 13 July 2010, Ballinskelligs

"Low tide was at one, so you'll have a few hours to wander the strand."

Kyle pulled into the small parking area at the public beach, shifted into neutral, and set the brake. They climbed out of the car and stood looking at the bay.

"See the sandbar to the castle ruins? That's as dry as it gets. It'll be under water by four—you'll find yourself on an island if you're not mindful." Kevin was charmed by the concern Kyle had shown him throughout the day. "Just up there are the abbey ruins—see them? And back that way is the inn."

"Kyle, thanks again for showing me around. I've learned a lot."

"No worries. Tomorrow at ten thirty, then?"

"I'll be ready this time."

Kyle nodded and with a laugh headed toward the car. Loose gravel spit from the rear tires as he drove off.

The castle held little interest for Kevin, although he understood its importance as the sixteenth-century home of the ruling MacCarthy clan. Seeing how close it was to the abbey, it was readily apparent how easily the abandoned monastery could have fallen under clan control after the Protestant Reformation. What intrigued him instead was whether the Augustinians who lived there for four hundred years had played any role in the tale of the cross. Strolling along with the bay to his left, ten minutes later he stepped under the point-arched doorway of the church ruins and into the realm of medieval monks.

It was an intimate space made infinitely tall in the absence of a roof. Unlike the much smaller chapel at Gallarus, mortar bound together the stones of these walls that stood as holy sentinels on the weather-beaten Iveragh coast. The angular eastern face rose to a jagged peak, atop which stood a vacant belfry. A crude support post had been wedged into the window that dominated the western wall, traversing from the curved Romanesque arch to the irregular sill scarred by partial deterioration. Occupying the floor of grass were several dozen unadorned grave markers, long erased of any inscription.

Kevin exited through the side door. Had it been the dark of night, in a few short strides he would have crashed straight into the end of a tiered stacked stone tomb, one of several massive age-old sepulchers queued widthwise along the building's length. Past these lay a cemetery, an open field of burial plots studded with Celtic cross memorials.

Lost in imagination, he leaned against the largest of the tombs and, eyes closed, lifted his face toward the warmth of the afternoon sun.

+++++++++

Aideen stepped back a few feet from the kitchen counter, critically eyeing the arrangement of perennials that burst forth from her Waterford vase. Purple coneflowers, daisies, and spikes of pale lavender each vied for attention. Not quite satisfied, she added a few short clusters of baby's breath, then placed it on the dining table.

Kevin's four-o'clock call had been brief: he was in town investigating leads and would she like to talk over dinner at a restaurant of her choice? Yes, she was free tonight, but instead please come by at seven for a home-cooked meal.

With a near-empty refrigerator, she had made a quick trip to the market in Waterville, where she bought a small rack of lamb, fresh vegetables, soda bread with raisins, and a mixed berry pie. The flurry of preparation was a thankful distraction from her increasing anxiety over Michael. This time at home was far from restorative: she could not maintain the forced separation much longer.

At a quarter before seven, Aideen heard Kevin's car pull up. She went out to greet him.

"It appears I'm quite early. I expected a longer drive." Swinging the door closed, he reached forward and accepted her warm handshake.

"Nothing is too far in a village this small. Welcome, Father."

"Thanks for inviting me, Aideen. I'd not intended to impose on you last-minute."

"It's the least I can do, really. Can I offer you a glass of wine? With such a lovely evening, I thought we might sit in the garden until the lamb is ready."

"Lamb? Now I know I've imposed."

"Not at all." They went inside, passing through the parlor and into the kitchen. "I grew up in this house. I raised Caitlin here." She tented a sheet of aluminum foil over the roasting pan and slid it into the oven, then poured two glasses of Bordeaux from the opened bottle and handed one to Kevin. "Michael's favorite Easter meal. It should be done in an hour."

Out back, sunlight filtered through the rounded leaves of an old alder tree, its canopy gently shading a wave of hostas in fragrant bloom beside the south-facing patio. They sat in two cushioned cast-iron chairs, a café table between them, and watched as sailboats chased their lengthening shadows past the rise on Horse Island into the bay.

"I walked through the old abbey today," Kevin said, pointing toward the ruins easily seen off to the left. "Haunting."

"In a way, I suppose. As a child it certainly made a dramatic playground. Now it seems more a place of resting souls." She raised her wineglass, breathed in the deep bouquet, and sipped. "My great-grandmother was drawn to it with a passion, perhaps even a spiritual addiction. We would go hand in hand at twilight most fair nights. I learned the comfort of silence while she prayed."

"She made an impression on you."

"Oh, yes." Her slightly inclined head swayed slowly in a broad, arcing nod that merged ambiguously with a wag.

"I was talking earlier with a seminary student. He has great reverence for the many monastic sites around here."

"A source of inspiration, I'm sure." Her brief pause ended with an abrupt thought. "Is he a student of yours? He's in town? Please call and ask him to join us—there's plenty."

"No, actually, he's local. He was at the pub with his friends last night."

"A local?" Her eyes widened. "You must mean Kyle Dorrian, then?"

"Kyle, yes. Quite coincidentally they sat at my table. So you know him?"

She laughed. "As I said, it's a small village."

"He's likable enough."

"He is. He's a very sweet boy." Legs crossed, she leaned forward and gazed at the horizon. "His father Brian was in Caitlin's class. She had quite a fondness for him. I was pleased when they became friends. He was a good anchor, through her whole life, actually."

In a far corner of the yard a family of magpies descended onto a low shrub, yakking loudly, then hopped to the ground and began scratching for food. Kevin glanced their way and noted for the first time the detailed beauty of Aideen's flowerbeds.

"Father, you said you were here tracking down leads on the cross?"

Sitting upright, he set his glass on the table and turned toward her, hands already in motion as he prepared to discuss his research. "'Threads of the story' is a better way to describe it."

Immediately a thin shadow of disappointment fell veillike over what had seemed hopeful anticipation in her eyes.

His voice softened with carefully chosen words. "Our first task is to trace its travels from Calvary to its last known location. Like an arrow shot into the sky, the trajectory may lead us to where it landed."

He sat back, giving her time to grasp the analogy.

"I think we can make a fairly strong historical argument that a relic—likely fragments of the original cross—was transported from Jerusalem to France during the first century, then brought to the oratory at Gallarus about four hundred years later." In the telling he realized how lame his progress must appear to her: to himself even, a failed effort.

Aideen's expectant stare disarmed him as she futilely waited for more.

"Its whereabouts after that are nebulous." Her eyes slowly averted, and he cleared his throat. "In the realm of Christian history, this is a major finding."

With that, she erupted.

"Father, I don't give a damn about Christian history. This is about my grandson."

The protracted silence that followed pained him, yet her stone-still profile bore a sorrowful expression devoid of anger. He let the fervor dissipate.

"Aideen, thank you for sharing your family's story with me. I know it is intensely personal and deeply important to you and to Michael." Placing his hand over hers, he continued. "Please trust that I'm putting all my energy into this. If the cross is to be found, we will find it."

Her head bowed in acknowledgment. "I'm sorry. Truly. I've been unfair, and unkind. And unappreciative. Not to mention surly." A meager smile formed on her lips. "It's difficult to be away."

"Is he all right?"

"As of five thirty," she sighed. "Dr. Thomson 'prescribed' a week at home for me—if I last that long. The not-knowing is the worst. His condition could turn in a minute."

"Stephanie was looking forward to visiting him today," he said with a lighter tone.

"Yes, she did this afternoon. It was all he talked about." Her smile broadened. "There was an enthusiasm in his voice that I haven't heard in quite some time."

As they finished their wine, she stood. "I should check on dinner. Please, come in and I'll freshen your glass."

Scents of rosemary and garlic filled the room as Aideen turned the roast.

"So what next?" That she was speaking of the cross was clear.

"The trail picks up at Gallarus. I went there yesterday. What impressed me was its vulnerable location. I doubt a relic that valuable would have been kept there for long."

"Actually, it was hidden at Skellig Michael."

"The island?" His thoughts rushed ahead. "Of course . . ."

"Later it came to the abbey here."

Of course . . .

"Aideen, how do you know this?"

"Father Finnian. He said it 'disappeared into the hills' with the Reformation, whatever that means." Her hands whisked in scoff at the air. "Sadly for Michael, he has no idea where it went after Maw Maw was cured."

"When was that?"

"She was sixteen—1866 or so."

Kevin quickly began to reconcile events with years. He knew Saint Brigid died in 525, and Kyle had told him that the Skellig Michael monastery was built sometime in the sixth century. At most the cross would have been housed in the Gallarus oratory for perhaps fifty years. If it were moved to Ballinskelligs in the twelfth century, that would mean six hundred years on the island, four hundred at the abbey, and three-hundred-plus elsewhere before being lost.

Thus far, he had no objective documentation of the relic's existence after Gallarus.

"I'd like to talk with Father Finnian—that's his name?"

"Yes. Unfortunately after his latest stroke he moved from the rectory to a nursing home in Killorglin. It's not far—I can give you the address."

"I'm very sorry to hear that. How old is he?"

"Oh, God, ninety? Old enough to have buried Maw Maw." She did not hide her scorn.

"Have the strokes affected his mind or speech?"

"No, not at all. He's as wily as ever. Good luck."

Unsure of how to reply, Kevin stood watching her in silence.

"I must sound terribly bitter. Believe me, I am." She reached for a tissue and blotted her eyes. "'Forgive me, Father, for I have sinned.' Repeatedly, it would seem."

Making eye contact, he gently said, "Bitterness comes from a hurt, an injustice."

She did not blink. "I've tried to forgive. And I've asked his forgiveness. He referred me to God." It was said with the flatness of finality. "Well, this is not the evening I planned. Let's leave my wallowing to me and talk of other things, shall we?"

In that moment Kevin fully understood how desperately Michael and Aideen—even he himself—needed the wood of the cross of the Christ.

Wednesday, 14 July 2010, Skellig Michael

The sea was perfectly still.

Kevin stood at the bow as the engine idled low, then stopped. They floated in a moment of observation. Above, gannets held aloft on the lightest breeze before plunging after easy prey unmasked by the absence of surf. Cormorants perched on rocks, wings outstretched. Nearby, puffins gloated, their oval orange beaks overloaded with silver strands of wriggling fish.

Even as the ferry left Ballinskelligs Bay and skirted the peninsula's escarpment, Kevin was transfixed with his first glimpse of the Skelligs, raw rock triangles seven miles to sea, piercing the ocean's surface and reaching heavenward. Now, a mere hundred yards away, he was unprepared for their magnitude, humbled by their magnificence, awed in silence.

There was no darkness in the ocean's depths. Endless beams of light carried the sun's spectrum to the roots of these island mountains, illuminating them in fiery white before spinning off colors in every direction.

There was no mistaking the spiritual symbolism of a medieval monastery wrought atop the pinnacle of Greater Skellig, itself an earthly representation of the Holy Trinity.

There was no doubting that Skellig Michael and its cherished hidden relic had inspired future monks to craft pendants of elemental shapes that, in their very simplicity, bespoke divine healing power.

They landed. Kevin followed at some distance behind Kyle and the other sojourners, content in solitude. The way was steep with no protective rail. He climbed the tall, irregular stone steps, arms out keeping balance. Often he paused to rest, immersed in the mystical union of nature and ancient human presence.

On this crag Fionán had led his band of faithful monks upward to a rocky outcrop near the apex, jutting to the east.

Flat stones were stacked at the perimeter, a retaining wall within which a firm ground was made of pebbles and grit. Smooth stones were stacked into beehive-like huts sealed against the weather, punctured only by the smallest of windows and lowest of doors, readily shuttered. Adjacent to a diminutive oratory, an echo of Gallarus, the dead were laid reverently in graves, eternal reminders that life on earth is but a shadow of life above.

From the cemetery's edge, the scalloped hills of the mainland coast rose emerald green beyond Little Skellig. Kevin gazed out in a sense of communion with the buried. Priests all, they were soldiers under Saint Michael the Archangel, defender of the Church and leader of the army against Satan. Saint Michael the Healing Angel, namesake of this sacred place.

He then turned, descended a cascade of stairs into a shallow valley, and began climbing rough terrain toward the more jagged and yet-higher southern peak. Ahead he could see a gently sloping path nestled along vertical stone parapets, demarcated by a low wall.

Expecting the walkway to broaden onto a plain similar to the monastery, instead he found himself suddenly at a six-hundred-foot-high precipice. He steadied himself against the wall and set his eyes on the vast horizon of unbroken open ocean.

"You like heights, then?"

Already a bit shaken, the added surprise of a disembodied voice calling out completely unnerved him.

"It's just me." Kyle grinned impishly as he approached. "Sorry to startle you."

"I may survive." After a big breath, Kevin slowly dropped his hand from his chest.

"Lots of gawkers today. Best time to visit is with the clouds coming in—threatening weather scares 'em off." He returned to the railing and looked down at the cliffs. "This was a lighthouse back when, not part of the monastery. Nice view, though."

Kevin moved forward and looked about, noting immediately many telltale clues that these were more recent ruins. "The view from your room must be unbelievable."

"It's a zillion views—the sky's always changing." His eyes grew animated. "Shadows drag purples and blues across the serrated relief of the crests, then the sun follows with yellows and greens. God's canvas out my window."

"Kyle, you speak in poetry."

"Like I said, I just pay attention."

A gift shared by too few, Kevin thought to himself. "Do you come out here often?"

"Not much anymore. The summer after high school I was on the boat crew, back and forth most days. When we were done 'swabbing the deck,' meaning the johns, we were free to roam. Never got bored exploring."

"So tell me: If you were a medieval monk living on this island and were in charge of keeping a treasure safe, where would you hide it?"

Kyle's reply was immediate. "Right there." With his back to the sea and head raised high, he extended his right arm upward, finger pointed at the tip of the southern peak.

Kevin strained to see a structure, the ruin of a hut, some clue of earlier habitation. "What am I looking for?" he said, hand over eyes to block glare from the midday sun.

"See those two patches of green?" He motioned to an area about forty feet below the summit. "Two narrow ledges. See 'em?"

Kevin nodded. "I think so. People climbed there?"

"Exactly. Vikings were the problem, right? The monastery was easy pillage, out in the open with stairs leading up from every landing. But the hermitage," he pointed again to the ledges, "that's a different story. First they'd have to discover it. Then they'd have to scale the mountain." His finger traced a winding path along the shear rock wall that was the peak.

"The monks did it . . ."

"Yeah, but they were super clever. It was lost to history until a few years ago."

Kevin was totally captivated.

"Best of all," Kyle said, virtually bouncing, "is that a single monk could hold off an entire raiding army. The only way up is through the needle's eye, a whisper-thin passage between huge vertical rocks. If invaders were lucky enough to get that far, they'd be knocked to their doom as they emerged, one—by—one." He beamed, relishing the victory of an imagined medieval hero.

"This is for real?"

"Well, yeah. Archaeology and all." Kyle's eyes squinted as he thought. "Why are you asking about this? And you said a treasure—is that for real?"

"Good question." Kevin looked at him with a sober smile. "Kyle, my research is on more than just old stones and huts." He paused. "A certain relic was sent to Ireland, to Patrick, for protection. I believe it was kept briefly by Brigid at Gallarus, then brought here by Fionán."

Kyle shrugged. "A saint's bone? Doesn't every church have one?"

"Not every relic is a bone."

"Okay. So what was it?"

"Wooden fragments, Kyle. Fragments of the cross of Jesus."

They looked at each other in silence for a long moment.

"I believe you," Kyle replied with a subdued voice. "I've always felt that something extra-spiritual had happened around here but never understood. Now I know." He turned and looked to the sea. "They found a rock slab up there. A ringed cross."

Kevin nodded. It was a simple validation, yet another historical witness to the truth of Aideen's story.

PART II

CHAPTER ELEVEN

ANGELUS † ANGEL

To: Marco Giordano <m.giordano@arcsacra.va>
From: Kevin Schaeffer <kevinschaeffer999@yahoo.com>
Date: July 15, 2010 06:44:59 IST
Subject: Per un favore . . .

Buongiorno, Marco!

It has been a remarkably productive week, I am pleased to report.

Allow me first to capture your interest with some tantalizing bits of discovery. I will then entice you with a proposal for collaboration that will no doubt prove irresistible from an intellectual perspective. If not, perhaps as a favor to an old friend.

Awaiting my return to Dublin three weeks ago was a note from the grandmother of a ten-year-old boy who is dying of leukemia. She suggested I might be able to save the child. Curiously, it was not a request for prayer but for my expertise as a New Testament historian and detective of sorts.

When we met she showed me two interrelated family objects that sent me traveling to opposite ends of the country: a 300-year-old Bible and a silver pendant.

The Bible contains a baptismal record going back twelve generations, ending with her grandson. As one would expect, the dates of birth and death are documented. In addition, some names are marked with a cryptic symbol—a cross within a circle within a triangle. Even more cryptic, the marks only appear in the first seven generations.

The silver pendant is, as you may have guessed, a cross within a circle within a triangle.

So what, you say?

It turns out that all the ancestors marked with this symbol were cured of cancer by Christ's cross. Not by faith alone, the woman claims, but by physically touching the wood of the cross. The cured were given pendants as blessed scapulars. These events happened here, in western Ireland.

Any initial skepticism I may have had vanished once I started to investigate.

Among Saint Patrick's personal effects in Armagh is a letter written by Saint Brigid describing a chapel she built to safeguard a relic sent from France. This was on order of the pope during the dissolution of the Roman Empire. I believe she meant the oratory at Gallarus. And I believe the relic was in fact pieces of the true cross that were saved by Mary Magdalene, taken from Jesus's tomb and brought with her to the grotto where she lived out her life at La Sainte-Baume.

Over the past few days I visited the ruins at Gallarus and at Skellig Michael, where the relic was kept for many hundreds of years. It is likely that Saint Patrick himself created the famous Celtic ringed cross to symbolize the eternal healing power of this most sacred object. Original stone slabs bearing his mark can still be seen at both monasteries. And as any picture of Greater Skellig will attest, the triangle is an image of the island itself, a significant third element that evokes the trinity of Father, Son, and Holy Spirit.

We now arrive at a great mystery: the relic has been missing since the last ancestor was cured in 1866. Five generations of this cancer-ridden family have sought in vain to touch the wood of the cross. A child waits in hope that it be found.

I am compelled to act.

Tomorrow I will meet with a very old parish priest who is a member of the dwindling Augustinian order established by the monastery monks here 1500 years ago. He has deep knowledge of their history and of the healings. I've been told he knew the child's great-great-great-grandmother toward the end of her long life, many years after her cure. He may be the only person alive who can help fill in some of the blanks.

Marco, my friend, I ask for your help in searching the Vatican documents for any reference to the relic or its journeys. I will continue my efforts here. That Pope Benedict has assigned you to the Secret Archive seems providential indeed. Our task is daunting. We do not even know if the relic remains in Ireland.

If I may indulge you with one more request. There is a bright college student from Ballinskelligs who would be of spectacular assistance to you. He is at a crossroads in his calling—I believe that broadening his horizons beyond home and school would benefit him greatly. What better place than the Holy See to discern God's will? With your permission, I'll see if he agrees.

My sincerest thanks and appreciation . . . Kevin

Sunday, 18 July 2010, Florence

It was as though dawn had chosen to ignore the sun's rising. Overhead, dense gray clouds lay one upon another, bloated and low, refusing any upward escape of yesterday's heat. Doors stood open, hopes unfulfilled for a breeze.

Marco stared at the starkly unfinished fifteenth-century striated brick facade of the San Lorenzo basilica, oblivious to the blur of tourists around him. He had walked alone from his father's funeral, thoughts whirling mournfully—glimpses of memories flashing in random succession like windows of a passing train.

With only a few outsized drops as warning, rain suddenly poured forth. The pavement was instantly wet, submerged under a sheet of moving water. People scattered for shelter, many crowding under the countless vendor tents lining the street market. Startled whoops gave rise to laughter and boisterous chatter.

In a useless gesture to remain dry, he flipped up the lapel of his clerical jacket and ran toward the Medici Chapel entrance at the rear of the basilica. There was general confusion as those rushing to get in pushed against others rushing opposite to see the cloudburst.

Abruptly, the rain stopped.

Eyes looked skyward. No shadows were cast by the dark clouds now moving apace to the northeast. Sensing that the dry spell would not last and with the Sagrestia Nuova about to close for the day, a hurried shuffling left the lobby deserted and quiet. He shook off what wetness he could and, waved on at the gate, entered the chapel.

He was alone in the presence of the entombed.

He moved to the center of the small sacristy and stood, turning slowly to absorb the stunning miracle of Michelangelo's creation. There was no architectural detail unknown to him, no bodily twist or draped fold of Carrara marble that he had not observed before in his many visits to this sanctuary: a mortuary of dukes, a sacred refuge for mortals.

His gaze paused on the Christ child, a cherub on Mary's knee. He yearned for the figure to breathe, to awaken, to relinquish but for a moment the comfort of his mother's breast and reveal his radiant face.

A wash of light filled the room as the clouds passed and sun shone through the opening at the dome's apex. Reclined on the arch-topped sarcophagus before him, personified Night looked down, her sorrow hidden in the shadows, while Day displayed his nascent features proudly, confident that an expression of sculpted muscular strength would suffice.

A hand gently pressed on his shoulder. He grasped it with his own.

"'Day and Night speak, and say: We with our swift course have brought the Duke Giuliano to death.' All this, and the artist graced us with poetry as well."

"I knew I would find you here, Marco."

"You've always known my heart."

"And you mine." They stood together in silent grief, brother and sister.

"There is no death in this statue. He sits, forever arrogant and invincible."

"Yet none escape death." There was a mature acceptance in her voice.

A quiet clinking of keys near the exit alerted them to the chapel's closing.

"I want to remember Papà laughing. I want to see him through five-year-old eyes." She smiled wistfully as they walked outside, arm in arm. "That he will forever sing us to sleep."

Like Night, Marco's head hung in unremitting sadness. "We're orphans now, Talie."

"They're together again, Mamma and Papà. They belong together." Stopping, she looked into his eyes. "And we have each other. Never forget that."

He acquiesced with a nod.

"A houseful of guests awaits, *mio caro*. Let's go home."

Tuesday, 20 July 2010, Fiesole

At the southernmost corner of the hillside farm, a wooden swing hung suspended between two hundred-foot-tall Tuscan cypress trees. Its densely grained slats were grooved from a century of weather but remained sturdy, cut from the trunk of an olive tree that had long before yielded its last harvest.

Marco sat, exhausted. Below, Renaissance Florence stood in a terra cotta relief that only grew more intense as the sun dipped, while in defiance the River Arno darkened to greenish black. Above, a crested lark reached its peak of flight and celebrated with a song of triumph.

"Tell me again you will be okay here alone. There's so much to manage."

"I will be okay here, Marco. And I'm not alone." Natalie scratched behind the mastiff's right ear as he languidly leaned his full weight against her thigh.

"Paolo's way of pressing olives is to stand on them. That's hardly helpful."

"*Sta' zitto*, now—you'll hurt his feelings." The dog's jowl drooped even lower in a state of complete relaxation. "*Caro*, the workers have been with me for four seasons. They're good people. To be honest, caring for Papà had become the biggest job." Her sigh was part relief, part sentiment. "I will be okay."

She sat next to him and set the swing swaying.

"When did our childhood recede so far into the past?"

"Sometime between seminary and the Vatican," he lamented. "I should have requested an assignment here. It wasn't right to leave."

In her wisdom she let the words drift away on the evening breeze—and with them, a portion of his undeserved remorse.

Marco, don't leave me.

I'll take the last train out I can tonight, Papà. I'll be back on Friday.

Don't leave.

Papà . . .

Ti amo, Marco. I love you.

Standing, he turned and looked at the remaining family acreage. Once ten times this size, it had been ravaged by the economic collapse of two great wars. These nine acres, bordered by Etruscan walls and blessed with fertility, were their earthly inheritance. High on the hill were the oldest trees, of sufficient girth to suggest that perhaps Michelangelo himself had tasted their fruit. Nearly a thousand younger trees grew in an orderly grid toward where he now stood, spikes of gray-green foliage emanating in every direction to capture the sun.

Don't leave.

"Come. There's a bottle of limoncello in the icebox. Tomorrow you can sleep late while I make a wonderful frittata you will not forget."

Together they meandered up to the family home, reminiscences weaving sporadically through strands of silence.

Ti amo, Papà.

Wednesday, 21 July 2010, Umbria

On its volcanic plateau, Orvieto seemed a sparkling island hovering above the midnight black of the countryside. Marco peered out his window at the illuminated cathedral that held dominion over the ancient village. It faded like a passing vision as the tracks veered southeast.

The train issued no warning but the squeal of brakes to signal its pause at the station. A few dozen passengers waited to board, either too tired or restless to heed a safe distance from the platform's edge. In retaliation, the cars lurched without allowing even the briefest opportunity for the new riders to sit.

Underway once again, slumber quickly pervaded the cabin. Marco sat enveloped in the swaying solitude of whooshing air and the steady drone of wheels spinning along seamless rail.

He toggled the reader lamp switch and looked at the leather-bound book on his lap, its cover burnished with use. *Le Rime di Michelangelo Buonarroti, Pittore, Scultore e Architetto,* "Poetry of Michelangelo Buonarroti, painter, sculptor and architect." Natalie had pressed it into his hands earlier as he was making ready to leave.

A folded note protruded from between the pages.

Mio Marco—
    This book is now yours.
    Papà knew you would cherish it as he did, and his father and grandfather before him.
    The original inscription, to Faustino Giordano, is dated Natale 1863, Christ's birthday. "'I saw the angel in the marble and carved until I set him free.' My son, this I wish for you."
    It is an eternal wish, that each may find the soul within.
    Michel' Angiolo revealed his soul in these words and in his works.
    I have added your name beneath Papà's, his gift to you, with love   —Talie

Holding the note close, a memory rose in his thoughts. It was of a school morn during his fifteenth year, to him yet another day in the interminable trudge toward an adulthood that had not yet revealed its direction. He sat sullen at the breakfast table while Natalie prattled over friendship woes. Lovingly, his father leaned toward him, arm outstretched, and lifted his son's chin. In a voice only Marco could hear he counseled, "Close your eyes and you will remain blind, your ears and you will remain deaf."

Thirty-five years later, he pondered anew the wisdom expressed in such few words.

His hand lay on the open book, perchance fortuitously at Sonnet LXV.

"Giunto è già 'l corso della vita mia,
Con tempestoso mar, per fragil barca . . ."
Now hath my life across a stormy sea
Like a frail bark reached that wide port where all
Are bidden, ere the final reckoning fall
Of good and evil for eternity.
Now know I well how that fond phantasy
Which made my soul the worshiper and thrall
Of earthly art, is vain; how criminal
Is that which all men seek unwillingly.

The poet spoke as though he had been led through the gates of hell, having abandoned all hope and languishing on the verge of everlasting darkness. Yet to this creative genius, from whose human hands spirit coursed into stone and pigment, salvation had been revealed.

Painting nor sculpture now can lull to rest
My soul that turns to His great love on high,
Whose arms to clasp us on the cross were spread.

The cross.

In his deepest moment of sorrow, Marco was placed at the feet of the crucified Christ.

Praying for an understanding that only comes through faith, he turned off the lamp and watched the amber lights of Rome approach from afar.

CHAPTER TWELVE

CALURA † HEAT

17 Nisan, AD 33, Jerusalem

M ark awoke at first light, rolled his bed, and placed it in the corner. Stepping quietly over the apostles, one by one he propped open the windows of the upper room. Cool spring air seeped over the sills and spread across the floor. Simon Peter stirred, drawing his blanket close about his neck as he turned onto his side and resumed an uneasy rest.

Downstairs Mark's mother and the wife of Clopas were in hushed conversation while they prepared the breakfast meal. Each reaffirmed with wonder and astonishment that late the prior evening Jesus appeared alive in their midst. Had they not stood together at the cross just three days earlier and witnessed his death?

Sun was beginning to filter into the garden. The young man walked along the diagonal path to the stone cistern, set its cover on the ground, and lowered the small wooden bucket into the water, not seeing Mary of Magdala standing nearby under the fig tree.

Why are you not asleep with the others? It has been so few hours since we retired.

Startled, he felt the rope slip roughly through his loosened grip.

I must tend my duties. Shy and dressed only in a linen cloth, he did not meet Mary's eyes. The weight of the full bucket tugged downward as he raised it, hand over hand. He then filled the clay jug standing ready and, with effort, hoisted it by the handles to carry inside.

Mary watched as he slowly plodded, sandaled feet straddling the vessel, an occasional splash wetting the ground. Her heart surged, recognizing in him a passionate belief in the truth of the Master's word and an unshakeable commitment to share it with the world. She combed through her hair unconsciously, fingers lifting the trusses up and back. They cascaded to her waist.

Alone in silence, the tumultuous events of the past week engrossed her thoughts. Gone was the previously inescapable plummet of emotion from triumphant exultation to barren void. She could neither conjure pain nor detect its scar. All had been eclipsed by a new reality, a new meaning, a new forgiveness. A new peace.

John approached with soft, measured steps deferent to her meditation. She smiled meekly and embraced him warmly in mutual kinship, their futures wedded in selfless devotion to Jesus's mother.

How fares she this morning?

A serenity is upon her that I have never seen.

Together they left the garden, latching the iron gateway securely behind them. The few who scurried about so early were mostly shopkeepers. Fearful that they might arouse the attention of Jewish officials already incensed by the disappearance of Jesus's body, their route skirted neighborhoods of the prominent and wealthy and led them to the lesser-used Gate of the Essenes.

Outside Jerusalem, the path to Golgotha hugged the great city's western wall, shrouded in shadow at this hour. They walked quickly, following it north then northeast. Nearing the final eastward turn, Mary slowed, her head buried in the young apostle's shoulder.

The Place of the Skull was deserted, studded with bare vertical stakes rising ten feet in the air. The rock beneath bore stains of death, burgundy against black.

They did not dwell at this scene of violence.

Beyond, the terrain dipped toward a grassy hillock whose cluster of scraggy trees gave poor camouflage to a broad horizontal outcrop. Wild roses matted densely against the stone, vining branches entwined, thorn spikes protruding menacingly from between deep red petals. Bordering steps led to an earthen terrace below.

They were alone.

The tomb stood open.

John bent low and entered. Gray light diffused in, reflected weakly off the floor and cast softly upon the walls. A fragrance of myrrh and aloes sweetened the air.

The burial linens and face cloth lay undisturbed on the stone shelf where Joseph and Nicodemus had placed Jesus's body. Despite his rising, perhaps intensified because of it, images of the dead Savior would remain vivid in John's memory, to be recorded in his writings sixty years hence as though fresh.

Let us gather his things. She asked to keep all. The tomb darkened briefly as Mary passed through the portal. In the corner to her right was the amphora of precious oils purchased at extraordinary cost by Nicodemus. It was empty, all hundred pounds having been used to anoint Jesus, as would befit a king. To its side was the loincloth, soiled with blood. Upon it lay everything John and Joseph had removed in cleansing the body.

Mary reverently wrapped the items in her scarf, set them in the amphora, and pressed the lid firmly onto the supple wax seal.

A miracle had occurred in this cave, written by the prophets and foretold by Jesus.

A miracle that now lived in their hearts.

Saturday, 24 July 2010, Rome Fiumicino International Airport

It did not at all feel as though the heat wave were lifting. Nor did it help that the Vatican vehicle office had assigned to him for the day a black Punto with a coordinating black interior. Marco defied policy, locking the doors but leaving the windows and sunroof full open. He considered it a humanitarian gesture for his guest, given that the only available parking space in the airport's D structure was on the sunbaked top deck.

Kyle's plane arrived twenty minutes early. The young man stood just beyond passport control, bouncing his carryon bag repeatedly off his right knee as he looked about for the man Kevin had described vaguely as "Italian with dark hair." No mention was made whether this priest wore a collar.

"I hope you haven't waited for long. *Prego*—" Marco reached and took the bag before Kyle had a chance to object. "Welcome to Roma."

"Thanks. I can take that," he protested, the priest already several steps in the lead and waving his hand to prod the young man forward.

"This is your first visit, no?"

"Yeah—yes, it is." He quickly became out of breath trying to keep up with the older man's long strides. Relieved to see a moving walkway ahead, his look of disbelief went unnoticed by Marco as they continued instead along the terrazzo concourse.

Coming to the lobby some minutes later, they stopped. "I'll get us water for the drive. *Frizzante?* With gas?"

Kyle scrunched his nose, as though being offered strychnine. "Is it any good?"

Marco was momentarily confused, then laughed at the unintended humor. He sidestepped the crowd vying for the barista, set six euros on the counter, and pointed to the half-liter bottles of Pellegrino.

The air warmed significantly as they approached the exit doors. Once they were outside the heat hit without apology.

"Holy shit it's hot!" Kyle had clearly not prepared for the dramatically different weather compared to Ireland. He quickly pulled off his sweater and rolled the sleeves of his shirt as far up as they would go. "You have A/C, right?"

"In the car, yes, but not in the seminarian residence." He smiled slightly, leaving Kyle to wonder. "They say it will be cooler tomorrow. Come, *andiamo*." Marco thoughtfully slowed their pace on the lengthy walk to the structure, and resisted the stairs for the elevator.

Even with the cloth seats, Kyle shifted uncomfortably at first as they drove down the spiral of rectangles. By the time Marco merged onto the autostrada, the fan quieted and they were able to resume conversation in relative cool.

"Kevin said you work in the Secret Archive."

"*Sì*, the Archive." Glancing in the rearview mirror, he maneuvered into the left lane and sped past a Peugeot. "The press—they prefer to repeat the drama of fiction. I'm afraid the truth will be a disappointment to those searching for conspiracies."

"So why the secret?"

"*Archivum Secretum Vaticanum*. The correct translation isn't 'secret' but 'private.' It's an irresistibly easy error to exploit. I confess that until recently the Church has done little to dispel the mystique."

"And I'm allowed in because Kevin's a friend of yours?" he asked naively.

"Not quite." Marco began to suspect that Kevin had been less than forthright with Kyle about the practical details of this project. Did Kyle appreciate the degree of circumspection needed when probing the historical Jesus, or the distinction between mere secrecy and absolute confidentiality? Had he been told of Marco's position in the Vatican, or that his access to the papal archives had been approved not by Marco, but by the prefecture—in consultation with the pope himself?

This was fast evolving into a delicate yet necessary conversation, requiring finesse.

"'And the Word became flesh and dwelt among us.' What does this mean to you?"

Kyle squirmed once again in his seat. "Isn't it obvious? Jesus was God, right? And man."

Marco smiled. His new charge spoke with the abruptness of youth and the conviction of an evangelist.

"Well said. A near quote from Thomas, the doubting apostle. 'My Lord and my God.'"

The engine revved as Marco downshifted, darted into the exit lane, and rounded the cloverleaf northward onto A90. They would approach Vatican City from the west along Via Aurelia, pass through the security checkpoint, and enter on restricted roads.

"Kyle, from that first declaration of Jesus's divinity, the Church has been the guardian of Christianity. Peter was entrusted with the keys to heaven: Faith. Revealed truth. Free will." For several miles he remained silent, letting the deep meaning of these theological concepts become manifest.

"Okay. I get it. But what does all that have to do with the cross?"

Marco sighed.

"The essence of the cross is not contained in wooden fragments. There is nothing in the archive that can compel faith."

It was Kyle's turn to sigh.

Saturday, 24 July 2010, Vatican City

Cristina De Lecce was simply the most stunningly beautiful woman Kyle had ever met.

From the beginning in the Pio XI Reading Room where she sat awaiting their arrival, he was enthralled. His eyes volleyed unceasingly between a naked stare and a contrite, shy downward averting. Face flushed, he inexplicably grew aware of his every motion and the effect of what seemed to be excess gravity on his limbs. His self-consciousness intensified when Marco quickly completed the introduction and left her in charge of the private tour.

"So, Kyle, be sure always that your guest ID is showing, right?" She reached forward and clipped the badge to his shirt placket just below the third button. "Now, let's go upstairs. I will show you the Piano Nobile first. They are the oldest rooms of the archive."

Following a close step behind, he felt lost in her allure.

She turned her head slightly and spoke softly as they walked. "My English is sometimes a little weak, and my accent a little strong. Please, ask if you don't understand, okay?"

"I understand fine. And it's lovely, your accent."

"Ah, *grazie*." She smiled. "And we are here."

The room opened before them as they passed through the entry. Darkly stained walnut document cases stood tall, overshadowed by ornate frescoes covering the ceiling and walls. Additional rooms lay beyond an identical doorway directly opposite.

"It's small," Kyle said, surprised.

"Yes, these chambers are more intimate than the main archive. You can understand why they needed more space after a few years. But remember, they were meant for the personal use of the pope." As he looked about she wandered slowly toward the east windows and into the beaming sunlight. Her wavy chestnut-brown hair shimmered, highlights aflame. "The library courtyard is below. Come see."

Kyle joined her, squinting into the midday brightness. A narrow rectangular patch of green lawn lay bounded on all sides by the characteristic pale yellow facade of the palace complex.

"To the right—there—is the library." She painted the air with broad, openhanded strokes. "And left—over there—is the Braccio Nuovo. Do you like, how you say, *scultura?*"

"Uh . . . you mean sculpture?"

"*Sì*, of course. There are many, many ancient sculptures in the gallery. They are not the most famous, but it is an extraordinary collection. You should visit during your stay." She checked her watch, then motioned forward. "Next I will show you the Tower of Winds. It was once the Vatican observatory."

They strolled slowly through the adjacent rooms as Kyle took in the magnificence of the scenes above, vibrant with pigments that had been applied to wet plaster four hundred years before. All the while he listened to the texture of Cristina's voice narrate the history.

"Thank you for showing me around."

"*Piacere mio.* It is my pleasure, Kyle. I am happy to assist you with your project."

After a few steps Kyle stopped, caught off guard by the unforeseen prospect of their working together.

"Assist me? I thought you were a tour guide."

"*Guida turistica? Dio!*" The sweetness in her laugh was like a caress. He smiled.

"What? What's so funny? Isn't that what Father Marco said?"

"He said I would give you a tour, *sì*, but I am not a guide. *Dio!*" She laughed softly again.

They climbed the stairs in silence, the echo of their footsteps trailing behind.

"Now, Kyle, on the first floor of the tower is the Sala della Meridiana. You will see that the frescoes are even more *vibrante*, more colorful, than those downstairs."

There were already two tour groups filling the room when they entered. Cristina led him along the perimeter of the confined space to a corner. The walls were indeed saturated by the deep blues of sea and sky. Figures abounded, humans below and angels above.

"Too many people today! It is sad you cannot see the sun clock on the floor. But look up." The ceiling teemed with figures surrounding a perfect circle of indigo. It was a dial of sorts, a single hand pinned at the center. "The hand is at the mercy of the winds," she said in a whisper, her breath washing over him.

With a quick gesture, she beckoned the guard and showed her badge. "*Prego*—" Kyle watched as they walked away in animated exchange. Moments later her eyes were on him, calling him over.

"He will let us onto the balcony."

Outside they leaned on a balustrade overlooking the courtyards, the air still and hot. Neither spoke. Off to the south, Saint Peter's Square was filled with thousands of summer visitors held in the regal embrace of Bernini's colonnades.

Straightening to a full stand, Kyle broke the silence.

"If you're not a guide, what do you do here?"

Cristina was gradually becoming accustomed to the brevity of Kyle's remarks. She, in contrast, relished the expressive sensuality of Italian conversation.

"My mother, she too asks why I am here. '*Crista, il Vaticano? Will you never marry?*' I tell her, '*Vai tranquilla, Mamma.*' Chill, right?"

There was subtle restraint in his smile.

"No matter. I continue my studies."

"Studies?"

"Graduate school, *sì*. This will be my third year at the archive. My thesis is on Saint Malachy of Armagh." She paused. "Do you know the Papal Prophecy?"

"Sure. A little. I'm Irish, aren't I?" This time his smile was genuine and full. "Why the prophecy?"

"First tell me what you think about it—if you think it's true."

He hesitated, wanting his reply to sound scholarly. "Well, I was raised believing it's true, no question, him being the first saint born in Ireland and all. The professors at college, they weren't convinced."

"*Scusa*—I didn't understand. Your professors, they weren't what?"

"Convinced. You know, they thought it was fiction, a fantasy." Again, a smile.

"Ah, *fantasia—sì*. And why?"

"Politics, I guess. They said Saint Malachy didn't write it, that it was made up later to get a pope elected. They said none of his prophecies about future popes was real."

"That is the story, yes." Her eyes met his. "But you believe?"

"Maybe. I don't know." He shrugged, looking away. "I guess it doesn't matter. What will be will be. *Que sera*, like the song."

"*Che sarà*. Perhaps."

She walked the length of the balcony toward a grand courtyard, waiting for him to follow.

"My favorite—the Cortile della Pigna. So peaceful." Paved walkways crisscrossed the grassy expanse, dominated by an imposing polished bronze sphere at the center. "Do you know that word—*pigna*?" He shook his head. "The fruit of a pine tree," she said, pointing to the statue of an immense pinecone standing tall on its pedestal at the far end. "A symbol of eternal life."

As she spoke, the sun inched westward just past the roof's peak, casting them into the slightest cool of shade. Kyle puffed his shirt in and out with a sigh of relief. Cristina seemed unaware.

"One would not guess that the archive is buried beneath this court."

He was immediately confused.

"It's underground, not over there?" he said, indicating a structure behind them.

"*Si*, underground. That building is the Apostolic Library. It is open to the public for research. It is big, but the archive is much bigger, with many thousands of very old, important papers. No one enters without special permission. College students are usually not allowed. Father Marco assigned me to accompany you and request the documents you need."

She saw him wince, as though his manhood had been questioned.

"Kyle, your project must be of great significance to have the pope's support."

He looked up, eyes briefly wide, then narrowed.

"I don't know if that makes me feel better or nervous. And you still haven't told me why you picked Saint Malachy for your thesis."

"So, the prophecy," she nodded. "It is a tale of controversy, *intrigo*. Some believe that Saint Malachy was visited by an angel in 1139 and was told a saying about each of the next one hundred twelve popes—predictions up to the end times. Most believe it was just, how you say, a *schema*, a story, made up in 1590, hundreds of years after Malachy died and nothing to do with him, all so that a certain cardinal they said was chosen by God would be elected pope. *Fantasia* or no, that cardinal lost."

Kyle thought for a moment, fingers slowly stroking his lower lip. "If it was written by Saint Malachy, where'd it disappear to for four-hundred-something years?"

"Precisely. That is the work of my thesis." Her eyes danced as she spoke. "Disbelievers say that a forger, writing later, already knew everything about the popes before 1590, so of course those predictions would be true. Anything after 1590 would be fiction, no more, and they list the errors they find."

"You're a disbeliever, then?"

She spiritedly shook her head. "No, I am not a disbeliever— nor yet a believer. They make arguments, *sì*, but perhaps they are wrong. What if there is *prova*—"

"Proof?"

"*Sì, prova*, that the prophecy was hidden right here, in the archive, from the time Saint Malachy transcribed it in Roma until it was found again in 1590?"

Kyle grew excited. "What proof?"

She reached forward suddenly and placed her finger across his lips.

"*Sfortuna!* That is my research. Don't bring a bad omen to me!"

He laughed. "A bad omen to you! What about the future popes? Wouldn't they care even more? Seeing as it predicts the apocalypse."

"You speak truth," she said, her tone deliberate and without humor. "*Papa Benedetto*—Pope Benedict . . . he is number one hundred eleven."

Kyle was stunned to silence with the same sense of foreboding that was rampant at the turn of the second millennium, when uncertainty bred an alliance between myth and fear.

"*Vai tranquillo*, Kyle," she soothed. "No worries. It is only a thesis. If I find no proof, I will be in the good company of disbelievers, including number one hundred eleven."

"But what if—"

"*Sì*, what if. Then I will be in the very good company of a handsome young man who once told me, '*Che sarà.*'" She traced the line of his cheek with her finger and smiled. "So, now your *guida turistica* will finish the tour, and on Monday the archive will begin to reveal its secrets of the cross."

CHAPTER THIRTEEN

ALYSCAMPS

Sunday, 1 August 314, Arles, Gaul

The emperor strode to the podium firm of foot, each step commanding deference. He did not acknowledge Marinus, the local bishop whom he had ordered to lead this *concilium* and whose eloquent introduction had precipitated prolonged table rapping by most of the other thirty-three bishops in attendance. Nor did he bridle his ridicule of the ecclesial schism roiling within the Roman Church that forced this meeting.

"When certain men began wickedly and perversely to disagree among themselves in regard to the holy worship and celestial power and catholic doctrine, I wished to put an end to such disputes." Brow furrowed, he scrutinized each man's reaction for any betrayal of righteous indignation. "But some, who seem to have forgotten both of their own salvation and of the reverence due to the most holy religion, have not yet ceased these hostilities."

The dramatic pause was met with silence.

"Therefore I provide that this dissension, by the presence of this great number of bishops from throughout the realm, should now be brought to an end, that the division be healed."

Constantine Augustus returned to his seat.

At age forty-two, the successor and son of Emperor Constantius Chlorus was rapidly extending his reign to the east. The Church fathers prayed ardently that the tolerance he displayed thus far toward Christianity might one day culminate in a public declaration of faith. It would be truly miraculous to witness Catholicism ascend from the still-warm ashes of intense persecution and prevail as the de facto state religion.

Today, however, whether the Church would even survive its greatest internal fissure was doubted by many in the room.

Murmuring began in the back, spreading forward like flame among dry leaves.

Rhétice grew anxious. He and the other bishops of Gaul, including young Austromoine here at his side, understood well the pagan threat to evangelization that confronted them. They knew their influence among the peasants was already tenuous. Offering a promise of eternal life was their greatest strength, a promise that poured forth from the merciful heart of a single loving God. Accepting the false—even heretical—notion put forth by some at this council that Catholicism was "a church of saints, not sinners," denied the hope of salvation to the masses.

Yet this was not simply a theological debate. If Donatus Magnus and his adherents were not routed, the Church in Gaul and other border regions would likely fail. Much was at stake.

Austromoine stood silent, unblinking.

"The number who foment trouble is greater than was foretold," Rhétice whispered of his observation. Almost imperceptibly, the younger man nodded, his upraised eyebrows acknowledging concern. "Come."

Rhétice led him through the heavily draped egress and into the rear passage. It was not until they had entered the elder man's chamber and secured the door that they spoke openly.

"I have received a directive from our holy father Silvester." Rhétice intoned the words with gravity. "He implores us to raise voices in accord and excommunicate the schismatics. He fears for the sanctity of the Church."

"Rightly so. He should as well fear for his safety," exhorted the younger.

"Those around him do. For himself, there is no unease—he appears quite prepared for martyrdom."

Austromoine raised both hands, finger pressed tensely against finger, and shook his head slowly in consternation. "Such would perhaps deposit him before heaven, whereas we would most assuredly be deposited before hell: the Church will not survive the duplicity that would beset us in choosing yet another pontiff."

"Brother, do not discount the absolute resolve of the emperor toward unity. He wields the reigns of Rome brazenly and defers to no one. He will do the same against division in the Church."

Exasperated, Austromoine's reply was sharp. "He is a politician! Did you not perceive the zealotry among our brethren just now? There will be no swift victory. And the wolves prowl all the while."

"On that we are of one mind with the pope." Rhétice stood close, his voice once more a whisper. "These are times of danger in Gaul—for us, yes, but also for treasured relics long concealed in the nearby mountains." His gaze was direct. "They are for us to protect."

The younger man's disposition grew somber, head bowed in assent.

"We shall meet again at dusk near the tomb of Trophime in the Alyscamps. Talk to no one, and arrive alone."

+++++++++

Just beyond the town walls, three thousand troops were encamped. One thousand were cavalry, twice that number foot soldiers, all sworn to defend their emperor to the death. An orderly city of tents flanked the Via Aurelia, with horses quartered close at hand.

It had been two years since Constantine defeated Maxentius and his loyal praetorian guard in battle, and Roman military might had grown by legions. Infused with conscripts whose skills were perfected through use of the sword, the Eternal City and its royal palace were secure against invasion. The elite of elite surrounded the emperor at every moment, regiments of Palatine *scholares* whose magnitude alone wholly averted the boldest of would-be usurpers.

Austromoine hastened along the paved walk that abutted the stone highway. Cassock in full display and eyes down, he hoped to reach the necropolis unnoticed.

Without forewarning a six-foot wooden spear was brought down forcefully across the path before him. He halted, the weapon flat against his waist.

"Certificate." The order was dictated with a deliberate tone, ambiguous as to threat or intimidation.

Raising his left hand high to signal deference, the bishop slid his right through the side opening of his outer garment and withdrew a folded leather sheath of documents in Latin.

In the fading light of early dusk, a stream of torches burned along each side of the road, creating an illuminated tunnel of amber off into the darkness.

"'Stremonius Romanus.'" The soldier leered at him with overt skepticism. "You claim to be a citizen of Rome?"

Austromoine blanched at the affront. "I claim not. It is that which I am. The certificate attests to the fact."

Trained to fight and also subdue, the soldier tempered his authoritative response. "Germanus, guard this man." He then stepped away and paced toward a large canopied tent several hundred feet from the road. After a lengthy interval he returned, accompanied by a man wearing not segmented armor but a white tunic sashed with a leather belt.

Immediately the commander ordered Germanus to lower his sword.

"Citizen, I bid you explain your presence in Gaul and your reason for travel this night. We seek not to breech your rights, yet our obligation is to the safety of the emperor."

"May I approach?" The familiar voice emanated from directly behind Austromoine.

"If you have knowledge of this man's intent."

Rhétice bowed and showed his certificate as being a resident of Provence. "Sir, we are bishops of the Church attending the *concilium*. At its conclusion we will resume our posts in Autun and Auvergne."

The commander inspected the document briefly and handed it back. "Your purpose for being outside the city walls at this hour?"

"To honor the tomb of a fellow bishop at Alyscamps. The entrance is not a tenth league from here." His eyes turned to the brash young man, bidding him still.

A sharp nod confirmed the commander's approval. Without further word, he left for his tent.

The soldier uncrossed his arms and reached toward Austromoine with his documents. "You are advised to carry certification of your post. As such, you are in violation of Roman law." He slowly released his hold on the sheath and stood back. "Let them pass."

Rhétice pushed his companion forward and hurried them along the path.

"'You are advised.'" The elder man's derision was not masked by the quiet of his speech. "May this be a lesson not readily forgotten, lest you draw suspicion upon yourself and the Church. Never risk that with which you have been entrusted."

Shortly they came upon a side road that branched to the right. The narrow path was of crushed stone packed tight, strengthened with fine silt. Deep grooves revealed the course taken by thousands of casket-laden wagons carrying the dead for burial in this vast, ancient cemetery.

Torches lit the hammered iron portal. Rhétice bent forward and retrieved an oil lantern left by the caretaker for their use, as well as a kindling sprig to set its wick aflame. With effort, Austromoine pulled open the massive door, and they entered.

The passage before them was forbiddingly dark, shrouded by an allée of plane trees. Faint light at its end beckoned them onward.

In the brilliance of day, one could readily become lost amidst the acres of monuments and intersecting trails. Now, as dusk deepened to night, how they would find their way seemed to Austromoine beyond imagining.

"We wait." Rhétice stood patiently, lantern at his side.

Slowly, even the dimmest glow disappeared from the clouded sky. Still they stood.

"There! Follow me." Rhétice moved ahead determinedly, without apparent caution.

Austromoine followed at his heels, eyes on the lantern that swung at the older man's knee. "What did you see? How are you leading us through this blackness?"

A hundred paces later he too saw that which moments before had been masked to him by the lantern's glare: mounted high on the trunk of a linden was a hand torch, its small flame visible only against the absolute darkness that surrounded it.

The beacon stood at the junction of three trails. Rhétice hooded the lantern and stared in each direction, searching for the next pinpoint of light. "There!"

This time both men could make out the signal, far down the leftward trail.

After a succession of seven such turns, they were at last in sight of Trophime's tomb.

As a memorial to the first bishop of Arles, what Austromoine had expected to be a low crypt was in fact an ornate chapel sited on the rise of a hill. Lamps guttered within, casting an ethereal luminescence that pulsated lifelike through rose-red panes.

Holding the lantern shoulder high, Rhétice ascended the long, stepped walkway to the portico and rapped thrice. Soft thuds were heard as a plank barricade was removed from its frame and the door creaked open. A cloaked man greeted Rhétice who, with a swing of the lantern, motioned for Austromoine.

"Did you meet with trouble? It is late."

"A minor inquiry, Daphnus. Nothing more."

"I have seen no one, else yourselves." He waved them into the chapel, then closed and barred the door. "What is the news? Did our brethren from Carthage concede on any issue after I departed?"

Rhétice shook his head. "You will not be surprised when I say no."

"Sadly, that is true. Let us pray for unity in the Lord's Spirit."

"And for his protection in our present task."

An altar stood against the far wall—and in the center of the room, Trophime's sarcophagus. Twice yearly a Mass was offered here in observance of the saint's birth and death. Fresh flowers were placed on the tomb, left to dry until the next celebration as a symbol of mortal life.

Daphnus walked to the altar and knelt. Assuming it a genuflection, Austromoine's eyes instinctively searched for a tabernacle and found none. Rather, the bishop from Vaison drew aside the brocade antependium that hung to the floor. Rhétice knelt beside him. Together they grasped into the shadows beneath the altar and, straining, brought forth an object that Austromoine knew at once must be the amphora brought to Gaul by Marie Madeleine.

"It is here? How can this be? I thought it was ensconced at La Sainte-Baume!"

The bishops rose, stood on opposite sides of the amphora, and carried it out into the candlelight.

With hesitant steps, Austromoine approached the sacred vessel and dropped to his knees in awe. Before him was not a piece of common pottery, but a fine ceramic container of exquisite proportions glazed pure white and flawless. Broadest at the top and narrowing gracefully downward, it was regal in stature. Curved handles, swanlike, adorned the sides and lid.

Yet in this moment he saw not magnificence but splendor.

He reached for but dared not touch that which caused his heart to leap.

There, embedded in a palm-sized circle of yellowed wax on the front of the vessel, four wooden splinters formed the shape of a cross. He gazed at it, lost in contemplation of Christ crucified, of sacrificial blood, of wood forever stained crimson brown.

He contemplated Christ buried, and resurrected.

He rejoiced in this divine act of saving grace.

After a time, Rhétice spoke under breath, his tone flat. "Austromoine, this is your charge: that the amphora be taken with you to Auvergne and hidden where it will be neither found nor plundered. Holy Father Silvester has so ordered."

"Auvergne?" The young man's voice quavered with an insecurity not earlier displayed. "I fear I am not worthy of this trust. Would not Vaison be safer?" He looked to Daphnus.

"All courses were debated. When our enemies were solely from without, there was naught but risk in translating the relics elsewhere." Daphnus breathed deep, then continued. "Alas, our world has changed. We face not Roman persecution but threats from within, from those who know of La Sainte-Baume."

"Of all options, Auvergne is the place of least risk." Rhétice raised his thumb, indicating the first of several reasons. "It is buried deep in Roman Gaul and furthest from pagan incursions. Unlike Lyon and Arles, there is little interest in it politically. The see is solid, you yourself having ably led it for half a decade. And," a benevolent smile formed as he spoke these words, "it must be in the care of someone not readily defeated."

Austromoine stood, looked at each man in turn, then once again let his gaze fall upon the amphora. Its lid, set in wax by the saint herself, bore an inscription lettered in deep purple.

INRI

A crime of guilt under Roman law, nailed to the cross for all to see.
Jesus of Nazareth, King of the Jews
Words of shame.
Words of truth.
He touched the inscription, then his lips.
"There is an empty tomb in Issoire. It will be safe."

CHAPTER FOURTEEN
PONTE SANT'ANGELO
†
BRIDGE OF THE HOLY ANGEL

To: Marco Giordano <m.giordano@arcsacra.va>
From: Kevin Schaeffer <kevinschaeffer999@yahoo.com>
Date: July 25, 2010 14:22:06 IST
Subject: Papà Giordano

Marco, my friend, I am deeply saddened to hear of your father's passing and regret having not visited him while I was in Italy last month. It was unexpected news, despite his age. He was a righteous man whose virtues live on in you.

The week he spent in Boston after your mother died is all the more poignant to me now. I had expected to help a grieving man confront loss even as he fulfilled his dream of setting foot in America. But he did not need my counsel. His soul was aloft, his heart filled with grace.

Before leaving he asked if I'd found joy in life. Joy, not happiness. I had no answer. Yet in the peace of his smile was a father's love, ever perceptive, ever teaching. Such was his effect on me. For a moment he became the father I'd lost in third grade and whose absence looms ever larger.

So we have both lost parents in the span of a year—a mother, a father: a kinship of the grieving. It is true that even on the darkest night, the moon reflects the light of the sun.

I received an email from Kyle today. He seems sufficiently comfortable at the residence and is eager to dig in to the project. I still think it's best for him to approach this as purely academic research. Ties back home are strong—there's no need to make him feel responsible for saving a child's life. He'll hear the whole story soon enough.

Thanks for arranging his stay at the glorious Gregorian U. It has set me thinking back on our own years there as dissertation slaves. In reality, how spoiled we were! Cocooned in Rome, protected from worldly distraction, immersed in completing a monumental work with the greatest Church theologians and exegetes of the modern age . . . for that I am grateful.

Michael's doctor sounded vaguely encouraging yesterday. The leukemia is almost in remission, and she hopes that a course of more intensive therapy will help. I readily admit to not fully understanding the details but sense that "almost in remission" is a disappointment. My student intern has been a blessing to the boy—and a support to the grandmother. What an education in empathy she is gaining this summer.

The old Augustinian priest I mentioned earlier is a fascinating character. His memory is long and penetrates many facets of life in that small community. He appeared cautious in what he shared during our first meeting and revealed no new leads to help track down the relic. However, we established some rapport so perhaps he will entrust me with additional insights next week.

Interestingly, he did not hold back on a vivid retelling of the last known cure by the cross, that of Michael's ancestor in 1866. It was as though Maire herself were speaking. I suspect there was much embellishment, yet I found it engrossing.

Unfortunately we now have two differing versions of the tale. The priest describes an ill and delirious Maire touching not wood, but a wax seal on the lid of a cask—a seal placed by none other than Saint Patrick to preserve a most holy relic inside. Michael's grandmother is convinced that Maire touched the cross itself. We may not know until—and if—we find the vessel.

I send with this message my endless gratitude, condolences, and prayers.

Ciao, amico mio . . . Kevin

Monday, 26 July 2010, Pontifical Gregorian University

Kyle stood in front of the Central Building and scanned the piazza nervously. Streams of pedestrians converged toward the entrance as the eight o'clock hour neared, intimidating even Vespa riders to wait quietly to the side.

Soon bells tolled, from steeples and towers and cathedrals. Then they were silent and the noise of nearby traffic could be heard once again. Sidewalks cleared, leaving the gray cobblestones to leashed dogs and passing bikes.

If asked, he could not have explained why he thought Cristina would appear from across the piazza, nonchalant in a slow promenade, sundress billowing gently about with the morning breeze.

"*Buongiorno*, Kyle."

The voice was like air, drifting softly into his vision as if real.

"Shall we start with coffee, perhaps?" She touched his arm. He jolted alert.

"I'm sorry. Did I frighten you?" Her head inclined in a look of tender concern.

"What? Nah, I'm fine." Turning, he shifted his weight from foot to foot, clearly more startled than his reply suggested.

"There is a nice café here. We can get our drinks and sit in the garden. *Sì?*"

"Sure, *sì.*"

The building was spacious and evoked a modern, neoclassical grandeur. They made their way past offices and lecture halls, strolled through the central atrium, and eventually stood in queue with a dozen other, mostly clerical, patrons.

"So, Kyle, tell me about your home."

"My home? With my parents?" He felt uncomfortably like an adolescent whose guise of maturity had been stripped away.

"Yes. I would love to hear all about your family. Maybe they are a bit like mine."

"That I doubt," he laughed. "It's just me—I don't have any sisters or brothers. We live in a small city, a village, really, on the Atlantic. Have you been to Ireland?"

"I want to, someday."

"Well, we're over here." He held out his right hand, upright with fingers half-flexed, and pointed to the base of his thumb as southwest. "Where are you from?"

"Ah, from the most beautiful part of Italy, of course. Our little village is named Cagnano Varano, in Puglia, here." Leaning down, she touched a spot low on her right calf. "If we want to swim we can choose the sea or, much better, Lago di Varano—it is warmer, with no salt."

"What about your family?"

"I was the only child too, but only for a year. Now there are five. Lucia and Ricco are still home. Terese, Camilla, and I are at university. Our parents are happy that the government pays for tuition. Is it the same for you?"

He shook his head emphatically, as much astonished at the family size as the notion of free college. "Not a chance. I have a scholarship. I did, anyway."

"I don't understand."

He shook his head again, this time with a slight shrug and prolonged blink.

"*Scusate, cosa desiderate ordinare?*" the server interrupted.

"*Sì, un attimo, prego.*" She turned to Kyle. "Do you know what you want?"

"Uh, I guess a latte."

"*Un caffè latte e un cappuccino. Grazie.*"

The cashier line moved quickly, and a moment later their order was ready. Outside, they found an empty table on the patio and sat opposite each other.

"Please, you were telling me about school."

Kyle blew lightly on his drink several times, sipped, and set it down. He looked out at the garden, eyes passively tracking a ground squirrel until it disappeared under a shrub.

"I dropped out."

Cristina held her cup with both hands and let it hover near her lips, saying nothing.

"I'm not sure what's happening with my life, or even if they're holding the scholarship." He turned the glass in slow circles on his napkin. "My father's cool with it—better this way than making a big mistake. I think my ma's disappointed. But she doesn't say much."

He gradually lifted his eyes and met her gaze.

"It is good you are here, then." Her smile was warm and encouraging. "The world is big, no? And there are many tomorrows."

"*Que sera.*"

"*Sì!* That is right." After a minute or two with no response, she touched his arm briefly, then rose. "Now, I will find some paper cups and we can finish our coffee while we walk."

He watched her return to the counter. Her hands moved expressively as she spoke with the clerk.

The day was young. He breathed deeply and prepared for the journey ahead.

+ + + + + + + +

Kyle was in awe as they passed the Pantheon. When they reached the Ponte Sant'Angelo and looked over the Tiber to Hadrian's castle, he was speechless.

The bridge itself was a spectacle. Statues of Saints Peter and Paul flanked the entrance, greeting pedestrians. Spaced evenly along the span stood five additional pairs of statues: ten angels of heaven with wings resplendent in the rising sun. Beneath, the murky green water of the river plodded by, confined to its ancient course.

Cristina visibly delighted in Kyle's excitement. Her world was fresh anew.

"I never thought I'd be here. Until now this was all just part of a history book."

"It is a wondrous city. When I close my eyes I can feel the spirits of the many centuries crowding near, filling the streets." Standing with her arms back, palms up, forehead high, it was as though the moment of rapture had arrived.

She sighed in an indulgent stretch, then took his arm and together they meandered from figure to figure. "A choir of angels, no?"

Midway across, Kyle stopped and examined one in detail. He paused, looking again at those behind and others up ahead. "Cristina, these angels were with Jesus at his crucifixion. Can you see what they're holding?" He pointed out the nails, lance, sour sponge, crown of thorns. "And look at their faces. They mourn."

Her eyes went not to the statues but to Kyle, whose own face was in sorrow. "I will always think of this bridge now with sadness," she said.

Dropping his gaze back to her, he replied in soft tones, smiling, "They mourn that he had not yet risen."

Comforted, she took his arm once more and they continued on.

"Near our village there is a famous mountain *caverna* where it is said that San Michele Arcangelo appeared for the first time in all of Europe. He promised to protect the faithful. And he did. When pagans attacked he returned with his sword on fire. He is very powerful."

At mention of the archangel, Kyle turned, straightened tall, and focused intently on her. "In the Dark Ages, right? I know that story. I know all about Saint Michael. And you're from there. How cool is that?!"

Seeing his youthful enthusiasm, her smile broadened to a full grin.

"Then you will like this especially well." She withdrew a small red paper packet from her cross-shoulder purse. It opened like a square petal.

"This is from Monte Gargano, the sanctuary. It is an image of San Michele raising his sword." In her palm was a scapular, two identical postage-stamp-sized cloth portraits of the saint strung together with soft cording. "The same as the statue right up there." Together they looked at the bronze figure that reigned from atop the round second-century castle.

"Papa Benedetto blessed it for you. May it keep you from harm and heal you of all ills."

Reaching up, she placed it over his head, draping the images on his chest and back to envelop his heart.

He held the cloth in his hand. "A guardian angel."

"*Angele dei, sì.*"

"Thank you—*grazie.*"

"Ah, already you speak *italiano*!"

"*Un poco,*" he said with a laugh.

"*Benissimo!*"

As they resumed walking, Kyle tucked the scapular inside his shirt.

"You know, I can see Skellig Michael from our house. It's the tip of a mountain peaking out from the ocean. Kevin says the abandoned monastery there was built to hide the cross— well, fragments of it, anyway. The monks dedicated it to Saint

Michael, with him leading God's army against Satan and all."
Again he touched the scapular. "Growing up and seeing it every day, that's how I learned so much about him."

She smiled, content. "So we share an angel. That is nice."

They had come to the end of the bridge and stood in front of the castle.

"One day I will give you a tour here. But today is for research, *si*?" Turning left, she led him across the small square and onto Via della Conciliazione. The Basilica of Saint Peter rose in the distance, Michelangelo's dome gleaming white.

"Kyle, you said a name just now that I don't know—when you told about the island."

"Kevin, you mean? Father Marco's friend? He's the priest I'm helping."

"*Va bene*. Now I understand."

A large flock of tourists approached from behind, talking loudly in a language Kyle couldn't identify. The two stepped aside, letting the group pass, and with it, the din.

"*Dio!* The *chiasso*—it's not easy to think!" She stopped momentarily, taking a pair of stylish jewel-tone sunglasses from her purse. "*Molto meglio.*"

They walked a block, enjoying the quiet. Soon, she spoke again of the archive.

"Have you decided how you want to start your search for the cross?"

"Well, I was hoping you'd have a suggestion."

"Me? You are clever . . ."

Kyle beamed.

"Okay. For me, it is always good to start with what I know." Brows raised, she eyed him provocatively over the rim of her sunglasses and waited.

"What I know. Hm." His smile changed to an earnest look of concentration. "The only for-sure date we have is 477. Oh, and 1866."

"Why those dates?"

"477, that's the year of Saint Brigid's letter. And 1866 was when the last cure happened."

"*Aspetta, aspetta.*" She shook her head in confusion. "First, everything about 477."

"I'm sorry." Embarrassed, he stopped, head bowed as if scolded.

Cristina's breath caught at having hurt his feelings. In apology, she brushed the back of her hand affectionately across his cheek.

"*No, è il mio problema. Prego*, I want to hear more."

Gradually they set out again, walking slowly.

"Kevin found a letter from Saint Brigid to Saint Patrick. It was written in 477. I guess it was about the cross being sent to Ireland by the pope. That's all." He looked up to see her response. She was smiling fondly.

"That is a very good lead, Kyle. Now, tell me about the other date—1866?"

"Yeah. Anyhow, once the cross was in Ireland, a lot of sick people were brought to it and cured. The last was a girl back in 1866. Then it just disappeared. That's why I'm here."

She nodded so exuberantly that her whole body swayed. Her obvious passion in working with him on his project erased from Kyle any remnant of insecurity. He had never before experienced such elation.

"*Magnifico!* We have much to go on! The archive is filled with records from the popes. *Dio*, they keep everything! What do you say we start at the beginning, then, in 477? There are not so many early documents, but we need only one, *sì*?"

With that, she grasped his hand and playfully tugged him forward.

He had long since decided to follow her anywhere.

CHAPTER FIFTEEN
CRUX DE CRUCE
†
CROSS OF THE CROSS

Thursday, 28 July 477, Issoire, Gaul

Clovis stood balanced on one leg, his other poised to leap. The rocks were thick with moss, and he had already fallen once into the shallow water. Uttering a token prayer to Volturnus, the river god, he grunted loudly and flung himself forward, barely lighting on the three remaining stones before tumbling into a bank of reeds.

Beneath him the ground was damp but firm. He rolled onto his back and listened, eyes closed, for the croaking of summer frogs. The silence seemed unnatural. At dusk in Tournai there would be such reverberation that the air itself would shudder. But they were far from the marshes of home. Here the waters ran low in drought and the blackened stubble from grassland fires was harsh on the foot.

"Come now, boy—out of hiding." Rémi had not seen the child run off, his eyes trained instead on the tomb of Austromoine a hundred paces distant. Three companions were still at task within. Hearing no reply, he trekked to the river's edge in search.

A soft rustling in the reeds was the only sign of ambush. In a pounce, arms suddenly contracted about Rémi's ankles and he was down.

Clovis sprang up, planted a sole on the man's chest, and declared victory.

"You have trounced me, nigh to the death." His kindly face looked up at the scraggy silhouette that hung over him. He had grown fond of his ward, the future king—whose brutish impulse was ever more tempered by warmth. "Oblige your wounded foe a hand and together we will make haste. Your father needs our service."

They walked back across the dry floodplain, Clovis trailing behind the bishop of Reims.

Childeric had left the tomb and stood in the wagon next to a slatted wooden crate that rose even with his waist. He appeared more a laborer than the august Frankish king of coastal regions to the north. Seeing them, he called out. "Indeed, a well timed return."

Rémi prodded the boy along. He broke into a run, now leaving his mentor to follow.

The horses bridled as the eleven-year-old passed, sensing an imminent departure.

Clovis clambered up next to his father. In two motions they heaved the crate forward and stowed it securely in place.

"Good. Now, split this bale for the team. And stay near. We leave soon."

Rémi waved his old friend hither, at most fifteen paces from the tomb, and spoke softly. "While we are alone, tell me your mind on Syagrius. We cannot make the ten-day journey across his lands absent him, yet I harbor a measure of distrust—truce or no."

Childeric shook his head decidedly. "Your concern is unfounded. Rivals we may be and our militaries may yet clash. But it cannot be denied that he has steadfastly protected the Church throughout Soissons, like his father before him." Gesturing assurance, he rested a hand on the bishop's shoulder. "Do not fear that Rome's fall will risk your safety. He is a Roman commander true to his word."

"Still, he will not stand for long," Rémi warned. "Arian Goths press from all sides. Need I mention your own banishment by them at point of spear?"

"Yes, and who came to my aid? Syagrius is an ally against common enemies."

Rémi now clenched his friend's shoulder. "I am always at the ready to baptize you and the boy." He smiled. "Clovis will be a worthy successor. He has the heart of a great leader."

"I would die well knowing you are his sworn regent." It was not said lightly by the king.

"Enough of talk that will not come to pass."

Childeric irked at the deflection, yet knew there were more urgent issues. "In my sight, both have acted with honor." His glance went to the tomb: neither the Roman commander nor the bishop of Auvergne had yet emerged. "Syagrius pledged Sidonius safe passage north to the shore where a boat awaits. By journey's end I expect the two will be wedded in any future need against the Goths."

"That is good, that is good." Rémi paused, then spoke in even lower tones. "The sacred vessel here retrieved, long buried with Austromoine—what was said of it?"

The Frank shrugged. "Syagrius's interest seemed not aroused. He and I are pagans—to us it is a vessel, nothing more. Sacred to you and to Sidonius, to the Holy See—that we know. As rulers, we have vowed to guard you both en route and to protect the object that you hold holy. This we will do."

Rémi bowed deeply. "May your compassion one day be rewarded in heaven."

A fleeting radiance shone on Childeric's face as he nodded in reply.

+ + + + + + + + +

He had never been to sea.

Although enchanted by the sandy coast, where a thousand golden plovers skittered, Sidonius grew perturbed as they lost sight of land. Soon he was seized by apprehension, which yielded quickly to fear. His hands gripped the rail, his body immovable.

"You'd best retreat inside," shouted the aging Welsh boatman brusquely from the stern. Brieuc had traversed these waters even as a child. Of late he had been ferrying monks to and from Ard na Caithne, sufficient to deplete all tolerance. "Moninne, move him along and give him a pail—he'll need it, to be sure." The boat swayed deeply into the wind as he thrust the paddle rudder against current. He looked back toward the mainland. *Anon, Ar Y Môr, I shall return to stay.*

Spray washed across the deck. Sidonius suddenly lurched, feet splayed. The diminutive nun lost her hold on the rail and they slid, one upon the other, past the cabin and into the bow. Slowly he crawled aft, lifting neither knee nor palm off the planks. Only when the sails luffed was Moninne able to coax him through the hatch and onto a narrow berth.

After some time she emerged, patting her brow with a stained square of cloth. "God's grace be with us. This one is not fit for voyage."

"Aye, sister. By my word, neither will he venture out until the morn, and weakened at that. The sea humbles the proudest of men."

An ebb tide had carried them swiftly into the channel. By noon the weathered wooden boat would be coursing smoothly with the Atlantic's strong northern stream.

"If the winds stay with us, we will easily reach harbor on the third day."

+ + + + + + + +

"I can scarce believe such wonders exist." Sidonius leaned far out over the bow as though the effort would draw him nearer. The sun, squat and full, continued its nightly descent toward the horizon. Soon it would transform into a halo of fire melting behind the rocky pyramids: islands cast black in shadow. To the east, the Celtic coast was alight.

Seeing the Sceiligs, Brieuc pegged the rudder fast and strode to the cabin. He returned holding two lengths of wood hinged at their ends and handed it to Moninne. "Sentries will be posted at the headland. When we round the last point near the harbor, clap thrice."

She pried the damp boards apart and worked rust from the hinge. "They have been instructed to advise Brigid of our arrival, no matter the hour. Padraig may also be there to greet us."

"Padraig?" Brieuc whistled low in surprise. "Sister, what is it that Sidonius brings?"

Moninne set down the clapboard and stepped close. "He asked that it not be discussed at sea." She waited to speak further as he adjusted the rudder and again set the peg.

"All of Europe is in turmoil with Rome's fall. In its stead is a fragmented rule of pagans and heretics. These things you know."

Brieuc nodded for her to continue.

"The Church is at risk of plunder and destruction. Nowhere are its relics safe. But Éire stands apart, separated by ocean and strong in faith. The pope turns to us in his hour of need." Her voice wavered with words hitherto unimaginable. "For a time the amphora of Nicodemus will be in our care."

Brieuc stood silent, contemplating what had been said. Then: "May God forgive me, but I wonder, how is it known to be the true vessel, four centuries after the crucifixion?"

"It is fact," came the definitive retort in brusque baritone.

Startled, they turned to see Sidonius at their side. He spoke firmly, with authority and certitude. "I will explain, that you may believe."

He allowed them a moment to calm.

"We carry to Padraig the very amphora of Jesus's burial, borne from his tomb by the beloved apostle John and blessed Marie Madeleine." Saying their names, he touched fingers to his brow, chest, shoulders, and lips. "Kept within were treasures from the earthly life of our Lord—not gold or coin but remembrances of his childhood and of his passion."

Moninne clutched the cross that hung from her neck, an emblem of Christ's suffering.

"There was then a great tribulation in Jerusalem. Marie fled to Gaul, taking with her the relics. She lived alone in prayer, tended by sisters. Before dying she sealed the amphora by her own hand, desiring that it never be disturbed. On its lid she painted the inscription of our Lord's crucifixion. On its side she set into wax a *crux de cruce*."

He saw from their expressions that neither understood the meaning of this phrase.

"A new cross created of splinters taken from Jesus's body. *Cross of the cross*."

For some time none spoke, humbled that objects of such holiness were in their midst.

Moninne reflected on their months of preparation at Gall Iorras. "Padraig and Brigid do not know what comes. I myself learned of the vessel only by Rémi, and he said nothing of what it holds."

Sidonius nodded. "Thus was the order of the Holy Father. Yet on this night all will be revealed, for to them passes the sacred privilege of its protection."

He turned to Brieuc. "Friend, I have freely given you my trust these three days for safe passage, knowing well what we bear. I ask your trust on the truth not only of my word but also the words here written." From his tunic he withdrew a limed parchment scroll laced in red. "Many have devoted their lives to the guard of these most precious items, at La Sainte-Baume and at Issoire, as testified herein. By God's grace Éire too will prove itself worthy of this profound task."

"Aye, brother. We join in that prayer." Brieuc bowed reverently.

As twilight fell they entered the harbor. Moninne stood at the bow, torch raised. In the distance two lights burned, held high by those in wait.

Oh, Éire, bastion of monastic faith—what wondrous miracles might now be wrought?

Monday, 26 July 2010, Pio XI Reading Room, Vatican Secret Archive

"I have found nothing." Cristina turned over the small stack of documents and began straightening them. "The first Pope John died in *prigione*—jail, no? Do you know why?"

"Monophysitism?" Kyle laughed, stumbling over the word, and continued to search through the much larger folder of Pope Hormisdas.

"What? *Dio*, enough for today—they will lock us in if we stay much longer."

"It looks like this guy spent all his time on schisms." He lifted an inch-tall bundle of papers marked *Constantinopolis*.

"Many schisms, *sì*. Many temptations from the true faith." Pushing back her chair, she stood and filled her arms with files. "We have made much progress today, Kyle. Don't be disappointed—tomorrow we will begin again at the Gregorian archive. If the sixth century is not kind to us, perhaps our fortune rests in the nineteenth. *Un momento . . .*" She headed toward the distribution counter to return the first load.

Kyle labored through the documents on the Acacian schism, once more thankful that his years of toil in high school and seminary Latin classes were finally of some practical value. The pages below regarded various papal pronouncements that followed during what would have been the summer months of 519.

He did not notice Cristina collect a second armful and leave.

He sat alone at the table, alone in the room.

"Cóemgen." He spoke it aloud.

The creased sheet before him appeared to be of stretched animal skin, small patches of dense hair still showing at the edges. It was thick and irregular, with pigmented areas one would expect on unbleached hide. Kyle surmised it was the paper of an outpost, not the fine parchment of the elite.

I, Conlaeth, Bishop of Cill Dara, faithful servant of Most Holy Father Hormisdas, hereby present to His Holiness Cóemgen, devoted brother in Iesus Christus.

"Are you ready?" He did not respond. "Kyle?"

"Please, sit for a minute." His eyes did not leave the document.

She watched as he translated the letter and carefully transcribed it in pencil onto the top sheet of a legal pad. She knew from his intense concentration that he had discovered something significant.

Twenty minutes later he finished.

"This is incredible. You won't believe it."

"*Prego*—please, tell me." The excitement in her voice nearly matched his.

"Okay." He spoke in short bursts with breaths coming quickly. "A name on this letter leapt out at me: *Cóemgen*. Saint Kevin. You wouldn't know him, but I do. He was the first abbot of Glendalough in Wicklow. He started the damn place!"

"When was that?"

"I don't know for sure. A long time ago, must have been in the five hundreds." With a slight wave he dismissed it as detail. "He traveled here to Rome. He met with Hormisdas."

Cristina knew that Vatican pilgrimages were commonplace, even from the farthest reaches of Europe.

"So what was special about this visit?"

"That's the best part." Kyle sat forward in his chair, hands thumping the table as he spoke. "The bishop of Kildare sent him as a messenger. Kildare—that's Brigid's monastery." His eyes widened. "Conlaeth met with Cóemgen in Wicklow and gave him this letter, but never went to Rome himself."

She waited. There was more.

"Cóemgen was given a scroll to deliver to the pope." Kyle's demeanor suddenly tamed. "It was a scroll of the history of a vessel."

He paused.

"The amphora of Nicodemus had been hidden at Skellig Michael."

He took her hand.

"Cristina, on the amphora was a *crux de cruce*—a cross of the cross."

CHAPTER SIXTEEN
GLEANN DÁ LOCH
†
GLENDALOUGH

Monday, 3 May 519, Kildare

A chill wind swept across the field midday, its howl enough to herd the newly shorn sheep and trail of frantic lambs homeward. Soon, hawthorn branches hung low, blush blossoms crowned with snow. By evening, troughs were encrusted in ice. Angry bleats murmured among the thirstiest ewes, then grew to a chaotic uproar as others joined the protest.

From the study Conlaeth heard the scuttering of brothers quickly donning heavy cloaks and overshoes. Weeks before they had stowed away shovels and pickaxes, confident that the sustained early spring would gently turn to summer.

"Well it is to be old on such a night, Fionán." He leaned forward in the padded chair, took hold of the table's edge, and gradually pulled himself to a standing position. "In stealth the youth have made off with my strength. Let work be their reward." His step was slow, obstinacy his sole weapon against infirmity.

Once at the hearth, he jabbed the half-charred logs with the worn tip of his cane until they erupted into flame. He would miss this place, this room: for forty years his home. That his pilgrimage to Rome was finally upon him—favored by the company of Cóemgen, former pupil and founder of his own monastery in the Wicklow hills—tempered the loss.

Fionán strode to his side. "Let me journey with you to Gleann Dá Loch. I will rest better seeing you there in safety. At the least, delay while the cold persists."

Conlaeth placed his hand on the monk's shoulder. "No, Fionán, I must be off on the morrow. Cóemgen has already sent for our ferryman Bréanainn, and both wait. If I do not arrive when expected, they will fear the evil one has stricken at last. And you are not yet recovered from your own trek from Sceilig Mhór." He smiled. "Too few years separate us, my friend. Do not hasten to leave your new home quite yet, even for a brief while. Take your deserved rest."

Together they drew a bench close to the fire and sat. When warmed, Conlaeth resumed instruction of his successor bishop.

"Never neglect your abbess—Brigid is your greatest ally. She and Neacht will mind the sisters. Your eternal woe as bishop will be the novices."

"Aye—men they appear but rams they are." Fionán's nod was of experience. "Their passions will rightly burn only for God after years on the crag."

"My memory is dim of such longings." Conlaeth laughed heartily, content yet again with age. "Now, the day is 'most done and I have consumed it with talk. Tell me of the monastery. Last I risked venture you displayed two huts and an unyielding determination to create a civilization."

"A civilization indeed." Fionán looked caringly at the aged bishop. There was no other he trusted so fully, none whose wisdom had shone so brightly on his life. His eyes misted. "Your presence will be missed, Conlaeth. I pray that Holy Father Hormisdas discerns the treasure he receives in you—not solely the scroll you bring."

By his silence the bishop humbly accepted the homage.

"The crag—it nearly proved our death. Broccán lost footing more than once laden with baskets of earth. Three months of labor it took to make flat the small plot where the first huts were raised. With shelter, others from Gall Iorras joined and progress hastened."

"So with effort and grace the relic has been kept safe these many years."

"With all that it is in me, I dare say yea."

Conlaeth laid hand on Fionán's arm. "May God's blessings be poured out upon you here even as they have been lavished upon that desolate island."

"In his will are our strength and endurance."

The fire flickered and a cool draft swept the room. Fionán set fresh logs on the embers, draped a blanket about the older man's shoulders, and sat again at his side.

"As foretold by you ere we began our work, Broccán showed himself to possess the full measure of his uncle Padraig's tenacity. He is fit to ably lead the monastery and guard the relic from discovery and harm."

"Then I shall depart in peace." He motioned for Fionán to help him rise. Slowly they returned to their chairs. On the table lay a parchment—at its end a signature and seal.

"These are the papal orders appointing you bishop and abbot of Cill Dara. Bestowed upon you is the responsibility over all ecclesial matters in the see and authority to confer Broccán as abbot of Sceilig Mhór." He lifted a simple bronze crosier from the table and bade the younger monk kneel before him, head bowed.

"Fionán mac Rudraigh, at the command of His Holiness Pope Hormisdas, accept the mantle of shepherd." He touched the staff gently on each shoulder, laid hands on his head, invoked the Holy Spirit, and anointed him with chrism oil. "Wear this ring as a mark of your pastoral office." He removed it from his own finger and placed it on that of the new bishop. "It is a noble task. In the words of Saint Timothy, at all times be above reproach."

Fionán bowed low and with great reverence kissed the old man's feet.

++++++++

It was a day the Lord had made.

Conlaeth rode tall in the saddle, exuberant as he passed through the land of his youth, a joyful procession of one.

The air bespoke winter. The land was white. The trees were leafed in frosted green.

His woolen cloak was warm.

It was a day of reflection.

He thought of childhood, of parents, of family, none still living.

He thought of his years alone, content in prayer.

He thought of his calling to build with Brigid a monastery at Cill Dara, the firstfruits of their labor—which was to be overshadowed by the yet greater achievement of securing a sacred home for relics of the Lord.

The sun set. A new moon rose. Darkness covered the earth.

He entered the forest. There was no snow. The horse moved along the soft trail.

Crisp air greeted them at the clearing. In the distance, soot-red smoke drifted skyward from a stone flue.

Conlaeth gently spurred the horse to a canter as an outline of the small structure grew visible, pale light pouring from its windows.

Of a sudden the horse reared high, pulling the reigns from the old man's grip.

The horse moved from under him.

He fell.

Above, the firmament was replete with stars.

+++++++++

"Listen—a wolf howls."

Cóemgen raised a candle's flame to the window. Its heat melted the icy glaze into tears that streamed down and puddled at the sill. Outside, the expanse of snow shone gray. "I see it, Bréanainn, not a hundred paces off."

"It calls for others. Prey has been felled." He stood next to the young monk. "See how he lifts one paw high, the other held fast on its victim."

From afar they heard the frenzied response of the pack, then silence.

"They come."

No words were spoken as they hurriedly cloaked and lit torches.

The horse and mule were thudding the ground, their necks straining against leads that bound them to a post. The men rushed to unhitch the animals and move them close to the house where wolves would not approach.

At once a large shape rushed toward them, clouds of snow kicked up by its hooves. Bréanainn caught the reigns and brought the frightened horse to a halt.

The saddle was empty.

"It is Conlaeth! Run and scare off the wolf with your torch. Go!" He looped the reigns quickly over the post, drew them tight, and dashed off behind Cóemgen.

A halo of blood had seeped from the old man's wounds. His neck lay open. Yet he breathed.

Bréanainn planted the torches toward where the wolf stood panting, others nearing.

Cóemgen cradled the bishop's head in his arms, and together they carried him into the house, setting him on a cot.

Already the wolves lapped at the sodden snow where Conlaeth had lain, torch flames burning bright.

"I burden you." Conlaeth grasped weakly at Cóemgen's hand.

"Hush. Bréanainn brings water." He removed his cloak and covered the chilled body that had ceased to shiver.

"The scroll—it is for you now to convey. The Holy Father—Hormisdas . . ." With a feeble cough, reddened spittle gathered on his lips.

Bréanainn dabbed the blood away with a moistened cloth, dribbled a bit of water into his mouth, then placed a folded towel over the torn flesh.

"You know of the vessel. Bréanainn, you yourself have guarded it on the crag." He coughed again. "Listen now to what I tell. Write it as a letter, Cóemgen, in my name. With it the pope will receive you as he would me."

His voice was faint but steady and clear, his breaths frequent. The words came forth.

After much time, a deep sigh averred that he was done.

"Cóemgen, remember all that I have said, all that the pope must hear. Deliver the scroll. Will you do this for me?"

The young monk held the elder's hand firmly in his own. "I will."

Thumb extended, Conlaeth traced a cross on Cóemgen's forehead.

"May God's love be always in your heart, his peace ever in your soul."

Life complete, the bishop closed his eyes and rested.

+++++++++

Dawn came and the sun spread warmth over the land.

It was spring once more. Soon the fields were rid of snow. There was none to be found even in the shadows.

Cóemgen broke the earth with a spade. A mound of dark soil grew at his side. He did not pause in his labor nor prayer.

They laid the wrapped body deep on a bed of rock. Raised planks were set crosswise, stacked with stone, and blanketed with a portion of last year's hay. Then the earth was made whole.

+ + + + + + + + +

The bay at Aremorica glowed silver, its still water a mirror for the setting sun. Bréanainn dropped sail and let the curragh drift into Ocsimor harbor. As was his ritual, he knelt and spoke a silent prayer of thanks for another safe passage across the channel to Brittany.

"It was a fine crossing, brother," the younger monk praised. "I thank you. May God's presence now protect me along the many solitary miles ahead." Cóemgen thought of the epic voyage Conlaeth had prepared, of their time together at Cill Dara with maps spread broad on the study table under candlelight. The way was made ready. If but alone, he would endure and reach Rome with the scroll, thus fulfilling his promise to Conlaeth.

There was an abundance of vessels moored or tied at the dock. The two anchored some way off, hoisted a green flag, and waited for an oarsman to bring them ashore.

In the village, the cobbled streets were raucous.

"We will have a devil's time finding an inn this night. What has drawn such a crowd? And on a Sabbath?" Bréanainn led them to his favored lodge, where they gratefully secured a room that was unexpectedly to be vacated after the supper hour.

"Fortune rests on you, friends," the innkeeper said as he stowed their bags. "The guest who departs is physician to the court. Queen Mother Clotilde has taken ill and leaves anon: he is ordered to her side. King Childebert will follow on the morn with his retinue."

"The king is in Ocsimor?" Bréanainn was in awe. "On what occasion?"

"Being of the cloth, are you not aware? At noon this day he consecrated Paol as bishop."

"Paol—but he is a Welshman, not a Frank."

The innkeeper shrugged. "The king is devout, as Clovis before him, and yields to papal authority. Bretons swarm this land—the choice is not unforeseen as he may placate their animus against the Franks." He gave them each a token. "The tavern next door will serve you."

Outside it was dusk. A dozen men were gathered at The Saxon waiting entry.

Cóemgen spoke for the first time since coming ashore.

"I do not understand. How is it that a king has consecrated a bishop?"

"It is politick, no more." Bréanainn had witnessed many upheavals during his years as a monk and would try to explain the complexity.

"The Church has influence over souls. It is a powerful ally for those who rule armies." He drew the young monk aside. "They dance. The pope teaches spiritual solitude and moral virtue— Christians are docile to earthly authority when free to worship. Rulers genuflect before the pope, institute laws favorable to the Church, and install bishops according to papal edict."

The younger monk shook his head. "Is it politick to consecrate?"

"You are graced with a strong mind, Cóemgen." The older monk smiled. "Childebert performed a ceremonial consecration, that is all. Pope Hormisdas has yet to bless Paol as holy bishop."

"So he travels to Rome?"

"So he shall, Cóemgen, so he shall." Bréanainn's eyes lit. "And with you at his side."

CHAPTER SEVENTEEN
CENTOUNO † ONE HUNDRED ONE

To: Marco Giordano <m.giordano@arcsacra.va>
From: Kevin Schaeffer <kevinschaeffer999@yahoo.com>
Date: July 26, 2010 17:48:35 IST
Subject: Michael

Was it really just yesterday that I wrote with cautious hope that Michael seemed to be improving?

Not so today. An hour ago a nurse called—his temperature shot up again, now to 105°F (my math skills are limited but I think that translates to something like 40°C). He is also having trouble breathing and they suspect pneumonia. To make matters worse, his blood counts plunged, and the worry is that he won't be able to fight an infection even with antibiotics. It is heartrending.

His grandmother must be frantic. It occurs to me that I've never told you her name—it is Aideen. Life was cruising along smoothly enough for them until two months ago, and now it's not certain that the boy will survive the week. After dinner I'll head to the hospital and do what I can to help, which may be little more than sharing my presence. A curtain has dropped about her that has become increasingly difficult to pull away, as if she's preparing for inevitable loss.

Since returning from Ballinskelligs I've visited Michael most days. I hope he sees me as a friend, not a mere priest. Stephanie, my summer student, has also been spending time with Michael—more than with our project, which is for the best since she's someone he can relate to way better than a graying man like me. In reality, the center of gravity for finding the cross has shifted to Italy, whereas the child in need is right here in Ireland.

And that need is dire. I realize it's only been one day, but has Kyle found the cross yet???

Marco, I truly regret bringing these sorrows upon you during a time of personal grief. Perhaps in your doing for others the Spirit will hasten the healing of your wounds.

I will send additional news as I learn of it. Tell Kyle to behave himself (I know that he will).

Many thanks as always.

Ciao, amico mio . . . Kevin

Monday, 26 July 2010, Pio XI Reading Room,
Vatican Secret Archive

"What is a *crux de cruce*?" Cristina said with a hopeful, expectant look.

"I don't know. It just translates to 'cross of the cross.'" His chair skidded loudly on the tiled floor as he pushed back excitedly and sprang up. "I'm stoked! This is the first proof we have of the relic actually being in Ireland."

"The relic . . ." She half smiled as her gaze fell on the parchment before him. "So, Kyle, we should investigate to be sure. What else does the letter say?"

"What? What do you mean?" A look of bewilderment swept his face.

"The phrase. We don't know as fact that it refers to the cross."

"I've told you all." Exasperated at her lackluster response, he failed to hide a smirk as he paced. "Don't you see? How can it be anything but the cross? For Chrissake, we're talking about the amphora of Nicodemus!"

He turned away in a silent stance, arms crossed. Again he had bared his vulnerability and again he had been belittled.

At length she sighed.

"*Sì.* You are right." She rose, walked to his side, and looked up into his eyes—her own moist. "I'm sorry." She led him back to the table. "This is a very important discovery."

Kyle softened. "I should eat before I speak anymore."

She laughed. "*Primo!* I'm ready to die with hunger!"

+ + + + + + + + +

Kyle watched as the maître d' moved briskly from table to table lighting candles, pausing at one to shoo a petulant street violinist from imposing his sour notes on the amused diners. With equal efficiency their waiter Sergio emerged to clear plates. Dressed in black but for a spotless white towel tucked neatly at the waist, he drained the bottle of cabernet into their empty glasses, then presented a platter of elaborate desserts.

"*Prego, biscotti e vin santo, per due,*" Cristina ordered.

"*Certamente.*" Sergio bowed courteously, pivoted, and left.

She reached for her notebook on the empty chair between them and uncapped her pen. "We should finish this while I can still think. The vino . . ." She made doll's eyes while rocking her hand over her temple. Kyle smiled, unaware that his gaze had become a stare.

"Tell me if I have written something wrong, no?" she said, briefly catching his eye and adjusting the candlelight toward the page. "The names I have are Conlaeth and Cóemgen, Sidonus, Hormisdas, and of course Patrizio and Brigida. Here, check the spelling."

Kyle looked over the list, running his finger across the flowing script. "*Sidonius* is wrong—see, you left out an *i*." She made the correction. "And those aren't the Irish names of Padraig or Brigid." He took the pen and printed each in parentheses next to her notations.

"*Grazie mille*," she said as he handed back the pen. "Now, the years—we must guess a bit, right? You're pretty certain the letter is from 519, when Cóemgen would have come to Roma to meet with Pope Hormisdas. But so far we don't have documentation of that visit."

"Yeah, except the letter got here somehow."

"*Sì*, of course. Good point." She tapped the pen against her lips, thinking. "Now, what about the scroll?"

"Well, Conlaeth said it was sent to Ireland with the amphora, under the order of Pope Simplicius. He didn't say when that was."

"Ah, I forgot him on the list," she said, writing. "We can easily look up the dates of his papacy—that will be good enough for now." She made a show of waving her smartphone before him and quickly entered the search. "He was pope a long time—468 to 483. *Dio*."

They looked up as Sergio approached with two cordials and a silver tiered server filled with biscotti and wrapped chocolates.

"*Paradiso*," Cristina whispered as she dipped the end of a cookie into the dessert wine.

Kyle did the same and was quick to agree. "Can you imagine when we find the scroll? The secrets it will tell?"

"*Sì*. That would be amazing." She nibbled more. "You're sure it's not at the archive?"

"Not in the papers I slogged through. And I looked at every damn piece."

She nodded. "Then we will start at the Gregorian archive tomorrow, okay?"

"*Certamente*," he said, watching her eyes glisten in the flickering light.

Tuesday, 27 July 2010, Pontifical Gregorian University
Historical Archives

He stood in the corridor listening to the bounding echoes of animated dialogue that streamed forth from the reference room and reverberated along the high plastered walls.

"*Dio.*" The single word lingered in her wake as she marched toward the building's exit.

He waited a moment, then followed behind at a safe distance.

"I cannot believe it. *Stupido!*" Even in heels she outpaced him. Finally she stopped.

"Uh, what did the lady say?"

Hand on hip, toes tapping, she spoke in a subdued but deliberate tone. "Their collection starts in 1551."

He was clueless as to why this disturbed her.

"Kyle, I know that not to be true. I've done research there myself." She took his silence as support, an acknowledgment of her rectitude. "*Mi scusi.* I should not be so—*emotiva.* Ah, *sono italiana.*" With that she dismissed her outburst. "I need a cappuccino."

Twenty minutes later they were settling into the same garden seats at the GregCafé as the day before. Few words had passed between them.

"*Purtroppo*, there is no more to be done about it now. I will bring it to Father Marco—he wants to meet with us tomorrow after daily Mass. You may get to see Papa Benedetto."

Kyle's stomach tightened.

"No worries. He's a very kind man." She smiled.

With a shrug he asked, "So what about today, if we can't search here for the scroll?"

"The story you told of the cross has two ends, no? We start at the other end."

"I don't get it. I don't understand." His look was part wince, part befuddlement.

"We start with the last person to be cured. A girl, right, in 1866?"

"Yeah, but what are we looking for?"

The flat expression on her face belied an underlying impatience.

"I'll tell you at the archives."

++++++++++

"*Grazie. Buona giornata.*"

Cristina left the reference room and rejoined Kyle in the hall.

"She was much nicer helping with later dates." Jotted on a notecard were the locations of documents relevant to Pope Pius IX.

Kyle followed her into the archives and they found a secluded table. Cristina set down her bag and, card in hand, went to retrieve a 1916 general reference on the history of popes since the Reformation.

It was a massive volume covered in what appeared to be densely woven horsehair or flax dyed dark green. A coating of dust dulled the sheen of the upper gilt edge. The book seemed not to have been disturbed for some time. In the table of contents, Pius IX was the next-to-last pope in a list that started with Leo X and ended with Leo XIII.

She read at length in silence but for an occasional comment.

"Did you know that Pio Nono had the longest reign of any pope? Thirty-two years."

The weighty pages turned heavily and made a scuffing sound as one fell on another.

"He called for the First Vatican Council and they announced the Virgin Mary's, how you say, *Immacolata Concezione.*"

Kyle once again found himself staring without listening, noticing the smooth cup of her hand as she gently brushed back a wisp of hair.

"*Infallibilità papale* . . . the catacombs. *Caspita!* What didn't he do?"

A few pages later she straightened in her chair, nodding with heightened interest. "You will like this pope—he was first to bless the scapular of Saint Michael."

"I like you." It was spoken so softly that he was unsure if he had even said it aloud.

"*Prego?*" Her eyes did not rise.

"Nothing."

She sat back and smiled apologetically across the table. "I'm sorry—this must bore you crazy."

"No. Not at all. I just—." He fumbled for words.

"What?"

"It's just—you said something about catacombs. That got me thinking about relics. I bet there are a lot tucked away in all those tunnels, and maybe—anyhow, it was a stupid idea."

Her head tilted slightly as the impact of his inspiration seized her.

"*Brillante*, Kyle. *Brillante.*" She reached out and squeezed his hand.

"But we don't have any proof that it's true."

Cristina laughed and squeezed harder. "Kyle, you sound like me! Okay, maybe your idea, it is wrong—or, maybe Pio Nono had the same idea in 1866. Right? Where better to hide an amphora than underground?"

"Maybe." He looked up, eyes roving as they coursed the ceiling.

"So, what to do?" she stated. By the silence that followed it was clear she wanted him to take the lead.

"So . . . we should see if we can find anything in the pope's papers. Then learn more about the catacombs—try to narrow down where to search. Then go exploring." He half smiled, awaiting her response. "Oh, and we need that scroll—the cross could still be in Ireland."

"*Molto bene.*" With both hands she turned the tome in his direction. "Here—a long section on catacombs just for you." She pointed to the top of the right page. "And see this draw- ing? Pio Nono is standing at the Callixtus entrance next to Professore De Rossi, the archaeologist—he's the one holding the torch."

"Yeah, I figured the pope would be the guy in the gown." It was said lightly. But then, with a single glance at the text, he slid the book back across the table. "I don't read Italian."

"*Sono stupida!*" she said a bit too loudly, rapping her knuckles on her forehead. "*Sì,* of course. We will read it together. You make notes."

Tuesday, 27 July 2010, Pio XI Reading Room, Vatican Secret Archive

Kyle sat alone at the table, a single folder open before him.

All of the documents were in Latin except one—a letter in Italian.

It was handwritten in blue pen and dated *11 settembre 1870.* In keeping with the exaggerated European style of the time, each *1* was adorned with a dramatic leading flourish that scooped up to the digit's apex, rested sufficiently long to indent the paper, then rashly descended to its baseline. Inscribed a generous space below was the name *Giovanni B de Rossi,* and on the line following, *Università degli Studi de Perugia.*

Comunicazione Riservata!!

It began
Caro fratello—
and ended
Affettuosamente tuo, —*Michele Stefano*

Kyle stared at the terse paragraphs in the middle that he could not understand.

Within paragraphs he stared at the few words that he did: *San Patrizio. Croce. Irlanda.*

Anfora.

He heard her heels clicking before she rounded the corner.

"There's nothing here in the pope's papers. And almost all of De Rossi's are archaeology documents—hundreds, I mean hundreds—typewritten in Latin. It helped that they're organized by date." He watched her approach. "Did you find anything at the university?"

Cristina had barely reached the table and missed most of what he'd said.

"No, nothing. *Niente. Momento—*" She dropped her bag on the chair, tossed down her sunglasses, and dashed off to the bathroom. Her absence was brief. "Okay, much better. Now, say again?"

"I found this buried in Professor De Rossi's reports from 1870." He carefully handed her the yellowed sheet of stationery.

"A personal letter in his work files?" she said at once, wholly fascinated.

"It's from his brother—I looked him up. He was wild about seismology but had mapped out the catacombs with Giovanni."

Kyle watched her lips move, her hands flutter as she read, her eyes unblinking.

Finished, she remained hunched over it for some time.

"What does it say?"

Her head rose, a smile broadening on her flushed face. "*Angele dei*, Kyle—I believe an angel has guided you, yesterday and today." In her sigh was a sweetness of understanding, an awareness of the grace surrounding him.

She looked again at the sheet. "You are right. This is a letter from his brother—*fratello* in *italiano*. Giovanni was away visiting friends at the university in Perugia when Emanuele invaded Roma."

Kyle showed no change in expression.

"How much do you know about Italian history?"

He shrugged. "Not much."

"*Niente?*" Palms up, her hands waved shoulder-high in disbelief. "Ah, *non c'è problema*. I will tell you what you need to know."

She spent the next several minutes detailing the turbulent events leading to the Italian unification in 1861 and the unwavering refusal of the pope to relinquish hold on a swath of territory that cut across the entire peninsula from Tyrrhenian to Adriatic. Ultimately, King Vittorio Emanuele II defeated Pio Nono in battle.

"Do you see? The invasion started on *dieci settembre*—the day before Michele Stefano wrote this letter."

"And the amphora he mentions—it was no longer safe?"

"*Precisamente.*"

"Even in the Vatican?"

"*Sì*, Kyle. The Vatican was part of Roma, and Emanuele claimed it for Italy. Sure, he said he would leave it alone, but the pope, he did not want the Church under the king's power in any way." She waved her finger dramatically. "There was, how you say, a *stallo*, an impasse, for many years. Papa Pio said that his own palace was a *prigione. Pensa un po'!*"

Kyle could easily imagine the pope panicked with a fear of troops pillaging the Vatican.

"Tell me what it says." He tapped at the letter impatiently, knowing it held more clues.

"*Dio,* of course you're waiting to hear." Her finger scanned down the sheet and stopped at the third paragraph. "The first part is about the king declaring war on Papa Pio and their preparation to defend the papal palace. Then it says: *The amphora with the seal of San Patrizio*—Saint Patrick—*that was delivered to us by the* cardinale *from Ireland will be kept* sicuro sotto protezione di Jonas—secure under Jonah's protection."

"The cross. What does it say about the cross?"

"*Sì, la croce.*" Her finger moved to the fourth paragraph. "*The seal and cross are* non disturbati—not disturbed, *sì?*"

"*Sì,*" he nodded, voice drifting. "It had to be it," Kyle softly repeated to himself until the discovery finally felt real.

Across the table, Cristina's focus was on her iPhone screen.

"*Cristo!*" It was spoken so abruptly that he jumped. "Kyle, when do you think the first *cardinale* from Ireland was appointed?" The pause was brief. "In *giugno* of 1866."

Her thumbs flew from virtual key to virtual key as she continued her search.

"*Gesù Cristo!*" Her hands thudded down. Her mouth hung open.

"What?!" The pallor of her face scared him.

"Kyle." She grabbed his hand. "Kyle, the prophecy . . ."

"What? Tell me."

"Pio Nono. He is number *centouno*—one hundred one."

"And?"

"In the prophecy, *Centouno* is named *Crux de Cruce.*"

CHAPTER EIGHTEEN

TRINITAS † TRINITY

Friday, 24 October 592, Glendalough

The crystalline waters of the broad shallow lake were still, undisturbed even with the gentle landing of leaves wafting down from above. Áed looked heavenward as the sky blackened with geese, the beating of wings their only sound.

It was a warm day and the sun high. Beneath his feet the sand gleamed white. He knelt. The powdery grains felt soft between his fingers. "What Bréanainn said of here is true." He stood, rubbed his hands clean, and walked back to the horses.

Cóemgen beamed paternal affection. "Bréanainn surely spoke right of you."

They rode home south along a trodden path bounded by water and peak.

Let the color of the glass be of your choosing, not that of the sand.

"I am near twice as old as when he baptized me," Áed pondered. "I fear God would not judge kindly on my life."

"The harshness is solely from within: all know you to have been a king of compassion." His voice was resonant. "And your life is not yet spent," the elderly man said with some measure of envy.

The younger man sighed. "Perhaps, Cóemgen, but now it is of no consequence. With abdication comes peace."

"My son, you have been called to a new life. While I draw breath I vow to be your guide. As well, there will always be many brothers on whom you can rely. He doth provide."

The path narrowed. The old man led, the way being well known to him.

About them the mountains shone autumn gold. Soon the lake turned to a coursing river canopied by fir and spruce. Solitude reigned.

After a time the trees thinned. A large lake lay ahead. Shadows had grown long. A pale moon hung in the east. They rode onward.

With the deepening of dusk they arrived. Simple stone dwellings stood against the horizon. On the air was a scent of hickory. A lamp hung at the door of the farthest hut, awaiting their return.

Cóemgen strayed off path toward a well-tended plot. He dismounted, sat on the low fence, pivoted, and rose. Burial mounds radiated from a central marker hone with the image of a lamb.

He bowed over Conlaeth's grave and recited the Our Father.

From a distance Áed echoed the prayer, lifting his voice in remembrance of another monk who years before had taught him the Lord's words.

Pater Noster, qui es in caelis,
sanctificetur nomen tuum . . .

Upon the Amen, Cóemgen rejoined his novice and together they walked the animals slowly to their enclosure.

"You were fond of Bréanainn."

Áed nodded. Sadness overcame him.

"He saw in you a light, a heart that burned for Christ."

Cóemgen stopped and waited for Áed to meet his eyes.

"He left for you the window of Mary." An assuring smile formed on his lips. "He always believed its radiance reflected the love you poured into it on the day of its making."

Red, for his wounds.

An unutterable joy borne of hope in salvation filled his soul.

Wednesday, 28 July 2010, Vatican City

Already a sizable crowd had gathered. Soon it would reach beyond the ancient obelisk that stood in the center of Saint Peter's Square, itself a silent witness to the apostle's crucifixion at the hand of Nero. The just-risen sun cast long rays from the east, sending forth a tapered shadow from pillar to basilica that pierced the bronze doors with a sword of darkness.

Cristina skirted past those waiting and climbed the steps. A host of the Swiss Guard in full tricolor costume and bearing halberds was stationed at the entrances, while others were posted across the portico to direct visitors. At the far left, a guard uniformed in monochrome blue surveyed the piazza, expecting them.

She motioned Kyle ahead as she approached with their Vatican badges. "*Buongiorno. Philippe, no? Io sono Cristina De Lecce e questo è il mio collega irlandese Kyle Dorrian.* I believe you are holding our passes for today?"

"*Sì.* One moment." He inspected the documents, eyed each of them closely, then affixed the day's passes to their badges. "All is in order." With a nod he ushered them into the nave.

In the vastness of the cathedral, surrounded by immense marble pilasters reaching skyward toward a gilt vault glowing with morning light, Kyle felt as though he had crossed the threshold to heaven. Gradually his eye traversed the ceiling's length, traced the arc of the dome rung in gold, and descended to the bronze canopy that dwarfed the altar below.

"Kyle!" The faint whisper disappeared into the cavernous space. "Kyle!" Her voice seemed without source, a faint aroma that, once sensed, exists no more: the crescendo of sharp steps approaching from behind spoke otherwise.

Taking his hand she hurried them back to the guard, who stood holding open a black gate near the iconic stone-sculpted *Pietà* of Michelangelo. Kyle slowed deliberately as they passed the masterpiece. Cristina did not resist.

Once through the doorway, Philippe pulled the gate closed, confirmed it had locked, and escorted them wordlessly along private stairs and corridors.

Their abrupt entrance a short distance later into the Pauline Chapel was stunning.

"Padre Giordano will receive you here." He gestured toward the exquisite frescoes as they walked from the altar wall farther into the empty room. "The restoration was finished last year. Please, enjoy."

"Is there no morning Mass?" Cristina had noted the absence of pews.

"That is correct. The Holy Father is on holiday at the summer residence." He bowed slightly. "*Buona giornata, signorina.*"

"*Grazie mille.*" She watched him stride to the main doors, draw them open, and take stand in the bordering Sala Regia. "Well, Kyle, you will not see the pope today after all."

Her comment met no reply. Even as Philippe was speaking of the restoration, Kyle had gone straight to a fresco of Peter that dominated the left wall, transfixed by the saint's penetrating gaze.

It was a crucifixion scene that could only have been created by Michelangelo.

The apostle lies upon a cross, hands and feet pierced with nails but not yet bleeding. A youth kneels hunched, spade near, deepening a hole with his hand. Soon the cross will be set into the ground. He will be crucified head down, confessing he is not worthy to die in the manner of the Lord. His powerful torso strains upward, struggling to right itself.

She observed how intensely Kyle peered into the saint's staring eyes, his inspection of the furrowed brow and the incomplete ring of woolen-white hair encircling a bare scalp.

"His face—that is not a look of anger: it's panic. He fears for his salvation. See, he wears a broken halo."

Peter the Rock depicted as humility itself.

Depart from me, for I am a sinful man, O Lord.

Kyle's heart filled with dread of his own unworthiness and an unrelenting anguish of not knowing life's direction. Tears fell onto his cheeks, but he did not brush them away.

She stood close, her presence a comfort.

He stood close, his despair an isolation.

Neither heard Marco approach from behind. "Benedict described Peter's expression as one seeking the light of the risen Christ. It is a message for all to contemplate."

Kyle turned with a start. Cristina's hand dropped from his shoulder.

"Come. They wait."

Marco walked briskly.

No one yet roamed the public spaces, as the hour was early. Farther down, staff moved quietly about the private quarters performing daily activities. The décor became more residential beyond the utilitarian areas.

They paused in a small reception room, were promptly joined by another priest, and together filed into Benedict's personal chapel. Marco directed them to stand at a pair of chairs on the right. The two priests genuflected before the tabernacle, disappeared into the sacristy, and returned with the pope.

Mass began.

Afterward, Kyle remembered just a single detail of the unexpected event: receiving Holy Communion from the vicar of Christ on earth.

Marco's office was located one floor below the papal apartment. In it were crammed a broad desk, several ceiling-tall bookcases, a lateral-drawer file cabinet, one guest chair, and a late fifteenth-century globe. He cleared a stack of texts from a low wooden stool for Kyle, and they sat.

"The guard, he told us that Papa was at Castel Gandolfo." Cristina had been surprised by his sudden appearance.

"*Sì*, that is true, officially." Marco did not elaborate. "Kyle, it is quite a privilege to have attended a papal Mass with so few others, don't you think?"

Cristina roused him with a pat to the thigh.

"Sorry. What?"

"Father asked if you liked the Mass."

"Well, yeah, sure." He shifted on the stool, wishing it were a chair so he could lean back.

For a long moment Marco considered the young man's enigmatic nonchalance: without doubt a veneer masking deep awe. "Tell me how your project is going," he asked gently.

Kyle looked up. Both sets of eyes were on him. A nervous half cough escaped as he sat straight. "Okay, I think." He found himself glancing at Cristina for support. "We were pretty lucky on Monday—there's a letter at the archive from Saint Conlaeth to the pope. It's from when he was bishop of Kildare, like from the year 519, and he says that the amphora of Nicodemus was being hidden in the Skellig Michael monastery."

"The amphora of Nicodemus?"

"Yeah. You know, like in the Bible, with myrrh for Jesus's burial."

"The amphora was at Skellig Michael, the island?"

"Uh-huh." He was now looking directly at Marco. "And it mentions the cross. Well, a *crux de cruce* anyhow."

After a pause, Cristina leaned toward Kyle and whispered, "The scroll."

"Oh, right." He continued aloud. "There's also a scroll all about the amphora that was sent to Pope Hormisdas with the letter, but we couldn't find it."

"Kyle is being *così modesto*, Father. He discovered that letter—and then another one yesterday—by searching through hundreds of pages of documents. He is a very dedicated researcher. Kyle, tell him about the second letter."

He had already started speaking. "This one was from the brother of the archaeologist who discovered the catacombs."

"De Rossi," Marco said immediately.

Kyle was dumbfounded.

"You forget where I work." There was not a hint of irony in his voice. "And?"

"And . . ." He took a second to gather his thoughts. "So he writes his brother, who's away on a trip, that he'd had to move the amphora for safekeeping—this was in 1870—because Emanuele might invade the Vatican."

Cristina beamed at her student.

Marco sat thinking over what had been said, head rocking with each point, index finger simultaneously rapping the desk. Then he spoke in measured words. "Kyle, tell me if I understand you correctly: there are two letters here in the archive that document not only the existence of the Nicodemus amphora but its locations in 519 and 1870. Is that right?"

Kyle suppressed a laugh. "You got it."

"Except," Cristina stated emphatically, "except the De Rossi letter doesn't say where it was taken, only that it would be *sicuro sotto protezione di Jonas.*"

"That means 'secure under Jonah's protection,'" Kyle translated unnecessarily.

She nodded. "Kyle, tell him your *teoria.*"

He cringed at his idea being called a theory. "Maybe they hid it in the catacombs." The statement ended with a tentative tone.

A benevolent smile gradually emerged on Marco's lips. "Cristina is right. You seem to have a natural talent for research." Kyle reddened at the compliment. "Have you visited the Cubicles of the Sacraments in the Callixtus catacombs?"

Kyle shook his head.

"They are renowned for their third-century frescoes. Jonah is a common theme, whether being thrown from the boat or languishing in the belly of the whale."

"Why Jonah? What's the connection with the amphora?" He sat riveted.

Marco stood and appeared as though ready to pace before a seminary class.

"Jonah and Jesus shared something spiritual, did they not?" Fingers intertwined, palms open, he signaled with his hands the unity of meaning. "Rising from death on the third day, each brought about salvation. In the Old Testament it was God's prophet saving a city from destruction. Of course in the New, it was God's son saving man from his own sin—through death on the cross. You see?"

Kyle was visibly excited. "Yeah, that's cool. We already decided we want to explore down there tomorrow."

Cristina interrupted. "Kyle means we wanted to ask you if that is okay."

Marco flipped through his Rolodex and picked up the office phone. Kyle could hear a male voice answer, and a short conversation in rapid Italian ensued.

"It is arranged for Friday." He strode to the first bookcase, scanned several shelves, and selected a trilogy of volumes totaling more than two thousand pages among them. He placed them in Kyle's hands. *La Roma Sotterranea Cristiana* was imprinted on each spine.

"Tomorrow you will prepare for the expedition. These are the findings of Giovanni De Rossi, with his original detailed drawings and the maps by his brother." Reaching forward, he held open the front cover of one to reveal both men's autographs. "*Momento*— you don't read Italian." He returned to the shelf as Kyle grunted no. "I happen to have the condensed English version as well," he said, adding a fourth book on top of the others.

"So, Father, who will be meeting us on Friday afternoon?" Cristina had already taken down the time and place from what had been said during the call.

"Dámaso La Macera," he said, scrawling the name and mobile number on a notecard, then handing it to her. "He studied archaeology in Madrid and has been on staff with us for many years, working for the superintendent of the catacombs. I will talk with him again before Friday about the project."

"*Grazie.*" She tucked the card in her purse. "Can you help us with one thing else? The reference room assistant at the university archives has not been eager to let us see the more ancient documents."

"A search for the scroll you mentioned?"

"*Sì.* The letters, they're incomplete. We think the scroll will solve many mysteries."

"Like what?"

Kyle spoke up. "Like what's in the amphora, and what *crux de cruce* means."

Amazed yet again at the young man's brazenness, he sat with a plop and answered.

"I will take care of it today."

✦ ✦ ✦ ✦ ✦ ✦ ✦ ✦ ✦

On leaving the Apostolic Palace, Cristina led them zigzagging through the wall of tourists waiting to see the Vatican treasures. Their way was easier once past the piazza.

"We should walk down the Borgo Santo Spirito, then along the river. It is a beautiful morning. What do you think?"

"I dunno. Sure." The dark mood hovering about him that lifted temporarily in Marco's office had returned, a tenacious fog refusing to burn off with the heat of the day.

"This will be a good week for you, Kyle. I've never been to the catacombs either. We'll have fun, no?"

What could have been a pleasant stroll dragged forward sullenly. Head down, hands thrust in his pockets, it was clear Kyle was not interested in chatter.

The road curved gently and they reached the Ponte Sant'Angelo, its winged creatures ever steadfast in their angelic duties. At the crest of the bridge Kyle stopped. He rested his arms on the parapet and stared at the water coursing slowly beneath. She stood close, silent, waiting.

In time he spoke. "When we met, you asked if I believed."

For a moment she strained to recall what had been said. "About the prophecy, *sì*."

He turned and faced her. "Cristina, do you believe? In God?"

Sadness rushed upon her as the depth of his confusion, of his spiritual turmoil, revealed itself. At first she was without words, then her hand sought his and she spoke from her heart.

"Kyle, yes, of course I believe," she said, her grip tightening. "I believe all of creation was once but a speck—yet with power unimagined it burst forth from the palm of God to fill the universe. I believe he lived mortal among us—yet was resurrected into a whole new being in an explosion of light, as a shroud forever bears witness." Her gaze was intense, unblinking. "And I believe he pours his love into our hearts, even now."

In that moment he heard truth as never before.

Her eyes embraced him. He drew close and their lips touched. She let the tenderness linger, then placed his hand over her heart.

"Do not doubt, Kyle. Have faith. You do not need to probe his wounds to believe."

He looked down.

"Seek what God wants for you. There you will find joy." Her head tilted to catch his gaze. "Perhaps we will find joy together, no?"

Hands clasped, they continued over the Tiber.

CHAPTER NINETEEN

CALLIXTUS

Saturday, 21 July 1866, Basilica of Saint Peter

A kerosene lamp burned brightly. On each side of the marble stand, in half illumination, sat a Giovanni. The younger was renowned as discoverer of Roman catacombs. The older was Pio Nono—Holy Father, pontiff, pope.

In Pio's gloved hands lay a brilliantly white first-century parchment scroll, about which a cord of red and gold thread was drawn. Of gevil, it was supple with an herbed resin scent.

Reflected light glittered from a ninth-century mosaic of Christ before them, the visage gazing serenely from its niche above a shallow altar. As though cradled in his arms, a lavish silver-gilt chest graced the recessed shelf. Sheathed in marble, the entire space was no larger than a wardrobe. Yet but for this structure and the ancient tomb encased beneath, the cathedral built around it would not exist, nor the celebrated high altar above.

The bell tolled midnight, its tone pure and resonant, each clap rising louder to fill the basilica with singular song.

Pio unrolled the parchment. Latin script flowed line after line, penned in days of old in the imperial tongue. Together the Giovannis had first read this scroll upon its unearthing in the archive. Together their hearts had soared with an improbable hope that the amphora of which it spoke might be extant, that the most sacred relics within might be reclaimed.

Now, in this holy of holy places, after fourteen hundred years in Éire, the vessel stood resplendent near the tomb of crucified Peter and the papal altar of the risen Lord.

In a subdued voice, Pio read from the earliest entry.

Maria the Magdalene, beloved companion of our Lord, present at His death and rising, and Iohannes son of Zebedaei, to whom the Lord's mother was given in care, kept most precious and revered these objects, held close by the Lord's mother, from the mortal life of her Divine Son, Who was crucified for our sins.

He rose, lifted the thurible from its rest, and with reverence swung it methodically around the amphora, chains clanking softly with each pass. Sanctifying incense fragranced the air.

Sitting, he read further.

The time of her triumphal entrance into the Savior's kingdom not yet come, desiring these precious objects to remain undefiled unto the close of the age, did she seal the amphora in which they were kept, it being scented with the oils of His burial according to Nicodemus.

Again he rose. Again clouds of incense enveloped the vessel, emanating out, up, borne high into the lofty dome.

So that it may be known to all did she mark it with the offense for which He died, that which had been spoken of by the prophets, and so that all might bow in homage to His sacrifice did she mark it with a cross of the cross upon which He bled.

A third time the thurible was wafted about the vessel. Then together they knelt and prayed.

An ineffable passion filled their hearts, a sorrowful joy that could not be expressed. In the wood of the cross—the crucifixion here made visible—they were lifted up, transcended to a realm where faith and experience are one.

Pio stood and approached the niche altar. On it was a silver pendant, given to him early that day with the amphora by the newly appointed Irish cardinal. It was finely crafted, the central insignia unmistakably a Celtic cross of Saint Patrick set within a Trinitarian triangle. He placed it in Giovanni's hands, blessed it, and read a later entry from the saint.

When first I glimpsed the amphora, brothers Sidonius and Brieuc having unlatched the armarium and set it open, I fell as though struck dead onto the ground. I yielded to impulse and touched the wood of Christ's cross in its circle of wax, weeping. Through tears it became for me an image of His eternal love, the symbol of my flock.

Bowing, Giovanni hung the chain on the pope's neck. The pendant rested against his heart.

It was here at the harbor, our feet in the sand, that I set three seals of green upon the lid, impressed with the image of a clover leaf in which my authority is vested, in the witness of Sidonius and Brigid, brother and sister in Christ. These seals testify as truth that in our care the amphora remains inviolate, His Holiness may believe with certitude.

For many minutes they stood silent, each sensing his smallness in the empty darkness of the great cathedral, itself miniscule in the presence of the infinite.

Pio closed the scroll, looped its threads in place, then sat. "At dawn the vessel will be taken below to the crypt. With Emanuele afoot, I dare not count anything safe at Palazzo Quirinale."

Giovanni nodded: that the pope risked his own safety living outside the Vatican need not be stated.

With a grave face, Pio looked at his archaeologist. "Worse still, I have no trust in his intent but that he would reach even to conquer these lands in the name of unification."

"Vatican Hill?" He shuddered. "Truly, this you fear?"

"Do not forget we rely on French troops for our defense."

"Even here, then, the vessel is at risk." His head shook with despondence.

Pio sighed heavily. "Through worse times the Church has survived. Yet I cannot allow the most precious treasures of our Lord to be pillaged."

"In heaven's name, what would be our recourse?"

Shoulders sagging, the dual burden as pontiff and sovereign ruler of the Papal States weighed on Pio. He yearned to be unbound from the temporal, freed from politic and war to lead an independent, universal Church of Christ on its spiritual journey. Dawn of that day was not yet within grasp.

His brow softened. "My friend, we shan't despair. Rather, let us draw strength and endurance from Christ. Surely, this generation is an evil generation. In his words: 'No sign shall be given to it except the sign of Jonah.'" He raised the medallion symbolically. "So let us rest in his trustworthy promise. As Jonah spared the great city Nineveh from destruction with a call of repentance, he will certainly repel the enemies of God's earthly realm."

"The vessel will be held secure under Jonah's protection?" Giovanni questioned.

"*Sì*. This I know, this I believe."

Friday, 30 July 2010, Catacomb of Callixtus

Emerging from the cool of subterranean Rome and expecting the unbearable heat of late afternoon that had been the norm, Kyle breathed relief. Thunder rumbled in the distance, promising rain. Beside him, Cristina untied a silk scarf from her purse strap and draped it over her bare shoulders, shivering conspicuously.

Dámaso outpaced them toward the car with a false hope of speeding into town before the streets were thick with traffic.

"I'm sorry we didn't find any clues today, Kyle."

He strolled along, kicking the same stone ahead repeatedly, inches per pass.

"It's nothing. I really didn't think it would be sitting there waiting for us."

The disappointment in his voice was clear. She rubbed her hand across his back.

"*Dio*, what a maze! Can you imagine how lost we would have been without Dámaso?"

His spine stiffened perceptibly. Struck decisively, the stone skittered off to the side a few feet. Her hand hung midair then dropped as he stepped away in pursuit. Several strides later he had directed it again onto their path, and they continued.

"Thank God the weekend starts, no? Time to relax and forget about the amphora. What would you like to see? The Coliseum? Fountain of Trevi? Pompeii?"

"No more ruins, please. Anything else."

She laughed, seeing the subtle upturn of his lips.

"Okay, okay. I agree. Tonight we dance and tomorrow we go to the zoo. *Sì?*"

He stopped. Rearing his foot, he took aim and sent the stone flying.

"Deal."

Inhibitions gone, he turned, laced his fingers through her hair, looked into her eyes, then kissed her with an intensity that grew with each breath.

They walked hand in hand to the car, her head on his shoulder.

"Thank you," he whispered.

Once again she was without words.

Sunday, 1 August 2010, Vatican City

He sat facing the sun.

The piazza seemed oddly vacant absent the midday crowds, as though the surrounding architecture had no purpose. A few children romped in the open space, parents content to observe from the shade.

Kyle did not notice the freshness of the air or the mild breeze that had arrived in the storm's wake. He did not notice the obelisk at his back, the pigeons squabbling over a lone scrap, or even a photographer, eye to camera, who stumbled over his extended legs.

When the basilica bell rang seven, he rose.

As before, Philippe stood waiting. They traversed the corridors and stairs in silence.

The Pauline Chapel was again empty, the doors to the Sala Regia ajar.

Marco greeted them on their entering the regal room. "*Grazie, Philippe. Buona sera.*" The guard bowed and left. "Kyle, the chapel is not in use. Let's talk there."

Kyle turned, prepared to retrace steps. Instead Marco's arm pointed toward a pair of solid wooden doors to the left.

The glory of the Vatican stood beyond.

He walked under the lintel and was at once immersed in the very act of divine creation. Frescoes abounded, alive with the flood of evening light. Yet his eye was drawn up.

It seemed the whole of life radiated forth from a single painting centered high above: God reaching toward man, man reaching toward God—Adam, pure, made in his image.

Eyes not deviating, Kyle slowly stepped deeper into the Sistine until he was directly beneath the scene. His neck craned. His right hand met his cheek. With finger extended he gently traced the outline of God, draped in purple, then Adam, naked without shame. Last, he touched the space separating their fingers, his own distance from them a chasm.

Marco found himself quietly studying the youth, whose expression in a single moment professed understanding and doubt, longing and indifference. But unlike the child lost and crying in the dark, his eyes revealed a hidden determination: they sought truth.

Kyle's voice emerged a soft rasp. "He paints as he sculpts—using not chisel but brush. His figures breathe." The words were a spoken thought, an inner awakening that would forever color his perception of the artist.

Like a veil lifted, Marco suddenly saw a reflection of himself, an echo, in the young man who stood before him at a crossroads looking up: and in a revelation, saw that it was good.

Gradually Kyle lowered his gaze, twisting his head around to ease the strain.

"So, what is it you wanted to discuss?" Marco's tone was direct but accepting, neutral in a way that might invite confession from the penitent.

Kyle's eyes roamed the walls vacantly as he began.

"We failed." He paused, his swallow dry and exaggerated. "She couldn't find the scroll anywhere at the university archives, and we wasted hours in the catacombs searching for the amphora with Dámaso." He looked straight at Marco. "I'm sorry."

Marco nodded, trying to decipher Kyle's real motive for asking to talk with him now, alone, when the three were already scheduled to meet in the morning.

"For this an apology?" He smiled warmly.

A minute passed. Kyle remained visibly perturbed, head down.

"I need your help," he whispered.

Marco nodded again, this time with the solace of a father comforting his son.

"When I left school I figured I was done—not with college, maybe, but with seminary. I felt like I dodged a bullet, like I was saved from making a mistake." His weight shifted foot to foot as he dropped his face into his hands.

"Has that changed?"

"I don't know." His reply was swift and loud. "I don't know." He started to pace.

Marco watched Kyle course back and forth across the mosaic floor, no more than a few yards in either direction, slowing each time as he passed his confessor.

"Why now, Kyle? What has happened that makes you doubt your decision?"

"Her, of course. Cristina." He stopped. He pointed to the ceiling. "And him."

There seemed no logic in his answer.

"If you are in love with this woman, not being in the seminary should be a good thing."

"You don't understand." His eyes misted. He spoke so low as to almost be unheard. "I don't want to sin. I don't want to go against his will."

Marco sighed, head sagging, lids narrow. In the stillness he prayed for wisdom.

"Kyle, what do you see in this scene of the serpent in the garden?" The fresco was two panels away from the creation of man; between them God drew woman from man's chest.

With a dubious expression, Kyle grudgingly examined the painting above.

A lush tree stands at the center, its canopy shading Adam and Eve to the left, beautiful in their youth. In the tree rises a woman, hair flowing and innocent of face, legs wrapped sensuously about the trunk as a velvet cord might encircle a post, her left arm reaching out to Eve with succulent fruit even as Adam reaches to pluck his own. Hideously transformed by sin, to the right they are expelled from the garden beneath an angelic sword. They enter a barren land, arms up to hide their guilt.

Kyle made no reply but to look timidly at the priest, his face marked with pain.

Marco stood silent as the young man searched within. He then raised his eyes to Eden.

"The serpent is cunning, don't you think? She tempts us from the tree of knowledge in her pleasing guise. But she is fallen. She aches for us to taste the fruit of evil with her."

Kyle followed Marco's upward gaze.

"Temptation, Kyle. Turning from God's love. Rejecting truth. That is the essence of sin."

"'Lead us not into temptation.' Jesus knew." Kyle felt the scapular of Saint Michael beneath his shirt.

"He knew, yes. He knew temptation throughout his earthly life."

"And he won. He spurned it all and defeated Satan."

Hearing this reawakening of faith, Marco's heart lifted.

A tranquility settled on the young man as he pondered these thoughts. "So what should I do?"

Marco rested a hand on Kyle's shoulder as he remembered the book of poetry handed down to him in wisdom from father to son. "Michelangelo once said, 'I saw the angel in the marble and carved until I set him free.' These were not simply the sentiments of a sculptor, Kyle. God's will is to shower you with the joy of his presence. Set your soul free. Seek him and he will love you, no matter what you choose."

"Even if it's her?"

Marco laughed. "Not all are called to be priests."

"Thank God," Kyle said lightly, only half in jest.

The interior lights flickered on as evening turned to dusk.

"You have much to think about."

"I always do."

Together they slowly walked toward the altar wall with its soaring depiction of the Last Judgment: Christ triumphant presiding over a swirling mass of humanity, some rising heavenward, others descending into hell.

Tomorrow I will be here with Cristina, Kyle thought.

Marco led him through the Treasury, then out into the Vatican Gardens.

CHAPTER TWENTY

THE SEVENTH SEAL

To: Kevin Schaeffer <kevinschaeffer999@yahoo.com>
From: Marco Giordano <m.giordano@arcsacra.va>
Date: August 2, 2010 08:22:57 CEST
Subject: Kyle's Project

Kevin, mille grazie for sharing your memories of my father. They are now my memories too.

How is it that love's full depth is revealed only in death? But this you know.

And grazie for your wisdom in asking me to mentor Kyle. He is an earnest young man. Like the ancient Roman god of myth Janus, he sees the world from two faces but his head spins undecided over which path to follow. It is a hard lesson to accept that in grasping, one also lets go. In truth, even now I speak of this as a mere pupil. Together we learn, no?

You will be amazed at the progress Kyle has made on his project. Already he has discovered two letters in the Papal Archive that refer to the cross. I tell you they are quite remarkable—you must come see them with your own eyes—and they help explain the different stories you were told.

From them we know that an amphora—a cask—bearing a *crux de cruce* was sent to Ireland in the fifth century. This confirms the document you found in Armagh. We also know that sometime between 1866 and 1870 it was brought to the

Vatican by Irish Cardinal Cullen—1866 being the year of his installation, 1870 the year the amphora was hidden from Italian national forces. Sadly for the child whose illness prompted this search, where it was hidden remains a mystery.

What is truly stunning is that the older letter, from 519, calls it *the amphora of Nicodemus*. Can you believe it? In still another validation of your story, it says at that time the amphora was kept at Skellig Michael. The historicity of these concurring documents appears beyond doubt.

I admit the phrase *crux de cruce* is curious. By my translation it is clear the writer meant a cross set on, not in, the amphora. There is no mention of the contents, but do you not agree it would be logical for the disciples to save precious relics from the crucifixion in a container that stood ready in the tomb, especially one that had held the very oils of the Lord's anointing?

If all this is true, the child's grandmother and the old priest would both be correct. One could have easily touched the wood of the cross without unsealing the amphora.

Kyle is now looking for a scroll that might give some answers. It is a testament that dates to the earliest centuries with history of the amphora until 519. We will continue the search in hopes of learning the exact meaning of *crux de cruce* and what the amphora held. Finding the relic itself may require a miracle.

Let us pray for the Lord's healing grace to descend upon the child and his grandmother.

Vostro fratello in Cristo   —Marco

Monday, 2 August 2010, Vatican City

"Kyle, you will *love* the Sistine!"

He could not bear to tell her that he had already been, and so few hours before.

Taking his hand, she hurried them along the plain corridor leading from the ticket post to the tourist entrance. He recognized immediately that this door stood at the opposite end of the frescoed altar wall from where he had exited with Marco. Little did the many visitors crossing this narrow threshold suspect their figurative transit through the underworld, even as they passed beneath a murky River Styx where Charon ferried the damned.

Cristina stood back and allowed him time to revel in the riches surrounding them.

Unlike the rest, whose feet fought for space while their faces stared up, Kyle positioned himself at the center of the altar and peered at the perplexing scene that filled the wall. He knelt, hands clasped. The present receded. An interior silence pushed aside all distraction. The figure of Jesus loomed, one arm raised in judgment, eyes averted, mother meek at his side. There would be no plea on that day.

She leaned against his body, fingers stroking his hair. "Everyone looks at the ceiling, no? The apocalypse they avoid. I think it scares them."

"It scares me." His voice quavered.

She bent, rested her cheek on his head, and patted his chest where the scapular hung. "Do not fear God, Kyle. Trust him. Trust in Saint Michael, who protects you from evil."

The whispered words sank deep.

She pointed to a cluster of angels hovering on clouds amidst the judged. "When the last seal is broken and the trumpets are blown, Saint Michael will hold open the book of the saved. See? He leads the fanfare, Kyle—our *angele dei*."

The rapture was alive before him: the blare of seven brass horns radiated forth in all directions, awakening the dead and announcing to the universe the arrival of its King.

Kyle felt the humility of unworthiness.

His eyes returned to Jesus, who bore the wounds of crucifixion.

He believed, and began to understand.

His hands rose spontaneously as his gaze lifted up. Where ceiling met wall, he fixed on the towering image of a man whose colossal body arched back, feet dangling, face directed toward the creation scenes. At his leg rested the flaccid form of a large fish, its aqua snout and glazed eye tamed in the shadow of the prophet.

Writ boldly on the inscription below was a name: IONAS.

The beat of his heart paused, then pounded within.

He stood and clutched Cristina's hand. "We need to see Marco."

She checked her watch. "*Sì*, in twenty-five minutes."

"Now."

In the lead, he wove them quickly through the multitude and out.

+++++++++

Marco sat at his desk, left hand raised to shield the computer screen from the harsh glare of morning sun. With his right he scrolled through incoming emails and clicked to read a reply from Kevin. Strains of Respighi swelled from cup-sized USB speakers.

A soft rapping on the door grew persistently louder, finally rising above the symphonic crescendo.

"*Momento*," he called out, fumbling with the mouse to pause the music.

"*Ah, buongiorno.* Please—"

Kyle impatiently strode in and stood by the window. Cristina shrugged with a look of unknowing that perfectly mirrored Marco's.

They were barely seated when he blurted out his announcement.

"I think I know where they hid the amphora."

His eyes darted excitedly between the two, waiting for a response.

Cristina nodded in support. "Kyle was looking at the De Rossi books again yesterday. He found an unmapped area near the Cubicles—"

"That's not what I meant. Okay, sure, maybe there's a secret room at Callixtus—I don't know. But what if it never left the Vatican?"

"Kyle, the letter said it was moved for safety," she objected.

"No. It said the amphora would be kept *secure under Jonah's protection.*"

Marco leaned forward as thoughts coalesced. "You were at the Sistine this morning."

"Yes."

"So tell me your idea."

Cristina flopped back in her chair, not following the exchange.

"Under the altar, or in the wall. Or what about the treasure room behind—the sacristy I saw last night?"

"The Treasury."

"Right," Kyle said with barely a pause between words.

"You were here last night?" Her eruption was ignored.

"See, how could they hope to keep it from being found by troops way out there in the catacombs? But not even Emanuele would desecrate a church, especially with all those priests hanging around."

"*Scusi*, what are you talking about?"

"Huh?" Kyle looked at her quizzically. "Sorry. Jonah—he's painted right above the altar wall." He paused. "In the Sistine."

"Okay, okay, I understand." Hands up in defense, she sat back again and they continued.

"That's an intriguing hypothesis. Still," Marco's head bobbled, "I can assure you it is not hidden there now."

"Then where? And why couldn't it be *inside* the wall?"

"Kyle, we can't start making holes in the chapel, can we?" The admonition hung bleak, consuming the air.

Defeated, the young man's response was uncharacteristically calm. "How do you expect to find it if we're not allowed to look?" He faced the window in silence.

After several strained minutes, Marco tactfully changed the subject.

"I received a message this morning from your friend, Father Schaeffer."

"Your friend, you mean."

Marco let the retort pass. "He's visiting an old priest from your parish today."

"Father Finnian?" Kyle turned, brow furrowed. "What does he want with him?"

"*Sì*, I think that's the name." Slowly he logged back on and made a show of methodically scanning the email. "The nursing home, it is in Killorglin. Did you know he had a stroke?"

"'Course I did—that was in June. Is he worse?" There was heartfelt concern in his voice.

"I don't believe so." He caught his glance and added, "This is about a boy who's dying of cancer. Michael Callaghan."

Kyle's head shook in disbelief. "Mickey? He's supposed to be cured—what do you mean he's dying?"

Marco chose words cautiously, honoring Kevin's request to avoid any link between the child's illness and Kyle's search for the cross. "Apparently there was a relapse."

"A relapse. That sucks." Again he faced the window, forehead pressed on the glass.

"It sounds like you know the boy."

"A little, sure. Same as anyone in our village—fundraising and all that. My first year at college, I went up to Dublin a few times when he was in for treatment." Unspoken was the bond that formed during their hours together: to Kyle, Michael's antics and ails had been equally endearing. "Anyhow, I still don't get what Finnian has to do with this. Or Kevin."

Marco stood, moved to the window, and leaned his shoulder against the frame. "How well do you know Michael's grandmother?"

The young man looked up. "Not very. Why?"

"Father Kevin met her at the hospital. He said she hopes for a miracle."

Kyle held Marco's gaze with unexpected intensity, eyes frozen. "Then I feel sorry for the kid. She doesn't believe in religion."

Neither broke his stare.

"Why do you say that? What have you heard?"

"They had a falling out. She swore he'd rot in hell."

"You witnessed this?"

"Finnian told me. He said it happened when her daughter died. Bad blood, those two."

Marco was baffled. Nothing from Kevin had hinted at this antagonism.

"Why would she say such a thing?"

"Like I told you, she doesn't believe in religion. Or in Finnian."

For a moment all were still.

Cristina reached up and touched his arm. "Does she believe in God?"

His face flushed as he searched her eyes.

The words she intoned had once been his.

Monday, 2 August 2010, Allagheemore on the Iveragh Coast

The drizzle eased. To the west thunderclouds hung low, emptying themselves on the sea.

Kevin buttoned his jacket with a shiver and walked south along the isolated country lane. Tufts of loose wool littered the patchwork of grazing fields, each property neatly demarcated by stone fences into mostly square geometric shapes. An occasional stretch of barbed wire discouraged errant sheep from straying.

He could just make out the Skellig peaks in the failing light. Nearer, Puffin Island was visible with perfect clarity, its striated rocks bare against the assailing waves. This seascape and the land that descended into it: this place defined Kyle as fully as ancestral blood.

Yet it was the old man, late that afternoon, who had compelled Kevin to come here, even as Michael now lay in intensive care.

If not the cross, then, as their pastor, do you know of anything that might help the child?

The ailing priest had sat for a long while, eyes closed as if in slumber.

Kyle's father. Brian Dorrian.

He had said no more.

Rain borne on a raw ocean wind whipped the shore. Kevin turned and hurried along the darkening path toward the lamp-lit house.

PART III

CHAPTER TWENTY-ONE
AOIRE † SHEPHERD

Monday, 2 August 2010, Allagheemore

The driveway was firm but irregular beneath Kevin's feet. Ruts undulated haphazardly down its length. Spring's back-fill of gravel was now embedded deep in the base of each crater, hundreds in number, making impossible a smooth passage.

He stumbled over an unseen rock that jutted up several inches above grade, cursed under breath, then hobbled the remaining fifty yards to the door.

"Flat tire? Happens all the time." Brian motioned him in and pointed to a floor mat at the entry. "It's just passing through, the rain. Kick off your shoes—shouldn't be but a half hour afore the setting sun's out painting the sky red. Where're you from?"

Before he could answer, Brian shot around the center stairs, through a walnut-floored kitchen, and into what might have once been a large dining room but was now dominated by a billiard table set for nine-ball. Logs hissed at the hearth as remnants of kindling twigs smoked orange and fell into the ash below. With a quick motion he brushed back his shag of tawny hair, then grabbed the poker and flicked a chunk of flaming turf safely under the grate.

Kevin awed at the easy friendliness of his host, so clearly Kyle's father in appearance yet quite opposed in personality. "Sorry, I missed your question."

"You're driving a rental, right? I asked where you're from—the States, on my life."

"Boston, in Dublin for a year."

"Grand entirely." He rested the poker against the fireplace. To the right was a mirror-topped cart stocked with flasks. Pouring generously, he handed Kevin a whiskey and raised his glass. "Sláinte."

Kevin looked down, swirled his drink gently, then sipped. "Thank you for inviting me in. You're right the car's a rental, but no, the tires are fine." He inhaled, eyes drifting up beneath arched brows. "Actually, I stopped by to see you."

"Me?" Brian darted a quick glance to see that Kevin was carrying no sales pamphlets or catalogs. "My wife Shanon, maybe? She won't be long—"

Kevin extended his hand. "Brian, I'm Father Kevin Schaeffer, a friend of your son's."

He shook hands tentatively at first, then with vigor as recognition dawned. "Sure, sure, 'course you are. Glad to meet you, Father. Kyle—he's having quite a time in Rome, no doubt. First time away and all."

"He's a natural at research. I'm impressed with his passion."

Brian laughed. "Stunned me, that's the truth. First he's off to seminary, now research. I told him—Kyle, don't go rushing into everything, think it through. But it's good he's seeing a bit of the world while he can, don't you think?"

The priest offered an equivocal nod. "He doesn't strike me as impetuous."

"Don't get me wrong, Father. He's a serious sort—always been. Too serious, if you ask me." His smile changed subtly.

"How do you mean?"

"Broody. Closed in on himself." Falling silent, he turned to tend the logs.

Kevin let the thought linger a moment before probing further.

"He worries you."

Brian spoke into the fire. "'Course he does. He's my son." His shoulders rose and his face retreated from view.

"Kyle is a prayerful young man. He will find his way."

"Right you may be, Father, but the devil's in the detours." Brian swigged the rest of his drink and poured again.

Kevin set his still-full glass on the mantle and, fingers threaded, let his hands drop. "Tell me your thoughts on Kyle's spirituality. A child's faith usually reflects that of his parents."

"Well, he's an unusual child." Again he brushed back his hair, eyes now drifting vaguely in Kevin's direction. "We went to Mass and all, regular churchgoers. His ma, she's a strong believer, not that she talks about it. He soaked it up, though."

After a hesitant pause, he continued.

"Me—I had detours. 'Late have I loved Thee' kinda thing."

The unexpected reference to the fifth-century theologian and philosopher Augustine by this Irish sheep farmer was yet another sign to Kevin of the complex nature of both father and son.

"Enough of all that. You didn't come to ask on me." He gestured the conversation back to Kevin.

"To be honest, Brian, when I set out from Dublin today I didn't have this visit in mind. It's a detour of my own after speaking with Father Finnian."

"Finnian? What the—" He cleared his throat. "Is Kyle in some sort of trouble?"

"No, not at all," Kevin said, shaking his head in reassurance. "It's nothing directly about Kyle. Brian, are you aware that Michael Callaghan is in the hospital? He's had a relapse of his leukemia."

"Caitie's boy? I had no idea." Taking a step back, he steadied, then sat on a black leather stool near the cue rack. "Is he all right?"

"No. He's very ill." Kevin perched at the edge of the billiard table and leaned forward, elbows on knees. "He may die."

"That can't be. Shit." For several minutes he slouched over, eyes vacant, hands gripping continuously. He then shook his head and looked straight at Kevin. "You said this wasn't 'directly' about Kyle?"

Kevin nodded acknowledgment. "It's true. He knows very little about Michael's condition, and literally has no idea that his project in Rome is a desperate effort to save the child."

"A desperate effort? What's he doing down there?" he said, agitation rising.

Kevin pressed a hand firmly on Brian's shoulder. "Kyle is searching for a sacred relic, pieces of Christ's cross that were hidden here in Ireland for hundreds of years, on Skellig Michael and in this very village."

"The curing cross? That's what this is about?"

"Yes—you know of it, then. Michael's grandmother showed me her family Bible with a long list of ancestors who touched the cross and survived cancer. It's remarkable."

"Yeah, I've seen it," he smirked. "Caitlin's in the dead column."

"She died without the cross." He paused. "You don't sound convinced of its powers."

"Well, let's say the legend is more a myth in these parts."

Kevin stood and retrieved his drink. "Fair enough. It's likely of no consequence now, whatever one's belief. Despite the progress Kyle's made, we probably won't find it."

"So all this for nothing. And in the meantime, Michael's dying."

"Perhaps, perhaps not." He once more sat opposite Brian and spoke softly but emphatically. "Why did Father Finnian tell me to come talk with you?"

Brian flushed and looked away.

Kevin did not release his gaze. "Why? Is there something you know that can help Mickey?"

On hearing the child's familiar name, Brian teared but remained still.

As priest, counselor, and confidant, Kevin saw that the man clung paralyzed atop a precipice from which he would not soon descend. He reached for his wallet, withdrew Dr. Thomson's business card, and slipped it into Brian's shirt pocket. "Michael's doctor is a compassionate woman. You can trust her."

Standing at the bay window, he looked eastward. Dusk had settled on the hills.

"I'll let myself out."

Just then came the sound of footsteps approaching from the next room.

"Hey, Bri, there's a car parked at the road." Shanon's voice echoed through the kitchen, and she appeared at once in the doorway. "Oh, I'm sorry. I didn't know someone was here."

Brian shot up, reflexively checked his watch, and strode to her side. "Shanon, this is Father Schaeffer—the priest Kyle's been working with."

She smiled warmly and offered her hand. "What a nice surprise, Father. Thank you for being so kind to our son. He needed to get busy again, that's for sure." Then, "Have you eaten? You're welcome to join us for a bite."

"Thanks, but no, I had dinner before stopping by. I'm sorry to intrude unannounced—I was driving through and wanted to meet you."

"Driving through?"

"He was over to Finnian's," Brian stated.

"So you know each other? How is he? I've not heard a word at church for weeks."

"Quite well, it seems." He pulled out his car key abruptly and bowed slightly. "I'd better be going before it gets much darker outside, the narrow roads and all."

"Of course, we understand. Please, do visit when Kyle's back and you have more time."

"I accept the invitation with pleasure."

Moments later he stood at the car and gazed west across the water. Beneath a swath of black clouds the sky was indeed aflame with the setting of the sun.

+ + + + + + + +

"You're in luck—someone just canceled."

While Kevin registered, the innkeeper swiped his MasterCard then fetched the room key and the requested complimentary toiletries.

He climbed the stairs, entered the room, and flopped exhausted on the bed, refusing to think further about Brian until morning.

The familiar alert tones of an incoming text message roused him just as he dozed.

Please call when you can. It's about Mickey. Tnx . . . Steph

Fully awake, he dialed immediately and waited impatiently for her to pick up.

"It's me. What's happening?"

"Well, when I got to Mickey's room this afternoon they wouldn't let me in. He was having more trouble breathing— it's been getting worse for days—and they said he'd probably bought a tube, whatever that means. Later they came out and said he was on life support." She paused, cleared her throat several times, then continued. "I'm scared he's not going to make it."

"How long ago was that?" He spoke now with urgency.

"Um, I guess it's been about three hours. Yeah, it was a little before six. And Father," she said, hesitating, "this is really bad timing, but—don't forget I leave on the tenth."

In fact he had forgotten. Given their attachment, her absence would hit Michael hard.

His next call was to the pediatric intensive care unit.

"Yes, Father, I see you on the communications list. I'll patch you through to his nurse."

Then: "This is Margie. Can I help you?"

"Margie, I'm Father Schaeffer, a family friend. I understand Michael took a turn for the worse today. How is he?"

"Well, Father, he's stable at the moment. The ventilator will do the work of breathing for a good while so his lungs can heal."

"But he'll be okay?" he said, straining to sound calm.

"We're doing everything we can. Now we wait it out."

"And his grandmother?"

"I don't know her current condition. Let me connect you to Saint James's."

"No, wait—"

The silence of the line was interrupted every eight seconds by two loud, rapid tones.

"Bed Four. Who's calling, please?"

"Father Schaeffer. I don't understand—I was talking with Michael Callaghan's nurse and when I asked about his grandmother she transferred me to you."

"I'm sorry, Father. I can only share patient information with the immediate family."

"Patient? Aideen is a patient?"

Hearing his distress, the nurse's voice softened. "Did you say you were a priest?"

"Yes. Father Kevin Schaeffer. I'm already on the okayed list for her grandson—listen, can't you just ask her?"

"That's not possible, asking her. But under the circumstances, I'll share what I can." There was a muffled sound as she tucked the receiver under her arm and grabbed the ER chart. She continued with a tone of medical exactitude. "Mrs. Callaghan collapsed at seven thirty-five this evening when she was standing at her grandson's bedside, hitting her head on the floor and experiencing a brief seizure. There is no sign of a stroke or heart attack. A CT scan of the head has been ordered to be done stat."

Kevin tried to make sense of the detailed information, not knowing the significance of most of it but surmising it wasn't good. "They don't know what caused it?"

"Likely a vasovagal event—she probably fainted. The cause of her coma is unclear."

His mind froze at the word *coma*.

"Father?"

"Yes. Sorry, yes, I'm here."

"I'm afraid that's all I can tell you tonight. Given the uncertainty of her status, please do phone ahead if you plan to visit tomorrow. She should be admitted by then."

"I understand. I'll do that."

With a click the call ended.

Kevin's thoughts rushed sporadically in every direction, then spun and rushed again.

He found himself on his knees, hands clasped, prayers pouring out with an intensity he'd not experienced since he held his mother's hand as she breathed her last.

CHAPTER TWENTY-TWO

RESONANCE

Tuesday, 3 August 2010, Dublin

Kevin climbed out of the ice-blue Ford Ka, slammed the door, and stomped to the rear of the subcompact to inspect the bumper.

Never confident of parallel parking even in the States, after an aggravating forty minutes circling the hospital for a nonexistent space he finally sped off to a neighboring residential street and decided to maneuver into one he knew would be a tight fit. Judging angles from the right-side driver seat proved too much: the impact was slight but sufficient to trigger the other car's alarm. Fortunately the scrape had only left a trace of paint on the Audi that was easily removed with a swipe of his pant cuff.

He'd started out unreasonably early at dawn. Traffic along the drizzle-wet country road from Ballinskelligs to Limerick had extended the drive by an hour, but he'd made good time on the motorway and reached Dublin before one o'clock. It was now two as he set off for the main hospital entrance on James's Street, hoping to find a sandwich or scone at the coffee shop. Visitors were only allowed between 2:30 and 3:30; he intended to spend the full hour with Aideen.

Overhead the sky was layered thick with clouds. They appeared stationary, immutable in form, a monotonous shield against any chance of sunshine that day.

By peculiar happenstance, Aideen had been admitted to St. Kevins Ward. He'd learned earlier that she had regained consciousness before leaving the ER overnight and, although no longer disoriented, was asking repeatedly about her grandson's condition.

Twenty minutes later, Kevin brushed stray crumbs from his lips, then wrapped the napkin around the paper coffee cup as added insulation against the heat. He followed the corridors as instructed and soon found the blue route that led to the unit.

Aideen lay quiet in bed, a pillow propped low at her back and two behind her head. Her combed hair draped soft to her shoulders. She wore no makeup yet retained a pleasantly youthful complexion.

He knocked gently on the open door and took a tentative step forward.

"Oh, Father, you came." A wisp of a smile and an outreached hand welcomed him in.

"I should have thought to bring flowers," he said apologetically, accepting her grasp.

"Nonsense. Please, sit." The recliner already piled high with linen, she lowered the bedrail and patted the mattress.

"They said you fainted?"

"Yes, that's what I've been told. I'm so embarrassed." With a blush, she bowed her head down and away, then stopped, grimacing, her free hand cupped about her temple.

As the pain ebbed she opened her eyes to Kevin's overt expression of concern. "It's just from the fall—really." She could see he was not persuaded. "Now tell me, have you heard anything at all about Michael? You must know he's on life support. I'm frantic with worry." Her grip on his hand intensified.

"No more than that, unfortunately. When I called this morning it was shift change. His status was listed as stable."

"They've taken my phone, damn fools. I finally demanded they page Dr. Thomson, but she hasn't called. He must be worse." The cardiac monitor chimed, blinking in red her heart rate of 104.

"Aideen, it's important to trust those taking care of him. Have faith."

She looked away. "Have you found the cross?"

His head shook. Her grasp eased, and he felt her hand slip away.

A nurse donned in purple scrubs walked briskly to the monitor, pressed a button, and tore off the EKG strip when it finished printing. "Nothing to worry about, dear," she said curtly after inspecting it. Reaching the door, she stood aside to let Dr. Thomson enter.

"Mrs. Callaghan, what have you done to rate such exquisite accommodations?"

"Thank God. How is he, Doctor? I've been asking for hours. No one here knows a thing."

Her effort at courtesy undeterred, she gave Aideen a friendly scolding glance and turned to Kevin. "Father, good to see you again."

He returned the greeting and stood to the side.

"Michael is better," she said with a cautious smile. "His lungs opened up nicely on the ventilator and we've been able to keep the settings low. I expect he'll be able to breathe on his own in two or three days. Of course he's sedated."

The taut lines across Aideen's forehead softened and her eyes sagged in relief.

"Why did this happen?" Kevin asked in a deliberately low tone.

Dr. Thomson shifted toward him while still facing Aideen. "It is the irony of getting his leukemia under control. We did a bone marrow test this morning—he's managed to go into remission. Tenuous, yes, but a remission still."

"And that's good."

"It's very good. However, you must understand: he now has plenty of healthy white blood cells that are flooding into his lungs to fight the pneumonia."

Kevin continued her reasoning. "So while they're helping, they're hurting."

"Precisely." She looked at Aideen. "Do you see, Mrs. Callaghan? His lungs will heal. They just need help from us for a while."

Aideen's lips quivered, her voice shaky. "The leukemia—it will come back."

Dr. Thomson reached down and took her hands in her own. "Without treatment, yes."

"When? When is his next chemo?"

"A week, maybe two. First his body needs to recover. Too soon and—"

"He'll die." She spoke now with resignation. "Either way, he'll die. From the chemo or from the leukemia. What difference does it make?"

The doctor leaned in, capturing Aideen's gaze. "Tomorrow will bring what it will. Find strength in the good that exists to-day. Promise me you'll try."

Aideen forced a smile.

"Brilliant. Mend up and let's meet next time in Michael's room, then." She turned and left. Kevin followed, motioning to Aideen that he would be back.

Alone, sheets drawn up as if chilled, she wrapped her hand tight around Maw Maw's pendant, whispering a single word repeatedly: *remission*.

+ + + + + + + +

A sterile calm imposed itself on Aideen. The effect of the intravenous medication had been immediate: anxiety sucked up, distilled, bottled, set out for inspection. The sensation was disturbing, yet she did not care.

Nor did she mind the closeness of the scanner tunnel, mere inches from her face, as the thinly padded narrow bench inched her backward through the exact center of the machine, itself an immense metallic ring.

Even the ceaseless staccato of the electromagnetic coil that flogged her brain equally as intense as her worst migraine—even that did not rouse distress.

For a brief moment the banging paused and she was brought into the open air. A river of cold traversed her arm as dye flowed into a vein. Then once more, the tunnel.

Aideen's thoughts were distant. Another hospital, another MRI suite, another patient. Stripped of all metal objects, she had stood in the corner sobbing silently as her daughter lay claustrophobic with her head in a similar tunnel. There had been no treatment, no delay in the tumor's growth, no postponement of impending death.

No cross for Caitlin. No cross for Michael.

Today, alone, Aideen had been told that the CT done in yesterday's dark of night had revealed a shadow, an abnormality; that an MRI was needed—soon. She had not mourned the news but acknowledged it with a genuine void of emotion, no anxiolytic yet given.

Now drugged, she lay in painless anguish, robbed of tears. There were none she could cry for her daughter. None for her great-grandmother. None, pitifully, for her grandson.

CHAPTER TWENTY-THREE

AOIRÍN † LITTLE SHEPHERD

Friday, 6 August 2010, Over the Swiss Alps

Kyle peered out the window from his seat at the rear of the plane. Below, white-peaked Jungfrau rose tall to catch the rays of dawn. Beyond, Interlaken lay shadowed between the indigo waters of Thunersee and Brienzersee, themselves awakening to the sparkling light of another day.

I have a new assignment for you in Dublin.

With that brief message, he had scrambled to change flights, settling for an hours-long layover in Amsterdam and a hefty surcharge for Kevin. Whether the unspecified project was worth the price was irrelevant to Kyle—being returned as he was to the sameness of everyday life, where at night the drinks get longer and more frequent, the mind less sharp.

He thumbed through the hastily written summary that had occupied his final hours in Rome, finding stray incomplete sentences and an uncomfortable excess of misspellings.

Solid work, Kyle, solid.

Marco's stream of questions and multiple notations penned in the margins did not ease Kyle's fear that nothing would come of his labors. Unlike school reports, unlike any of the carefully crafted essays that had earned professorial superlatives, his search for the cross had transcended from task to mission: it was an intensely personal journey that had not yet reached its destination.

You're leaving.

The sorrow in her voice, the reluctant release of her embrace—these he clung to with such ardor as one holds on to breath when there is no air.

Cristina. My angel.

Friday, 6 August 2010, Smithfield

Petra rapped on Dr. Thomson's office door and waited. The dictation continued for another few sentences, then paused.

"Yes." The door swung open.

"Sorry to interrupt, Lenore," she said, adding several more charts to the knee-high stack that awaited the doctor's attention. "A man is holding on line three—Mr. Dorrian. Weren't you expecting his call?"

"Dorrian . . ." She quickly scanned her notepad jottings of the past few days. "Brian?"

"That's correct."

"Thanks. I'll pick up."

"Don't stay too late," the nurse said futilely, winking as she closed the door.

"Hello. This is Dr. Thomson."

"Uh, yeah. Hi, Doctor. I'm Brian Dorrian. Father Schaeffer gave me your card."

"Can you speak up, please? I didn't catch that?"

He exhaled loudly into the receiver. "You're taking care of Michael Callaghan, right? This is his father."

Kevin had only shared with her a suspicion: hearing it stated outright as a way of introduction caught her off guard. "Yes, he said you might ring, but he didn't mention your relationship to the child."

"That's because he doesn't know."

The line was silent.

"I see." She paused. "May I call you Brian?"

"Sure, why not."

"So, then: Brian, please explain who is aware that you are Michael's father."

"No one."

"No one?" There was clear surprise in her voice.

"Look, I haven't told anyone."

"Okay," she replied, lingering over each syllable.

"Sorry. I don't mean to offend. It's just—this is private."

"I understand. And so it will remain."

Again, silence.

"I know he's dying. Call me a cad, but I want to help him if I can."

Her comforting nod was unseen yet transmitted with full effect. "It is a brave thing to do—to come forward, Brian. You may in fact be the one person who can offer him any chance of survival."

"Tell me how."

She reached for a legal pad and started to document the conversation.

"All right. First, if I may ask, are you certain of your paternity?"

It was not a question Brian had ever contemplated. "'Course so. Why wouldn't I be?"

"I'm sure that's how you feel. Sometimes it turns out otherwise."

"You don't get it. Caitlin—his mom—she didn't mess around like they said." His story gushed forth unrestrained. "When she took off for Turkey, I didn't know she was pregnant. You won't believe me, but it only happened that once, her and me. Not even back when we were in school. Never. Anyhow, I caved when I heard she had a brain tumor. Then she said she was leaving. It just happened."

He wandered in thoughts for a moment.

"She started the rumor, that it was some guy she met in a bar over there. 'Course I knew it had to be a lie."

"You think she was protecting you?"

"Shit, yeah. I was married, for Chrissake, with a kid and all." He sniffled, holding back emotion.

"I'm sorry this is upsetting, but it is important." Dr. Thomson waited a moment, then continued. "When did you learn the truth?"

"Not until Michael's baptism, at the Easter Vigil Mass. She'd already confessed to our priest and thought I should know. I could tell as much, just lookin' at him."

In the quiet that followed this outpouring, Dr. Thomson quickly drew out a new plan of care for the child.

"Brian, you said you want to help your son."

He faltered briefly. Thinking of Michael as son, and not merely himself as father, was an entirely new perception.

"Yes. I do."

"Good. Be here on Monday. Stop first at the children's hospital for blood tests, then come directly to my clinic when you're done. This will take all afternoon. We have a lot to discuss."

"Blood tests? What are you talking about?"

She did not mince words. "Michael needs a bone marrow transplant, and you might get to be the donor."

Friday, 6 August 2010, Dublin

Kevin pulled up to the terminal half an hour late.

"Sorry—bad traffic. There's some kind of horse show in town." Closing the window, he pressed the trunk release and Kyle loaded his luggage. "How was your flight?"

"Flights," he corrected, slamming the door. "Better than the layover."

Darting around the line of taxis and onto the less busy linker road, Kevin raced toward M1, momentarily ignoring the probability of nighttime Garda speed traps.

"Right. You spent the day at Schiphol."

"Not by choice."

"Yeah, you got me," he cringed. "Okay, your project, then. What's happening?"

"Dead end. Didn't Marco tell you?"

Already exasperated with Kyle's attitude, he merged onto the highway, set the cruise control, and tried to invoke calm. "Look, my summer intern will be flying back to Boston next Tuesday—after that you can have her room until the fall semester starts. For the next few days you'll be staying with me. Let's be civil, all right?"

Kyle shifted so that his entire torso faced the side window, arms crossed. They were well into the northern Dublin neighborhoods before he spoke. "All right."

Not a minute later he spoke again. "I wrote a report for you. Marco has a copy."

"Excellent, Kyle. I'll read it tonight. To be honest, I'd love to hear highlights now. What do you say?"

The stress of the day ebbing and the ache of leaving Cristina beginning to dull, his spirit rose as he launched into the tale of the cross. It was filled with details and nuance that only the human voice could relate. At times during the narrative he sat so high as to bump his head on the small car's ceiling.

"The actual amphora of Nicodemus on Skellig Michael. Right where I showed you, remember? And at Gallarus. And in Ballinskelligs. Man." Kyle amazed himself with his own words.

"It's beyond incredible, really," Kevin said. "The letter of Conlaeth, that you found it—like God's hand was upon you."

"It was." Then, in a whisper: "I felt it."

What this young man expressed in awe, with a reverence so deep that could only be termed joyous fear, Kevin had glimpsed for himself on the rarest occasion, and then from afar. His heart rejoiced at hearing Kyle's spiritual encounter, that he had experienced this great blessing.

"Now, tell me more about the scroll—where you think it's hidden."

Kyle leaped in once more. "Of course it's got to be with the amphora and its *crux de cruce*. They belong together. Pio Nono needed to protect them both against discovery. Trouble is, he hid them too well."

Kevin considered this, then pushed further. "So your theories?"

"See, the archaeologist's brother wrote that the amphora would be kept *secure under Jonah's protection.* That means either the catacombs or the Sistine—because of the murals."

"And both are dead ends?"

"No. Marco is the dead end."

Their exit approached. Kevin flipped on his signal, descended the ramp, turned right, and slowly pulled to the curb. The car idled quietly.

"Kyle, neither people nor things are always as they seem."

Their eyes met, then Kyle looked down. Passing headlights streamed across the young man as he shrugged indifference.

Kevin put the car in gear, his left foot gradually releasing the clutch.

"Marco will do everything in his power to find the cross. This you must believe."

With a single halting nod, he replied. "I'll try."

It was nearing eleven by the time they reached the apartment in Rathmines. Kevin gave a ten-second tour and threw a pillow and blanket on the sofa.

"Jameson, right?"

"Sure," Kyle said, impressed with the priest's recall.

They sat at the freshly cleared table.

"Growing up, Kyle, did you ever hear people speak of the curing cross?"

"Cured by the cross, like in salvation? 'Course I did."

"That's not quite what I meant." Kevin edged forward in his chair. "Fragments of the true cross—did you hear anything about that?"

"Not until you set me onto it, no." He gave Kevin a puzzled look. "Why?"

"Well, there's an age-old legend in Ballinskelligs—and actually a deeply held conviction among some of the elderly—

that what you have now identified as the Nicodemus amphora, specifically the *crux de cruce* on its side, has healing powers."

Kyle scooted forward in his own chair. "What do you mean, healing powers?"

Kevin's expression was sober. "That by touching the wood of the cross, the ill are healed."

"Why wouldn't they be?" he scoffed.

His matter-of-fact reply surprised the priest.

"Good enough," he laughed.

"I don't get what's so funny."

"I'm just pleased at your response, that's all. But you're right to be serious. The power to heal, Kyle—finding the cross could mean saving a life. A child's life."

He understood immediately. "This is about Michael. From the beginning this has been about Michael."

"Yes, it has."

Kyle's disappointment was clear. "You didn't trust me enough to tell me."

Kevin had long anticipated his reaction. "Kyle, it was not fair to burden you with finding a cure for the child. That you agreed to take on this challenge was sufficient."

The young man would not be placated. "You're forgetting I failed. Knowing or not, I still let him down." He looked away.

Kevin's voice softened. "We've not reached the end yet, have we? Marco is continuing the search, even as we speak."

"If there's still a chance, then why did you call me back? What assignment could possibly be more important than finding the cross?"

The priest rested his folded hands on the table and spoke plainly. "Kyle, more than anything else right now, Michael needs your friendship."

CHAPTER TWENTY-FOUR

DÓCHAS † HOPE

Saturday, 7 August 2010, Crumlin

Aideen entered the room on tiptoe, pushed the door closed, then slowly released the handle with a quiet plunk of the catch. Michael stirred.

"Maw Maw."

He drifted to sleep again as she reached the bed. Brushing back his knit cap, she kissed his forehead and cupped her hand over his head—bare now but for a few wispy strands. Red marks on his lip and cheeks betrayed where until yesterday tape had held a breathing tube in place, their intensity inflamed against the pallor of his face.

She positioned the recliner close, grasped his hand, and watched him breathe.

In repose, the line of his jaw and slightly cleft chin set her thoughts on Caitlin, whose carpet of straight dark hair was so unlike her grandson's absent brown waves.

Why? Why take this child?

She sat in the silence of no answer.

Saturday, 7 August 2010, Smithfield

"Brian Dorrian called me yesterday."

Dr. Thomson crossed the empty waiting room and without greeting motioned Kevin to an armchair near the window. She placed Michael's chart on the small table between them. "He said no one knows he's the father except for his priest."

Kevin nodded. "That was certainly my impression, given his reluctance to talk and the little I was able to learn from Father Finnian."

She bounced the tip of her pencil softly against her left palm. "In my experience, walls of secrecy crumble when a child's life is at risk. Not all couples survive when the truth is revealed."

"Nor all families."

Each knew they were acknowledging the obvious.

"He said he wants to do what he can for his son. Being a marrow donor was probably not on his list." Her expression lent compassion to her laugh. "I've asked him to come over on Monday for tests and to go over details. It will take several hours. Can you be here? He'll need your support."

Like Brian, Kevin was unprepared for Dr. Thomson's request. "If you think—I mean, he doesn't know I know."

"No worries." She glanced at the appointment sheet clipped to the front of the chart. "Be here at one forty-five. We'll gather at two."

"All right."

She began to rise but, noting Kevin's downcast eyes, settled again in her seat. "You have concerns?"

His head dropped with a sigh. "Fears, to be honest." He slowly looked up. "What are his chances?"

"Chances . . ." A subtle shrug told all. "Father, we want to give Michael the best possible chance for cure. And cure is all-or-none with leukemia."

"I'm sure that's true. So then," he said hesitantly, "tell me what concerns you have as his physician."

The cleverness of his question impressed her. She smiled warmly. "Okay. If Brian is in fact the father—and we'll find out soon—he'll be a half match at least. If we're lucky, he'll be an even better match simply by being Irish."

Kevin interrupted. "Sorry—I don't follow you."

"I'll try to simplify. Matching is all about tissue type, and tissue type is influenced by ethnic makeup. You see? And the better the match, the fewer the problems."

"What problems?"

Again the knowing laugh. "Answering that will take up most of our time on Monday. It's enough for now to understand that not all patients survive—either due to complications or not being able to eradicate the leukemia."

"All or none."

She touched his arm. "Father, Michael had little chance of survival when his cancer returned so soon after he was diagnosed. Brian changed that. With him there is hope."

For the first time that day he smiled. "Thank you. Thank you for seeing me on a Saturday."

"Where else would I be?"

Their shared laughter brightened the room.

Opening the chart, she flipped to the treatment tab. "I've mapped out a schedule. While we ready for the transplant, Michael needs to stay in remission. Next week I'll start him on light chemo—pills, actually—that I hope will keep the leukemia at bay. If everything falls in line, his transplant could be in a couple of weeks."

"God willing."

"Of course."

As they walked toward the door, Kevin's pace slowed.

"May I ask about Aideen? I've visited her several times this week and not yet managed to meet up with her doctor. She says it was just a fainting spell—that seeing Michael on the ventilator was too much."

"That's all she told you? I shouldn't be surprised. She's a strong woman."

Kevin felt light-headed himself simply hearing her response.

"Aideen is not well." She leaned back against the wall on her right heel, hands holding the chart at her waist. "Yes, she fainted. I have no doubt it was triggered by emotion. And she did hit her head on the floor. But that isn't what caused the seizure."

Her pause was brief.

"Aideen has a brain tumor."

When she once again had his focus, she continued. "For its type it's quite small—but lethal nonetheless."

"Lethal? How do you know? What do you mean?" He stood rooted as she pulled over two nearby chairs.

"An MRI scan showed it's high-grade. That means it's growing aggressively and feeding off a network of blood vessels. Worse still, it's in a terribly critical location and has already bled into itself, undoubtedly jarred by the fall. Attempting to remove even a portion would risk uncontrolled bleeding—she could die during surgery. Father, it's simply not curable."

"You're serious. I can't believe it." His gaze darted about, his vision registering little.

After a moment, Dr. Thomson again opened Michael's chart and removed a stapled document tucked in loose behind the miscellaneous tab. "I've done some investigation into her medical history. That the records were still available is amazing. I found the original of this among them," she said, holding it out with a wave. "Her doctor was quite a pioneer back then—take a look."

It was a photocopy of a research article published by a Boston pathologist in 1948.

"'Temporary remissions.' That doesn't sound promising," Kevin said after scanning the top page. Most of the text was gibberish to him, but he recognized it was a report on the use of a new drug for children with leukemia.

"You must understand: this was a breakthrough, a genuine breakthrough. It was the only treatment until then to offer any real hope."

"But her doctor cured Aideen. How did he do that?"

"She—how did she do that," Dr. Thomson corrected. "Her notes say she had seen the report when it first came out. The April next, when Aideen was diagnosed, she placed a transatlantic call to Boston—your city, correct?—and coerced the authors to send what little of the experimental drug they could spare."

"Aideen turned eight in 1948," he confirmed.

"Yes—on the twenty-sixth of December."

"Saint Stephen's Day."

"That it is. Now," she continued without comment, "what has turned out to be crucially important for Aideen is this article." She handed him a second, folded to the summary page. Circled boldly in red was the word *radiation*.

He looked up, eyebrows raised in question.

"Aideen had responded immediately to the drug and was given monthly injections. The supply ran out by August. Her doctor knew the leukemia would worsen without treatment. This article prompted her to give radiation."

"It worked?"

"Miraculously well. So well, in fact, that she was cured."

With these words Kevin expected a look of satisfaction on Dr. Thomson's face. Instead, her brows furrowed and her lips pursed.

"She was cured, Father, at the expense of now having brain cancer. It was the radiation that caused the tumor."

Kevin felt the blood drain from his cheeks. He was unable to speak.

In his heart he cried, *Why, Lord?*

Saturday, 7 August 2010, Crumlin

"Please, leave the blinds open."

The evening nurse let go the pull and it tapped lightly against the window. She passed behind Aideen's chair, retrieved her clipboard, and trudged out the door.

It would be a long shift.

Michael had stayed awake most of the afternoon but fell asleep before his dinner tray arrived. Neither had an appetite, and it was taken away untouched.

Aideen leaned forward and quietly sorted the black-and-white backgammon checkers from the board into their dice cups. She smiled thinking of his impatience when it had been her turn to play. She set the game aside and sat on the bed, treasuring the memory.

As from a distance, she suddenly noticed what sounded like her flip phone vibrating. For a moment she was confused, believing they hadn't returned it to her when she was discharged from Saint James's that morning. Finally she realized it was coming from the bedside table drawer, where it must have been hiding since her fall.

"Addy, bless the Lord you answered! I've left a message every night this week, not wanting to bother you daytimes with the doctors about and all that. How is dear Michael?"

"Better, I guess. Peg, I so wish I could say he's going to be fine. He was on a ventilator. It was dreadful."

"A ventilator? Oh, Addy. I wish you'd called—I'd've had Danny drive me right up there in a flash. We'll come tomorrow, if we're allowed. How about that?"

Aideen reached for a tissue and blotted her cheeks. "Could you, please? That would be such a comfort. He's in a regular room now, so he's allowed visitors. Family, you're family."

"That we are, missy. Always."

+ + + + + + + + +

The day was at end.

Stray points of light skittered across the walls in the darkened room, filtered by the gray-glass window into muted shades of red. Michael's breathing was easy and regular, undisturbed by his grandmother's weeping.

In her tears she yearned for faith. She yearned for an assurance of eternal life, for a belief that the many who had abandoned her had not remained dust but had risen from death into a more perfect existence.

She yearned to reach beyond the impenetrable pain of loss but did not know how.

Heart empty, her tears stopped.

She gazed at her grandson's face. She ached for him to live, to grow, to grace the world with the excellence of his being and fill it with his love. For her love to live in him.

Please, God, spare this child.

In one fluid movement, she unclasped her pendant and hung it on Michael's neck.

Wear it always, my angel, my angel always.

CHAPTER TWENTY-FIVE

VERA CRUX † TRUE CROSS

Sunday, 8 August 2010, Maynooth

Kyle scooted his barstool forward, wiped the plate clean of mustard with the last chip, and finished off the pint in a few quick gulps.

The Roost was boisterous as usual, and why Kyle had chosen it for dinner. None of his former classmates were about, most off on holiday and not due back until late next month. In absence of friends, the noise was sufficient distraction from his ceaseless musing.

He left the hangout and walked up Parson Street toward campus. Just past the soccer field he crossed over to St. Joseph Square.

It was a clear summer evening and the waning crescent moon was nearing the horizon. A dozen re-sit students had unwisely chosen to play in the manicured gardens rather than prepare for their upcoming last-chance exams. Seeing them, he wondered how many would qualify for fall term.

The square was surrounded on three sides by an immense Gothic stone building that housed several academic departments and a conference center. Kyle traversed the yard, entered the structure at the Long Corridor, then strode quickly through the Stoyte House and out.

In the deepest corner of the property stood the thirteenth-century ruins of a castle's keep. He had discovered this place three winters past. Snowdrifts had reached halfway up the cathedral-like arches, all sound absorbed into white silence. With the onset of spring, it had become his sanctuary.

Wandering now in the long shadows of these broken medieval walls, he sought solace but found none: Marco's directive remained starkly incomprehensible.

Set your soul free.

Over and again he tried to reason it out and failed. Taunted by doubt, he left.

Dew had begun settling on the grass, and few remained in the square. At its center, paved walks radiated in the cardinal directions. He paused. St. Patrick's House lay straight to the west, its northern end terminating at the grand apse of the college chapel. Rays of sun poured out from behind the steeple, stretching across the lawns as a nightly farewell.

In the quiet, strains from the chapel pipe organ could be discerned. He was drawn forth.

A side door to the vestibule was ajar, and he entered. There were none within save the organist. An exuberant Bach fugue soared in major key. The air itself reverberated.

He walked up the aisle, stopped midway, and turned.

Dazzling with the strength of a summer sunset, the full spectrum of the mullioned rose window was on display above the gallery, its brilliance in harmony with the music. He lamented having never before seen its grandeur while residing on campus.

His gaze focused on the central figure: Christ the King, ascended in glory, his rule over the heavens and earth secure. Death defeated, the cross was fulfilled.

He then scanned the encircling ring of smaller panels. As his eyes passed upon the topmost figure of an archangel, they froze.

When the last seal is broken and the trumpets are blown, Saint Michael will hold open the book of the saved. See? He leads the fanfare, Kyle—our angele dei.

Kyle's hand searched over his chest for the scapular, and held it fast.

Yes, Cristina, I see. I see.

Finally at peace, he silently gave thanks and rushed to catch the 8:30 Dublin bus.

Monday, 9 August 2010, Crumlin

Kevin stood fidgeting as they waited for the elevator. Impatient, he pressed the call button a third time, annoyed that it did not seem to acknowledge his frustration. Finally he gave up, accepting grudgingly that they were in fact already late.

Kyle had stayed up late, awakened late, and dressed late. He did not seem at all upset by the circumstance he'd created. Rather, he appeared uncharacteristically tranquil.

Once on the ward they went straight to Michael's room. The boy was alone, playing a video game with total concentration. They backed out and asked after Aideen at the desk.

She was sitting forward on an upholstered chair in the family lounge, legs crossed and arms entwined, summer skirt draped casually to mid-calf. Facing her on a matching chair, so close that their foreheads might touch, sat Stephanie. Together they engaged in easy, intimate conversation. The scene was reminiscent of a young woman and her favorite grandmother.

It wasn't until Kevin neared that they saw him.

Aideen rose and graciously welcomed each, then looked long at Kyle. "You were just a boy, and now . . ." She ended her words with an embrace.

They settled at a small game table, Kyle opposite Stephanie.

Kevin apologized for their late arrival. "I hope we haven't missed Dr. Thomson—you said she wanted to share some news?"

"Yes, and I'm so sorry about mixing up the time. She was actually here at eight." Her eyes flittered in embarrassment, then she drew breath. "Father, they think they may have found a donor for Michael. Isn't it wonderful?" She clutched Stephanie's hand close with a trembling force.

In a practiced response, Kevin expressed happy surprise. "Aideen, that is indeed good news, and an answer to many prayers."

"Prayers or no, he needs this transplant," she said unflinching, then added, "before he gets worse." Seeing pity in his eyes, she instead glanced randomly about the room. "The donor—the anonymous donor—is having tests done today. And dear Stephanie is leaving tomorrow." Her arm enwrapped the young woman's shoulder. "Michael is already pouting."

Kyle shifted in his seat, anticipating he might be brought into the conversation. Kevin obliged.

"I was thinking, since Kyle will now be helping me here in Dublin, I'm sure he'd enjoy keeping Michael company. And they already know each other."

Aideen turned immediately toward the young man.

"Would you? He's fond of you, Kyle. He still mentions how you visited him before when he was ill. There aren't many men in his life."

"Sure, no problem," he said with a hint of enthusiasm.

"And Kyle, Father told me how you searched all of Rome trying to find that old cross. I don't know what came over me, really, thinking it could help." She brushed aside the notion with a headshake. "Desperate for miracles, I suppose. Forgive me."

He nodded slightly, then looked to Kevin, baffled.

"Why don't the two of you check in on Michael?" he prompted. "Aideen, tea?"

Kevin laughed as the pair left, suddenly remembering they'd never met. "I guess they'll introduce themselves."

A few people in rumpled clothes stood waiting in the café. Aideen lagged entering.

"I didn't want any either," Kevin admitted.

They went outside and found a sunlit bench, warm in the chill morning air. Each kept to their separate thoughts for a long while. Finally, in a soft voice, Aideen spoke.

"You've been so kind and I so selfish—sending you out on a pointless mission."

She had earlier mistaken compassion for pity in his eyes. He set on a different tack.

"Aideen, when you first showed me your family Bible, did you not believe in the power of the cross?"

Her head shook noncommittally. "As a child believes in magic, maybe."

"And miracles?"

"I stopped believing in those years ago."

"So why the pendant? Why wear it at all?" he pushed.

"For Maw Maw," she cried. "Don't you understand?"

She untucked a folded tissue from her shirt cuff, stood, and walked away.

CHAPTER TWENTY-SIX

PETROS ENI † PETER IS WITHIN

Sunday, 25 December 1938, Basilica of Saint Peter

Even as the octogenarian hobbled the mere five steps from pew to wheelchair, his breaths came with great effort. Ludwig held one arm across the ailing pope's back, the other firmly supporting His Holiness's weight as he shuffled foot to foot.

"You are good to me, Ludwig. Many are your indulgences for indulging a dying man." The prelate strained to hear the words, spoken with little air in short strings at the end of prolonged, wheezing expirations.

Pius XI had deferred most of his papal duties to others lately, although few were told of the heart attacks he'd suffered on the last Friday before Advent. Regardless, the headstrong man refused to let Christmas pass without venerating Saint Peter, upon whom Jesus built his Church and whose tomb by tradition lay here beneath the high altar of his basilica.

Ludwig steered the pope slowly along the empty marble aisles, pausing at the foot of many statues and honoring the radiant alabaster Gloria of the Holy Spirit with a lengthier stop. Each treasure was awash in nighttime illumination. Each received a whispered final blessing by the pontiff.

At last they reached the Confessio gate beyond which a pair of open stairs descended amidst a multitude of oil lamps to an ornate niche, long celebrated as the site nearest the great apostle's earthly remains.

"Achille, I fear I won't be able to take you farther in safety."

The pope nodded silently and patted Ludwig's hand in understanding. He brought forth his rosary, its olivewood burnished with use, and prayed, motionless but for the fingering of beads and the ceaseless flutter of lips. When done, he reverently signed himself and kissed the crucifix upon which his prayer had ended and begun.

"I wish to be buried near Peter. Will you see it done for me?"

Ludwig smiled, having known this was Pius's desire. "Of course, Achille. It will require some rearranging—the crypt is not large."

"Do what you must. I have granted you such authority as the basilica canon."

"Your Holiness—" He hesitated to burden an ill pope with what might appear a bold, even risky proposal, yet worried that Pius's successor would not be as progressive. "We may have need to expand the crypt."

The pope did not immediately respond.

"I've studied what is known of the original Constantine basilica and the plans for this structure envisioned by Bramante and Michelangelo. The foundations beneath lie on Nero's circus and the remains of a mostly pagan cemetery. It would require careful excavation, patience, and resources, but I believe it can be accomplished without desecrating Christian bones."

Pius's appearance looked grave. He placed his hand firmly on Ludwig's. "'Mostly pagan'? Come, now. What saintly relics rest below is pure surmise, would you not agree? Peter's tomb itself is taken on faith."

Ludwig bowed in deference. "Your Holiness, none would undertake this project with greater care or respect."

Upon consideration, Pius reluctantly conceded that progress was inevitable. "So be it," he uttered weakly, lifting his hand in blessing upon the canon's brow.

The future of the crypt decided, Ludwig led the fatigued pope quickly down the north aisle toward the exit.

"Please, the *Pietà*."

Ludwig leaned forward and spoke gently. "Achille, you are tired. We can return when you've recovered strength."

Pius pressed his head close. "Let my soul part from you in peace."

And together they contemplated the Virgin cradling her crucified son.

"Gaze upon her face! O, if I could but accept the will of God with such serenity. Yet how so? I leave a shattered world and a Church struggling to respond."

He motioned Ludwig near.

"The evil that is coming, that has arrived—do not rely on the Accords for our defense."

He pushed himself up, as though ready to rise and take arms.

"The most precious relics of our Lord's passion must be saved at any cost," he intoned with full force. "They know of the Sistine Treasury and will look there first. The Führer's appetite for Christian artifacts reaches to the depths of hell."

Their eyes locked in understanding.

"I give you my word," Ludwig vowed. "The amphora and scroll will never be found."

Thursday, 12 August 2010, Dublin

Aideen's bus pulled to the curb at Leeson Street Lower. She walked the few short blocks over to St. Stephen's Green and passed through the iron gates at the southeast entrance.

It was not yet six. She had an hour to wander the gardens, to freely imbibe the ethereal realm of Victorian perfection and become drunk on fantasy. Perhaps by then she would be emotionally prepared for her dinner with Father Schaeffer.

So had she wrongly imagined.

The treed path that initially led diagonally from the street corner toward the park's center soon splayed left and left and right, through and about the eastern quadrant. As if to mock the indecisive, three Fates dressed in bronze rose from a circular pool where the paths diverged. They appeared as fair maidens, goddesses holding the unbroken thread of past, present, and future in their hands.

At first their comeliness drew her close. Her heart lifted, their gentle beauty a seeming portrait of herself with Maw Maw standing wise and Caitlin sitting youthful at her feet.

Yet they disturbed, these veiled Norns of destiny.

Do you not know us, mortal one, we who haunt your dreams?

They beckoned, their voices thin, entwined, borne on an icy fog.

Come. Forfeit that will of yours disguised as free but cast in the flames of our deception.

Aideen shivered, engulfed by despair.

Come, creature of our desire: prostrate before us.

She looked away, barren and cold.

She did not notice the sun as it finally broke through the day's clouds, or the sudden onset of dusk when it retreated once again from view. Her course was without purpose.

Of what she perceived through blind eyes, Grafton Street might have been empty.

Once at Bewley's, the maître d' showed her to a window table upstairs, choice on a summer evening.

She sat, numb, and waited for the priest's arrival.

+ + + + + + + + +

"Please—"

Kevin seated, the maître d' draped a burgundy napkin on his lap, opened the menu to the evening's specials, and indicated the sommelier's recommendations.

"I had no notion this place existed. Thanks for suggesting it."

Aideen smiled faintly, then returned to watching passersby on the busy walkway.

He set down the menu and casually turned his water glass in place.

At length she alerted to his presence. "I do make a wretched hostess—no dissent allowed," she said, hand raised. "This being a thank-you dinner, one would expect better. I would expect better."

"As a meal between friends, neither thanks nor apology is necessary."

She demurred with a shrug. "A celebration, then. Dr. Thomson heard back this afternoon that Michael's donor is a match. Not perfect, of course, but she says it's close enough."

"I'm thrilled. Congratulations, to you and to Michael." Kevin's response was heartfelt. Left unstated was his relief that Brian's paternity proved true.

At that moment the waiter arrived. Neither was ready to order, but they made choices quickly and Kevin selected a wine. The waiter bowed and left.

"Aideen?"

She looked up with a start, only to let her head sink again. "I'm sorry. I should go."

Before she could move he reached and placed a hand over hers. "Aideen, please, tell me what's wrong. What's happened?"

"Nothing's 'happened.' It's just—I don't know."

His hand remained firm. She sighed in defeat.

"Do you ever just feel—screwed?" Her eyes revealed no abashment at the word. His were unwavering. "This curse on our family—there's no hiding from it. No one is safe. I thought, stupid me, that the cross would help Michael if we could only find it. Or the pendant—" She freed a hand and wiped tears with her napkin. "I counted on the pendant, on Maw Maw's promise."

He let go, bringing his hands together near hers.

Face now dry, she looked at him soberly.

"I'm dying, Father. I have a brain tumor."

Caught unawares by the sudden admission and plunged anew into pained sorrow over his mother's death, tears flowed abruptly from his own eyes.

"Do you see now? There is no saving Michael—transplant or no transplant. We all die."

The waiter discreetly set the wine glasses and bottle on the table. Long minutes passed before Kevin's emotions calmed. He then quietly poured.

In the silence as they took their first sips, Aideen's constant gaze probed him for any sign of insincerity, or worse, religious platitude.

The words he spoke were truth, no more.

"Christ is not confined to the wood of the cross."

It was a simple statement, without judgment or persuasion.

As with all truth, the simple was rooted in the profound.

Her gaze softened.

"None escape mortal death, Aideen. But remember: Adam's fall was only possible given free will." He let the thought linger, then quoted Scripture: "'I have set before you life and death, blessing and curse; therefore choose life, that you and your descendants may live.'"

Her halting words came as a whisper. "Father, I want to believe."

Visibly moved, Kevin enveloped her hands in his and raised them to his lips.

"Child of Christ, by your own confession it is so."

CHAPTER TWENTY-SEVEN

MISERICORDIA † MERCY

Wednesday, 18 August 2010, Crumlin

This should help, Mickey," the nurse said as she finished injecting a nausea medicine into his IV. "Now then, anything else?" With barely a headshake he turned away, queasy.

"Thanks, Erin," Kyle proffered with a knowing shrug.

"No problem." Her smile was attentive and subtly flirtatious. His eyes followed her to the door.

"Wanna watch the rest of *Ice Age*?"

Michael scowled. "Where's Stephanie? I want Stephanie."

"I told you—she had to go home. You're stuck with me." Kyle struggled against his growing impatience. He aimed the remote and pressed play, needing a diversion even if the boy didn't. He figured that it and the two sequels should carry him to midafternoon.

Ten minutes later his phone rang. Marco's number showed on the screen. He answered.

"So how is Michael?"

It had been almost two weeks since he'd heard an Italian accent. Instantly he longed for Cristina.

"Pretty good, I guess. He's getting chemo now and is ornery as hell." He rapped Michael on the knee and got an eye-roll in reply. "The transplant isn't for another week."

"I'm glad he has this chance." He paused. "And how about you, Kyle?"

A lot had happened since his hasty departure, and he couldn't think where to start.

"Better."

Undaunted by Kyle's stock-in-trade abbreviated answers, Marco continued. "Kevin tells me you're to receive research credit for your work here."

"Yeah—it helps having a friend who's a professor."

"A friend indeed, but you earned it."

"Not until I finish the report. Uh, sorry about that crap piece I left for you," he said, eliciting a laugh.

"As penance I expect a copy of your masterwork."

"You got it. Hang on—"

Michael was desperately looking for the plastic basin Erin had left. It was partly hidden under the blankets. Kyle grabbed it quickly and pushed it into the boy's hands.

"Man! Oh, geez—"

Kyle sounded distant over the phone, which he'd dropped abruptly to help Michael. An alarm chimed, and moments later a young woman's voice could be heard.

"It's okay. Why don't you wait in the hall?"

There were rustling sounds, then heavy breaths.

"Kyle? Are you all right?"

"He's puking his feckin' guts up. Oh, God." More breaths. "I am so not liking this. But he needs me."

What is uttered in innocence bears truth beyond comprehension.

Finally Kyle spoke again, now on a different topic. "You probably figured out I'm going back to school."

"I think that's wise."

"Yeah, me too. College, I mean. The other, I don't know yet."

"I think that's also wise."

The young man's gratitude toward his mentor hung naked in silence. Then tentatively: "Has Cristina asked about me?"

Marco considered his reply, which had the power to crush or elate a tender heart. "Kyle, your absence weighs heavily on her."

Elation.

"Do you think, maybe, not that I would, but if I ever wanted to study at the Gregorian, do you think I might be able to?"

The priest laughed. "I think maybe Father Kevin and I would be willing to help."

"Thanks."

Marco let a moment pass before getting to the main purpose of his call. "Now, let me tell you what I've learned about the amphora."

Not wanting to miss a word, Kyle pressed the phone to his left ear, closed his right with his forefinger, and walked out of the noisy lounge to the hallway.

"You were precisely correct in your interpretation about Jonah," Marco said, his tone suggesting mild surprise. In the background Kyle heard the distinct sound of pages turning. "It is recorded in Pio Nono's diary that he favored Callixtus as a secure hiding place for the amphora—perhaps in the uncharted area you identified—but De Rossi disagreed, arguing that the catacombs could not be adequately guarded."

"What? You found Nono's diary? Where?"

"In the pope's archive," he said flatly.

"But I searched there and found nothing!"

Marco's clipped reply ended further query: "His personal archive. Did you hear any of what I said, or must I repeat?"

"Sorry. Go on."

"Ultimately," he continued slowly, "they agreed on the Sistine Treasury."

At once Kyle forgot his chastisement and turned giddy with anticipation. "Is it there, where I thought?"

"We already knew it was nowhere in the room itself, remember. However, we did find evidence of rather poorly repaired plaster—on the Treasury wall that's back to back with the Last Judgment. It took five men to move the credenza away, and that after an entire day needed to empty it."

"Christ, don't tell me you didn't tear it open?" A passing nurse touched Kyle's arm and motioned him to lower his voice, to which he nodded mechanically.

"What if I told you we borrowed technology from the papal physician?"

The young man literally bounced, fingers crossed.

"Our friend Dámaso drilled a small hole in the middle of the repair and threaded a thin flexible scope into the space behind. It was empty. But—"

Deflated at the word, Kyle could not imagine any finding that could redeem this story.

"But what we did not expect to find was a wood-lined cavity."

"Large enough for the amphora."

"Yes."

"Empty."

"Yes."

"Damn." Then, in a small voice: "I wish you'd found it."

Marco sighed. "I know. As do I. Still, we cannot let disappointment spoil our progress."

"Yeah, I get it. This is big." He moped back into the lounge. "So what's next?"

"Next, the scroll sent from Ireland to Pope Hormisdas. It, too, is mentioned in the diary. Pio Nono instructed that it be hidden with the amphora."

"I knew it!" The excitement of hearing his theories affirmed was short-lived. "And that means they're both lost together."

"True."

"We're back to nowhere," he said forlornly. "Unless Nono wrote in his diary—"

"Unfortunately, no—it says nothing of the scroll's content."

Dejected, Kyle dropped onto a vacant couch and closed his eyes.

"Do you not want to hear the last bit?" Marco teased.

"Sure."

"It is what I found in Pio Nono's personal effects."

Kyle sat up, alert and unblinking.

"A scapular—a necklace that's worn—"

"Yeah, I know what a scapular is," he interrupted, touching his own.

Marco continued. "Most are cloth. This one is silver. It was inside a paper envelope labeled '*roccia sporgente*.' I suppose you know what that means too."

He snorted in reply.

"'Protruding rock,' Kyle. And below that was written 'San Michele.'"

Again Kyle touched the scapular Cristina had given him from her hometown. "Marco, Nono blessed the first-ever Saint Michael scapular. That must be it."

"I believe so. And 'protruding rock'?" Marco prompted.

"Skellig Michael," he whispered.

"That would be my assumption as well."

His gaze was lost on the ceiling's white. "Is there a Saint Patrick's cross on the front?"

"Yes. How did you know?"

Kyle sighed. "I've seen it before. There's one just like it around Michael's neck."

Thursday, 26 august 2010, Crumlin

Peg pushed open the door with one foot, steadying the overloaded cafeteria tray against her torso. Aideen had not left Michael's bedside all day except to use the adjoining bathroom.

"You're a dear. Thank you, Peg."

"Hush, now. Just let me see you eat. No breakfast or lunch—I daren't think of it!"

"He looks pale, so pale." She stroked the boy's cheek lightly. He did not stir.

"Think of tomorrow, how rosy he'll be after they pump him up with blood. The doctors didn't seem a bit worried, did they? So let's not worry ourselves for naught."

She watched as Peg set out the meal before her. She felt loved, cared for. Mothered.

"Kyle agreed to drive me home in the morning, if the car starts. I can't remember the last time I was home."

"Weeks and weeks, I'm sure. Danny's been over regular. You just go and rest."

"Sleep, if I can. My mind will be here."

"As it should be—but that's my job, now isn't it, to be with Michael? And Danny's, when I'm there with you."

Looking steadily into her friend's eyes: "I trust you both with his life, you know."

Peg opened her arms and wrapped them around Aideen's small frame.

"I made an appointment with my estate lawyer for next Wednesday—he scheduled three hours, but I told him I'd probably not last two. It isn't like I have many belongings, and they all go to Michael. Anyhow, he'll handle the finances until Michael is old enough to manage on his own." She spoke definitively, willing her grandson's survival. "I'd like the family house to be there when he needs it."

"Of course," Peg said as she wiped her face.

Aideen turned again to the sleeping child. "He didn't shiver once today as they gave him the transplant." She placed her hand on Maw Maw's pendant, draped over his heart. "Eleven days—that's when they expect him to recover." She laid her head on his arm. "And every one of those days I will give thanks to God for sending us a donor."

With that, Peg's tears became a flood.

Friday, 27 August 2010, County Kerry

The afternoon clouds were thickening and the air had turned damp. Kyle braked abruptly, arm out to protect Aideen, as he swerved into the Esso station just past the sparse village storefronts of Rathmore.

"I'll be quick."

He left the pump running and went into the mart, returning with two soft-serve cones. "A vanilla and a chocolate— your choice," he said, handing them to her through the side window.

He finished tanking up, then got back in the car. It was already half past three. If traffic around Kenmare was light and the rain held off, they had a good chance of getting home before six.

"This is delightful. Thank you, Kyle. You're a thoughtful young man," she said, tasting the chocolate.

"It's nothing." Edging onto the roadway, he waited for a red VW Golf to buzz past, then tried popping into second gear. The car stalled, ending his chance for pulling out in front of a motor home. He hit the steering wheel with his palm.

"I should have sold this car ages ago. My daughter bought it when Michael was little. Ten years . . ." Her smile was more wistful than sad. "He's been a happy child—my joy."

She offered Kyle the melting cone once they reached cruising speed, asking almost casually: "Do you remember Caitie?"

Kyle brushed his hand across his lips, swallowing. "Sure. She used to pick up Mickey from the nursery after church. And I remember her funeral—" He stopped midsentence.

Aideen touched his arm gently. "I don't mind. It wasn't much of a sendoff for her, was it? Rather awkward, really. No casket, of course—she was intent on cremation. I suppose I was just as stubborn, refusing a Mass. Father Finnian eventually forgave me. At least that's what he said."

The road curved slightly north. Seeing no oncoming cars, Kyle downshifted, darted into the right lane, and sped around the motor home. The VW had disappeared in the distance.

"So what's with you and Finnian? I mean, he's always been nice to me."

Silence.

"Sorry—none of my business."

"No, you're fine to ask." She sighed. "It's hard to relinquish old hurts."

"Forgive and forget, my da says."

Her eyes closed tightly as she tried to name the feeling that weighed within. Scalded or frozen, the pain was indistinguishable. She leaned back against the seat, head in hand.

They drove on. Soon the summer landscape was tufted by hills, and glimpses of the River Roughty appeared to the south, broadening in its run toward the bay. Kyle's spirits rose visibly as they neared the sea.

Even with N71 narrowing to a single lane on Henry Street, it took only ten minutes to traverse Kenmare center. Once beyond, there were unexpectedly few cars on the Ring.

"Kyle, would you mind if we stopped a moment?" She pointed to a dirt road on the left that dead-ended into a secluded dock. The bay opened westward.

"I'd come here alone when Caitie was sick. It seemed far enough away. It still does." Arms wide, her gaze floated out, out above the incoming tide. "The sky swirls—see?"

Her words caught the air and rode aloft.

She turned slowly and faced Kyle.

"I won't be returning to Dublin."

He stood rock-still, waiting.

"I have cancer. It's getting worse. Peg and Danny will be taking care of Michael now. They already love him as a son. But he'll need more than parents."

She took his hands. They were trembling.

"Michael needs a brother," she said.

His head bowed in acceptance.

+ + + + + + + + +

The untended mantel clock was silent. She walked through the lifeless house, turning out lights as she retreated to her room.

At length only the dimmed bedside lamp still burned. Her well-read copy of *Dubliners* sat untouched, on this night less likely to beguile than perturb.

She lay semi-recumbent, pillows soft behind, headache unremitting. The door stood open, kept so since Michael first became ill but tonight from habit. Shadows cast relief on plaster-patched holes where pictures once hung, a larger repair made after a fit of teenage frustration—old scars showing through layers of pale yellow paint.

She was home.

Outside the wind gusted and the house groaned in response. Chill air breathed through the window jambs. Shivering, she finally climbed from bed to shut the door.

Another gust, and the lamp guttered.

She stood in the dark overreaching, uselessly groping beyond the doorway into the empty hall for the knob.

As fast, light shone again. She looked, and she froze.

Directly opposite was reflected the chalk-white skin of crucified Jesus, dead upon the cross.

Her shoulder fell against the doorframe, mouth agape, eyes fixed on the lithograph.

How had she not seen before, never noticed despite tens of thousands of days having lived in this home, slept in this room, passed through this hall, that which inescapably cried out from the image?

The words sank deep and pierced her heart.

I do this for you.

CHAPTER TWENTY-EIGHT

ADUNATIO † ATONEMENT

Saturday, 4 September 2010, Ballinskelligs

P eg entered the house and immediately started opening windows.

"Can you imagine, on a lovely day like this! Addy, where are you hiding?" She moved from room to room with purpose, a fall-fresh breeze trailing in her wake. "Addy?"

Kevin followed as far as the bathroom. They'd not stopped since Cashel and he felt the urgency of his second latte.

The bedroom was empty but for a stagnance of over-breathed air. She gently billowed the damp linen, drew them taut, and folded back the comforter. Grabbing the used water glasses in one hand and the nearly full wastebasket in the other, she left the items in the kitchen and went out to the patio.

Aideen lay on the chaise, cowl neck of her teal wool cardigan pulled up tight, pajamas beneath. A roughly glazed ceramic teapot and jug of milk filled the small table at her side. Steam rose from her mug, warming her lips.

"Caitie made this," she said, touching the pot. "It's full—I didn't think to bring an extra cup."

"Don't you fuss, I know right where they are." She kissed her friend lightly on the brow and returned moments later with Kevin behind.

Aideen's look was distant, formalities expendable. "They said he's better. Peg, tell me how he looks."

"Like a star, Addy, a bright shining star. He smiled today—'course that made my heart sing. He looks like our boy again."

"And Kyle? I asked him to stay close."

"Every day, never misses."

"I'm glad."

Finally she acknowledged Kevin's presence. "Father, thank you for bringing Peg."

"Any excuse to visit." The words felt inadequate. Tea in hand, he sat down on the nearest chair. "Dr. Thomson wanted you to know that Michael's new bone marrow is starting to kick in. You should have seen how excited she was that he's eating."

"No leukemia."

"None they can see."

Her gaze drifted, alone in thought.

Peg leaned toward Kevin and said softly before leaving, "There must be something at home I can make us for dinner."

September was young but the earth knew summer had passed. The few plants still in bloom were fading, and color-fringed leaves could be found by diligent observation. Kevin wandered the gardens, her gardens, in awe at the beauty.

"Kyle told me to forgive and forget."

He'd not heard her approach, yet didn't startle. She slipped an arm comfortably through his and together they walked the lawn's edge. The sea was calm, prepared to accept the sun once more after a full day's absence.

"I think I can do that now: forgive. Maybe I'm old, or simply dying. I've lost track of why any of it mattered, why the pain."

She spoke in soliloquy.

"How do I forgive when I'm in need of forgiveness?"

When they reached the rose bed she stopped.

"Father, do you believe Maw Maw ever touched the cross?"

Kevin turned to see her looking up at him. Voice faltering, his eyes blurred.

"Yes, with all that is in me."

She smiled and touched her hand to his cheek, gentle as a breeze.

+ + + + + + + + +

"Just one, then?"

"No, Peg, please," Aideen said, pushing her hand away, and with it, the pill. Although her head throbbed intensely, she wanted nothing to dull her senses. "Sit and tell me more about your marrying Danny. I can't imagine, after years of being single—and he a widower."

Peg drew her chair near. "It was the most natural thing, really. I'd not planned to be an old maid—shush, that's what I was. After tenth grade I stayed home to tend Mum—she'd had the polio—and Beara isn't one of the most populated of places, now is it? So I didn't expect any suitors."

"Until Danny."

She nodded, sighing. "His dear, sweet Eanid brought us together in her own way."

Aideen squeezed her hand. "Nursing her after all those years caring for your mother."

"I was called to it, I suppose, helping others," she said, squeezing back. "Father Finnian sent word of their need for home care to parishes from Tralee to Skibbereen and wouldn't you know I was the only one to reply."

"As fate would have it."

Peg shook her head and pointed upward. "God," she corrected. "And a year to the day after she passed, Danny asked me to marry him."

"He'd have died of a broken heart, Peg. You saved him."

"Love is as love does." Smiling, she stood. "Now, I'm going to get you a glass of juice."

When she returned she carried a tray laden with crackers, slices of cheese, and orange marmalade.

"I'm at peace knowing Michael will have you and Danny as parents."

"Godparents, more like. He already has a mother and a grandmother, doesn't he? And believe you me, he'll not forget it."

Aideen took a sip of juice. "If you would," she said, motioning toward the package on the footboard bench. Peg handed it to her and sat. "Father brought this back to me today." From the paper sack she removed Maw Maw's Bible, enveloped in its protective satin pouch. "It's for when Michael's older—our family Bible."

Together they paged slowly through the baptismal record, Aideen explaining in what detail she could everything about Michael's ancestors. Then she spoke of the pendant, the cross, and the symbols next to those who had been cured.

"Here," she showed Peg. "Here, draw it here." Her finger rested at Michael's name.

An hour passed and the sun set. Peg closed the curtains.

"Can I get you anything, Addy?"

"I'm okay. Go rest awhile—you've not left my side for hours."

"If you're sure. I'll be back before you miss me, fresh and clean and ready for bed."

Alone, in solitude, Aideen lifted the Bible onto her lap.

She opened again to the baptismal record.

Maire, Siobhan, Aidan, Caitlin: each inked entry a life begun and ended. Soon, Aideen.

Last was Michael Sean Callaghan.

Covering his name with her palm, she closed her eyes.

Not this one, not yet.

CHAPTER TWENTY-NINE

AGAPE † LOVE

Saturday, 31 March 1866, Kildreelig

Seán stood tall at the peninsular ridge. Across the ocean inlet smoke rose in seven plumes from the chimneys of seven stone cottages that hugged the rocky cliff, drifting westward to Bolus Head on the light morning breeze. In the front-most, Da would have awakened before dawn to set the fire and tend the cow, udder swollen since its last milking. These tasks were Seán's as the oldest, but not today, or yesterday, or the day before—or tomorrow for that matter, which was Easter.

He stretched, then bent low, touched his knees gently, and raised the pant legs thigh-high. The skin was bruised, having deepened overnight from abraded red to violaceous black. Never in his thirteen years had he spent such hours serving the parish priest at altar, nor kneeling on flagstone in Eucharistic adoration while the village slept. Yet he bore these trivial wounds joyfully, reciting the gospel of the Lord's passion over and over, the true wounds of salvation vivid in his mind.

On this day sunrise and sunset would be celebrated with Mass. Few managed the early service, like Da burdened with chores both mundane and extraordinary, the holiday near at hand. Few would miss the ancient rite of the Vigil. *Lumen Christi! Deo gratias! Exsultet!*

And tonight, as the Paschal Flame leaped from candle to candle, so too would word of a bodily healing, that of a local girl, to commence at the toll of the midnight bell: a miracle to be witnessed by all.

He turned and followed the shoreline path toward Boolakeel, rounded the thin strand at the inlet's head, then climbed the road to Kildreelig. A flock of scraggy purple sandpipers, fewer than when they began their months-long migration, chitted along behind, hoping for any bit of food that might be upturned by his tread. Twenty minutes later he was home.

"Where's Da?"

His sister sat cross-legged on a matted pile of straw next to the hearth, kittens mewing as they tried to clamber away. "'Dunno." She lifted the tabby by the nape to arm's length above her and swooped it down repeatedly for pecks, giggling as forepaws batted unsuccessfully at her nose.

He stoked the turf logs into flame, drew down the oil-lamp wick, and cracked open the seaward window. Upstairs the younger boys finally stirred, lazily abed without an elder on hand to rouse them.

There was a thick layer of congealed lard in the pan from Thursday's supper. It melted then spat after a few minutes on the grate. The flat bread was already wedged and ready to fry, plumped sweet from an overnight soak in honey and cream: a passable use of week-old fadge. Soon the vapors reached the loft, and the three boys descended the ladder, hungry.

With the children's rising Seán's Gaelic tongue was loosed on family tales, narratives true in essence and embellished freely, the hearers never certain of the path a story might take. Yet unwavering was the purpose of the telling, of keeping fragmented memories of Ma alive even as they receded to myth. He was certain the littlest knew her only as the vibrant character he painted, the older perhaps more. For him, no detail was so inconsequential to not be hoarded, locked in his heart as a flower in glass.

++++++++++

The day had clouded but remained bright, a cirrus firmament above, scant of blue, rays diffused to an elated white that bounded with undiminished intensity from horizon to horizon.

Seán closed the cottage door softly, Da resting soundly after his early rise and the tots in forced slumber. The floor was swept, ashes removed, and clothes set out for the evening Mass. At the stoop he paused, making certain that he had not left any unnecessary burden for his father, whose visage and habitus were largely bereft of vigor now four years from his wife's passing.

As he walked uphill, sea to his left, he shifted the cloth bag from shoulder to shoulder, its weight balanced by the swinging of a one-stone mallet. Ahead the oratory ruins stood low on the terrain, early grass greening within. Stakes spewed from the tote onto rocky ground where he set it next to a worn cross slab. Older than the abbey yet not so ancient as the monastery on Skellig Mhór, the last healing performed at this site was a decade distant.

True to Father Sullivan's description, Seán found a foot-high stacked stone table where an altar might once have been. He brushed it clean, squatted to see that it was level, then cleared the area of twigs, leaves, and branches.

He had brought thirty stakes with him, guessing that twenty would be needed between here and home, where yet another twenty waited. The first was placed with difficulty after trying a half-dozen rock-laden spots. He strode fifty long paces, then placed the next into spring-soft earth. Conall, of Dungeagan, was to start in Boolakeel and meet him midway: the privilege of bell ringing at the late-night ceremony was the wager for who would be first to reach the overgrown trident maple at the road's bend.

A hundred stakes to hold high a hundred torches blazing in the dark.

And so the afternoon passed.

+ + + + + + + +

Maire lay flat on the stone tomb. Above, the full moon shone haloed behind gauzy cloud. Four figures towered at her side, their features lost in silhouette. She shivered in the cold, clothes damp with fever.

The air was still and the tide slack. Midnight arrived silent.

Dimly, dimly on the mist came whispered chant, tone compressed with distance to one.

Faintly the sound of handbells joined verse. The air grew sweet with incense.

Then the church bell rang, rang, rang.

Forty, fifty, many more flames appeared, each a sun about her, darkness dispelled.

Slowly she was raised, cradled in cloth stretched tight between poles.

Lord, have mercy on us. Christ, have mercy on us. Lord, have mercy on us.

The litany of Saint Michael began.

Glorious Prince of the heavenly armies, pray for us!

Leader of the angelic hosts, pray for us!

Three times the priest passed, encircling her in a shroud of incense. She breathed deep, tasting it as strong drink, heady, embalmed.

Warrior who thrust Satan into Hell, pray for us!

Defender against the wickedness and snares of the devil, pray for us!

The procession began, torchbearers ahead leading from the abbey graveyard along the bay out the village. Farther and farther into the distance they led, an eternal stream of light, the still water illuminated in a thousandfold echo.

Guardian of our souls and bodies, pray for us!

Healer of the sick, pray for us!

When all had advanced she too was moved forward, before her Father Sullivan voicing in clear tenor the Sorrowful Mysteries, Seán and Conall following with Bible and handbells at the ready. Fiona and Malachi looked down upon their ill daughter, cheeks wet with tears of joyful expectation, hearts filled with absolute faith in the power of the cross.

Their love a release, Maire closed her eyes and slept.

+++++++++

It was the earthen smell that woke her, the softness of dew-supple grass her bed.

She lay motionless, yet the darkness that surrounded her seemed to whirl.

She thought herself alone then heard the quiet breaths of those who stood thick about, their bodies trees looming skyward, their heads a canopy through which no star was seen.

The ground trembled with the footsteps of many approaching overhill from Coom.

"It is here. Raise the torches."

Six did as the priest bade, setting flames upright along the remains of the oratory walls.

Again, incense.

Again, chant.

Kyrie eleison, Christe eleison, Kyrie eleison.

Shadows shifted as people moved outside the narrow ring of light.

Maire glowed white, the pallor of death upon her.

Handbells chimed. Holy water sprayed across her face and chest.

Father Sullivan knelt and blessed her with the sacramental oil of the last anointing.

He rose.

Not ten steps up the road waited a throng, believers from myriad countryside hamlets dotting Prior and Killemlagh. They had followed two monks—old, kyphotic, preternaturally strong—who between them had borne the armarium these miles firm in stride, who would carry it again this night to its hidden sanctuary.

His bow a greeting, Father Sullivan spread a purple blanket at their feet. The monks inched forward to its center and set down the armarium.

The chest was opened, the amphora revealed—

The Lord is my shepherd; I shall not want.
and lifted before all to see.

He maketh me to lie down in green pastures: he leadeth me beside the still waters.

In a cloud of incense it was brought to the oratory.

He restoreth my soul: he leadeth me in the paths of righteousness for his name's sake.

The stone table was adorned with a chalice veil, red embroidered with gold—

Yea, though I walk through the valley of the death, I will fear no evil:

for thou art with me; thy rod and thy staff comfort me.
and the amphora set upon it.

Thou preparest a table before me in the presence of mine enemies;

thou anointest my head with oil; my cup runneth over.

The priest knelt. He wrapped his arms about her torso, one hand at her back, the other at her head, gently raised her shoulders, and whispered.

"Child, touch the wood of your Savior's cross and be healed."

She struggled to focus on the priest and could not, lids half closed.

He spoke again.

"Maire, touch the cross and be healed."

Her eyes opened. She looked at his face, then to the amphora beyond.

As she stared in awe, its brightness grew and approached that of the sun: brighter. Yet the light was backdrop for the cross, aloft and buoyant in a radiant sky. The wood moaned, crying sacrificial blood from its writhing fibers.

She yearned with her whole heart to be cleansed in the blood of the Lamb.

She reached, fingers outstretched, drawn to the cross.

She reached, reached, and touched.

+++++++++

The dawn from on high broke early that morn and bathed the apse in light. Seán rang the steeple bell. Music poured forth. The congregation sang.

It was Easter.

A bier stood before the altar, and on it, Maire.

Father Sullivan processed with the Paschal Candle, followed by Fiona and Malachi, and last, Conall.

None had slept. Not yet two hours had passed since their return from Kildreelig, and all had kept vigil with the child.

She had neither awakened nor died. Hope endured.

"'Greater love hath no man than this, that a man lay down his life for his friends.'"

With that proclamation, Mass began.

The readings were many, the songs plentiful, the praise abundant.

She rose during the Sanctus.

Hosanna in the highest!

They erupted in joy.

They gave thanks for the healing, thanks that one more among them had been cured, thanks for the generations-long presence of the relic.

They prayed that the cross remain near for all time.

Of that certainty Scripture would attest.

Surely goodness and mercy shall follow me all the days of my life:

and I will live in the house of the Lord for ever.

Sunday, 3 June 1866, Coom

Even as Archbishop Cullen's carriage disappeared around a northeasterly bend of the River Flesk on its return journey to Dublin, the aged monks were already deplete of tears. Sorrow settled deep. Broken—life's purpose taken in a moment, they were not long for the earth.

So it was that stain came upon this most solemn feast day of Cóemgen, holy messenger to the pope. The amphora of Nicodemus—fourteen centuries secure in Éire—would soon be received by Rome: hand-delivered as the first official act of a grateful new cardinal.

CHAPTER THIRTY

UNSEARCHABLE RICHES

෴

Monday, 6 September 2010, Ballinskelligs

All day wind battered the house, rain driven across the expanse of sea assaulting trees and roofs alike, the earth drenched.

The storm had arrived early. Aideen watched its approach, mountains churning dark in the distance, overwhelming the false start of first light. Peg awoke with a thunderclap and finally persuaded Aideen to accept pain medication. Eventually both found rest.

Now past noon, Aideen's bedroom window was opaque, masked with a dense curtain of ever-flowing water. She wondered what would be left of her shellflowers—yesterday lacey green bells drooping full of delicate white petals, tomorrow dusting the grass as if snow.

"Here you go, Addy. Peppermint should brighten your spirits," Peg said cheerfully, her heart torn. "We'll let it steep a bit." She sat, toggled the floor lamp to high, and continued reading *The Beginning of the Armadilloes* from where she'd left off, her voice in animated cadence through to the end.

"'Roll down—roll down to Rio.' How Michael longed to go, Peg. 'Some day before you're old,' I would promise him." Neither acknowledged that Aideen's subtle slur had worsened overnight or that she was dabbing her chin more frequently.

"All boy, that one. The Amazon!" Peg said, pouring. "Of all places. Can you imagine? Danny, he'll keep up with him, now won't he?"

+ + + + + + + +

The mantel clock chimed four. Outside the rain had turned to an apathetic drizzle and the western sky hinted at clearing.

Peg leaned forward, pushed herself to a stand, and tiptoed from the room, leaving the door ajar. Aideen slept, again only with medication. She scurried to the parlor and watched as Kyle helped pivot Father Finnian from the low-set passenger seat to his wheelchair.

"Come in out of the rain, you two! Careful up that step—" She opened the umbrella and fussed to cover them both as they entered the house. "You'll get a chill! Dear Kyle, how are you after the long drive? So kind to get Father, out of your way as it is."

Soon they were sitting comfortably at the kitchen table, tea and biscuits before them.

Father Finnian sipped, placed his hand in his lap, and sedately asked after Aideen.

Peg shook her head, voice low. "The life is drained from her, Father. They know these things, don't you think? They sense it." She brushed a tear. "The doctor says it more than likely bled again, the tumor—what with the weakness and all. That's why I called for you."

"It's right you did. I've been at the passing of five generations," he sighed, tired. "I don't intend to be here for the next."

Kyle immediately pictured Michael. Even if the boy continued to improve, today the grandmother and the fading old man had made loss real. Death scared him as never before.

The five o'clock hour neared. Father Finnian asked Kyle to ready the ampulla and pyx.

Aideen was sleeping when they gathered at the bedside. Peg touched her cheek. "Addy, Father's here to see you."

She looked into his eyes, at first confused, then understood the meaning of his visit. Moved to repentance, she grasped his hand.

"Be at peace, Aideen."

He had said these words to her in the past, but her heart had not been prepared.

"Forgive me, Father, for I have sinned against God—and against you."

Even as she spoke, he believed her confession to be true.

He turned to Kyle. "Son, please lead us in the Act of Contrition."

The young man blanched in face and mind. Slowly he breathed, focused on recalling the familiar prayer memorized ages ago in primary school, and began. "O my God, I am heartily sorry for having offended thee . . ."

Aideen observed his posture and vocal inflections, the tilt of his head and slight shrug of his shoulders. *So like Michael*, she thought, mourning anew that she was to be robbed of seeing her grandson reach manhood, but trusting he would be loved.

Kyle uncapped the ampulla. Using his good arm, Father Finnian dipped his thumb in the oil of the sick and touched Aideen, filled with emotion.

"May the Lord in his love and mercy help you with the grace of the Holy Spirit."

He anointed her forehead with a cross.

"May the Lord who frees you from sin save you and raise you up."

He anointed her hands with a cross.

Their eyes met and she felt within a peace that had long eluded her.

He then took a consecrated host from the pyx and placed it on her tongue.

"Receive the body of Christ."

Finished, he slumped and offered a silent prayer that another soul had been saved.

+++++++++

Aideen awakened gradually as the narcotic wore off and the pounding returned. Draping her robe loosely about her shoulders, she shuffled in near darkness to her writing desk, once Maw Maw's, and looked out into the night. Mist had settled on the water, a blanket that heaved with each swell. Tomorrow promised still more rain.

Determined but with energy fast waning, she lit the pull-chain lamp and reread the note penned earlier. She labeled the envelope *To Michael, on Your Twenty-Second* and placed it with the others: twelve birthdays' worth. There were none written for later years, when it would be time for him to give up childish ways.

She next chose a handcrafted card of two hedgerow fuchsia blossoms dipping toward earth, seemingly plucked from the profusion that perennially embraces the green summer landscape with confiding love. *Dearest Kyle*, she began, *your father visited this morning*. She emptied her heart. When she had filled the inside of the card, her thoughts flowed onto the back. Not yet done, she continued on stationery.

For Kyle, the envelope read.

Finally, she slept.

+ + + + + + + + +

She stood dizzy in the highest window of the Round Tower, hands gripping the smooth slab stone frame. Wind rushed through the Wicklow Hills, setting sway the trees. The light was low and the shadows long—day near its end.

Away to the east, beyond the valley but not yet to the sea, a speck of air glittered once, twice, then grew as it swept westward, sparkling as a whorl of mirror-dust in the sun, rising and sinking and rising again.

At once it was upon her, skin and hair luminous, soft as caress, and as swift it drew off, now an orb, floating, twisting, distorting, hurtling to the lakes, kissing the water, then on to the graves, hovering, humble, effaced.

From the west came a second orb at great speed, opaline, spectral, whisking the first to spin in its wake. One north, the other south about the tower. Together they joined an arm's reach before her.

Spirits: transcendent souls.

She peered deep, searching, seeking, with a sense not her own.

Caitlin, diffusion coalesced, reaching back, touching.

Maw Maw, embracing, infused warmth.

Youthful, dancing, joyous.

Aideen awoke.

She passed a hand slowly across her face then into the void of the room.

She felt its constricted dimensions, arbitrary and superfluous.

She had tasted afterlife and prayed for release.

A searing pain overtook her and she crushed her head in her hands.

It stopped.

Time paused as with the moment before lightning, and she was gone.

CHAPTER THIRTY-ONE
CARITAS † CHARITY

∞

Friday, 10 September 2010, Ballinskelligs

At Father Finnian's request Kevin celebrated the funeral Mass.

Aideen had rarely attended church after Caitlin's death and never warmed to Father Liam, the curate. Despite her late-sprouting personal disdain for religion, she was avidly determined that Michael be raised in the faith. It was thus that the child had endeared Danny and Peg, sitting angelic between them in the third pew from the front on Sunday mornings.

The day was sunny and pleasantly warm, the winds calm. All but the elderly processed behind the hearse on foot, more than two hundred strong, following the somewhat longer rural route from Saint Michael's to the abbey cemetery. Pretty much everyone knew she'd spent the summer at the children's hospital, but her own illness surprised most save those whom whispered rumors had reached.

By four o'clock they stood at the gravesite. With this burial the Reid-Reilly family plot would be filled. Her husband Sean was interred to her left, ground sunken and soggy from earlier rains, and Maw Maw lay at rest two rows distant with the oldest of the clan.

The ceremony was simple: a sprinkling of holy water and swinging of the thurible.

Kevin recited the final petition: *May her soul and the souls of all the faithful departed through the mercy of God rest in peace. Amen.*

Peg laid a bouquet of purple callas on the casket, Aideen's favorite and always in lush bloom at the Cahersiveen florist shop.

She was buried holding Tigger, shabby with lumps, more beige than orange from its many washings—Michael's companion from the crib and now his gift to her "so she won't be alone."

Friday, 10 September 2010, Allagheemore

Shanon reached up and combed her fingers through Kyle's hair as she had so often in the younger years. This time he allowed it, the need for maternal comfort strong.

Sunlight filtered through the house from the west, shedding its brightness on the foyer then beyond to the kitchen where they stood. The oven was warm and dinner would be at seven thirty—not unusually late with ninety ewes still on summer time and the fall lambing near. Soon the flock would dwindle, night would encroach on day, and the shepherd would assuredly arrive home earlier.

"What's next for you, Kyle? I've barely heard about your trip."

It was true: with Aideen passing and his spending weeks at a stretch with Michael, Kyle had been away but for an evening or two since July. He'd even missed the funeral to be with the boy. Now here until Wednesday next, he could finally begin to heal from the experience of loss—Cristina, Aideen—and the extraordinary weight of carrying out a grandmother's dying wish for him to befriend an ill child.

"Kyle, honey?"

"No big deal." He at once regretted letting the stock reply slip, having just resolved to be fully son, to hold close his parents while they were here, within touch. "I met a girl."

Her surprise was obvious. "Really? In Rome?"

"At the Vatican. She's getting a PhD. She helped me on Kevin's project."

"So, a fellow student?"

"Yeah, I guess you could say that. We—" He fumbled, not knowing how to continue.

Shanon shifted weight. "She's Italian?"

A quick smile rose on his face. "Yeah. Gorgeous." He'd dreaded this conversation—the first they'd ever had about relationships—but felt oddly at ease. "She grew up on the other side of Italy. Her family's from Puglia," he said, pointing to his calf exactly as she had. "Here, she gave me this." He pulled the cloth scapular from beneath his shirt and showed her. "It's Saint Michael. Our guardian angel."

"It's lovely." Her pleasant tone of voice belied an underlying concern of how serious—or better, infatuated—her son seemed about the woman.

"Cristina. Her name, I mean. 'Course this is Saint Michael," he repeated, blushing.

"You like her quite well?"

As his smile grew he could only manage a shy voice. "Yeah, I do."

She waited while he positioned the scapular in place.

"Father Kevin mentioned you'll be starting back at Saint Patrick's this year." Her voice was of suppressed buoyancy: a breath held shallow beneath the water's surface.

He waffled, head swaying. "They said they'd give me research credit for my report, at any rate, so last semester won't be a total waste. Starting back—I don't know yet. Maybe." He wasn't quite ready to share the conversation he'd had with

Marco about the Gregorian, nor secure enough in the dream to risk its loss.

"I hope so, Kyle. I hope your every desire comes true." She kissed his cheek. "Now, what do you say to helping your father so dinner's not delayed?"

+ + + + + + + + +

Kyle's dungarees had retained the smell of sheep despite washing and that made him glad. He was home, climbing the hills of his family's farm, breathing ocean air. He took it all in as if tomorrow it might be memory.

Over the rise, past the gorse, down through the glen he strode, knowing the flock would be drinking from the pond at this hour. And they were, half carrying their pregnant bellies no more than a hand span above the ryegrass, itself foraged low.

Bent at the waist, his father was deep in their midst, palpating the largest for twins.

"Here you are, then." He looked up, smiling. "Have you ever seen such a motley pack of ewes? Me included, 'course." Kyle laughed along, his mood considerably lighter than the day would have predicted.

"How many do you figure we'll birth this time?"

"Fifty at least," Brian said. "That ram's an ace—horniest devil I've seen for a long while, and God bless him. Worth twice what we paid. Don't go telling Malone, now."

Kyle patted the dense fleece as he forged a path through the animals, all in dire need of a good shearing.

He stood next to his father, waiting for instructions.

"I'm glad you're home, son. I missed you."

Together they finished the inspection. Brian looped a rope about the neck of one that he wanted to watch overnight in the shed, and they headed back at a leisurely pace.

At the rise they paused. The ewe took to grazing.

"Father Kevin's a good man, Kyle. You're lucky to have happened on him. And at Cables, of all places. I wish I'd been there."

Minutes passed and the sun neared the horizon. Soon the ewe was tugging Kyle forward, eager for grass just out of reach. Several paces away he turned to see Brian rooted in place. "Ma's waiting on dinner," he called.

Brian remained frozen.

Even from a distance Kyle could see tears on his father's face. He let out some rope and approached. "Da, what's wrong?" He put a hand on his shoulder and tried to shake a response. "It's been a rough day. Let's go home."

"Kyle—"

Silence.

"Kyle, I've kept something from you for a long time that you deserve to know."

The young man went pale with no clue what his father might mean, but fearing illness.

Brian grasped his son's hand, his eyes tight. "It's about Michael."

Again, he thought. *It's always about Michael.*

Still hesitation.

"What? Just tell me."

He faced Kyle and exhaled.

"Michael is your brother."

Kyle's eyes glazed, his mind sorting out this revelation until the truth dawned.

"You slept with her? With his mother?" He flashed back ten, eleven years. He would have been Michael's age. "You bastard. You slept with her."

Brian's head fell, shamed as if naked before his son.

"You cheated on Ma, goddamn you. You cheated on me."

He threw down the rope and walked off. Not twenty feet away he returned.

"Does Ma know? Were you man enough to tell her?"

Brian nodded. "She was with me when I donated the marrow."

Kyle raged. "You're the donor? I can't believe she forgave you. How could she?"

"I'd hoped you could find it in your heart to forgive me too, son."

"Fat chance of that ever happening. You're a stinkin' liar." He wiped spittle from his mouth and glared into Brian's eyes. "And do you wanna know what I've been meaning to tell you? You drink too much."

In total defeat Brian whispered, "I haven't touched alcohol in six weeks."

Stunned, Kyle yelled, "Well you're just perfect then, aren't you?" and left him.

Far distant, at the property's northeastern corner, he stopped. These hills, these hills of his childhood had forever changed.

CHAPTER THIRTY-TWO

WONDROUS LOVE

Tuesday, 14 September 2010, Skellig Michael

The calm waters of the bay yielded to ocean wakes. Still five miles off, Skellig Michael was lost in haze. Winds picked up, salt spray rained on deck, and tourists turned green.

As the landing neared, Captain Burke announced they would circle the islands first to view the spectacle of seabirds. Unsaid was his hope that the waves would settle with the change of tide, else there would be no visiting the historic site that day.

The boat rounded westward and the passengers hushed, then yelled excitedly at seeing a large pod of northern minkes breach, dive, and breach again: a privileged sight that alone was worth the trip, the captain exclaimed.

Three times about they went and finally docked safely. By then a dense flat cloud, no mere fog, had descended on the peaks and was slowly advancing downward. Few dared to risk the climb, expecting that it might clear before long.

Kyle bolted up the steps, yearning for solitude that was now within reach.

His ascent was hindered by treads covered in a slippery wet sheen. Once enveloped in vapor, he could barely see the ground to the right or the steep drop to the left. Then suddenly he broke into sunshine with nothing below but a blanket of white.

Never had he wandered the abandoned monastery in such utter silence. Above the dome of sky, he had entered the realm of heaven.

He knelt, crawled into a stone hut, and peered out in spiritual kinship with the monks of old. Now as then, the world was equally remote, its cares as distant—and as tempting a source of fleshly distraction to eschew. Here was contentment and peace.

A hermit at one with himself.

One with himself.

One.

Was this his calling, God's will for his life?

He looked up into the hut's vault, dark and without light.

He roamed the bordering graves, a scant foot's width from the threshold.

He stood alone in stark desolation. Abandonment surrounded him.

Where have they gone?

A voice spoke, whispering as from a seed buried deep.

Why do you seek the living among the dead?

Two angels, an empty tomb.

Another voice, clarion, eternal.

One.

Love one another.

Love one another as I have loved you.

A command calling him home.

Tuesday, 14 September 2010, Allagheemore

He sat on the floor with his back against the beanbag chair as he always did to read, gray gooseneck lamp bent just so, and opened the letter from Aideen.

Dearest Kyle, your father visited this morning. He surprised me. It had been years since we talked, and then just the niceties one speaks at the market or some public place. I told him how kind you've been to Michael, how grateful I am for you to be friends. I guess you may have told him of my illness, or perhaps it was Father Kevin. In any case, it spared me having to explain. I'm sure you know by now that he is Michael's father. That was the reason he came to see me, to tell me. He wanted me to know he'd kept it a secret from everyone, not just me, thinking it was best, until he learned that Michael needed a bone marrow donor. To be honest, it came as a relief, knowing that it was Brian and not just a man she met on a trip—that's what she'd told me years ago. Not that this is easy for you, Kyle. I understand that. He'll probably not say this to you, but you're the reason he kept it secret. Husbands and wives have a way of working things out. It's harder for children. I told him you deserve to know, and he promised me he would tell you soon. He saved Michael's life— never forget that—and risked losing the two people he loves most. Michael does not know, and I think that's best for now. He is your brother after all, and you should have some say in when he's ready to hear that kind of news. But I am rambling.

He read over the rest rather quickly: details about Michael's childhood, her hopes for his future, and lengthy reminiscences of Caitlin. He stood, stretched, and tucked the letter in the carved wooden chest that contained his most private belongings.

+++++++++

Light shone from beneath the bedroom door. He knocked, hoping his father was still out.

Shanon sat in bed, readers on and hardcover opened. She placed a bookmark and called him over. He lay down, curled, and rested his head on her lap.

"Kye, my sweet child," she said, scratching his back lightly as he'd always liked but long outgrown. "You worry me."

"I'm okay." He nuzzled. "I'm just trying to figure things out."

Her shoulders rocked. "We've made your life a lot more complicated, haven't we?"

"Not you. You didn't do anything."

She sighed. "We're married, Kyle. We're both responsible for our relationship."

"But he hurt you."

"Yes, he did." She sat him up. "And I forgave him."

"So that's that?"

"No, that's love. The hurt will fade."

He stood, arms crossed, and slowly paced the carpet.

"I decided to go back—to Maynooth. I can still finish this year if they let me overload."

"That's good, Kyle. I'm glad you're focusing on the future."

"And Michael needs me around—for a while, anyway. After that, I don't know." *Please, God, Rome*, he longed to himself.

"*Que sera, sera*," her voice lilted.

The scent of Cristina washed over him and he breathed deep.

He walked over to his mother, leaned, and kissed her good-night.

"I want to forgive Da too," he said softly.

She stroked his head and whispered, "Why not right now?"

He turned and saw Brian standing at the door.

+ + + + + + + + +

Kyle opened his contacts app and scrolled to Cristina's name. Her photo was a close-up profile taken at the archive. His wallpaper was his favorite—from their trip to the zoo.

He tapped on her mobile number and waited for the call to connect, all the while trying to suppress excitement and calm his voice. This would be their first time speaking since his departure more than a month ago; he only now felt ready to talk.

The ringing stopped and he heard a click. Her voice came on and his heart rose, only to sink when he realized it was her voice-mail greeting. Unprepared, he panicked and his mouth went dry.

"Hi, it's me—Kyle. Uh, I thought you'd wanna know I'm going back to school in a couple of weeks—on Michaelmas, kinda cool. Yeah, and I found out I have a brother. It's that kid with cancer. Long story. Anyway, he's been in the hospital for a while. They're pretty sure he's gonna make it. That's good. I didn't think I should leave just yet, I mean like back to Rome. I'm hoping for next summer, maybe. Marco said he could help me get into the Gregorian and I wanna talk with you about that—a master's? I kinda liked the research thing. At least with you. So, I'm wondering if you might wanna spend Christmas up here, seeing as you've never been to Ireland. I better hang up before your phone goes dead. Call me when you can. Love ya—I mean, I love you."

For an hour he lay tortured over what he'd said and how he'd said it, worried that she wouldn't call back.

Startled, he dropped the phone when her ringtone played, the volume set on high.

"Kyle, *sì*, I will come for Christmas! Of course!"

He beamed. "What took you so long?"

"*Dio*, your message went on and on and on. I had to suffer it twice—you talk so fast! I'm teasing, you know." She paused. "Kyle?"

"I'm here. I was just listening to your voice."

"*Mio Dio*. Now, I teach you a new saying: '*Ti amo*.' You try."

"*Ti amo*."

"*Precisamente*."

"And what does that mean?"

"I love you, Kyle. I love you."

CHAPTER THIRTY-THREE

THE SIGN OF JONAH

Thursday, 23 September 2010, Vatican City

T he driver pulled up to the private entrance, set the
emergency brake, and made his way about the limousine
so efficiently that Kevin was still working at unbuckling his
safety belt when the door opened.

"Here, I help you."

"Thanks, I've got it," he replied. Grabbing his bag, he
climbed out into the incomparable midday Italian sun. At that
moment he wished he could live here always.

"*Mio caro amico, bentornato a casa!*"

"Marco, good to see you."

"Come, let's go inside."

"What? I didn't leave behind a chilly rain to be cloistered
quite yet."

"*Prego*, Carmela can take your things to my office."

Minutes later they were strolling the Vatican Gardens,
catching up on family matters in a way that is only possible in
the leisure of personal visits. The path meandered south then
west to the far corner, under a grove of palms, and farther along
a ninth-century defensive wall. Marco led them to a bench near
the Saint Thérèse shrine, and they sat.

"Aideen's soul is at rest, Marco. She journeyed back."

"Without bitterness at never finding the cross?"

Kevin's hands met at his heart. "But she did."

"As it should be," he nodded. "For us all."

"Truly, my friend," he sighed. "Now, tell me what you refused to share on the phone."

Marco smiled slyly as he gradually meted out the information.

"The letters Kyle found are waiting inside—you already know everything about them. And there is also Pio Nono's diary, of importance in revealing where the amphora was last hidden—exactly where Kyle guessed."

"I'm pleased my intuition about that boy was right," Kevin interjected, echoing Marco's overt praise of Kyle's talent.

"This," he underscored as he reached into his pocket, "you need to see for yourself."

Kevin immediately recognized the envelope by the description Kyle had passed along.

Roccia sporgente—Skellig Michael.

He held his hand palm up. Marco opened the flap and let the pendant slide out.

He examined it as closely as he had Aideen's that first time: they were identical.

"You told Kyle this was found among Nono's effects?"

"*Sì*, with the diary. An entry dated the fifth of August 1866 confirms it was his. He also wrote what he knew of its history, which is quite fascinating. The pendants were crafted in a single lot by the Augustinian monks soon after they left Skellig Michael, using native silver mined along the coast at Ardtully."

"They moved to the Ballinskelligs Abbey eight hundred years ago. Wow." He looked again at the pendant. "How many were made?"

"That we don't know."

"Well, at least enough for each of Aideen's ancestors marked in her Bible as cured."

After a few minutes of quiet, Kevin looked at his friend with a feigned glare. "And?"

Marco laughed. He reached again into his pocket and withdrew a folded sheet of paper.

Kevin opened it and looked quizzically at what he saw: a six-inch circular image—what he took to be a digital print—of the initials *LK* and the date *9 marzo 1939*.

"I don't understand."

"Shall I give you a clue?" Marco goaded.

"Pass."

"Okay. What do you remember about Ludwig Kaas?"

Kevin thought for a moment and came up blank.

"Monsignor Kaas was an aide and confidant of Achille Ratti—you know, Pope Pius XI. He was the secretary in charge of the basilica, including the structure itself and the crypts below. This photo," he tapped on the sheet, "shows what we found written on the inside of the Sistine Treasury wall—it's round, as are all images taken by a flexible scope. This is the date when the plaster repair was made: the date Kaas moved the amphora."

"You're serious? Marco, that's incredible." He again studied the print. "And Cardinal Pacelli had become the next pope, what, in February?"

"Pacelli was named Pius XII just seven days before. Importantly, Kaas kept his post."

Kevin leaned in. "Where does all this lead?"

Marco stood. "That we will discuss inside."

Twenty minutes later they were sitting at an oak table in a spacious room within the pope's private chambers. On it was the sixth-century letter of Conlaeth and the one written to Giovanni De Rossi by his brother. The Pio Nono diary lay at their side. At once Kevin poured into them.

Marco prodded him after half an hour. "The room is yours for as long as you like."

He glanced at his watch, unaware of the lapsed time. "You should have interrupted far sooner. These are—'incredible' falls short."

"I agree." With a pause he segued back to their earlier conversation. "So, where does all this lead? I believe directly to the crypts—what were eventually expanded into the grottoes of today. Let me explain," he said in response to Kevin's raised finger. "By the time Pius XI died in 1939, it had become clear more space was needed for entombments. Kaas was the administrator in charge of these excavations. It was also Kaas who ordered the amphora to be moved from the Treasury wall, to keep it out of Nazi hands. You see?"

"Bingo." Kevin looked conspicuously about the room. "It's here, right? You found it?"

"My friend," he laughed, "that major a discovery I would have told you by phone. But I will say I have a much greater knowledge of the grottoes after participating in the grueling failed search for it."

"Well, I guess that's that—barring a miracle. You can't blame me for hoping." Kevin stood, stretched, and yawned. "How in the hell am I going to get a sabbatical out of this—let alone a book?"

"I trust in your infinite talents," Marco said as he walked toward a tiered console. "This may help."

He placed a small leather-bound notebook in Kevin's hands.

Inside it had the appearance of yet another diary, hand-written on ruled pages and more recent than Nono's. He saw that the same ink had been used throughout, suggesting it was completed over a relatively narrow timeframe. It was untitled and in Latin.

"Tell me," he chided impatiently as they took their seats.

"When we found nothing in the grottoes, I searched what we have from Kaas. This was among his items. I might have overlooked it as a transcription of a favorite classic text, but my mind was on the amphora—and the scroll."

"Seriously?" His voice was thin. "This is a copy of the scroll?"

Marco nodded so slowly and deeply it was almost a bow. "According to Nono the original was to remain with the amphora, which was in fact marked by a *crux de cruce*: wood of the cross and inspiration for the cross of Saint Patrick."

Kevin paged through quickly, catching words and phrases. It would require study.

Marco motioned for the notebook, thumbed to a particular page, and handed it back.

On it was a list.

Nails. Wood. Title. Crown.

Kevin's eyes refused to leave the words. He sat in astonishment.

"Not just the cross. Not just the cross but the very relics of the crucifixion."

Marco replied soberly, "Note well that the burial cloths were not present."

"The shroud—of course that stayed with the apostles in Jerusalem." Kevin pondered the rest a long while, then posed a conundrum. "But what of competing claims for these other relics—even from some here at the Vatican?"

"I've argued this with Benedict," he said. "We must begin with what is most likely fact and work backward. If the scroll is accurate, that the Nicodemus amphora contained the true relics when sealed by Mary Magdalene and that seal has never been broken, then other claims must be carefully scrutinized."

"That," Kevin replied, "is begging fury."

"It certainly would be. But remember, without the amphora there is no news and no controversy. For now it amounts to academic intrigue. As well, the scroll mentions 'nails,' meaning perhaps just two, and 'wood,' clearly implying not the entire cross. So for these, other true relics may also exist."

"Okay." The pause was brief. "So what about the *titulum*? And the crown of thorns?"

"A different answer for each. Already there are several crowns purported true, so it is less an issue. As for the INRI *titulum*, to date only one half has been reported found, and it could plausibly be a first-century rendition made for the faithful prior to the destruction of Jerusalem, when at some point the amphora had been taken for safety from Israel."

Kevin leaned back and sighed. "You've thought this through."

"Did you expect less?" He laughed. "Now, I will leave you in peace. Tonight we dine at the finest restaurant in Roma—"

"Papà Marco's again?"

"—and we must leave here not after 7:30. Carmela will stop by to remind you on her way out. *Bene?*"

"*Molto bene*. Marco, thank you." He rose and grasped his hand with warm appreciation.

"One thing more—" He handed him an envelope and left.

Kevin sat and opened the card. Benedict's coat of arms was emblazoned on the front. Inside a handwritten note began with warm greetings and closed with a blessing. He sent a personal message to Kyle praising his dedication and enjoined him to *contemplate well the words of Jesus when he said "no sign will be given except the sign of the prophet Jonah." There is, in fact, no other way in which one can be saved than by the cross.*

The message would be a treasure indeed for the young man.

As he slipped it into the envelope, he noticed a holy card inside: the faded sepia face of Jesus on the Turin shroud at the moment of his resurrection, and on the back a few words in Benedict's script.

Kevin—Seek always the light of Christ!
Come visit when you have completed your sabbatical.

Mystified, all thought of the documents before him was lost. He stared blankly ahead.

Soon the sun dipped far past its zenith. At last natural light spread across the room, its rays catching bits of jasper, amethyst, and carnelian from a small stained-glass window. The dove-white walls danced with color.

Kevin absentmindedly let his gaze float from violet to red then brown. Still pondering Benedict's invitation, his eyes slowly turned, seeking the source of such brilliance.

At first he saw only individual glass jewels—tones dazzling and saturated, each fit for a diadem. Gradually his focus relaxed, gradually the mosaic symphony came into view.

And in a single moment: recognition.

Mary. Jesus. Mary Magdalene.

Wood of the cross. Crown of thorns.

Brigid's masterpiece—crafted by the hands of Bréanainn and young Áed—found.

Hope filled his heart to overflowing.

EPITAPH

AIDEEN FIONA BRENNAN CALLAGHAN
26TH DECEMBER 1940 – 6TH SEPTEMBER 2010

FOR I AM CONVINCED
THAT NEITHER DEATH, NOR LIFE,
NOR ANGELS, NOR PRINCIPALITIES,
NOR THINGS PRESENT, NOR THINGS TO COME,
NOR POWERS, NOR HEIGHT, NOR DEPTH,
NOR ANYTHING ELSE IN ALL CREATION,
WILL BE ABLE TO SEPARATE US
FROM THE LOVE OF GOD
IN CHRIST JESUS OUR LORD.

† ROMANS 8:38–39 †

For God did not make death,
nor does he delight in the death of the living.
—WISDOM OF SOLOMON 1:13

AFTERWORD

Readers may be stunned to learn that the rare cancer syndrome afflicting the Callaghan family is real. It was first described by Drs. Frederick Li and Joseph Fraumeni in 1969, and the inherited genetic mutation was identified in 1990. As correctly noted by Michael's pediatric oncologist in the novel, carriers of this autosomal dominant disorder have an extraordinarily high risk of developing cancer, often at an early age—and in some, more than one type. A host of other predisposition syndromes exist. More information can be found on the Li-Fraumeni Syndrome Association website (www.lfsassociation.org).

ACKNOWLEDGMENTS

The author is indebted to Jon Sweeney, publisher and editor-in-chief, and the entire team at Paraclete Press, without whom inspirational literature as a genre would be all the poorer. Thanks go to Hollis Seamon, Cliff Ennico, and Stephanie Rosally-Kaplan for their thoughtful advice and expert services. Special thanks to good friends Denis Sobieray, Marie and Barry Saluk, and Veronica LaVista, who provided crucial encouragement on reading the first draft, and to Daniel Varholy for his ever-insightful suggestions on getting this work into the hands of readers. I am forever grateful to Dr. Raymond J. Hutchinson and Reverend Thomas F. X. Hoar, mentors extraordinaire and extraordinary friends. This story was immeasurably shaped by the strength, resilience, courage, faith, and love that I have witnessed with awe in the many children and families I have been privileged to care for: there would be no story without you. To my medical friends and colleagues, your role in this story is immensely more profound than words on a page. I thank my entire family for their endless love. Lee, thank you for introducing me to art, history, and the works of the Spirit as both sister and confidante. Marie and Clara, thank you for endowing me with the wondrous miracles of parenthood—including hugs. And Sue, thank you for being my one, my only.

It is important to acknowledge with respect and gratitude the many institutions—public and private—and the following businesses that were mentioned or served as real-world venues for the fictional characters and events portrayed in this novel: Charlemont Arms Hotel, Hester's Place Restaurant (Armagh); Ballinskelligs Inn, Cable O'Leary's Bar and Restaurant, Nicholas Browne's Filling Station and Foodstore, St. Michael the Archangel Church (Ballinskelligs); Alan Hanna's Bookshop, Bewley's Oriental Cafés, Insomnia Coffee Company, Our Lady Children's Hospital, St. James's Hospital, St. Luke's Hospital, The Old Jameson Distillery (Dublin); St. Joseph's Nursing Home, Jack's Bakery & Deli, Laune Health & Beauty (Killorglin); The Roost Maynooth Restaurant & Pub (Maynooth); Esso Petrol Station (Rathmore); GregCafé at Pontifical Gregorian University (Rome).

HISTORICAL EVENTS

YEAR AD	EVENT
33	Crucifixion of Jesus
44	Martyrdom of James the apostle; Mary Magdalene fled to Gaul*
314	Council of Arles; Donatism condemned
457†	Church founded at Ard Mhacha [Armagh] by Padraig
474†	Drum Criaidh oratory built by Brigid; later christened Cill Dara [Kildare] Abbey
476	Fall of Rome; Romulus Augustulus deposed by Flavius Odoacer
477	Gallarus oratory established; creation of the Celtic cross*
512†	Skellig Michael monastery established
519	Cóemgen departed Gleann Dá Lough [Glendalough] for pilgrimage to Rome*
576	Stained-glass window based on Brigid illustration crafted at Kildare*
1191†	Ballinskelligs Abbey established
1517	Protestant Reformation
1578	Priory at Ballinskelligs Abbey dissolved by Queen Elizabeth I
1861	Vittorio Emanuele II proclaimed king of Italy
1866	Italian Third War of Independence; Paul Cullen named first Irish cardinal
1870	Dissolution of the Papal States; Pope Pio Nono confined to Vatican
1929	Vatican City State established by Lateran Treaty
1932	Adolf Hitler appointed chancellor of Germany
1939	Death of Pope Pius XI six months before start of World War II

---

* Fictionalized   † Approximate

HISTORICAL CHARACTERS
AND FIGURES

Brother Murrough*	Lone monk protecting relic on Skellig Michael as monastery moved to Ballinskelligs
Mary Magdalene†	Follower of Jesus; cured of seven demons
Mary†	Mother of Jesus
Brigid of Kildare [St. Brigit]	Abbess; close friend of Padraig
Padraig of Armagh [St. Patrick]	Abbot; originated Irish monastic movement
Brother Tomas*	Monk; pupil of Padraig; with Brigid founded Gallarus oratory and Reask monastery
Pope Simplicius	Papacy 468–483
Romulus Augustulus	Roman emperor deposed by Odoacer at fall of Western Roman Empire (476)
Conlaeth of Kildare [St. Conleth]	Abbot and bishop; friend of Brigid
Alill mac Nad Froich	Brother of Óengus mac Nad Froich, first Christian king of Munster (Cashel)
Simon Peter†	Apostle of Jesus
Jesus of Nazareth†	Emmanuel and Christ, the Messiah
Andrew†	Apostle of Jesus; brother of Simon Peter
Fionán [St. Finnian]	Monk; founded Skellig Michael monastery
Broccán [St. Brogan]	Monk; nephew of Padraig
Brother Weylyn*	Monk; one of ten to assist Brigid in building Gallarus oratory and Reask monastery
Clovis I	First king of the Franks; son of Childeric; baptized at prompting of wife Clotilde

Pope Symmachus	Papacy 498–514
Zebedee†	Father of apostles James and John; Salome's husband
John†	Apostle of Jesus; son of Zebedee, brother of James
Salome†	Mother of apostles James and John; Zebedee's wife
James†	Apostle of Jesus; son of Zebedee, brother of John
Martha†	Sister of Jesus's close friend Lazarus (and possibly of Mary Magdalene)
Áed Dub mac Colmáin [St. Áed]	Distant cousin of Brigid; king of Leinster; later entered Kildare monastery
Bréanainn [St. Brendan]	Monk; pupil of Fionán; traveled extensively by boat; founded an early Brittany monastery
Cóemgen [St. Kevin]	Monk and hermit; founded Glendalough monastery
Nicodemus†	Jewish Pharisee and member of the ruling Sanhedrin
Gamaliel†	Jewish Pharisee and member of the ruling Sanhedrin
Caiaphas†	Jewish high priest at time of Jesus's crucifixion
Joseph of Arimathea†	Jewish Pharisee and member of the ruling Sanhedrin; Jesus's body was laid in his tomb
Rhoda†	Maid at the home of the Evangelist Mark's mother Mary
Mark†	Disciple of Jesus; author of the second canonical Gospel
Malachy of Armagh [St. Malachy]	Twelfth-century purported author of *Prophecy of the Popes*
Pope Benedict XVI	Papacy 2005–2013; personal name Joseph Aloisius Ratzinger
Constantine Augustus	Roman emperor Constantine the Great; decreed Christian tolerance (313)
Marinus of Arles	Early bishop in Gaul; led First Council of Arles condemning Donatism (314)
Rhétice of Autun [St. Reticius]	Early bishop in Gaul; attended First Council of Arles
Austromoine of Auvergne [St. Stremonius]	Early bishop in Gaul; attended First Council of Arles

Pope Silvester I	Papacy 314–335
Trophime of Arles [St. Trophimus]	First bishop of Arles (ca. 250); entombed at Alyscamps necropolis (relics later moved)
Germanus*	A Roman soldier guarding the Via Aurelia during the First Council of Arles
Commander*	Officer in Roman army accompanying Constantine to Arles (314)
Daphnus of Vaison	Early bishop in Gaul; attended First Council of Arles
Rémi of Reims [St. Remigius]	Bishop; mentor to Sidonius; baptized King Clovis (496) thus Christianizing the Franks
Childeric I	First Merovingian King of the Salian Franks; father of Clovis I
Syagrius	Last Roman military commander in Gaul; defeated by Clovis I (486)
Sidonius Apollinaris of Auvergne [St. Sidonius]	Bishop; Gallo-Roman aristocratic diplomat and prolific author
Brieuc [St. Brioc]	Welsh cleric; studied in Ireland; later founded an oratory in Brittany
Moninne of Killeavy [St. Moninne]	Abbess; raised by Brigid; baptized, confirmed, and likely veiled by Padraig
Pope John I	Papacy 523–526
Pope Hormisdas	Papacy 514–523
Neacht of Kildare*	Nun; inferior of Brigid
Timothy†	Apostle of Jesus
Innkeeper at Ocsimor*	Provided lodging for the retinue of King Childebert
Childebert I	King of the Franks (Paris, Órleans); son of Clovis I and Clotilde
Paol Aorelian [St. Paulinus Aurelianus]	First Bishop of Léon, Brittany
Pope Pius IX [Pio Nono]	Papacy 1846–1878; personal name Giovanni Maria Mastai-Ferretti

Giovanni Battista De Rossi	Archaeologist and Vatican archivist; rediscovered Callixtus catacombs (1849)
Michele Stefano De Rossi	Seismologist and topographer; Giovanni's younger brother
Vittorio Emanuele II	King of Italy (1861–1878)
Cardinal Paul Cullen	First Irish cardinal (1866)
Augustine of Hippo [St. Augustine]	Bishop; early Christian theologian and philosopher
Pope Pius XI	Papacy 1922–1939; personal name Achille Ambrogio Damiano Ratti
Ludwig Kaas	Vatican priest; papal prelate and canon of the Basilica of Saint Peter
Seán Ó Conaill (fictionalized)	Ballinskelligs altar boy from Kildreelig; oldest child of widower father
Father Sullivan*	Ballinskelligs parish priest
Conall Mag Aonghuis*	Ballinskelligs altar boy from Dungeagan
Fiona Reid Reilly*	Maire's mother
Malachi Reilly*	Maire's father
Pope Pius XII	Papacy 1939–1958; personal name Eugenio Maria Giuseppe Giovanni Pacelli

* Fictional   † Biblical

CELTIC CROSSING
DISCUSSION GUIDE QUESTIONS

1. In the opening chapter, Aideen bluntly tells Kevin that she's not looking for religion—then implores him to find the curing cross for Michael. Does this seem contradictory to you? Many today claim no religious affiliation or have left the Church. Do you think this reflects an absence of faith? Has the secularization of society influenced your views on religion or your faith in God? (Chapter 1)

2. Have you or a loved one faced a life-threatening, debilitating, or chronic illness? Did the experience change your perspective on faith and spirituality? In what ways?

3. Kevin dreams that he is visited by his mother's spirit in Iveagh Gardens, where he first met Aideen. What does the poem express about birth, death, purgatory, and eternal life? Might this have been more than a dream? In what ways is Aideen a maternal figure for Kevin? Contemplate how she too later touches his cheek, gentle as a breeze. (Chapter 5)

4. In the novel, Mary Magdalene is cured of seven symptoms that are described as demons. How might this biblical characterization of disease be relevant to the story's premise? (Chapter 7)

5. Marco inherits a book of poetry by Michelangelo that is inscribed with the quote, "I saw the angel in the marble and carved until I set him free." He later shares this quote with Kyle. How are Marco and Kyle alike? What are they both seeking? Discuss the ways each helps the other. (Chapter 11)

6. Kyle and Cristina are immediately attracted to each other. Why? Do their age and cultural differences seem to enhance or hinder their relationship? What do you think is the significance of their sharing Saint Michael as a guardian angel? (Chapter 12)

7. In the novel, it is significant that Mary Magdalene brings the relic to Gaul. Just as important is what her character gradually reveals about Jesus of Nazareth in earlier scenes. Trace that storyline and discuss its relevance to the main plot. (Chapters 2, 6, 8, 12)

8. Kevin and Marco's friendship began in graduate school. What subsequent life experiences do they have in common that foster this bond? In what ways are they like brothers? Do you see any parallels with the emerging friendship between Michael and Kyle? (Chapter 14)

9. Michael's illness triggers a cascade of events affecting multiple characters, each of whom has a different perspective on faith. What impact does the illness have on their individual spiritual journeys? In what ways are their lives intertwined? What does this say about our shared humanity? How does this propel the narrative?

10. Cristina had crossed the Bridge of the Holy Angel many times but never noticed the sad expressions of the statues. Kyle does so immediately, seeing that they hold the instruments of Christ's crucifixion. Earlier, Kevin had praised Kyle on his awareness of local history, which Kyle shrugged off. To what does the young man attribute his knowledge? Do you think he's being modest, or humble? (Chapter 14)

11. After seeing the Sistine fresco of Saint Paul's crucifixion, Kyle asks Cristina if she believes. Initially she thinks he's referring to the Malachy prophecy, then understands. How does her belief in the Trinity differ from her skepticism of the prophecy? What effect does this seem to have on Kyle? (Chapter 18)

12. In the Sistine Chapel, Kyle confesses to Marco, "I don't want to sin. I don't want to go against his will." Marco responds by pointing to a fresco of the Garden of Eden. Explore the relationship between temptation, sin, and free will. What role do you believe grace plays? (Chapter 19)

13. Many characters are profoundly affected by death in the course of the novel, including Aideen, Kevin, Marco, Kyle, Michael, and Brian. In what ways are their coping strategies similar? Different? Contemplate how hope borne of faith can be a powerful antidote against despair. Do you believe that hope plays a role in physical healing?

14. During her pivotal stroll through St. Stephen's Green, Aideen comes upon a statue of the Three Fates—Past, Present, and Future—in which she sees Maw Maw, herself, and Caitlin. Why do their taunts trigger a spiritual crisis? How does she express this to Kevin? In a later scene, what bit of wisdom does Peg share? (Chapter 26)

15. In recounting her life to Aideen, Peg says, "Love is as love does." How does Peg embody this truth? What does the saying suggest about forgiveness? Might this have been a lesson for Aideen? Has anyone ever shown you such kindness? How did you respond? (Chapter 28)

16. During the healing ceremony in 1866, Maire first appears on a tomb and later on a bier. She awakens on Easter morning. What other images of death and resurrection are presented in these scenes? What is the meaning of Maire's vision of the cross? (Chapter 29)

17. Through most of the novel, Aideen blames Fr. Finnian for having failed to heal Maw Maw and Caitlin with holy oil and even dismisses the sacrament as magic, yet she later allows herself to be anointed. What does this suggest about the evolution of her faith and her understanding of forgiveness? Compare a similar faith situation you've experienced in your own life. (Chapter 30)

18. In Aideen's dream, she is visited by two spirit orbs as she peers out from the Round Tower at Glendalough. Caitlin appears as a whorl of mirror-dust from the Wicklow Hills and is described as "diffusion coalesced." Thinking about the circumstances of Caitlin's death and funeral, what might this imagery symbolize? (Chapter 30)

19. With his home life shattered, Kyle flees to the solitude of Skellig Michael. Discuss the spiritual symbolism of his ascending the mountain on slippery steps, emerging through a cloud into the sun. To whom is he referring when he asks, "Where have they gone?" Whose clarion voice responds, and where does it beckon? (Chapter 32)

20. Light is a recurring motif in the novel. Explore its symbolism as a source of illumination in various settings, such as Alyscamps (Chapter 13), Saint Peter's Square (Chapter 18), Kildreelig (Chapter 30), and the papal chambers (Chapter 33).

SOURCES

SCRIPTURE

Revised Standard Version, Catholic Edition.

Gaelic Bible. An Biobla Naomhtha. Translated (from Gaelic to Roman characters) by Uilliam Bhedel (Old Testament) and William O Domhnuill (New Testament). London: Printed by J Moyes, Greville Street, for The British and Foreign Bible Society, 1817. https://ia800207.us.archive.org/26/items/bioblanaomhthaan00bede/bioblanaomhthaan00bede.pdf

QUOTED WORKS

Constantine's Letter Summoning the Council of Arles (AD 314). In Eusebius, *Church History*, 10.5.21–24. Modern edition: G. Bardy, *Eusebe de Casaree: Histoire ecclesiastique*, vol. 3, *Sources chretiennes 55*. Paris: Editions du Cerf, 1958. https://www.fourthcentury.com/arles-314-summon.

Guasti, Cesare. *Le Rime di Michelangelo Buonarroti, Pittore, Scultore e Architetto*. Firenze: Accademica della Crusca, 1863. Italian-English translation: *The Sonnets of Michael Angelo Buonarroti*. Translated by John Addington Symonds. London: Smith, Elder, & Co.; New York: Charles Scribner's Sons, 1904. Digitized by the Internet Archive, contributed by Cornell University Library. https://archive.org/details/cu31924014269975.

Kipling, Rudyard. *Just So Stories*. London: Macmillan, 1902.

MENTIONED WORKS

Joyce, James. *Dubliners*. London: Grant Richards, 1914.

Lewis, C. S. *The Lion, the Witch, and the Wardrobe*. New York: Macmillan, 1988.

Northcote, J. Spencer (1821–1907), and William Robert Brownlow (1830–1901). *Roma Sotterranea: or Some Account of the Roman Catacombs, Especially of the Cemetery of San Callisto*. London: Longmans, Green, Reader, and Dyer, 1869. Digitized by the Internet Archive with funding from The Getty Research Institute. https://ia802505.us.archive.org/19/items/romasotterraneao00nort_0/romasotterraneao00nort_0.pdf.

de Rossi, Giovanni Battista (1822–1894). *La Roma Sotterranea Cristiana*. Roma: Cromo-Litografia Pontificia. Digitized by the Internet Archive in 2009 with funding from Research Library, The Getty Research Institute. Volume (Tomo) 1, 1864: www.archive.org/details/laromasotterrane01ross. Volume (Tomo) 2, 1867: www.archive.org/details/laromasotterrane02ross. Volume (Tomo) 3, 1877: www.archive.org/details/laromasotterrane03ross.

Cover image: *The Skellig Michael*, adapted from the original photo by Jerzy Strzelecki https://commons.wikimedia.org/wiki/File:Skellig_Michael03(js).jpg

You may also be interested these titles from Paraclete Fiction

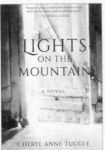